WIVES OF
WAR

ALSO BY SORAYA M. LANE

Voyage of the Heart

SORAYA M. LANE

WIVES OF WAR

Text copyright © 2017 Soraya Lane
All rights reserved.

Published by Lake Union Publishing, Seattle

www.apub.com

Amazon, the Amazon logo, and Lake Union Publishing are trademarks of Amazon.com, Inc., or its affiliates.

ISBN-13: 9781503942769
ISBN-10: 1503942767

Cover design by @blacksheep-uk.com
Cover photography by Richard Jenkins Photography © 2017

Printed in the United States of America

For Mackenzie and Hunter.
Thank you for all the cuddles, laughs and 'I love you's'.

PART ONE

London, 1944

CHAPTER ONE

Scarlet

Scarlet Alexander shut her eyes tight, one hand held high in the air as the wind brushed cold against her skin. She was clutching a letter between her fingers, waiting to let it go, because she had nowhere to post it to, no way of knowing whether her fiancé would ever receive it if she did send it. She knew the words by heart, had recited them so many times that she was certain she'd never forget them.

> *Dear Thomas,*
> *I don't know where you are, and I doubt you'll ever read this, but I want you to know that I'll never give up on finding you. I wish we lived in different times, that we could have already married and had a family, and that you didn't have to fight so bravely for our country. One day. I keep telling myself that one day we will look back on this as a distant memory, surrounded by our children and sharing tales of the time when everyone else told me*

> *to brace myself for the worst kind of news, before you*
> *walked back into our lives.*
>> *Yours for ever,*
>> *Scarlet*

The wind whistled, ice cold now, making her knuckles ache. She shouldn't have told the driver to go, shouldn't have been so insistent on making her own way to the station. But if she couldn't stand the cold now, being alone and having to fend for herself, then she knew she'd never have the strength to survive wherever it was she was posted.

Taking a deep, shuddering breath, Scarlet slowly let the letter go, allowed it to slip from her fingertips. She turned and watched it soar, violently taken by a gasp of wind, slowly disappearing from sight. This was it. She'd held on to the letter for weeks now, wanting to send it but not knowing where. It had been so long since she'd had a letter in reply that she was afraid Thomas was gone, that she would never see his smile ever again. Except for the tiny voice inside her head, the one that kept telling her not to lose hope. Even his own mother seemed uncertain, but Scarlet wasn't going to give up so easily.

'Miracles happen every day.' She murmured the words, bent to collect her bag and straightened her shoulders. Scarlet took a deep breath and started to walk. She could do this. She just had to swallow her fears, stay focused, and do her bit. She was new to nursing – it wasn't like they were going to make her do anything she wasn't prepared for, and if she found Thomas along the way . . . Scarlet walked faster, head ducked down as the wind slapped her cheeks.

If she found Thomas, it would be worth anything.

Scarlet dug her fingers into her palm as she fisted her hand, the other clutching her bag tight. This was it. This was her chance to do her bit, to be part of the war effort. She only hoped she was stronger than her family gave her credit for, because not even her mother had seemed to believe she would go through with becoming a military nurse. She could still hear the high pitch of her voice, snapping at her over afternoon tea that she hadn't exactly been bred to care for others.

But she'd done it, and there was nothing her mother or father could do to stop her now that she'd made her mind up. All she had to do was believe in herself.

She looked up at the sky, breathed in the cold, damp air, glanced at the oak trees as they waved their branches in greeting to her. It was as if even the weather knew they were at war, it was so unseasonably cold. Scarlet had no idea where she would end up, but she doubted that anything about where she was going would seem familiar to her. Would she be able to sleep at night with the sounds of war so close? Would she be able to do her job, have a strong enough stomach for the wounds she knew she'd be tending? Scarlet swallowed a lump in her throat, digging her nails deeper into her palm as she walked.

She could do it. For Thomas, she could do it. Just like she'd already survived her military training on the outskirts of London that she'd been certain would kill her at the time.

The railway station was unbearably loud – too many people in a small space, the sound of a train pulling into the platform and being loaded until it was brimming with humans and baggage making Scarlet want to run. But she didn't, because she'd left home now and she wasn't going to run back to her parents and admit she'd been wrong.

She folded her arms tightly around herself, thankful for her warm coat as she found a bench to sit and wait on. She wondered if Thomas was warm, then sighed. More likely unbearably cold and lying in a trench. She understood from his early letters that the conditions weren't great, even though as an officer he most likely had it better than some, but she hadn't received a letter for months now, so she had no idea what it was like for him. He'd endured almost eighteen months before she'd met him when he was home on leave, but she still worried.

Looking around now that the station wasn't so busy, she noticed other women, some alone, others with families. She tucked a loose strand of hair back behind her ear and took a slow, deep breath. What she needed to do was make a friend, someone to talk to, so she could stop worrying. Too much idle time, her mother had always said, was a very dangerous thing – although her mother would have preferred she fill it with socialising and ladylike pursuits – and the last few hours, even days, she'd had far too much time to think.

Scarlet was about to stand up when someone sat down next to her and stuck out a hand. She looked up into dark eyes and a huge smile.

'I'm Ellie. Are you waiting for the train?'

Scarlet laughed. She couldn't help herself. 'Well, I'm not just sitting here for something fun to do.'

Ellie stared at her blankly, and Scarlet quickly took her hand. 'I'm Scarlet. Sorry, I'm nervous and that was supposed to be a joke.'

Ellie laughed and shook her hand up and down before letting go. 'Bloody hell! I thought you were just rude.'

Scarlet's hand flew to her mouth, stifling a shocked laugh. She wasn't used to women cursing, and the fact that such a pretty girl had spoken like a man made it even funnier. Her mother would have been horrified. Strangely, Scarlet found that thought comforting, how her mother would have reacted, or maybe it was just a nice kind of distraction from her darker musings. Ellie immediately reminded Scarlet of her family's servants. Back at home she'd spent plenty of time with them without her mother knowing, especially those in the kitchen.

'Where are you from?' Scarlet asked, folding her hands in her lap. Ellie had an accent, but Scarlet couldn't place it; it was a mixture that was hard to decipher. They looked the same to any onlookers, she suspected, both in their smart grey uniforms and capes, with their Red Cross armbands, even though prior to the war she doubted she'd have ever crossed paths with Ellie. Hers had been a life of parties and picnics, young women being prepared to meet their future husbands. But even in their very short acquaintance, Ellie seemed so much more real than many of the friends Scarlet had met in that world. Scarlet suspected that she was poor, but her smile was huge and genuine, not dainty and controlled.

'Can't you tell?' Ellie said with a laugh. 'I'm from Ireland, but we've been here almost five years so I guess it's become a little muddled. My father fell in love with an Irish lass when he was working over there, but we moved home for him to take over his family's farm. My mother's never forgiven him for making her move.'

'Will she forgive you for leaving home and doing this?' Scarlet asked, her voice low, thinking of her own family. She understood why they didn't want her to go, that they imagined a society life for her that consisted of little other than pretty dresses, marriage and children. But she couldn't just sit at home praying for a miracle when there was so much more she could do to help.

'Why would you say that? Isn't your mother happy that you're helping our lads when they need us? I sent my letter away requesting to join just as quick as I could.'

Scarlet sighed. 'Has your mother told you she wants you to help the lads?' she asked, repeating Ellie's words, and suddenly aware of her clipped English accent.

Ellie frowned. 'Of course.'

'Mine isn't happy,' Scarlet confessed. 'She didn't speak to me for two days when I told her what I was doing. She didn't mind me training to be a nurse, but when I said I wanted to help, to go anywhere the army might need me, she was so angry I thought she was going to explode!'

Ellie frowned. 'We have three boys away at war. Some nights I lie shivering, thinking about them, wondering how bad it is. But I still want to help. I volunteered before I was enlisted into any other work.'

Scarlet felt tears well in her eyes. 'Me too. I can't . . .' She sucked back a big breath and looked up when Ellie's hand slipped into hers. 'My mother said we've lost enough men to this war without losing our women, too. She told me that it's not a woman's place.' Her mother had actually said that it certainly wasn't the place of a woman *like her*, but she wasn't about to tell Ellie that. They all had to do their bit, no matter where they were from.

'We'll be fine. I promise, we'll be just fine,' Ellie said.

Scarlet didn't know what to say, how to explain the heaviness inside of her, the pain of not knowing where Thomas was. But she was lucky, wasn't she? Her sister was safe at home; she had no brothers away fighting like Ellie did. Everyone had lost someone to this war, or more than one someone, and she needed to keep telling herself that. Even if she didn't find Thomas, she was helping. She just had to keep believing that he was alive, that she would miraculously find him or someone who knew where he was.

'So tell me, what was your training like?' Scarlet asked, wanting to change the subject.

'Me?' Ellie laughed and the sound was contagious. 'You really want to know?'

'What's so funny?' Scarlet asked, grinning back.

'I'm supposed to be delivering babies, not stitching up soldiers' legs!' Ellie said, shaking her head. 'My ma's a midwife and I've followed her around and seen babies born all my life, so the last thing I expected was to be nursing men.'

Scarlet felt her eyebrows raise up. 'And you were all right seeing that, when you were a girl? That must have been terrifying.'

'No different than a cow having a calf, and we saw plenty of that on the farms back home. Only difference is that a woman makes a whole lot more noise!'

Scarlet laughed again. Thank goodness for meeting Ellie. 'You're so funny.'

'Me? Because I'm not afraid to tell the truth?'

'Yes, I think that's exactly why.'

Ellie was nice; she might be bold with her words and stories, but she was kind and charming, too. Scarlet could tell that right away. She was different from her friends at home, and in a refreshing kind of way. Scarlet adored her friends, even if they had all raised their eyebrows at her choice to nurse, each and every one of them, but Ellie was a breath of fresh air and it felt nice to be sitting with her and talking, sharing. Scarlet had grown up in a beautiful house with servants to assist them, but she'd been sheltered from so much. Maybe that was why she'd spent so much time with the servants, why she was so curious about the rest of the world.

'So how bad do you think it's going to be wherever we're going? As bad as they say?'

Ellie grimaced. 'Worse, I reckon.'

They were both silent for a long minute, sitting side by side, staring ahead. The station was starting to fill up again, the noise level rising once more.

'I feel like this should be an amazing adventure, but . . .'

'It's terrifying,' Ellie finished for her. 'It's absolutely bloody terrifying, and I don't know what to think. But we just put our heads down and get on with it. You and me, we'll be fine if we stick together. We need to do our bit and make it home in one piece for our ma's.'

Scarlet reached for Ellie's hand this time. It was nice to know that someone else was as scared as she was.

'So do you have a man off fighting?' Ellie asked, wriggling closer so they were shoulder to shoulder on the narrow bench. The proximity reminded Scarlet of her sister, who was volunteering close to home so she didn't have to move away, and it was nice to have the warmth of Ellie against her. She sighed, holding Thomas's memory within her, trying not to worry about how long she'd gone without hearing from him. Everyone around her lost hope too soon after the letters stopped, or at least that's what she thought. She would never give up, not until the very end.

'I have Thomas,' Scarlet shared in a quiet voice. 'He's my' – she gulped – 'fiancé.'

'Ah,' Ellie murmured. 'And is your Thomas away fighting?'

Scarlet nodded. 'Yes. Only I haven't heard from him in a while and I have this mad idea that I might be able to find him if I'm closer to where our boys are.'

Ellie squeezed her hand. 'Doesn't sound mad to me.'

'Truly?' Scarlet asked, a wave of emotion running through her. She hoped Ellie wasn't just saying that to be nice.

'Truly,' Ellie repeated. 'There could be a hundred reasons why you haven't heard from him. And who says you can't find him while we're nursing? It sounds like a perfectly good plan to me.'

Scarlet liked Ellie more as every minute passed. 'How about you? Do you have a special someone? A sweetheart away fighting?'

Ellie laughed and it made Scarlet smile again. 'Ask me that again after I've been surrounded by gorgeous doctors and soldiers. If I can't find me a dashing man while I'm nursing, I don't reckon I'll ever find one.'

Scarlet laughed again. 'So that's the truth? You've joined up to find a husband?' She was sure Ellie was joking. She was beautiful, with glossy dark hair pinned up, a wide, full mouth and chocolate-coloured eyes. There was nothing about her that wouldn't appeal to a man as far as Scarlet could tell, so she doubted she had to go away nursing to meet someone.

'What can I say?' Ellie said, slapping her hand to her heart and making them both giggle. 'No, I'm just being silly. I'd love to come home with a husband, I'm not going to fib about that, but I want to help. Some nurse might have stitched up one of my brothers or saved one of them, and I want to do the same for someone else's brother. I want to do my bit I suppose.'

Scarlet did, too. Even if she'd started out simply hoping to find her fiancé, becoming a nurse had changed her. Why couldn't women be more involved in the war if it helped to bring more of their boys home in one piece? She was only nursing, doing women's work, but many young women she'd heard about were doing so much more, things they would never have been permitted to do if it wasn't wartime.

'Do you know how long the journey is?' Scarlet asked.

'No,' Ellie replied. 'I want to get to where we're staying and find out if we're going to Europe or not.'

'I've always wanted to go to France, but . . .' Scarlet looked down and grimaced. 'Not dressed like this or in some manly battledress.' She had to admit that her uniform was smart, and the day she'd gone in to be measured at Harrods she'd been so proud, but the only thing to like really was the scarlet-trimmed collar of her greatcoat.

'Do you really think they'll send us there?' Ellie asked. 'I've heard so many rumours, but you never know.'

'I'm sure Matron will tell us when we arrive. But maybe they'll need us here for a bit?' Scarlet wasn't sure whether she wanted to stay in London or if going abroad was more appealing; truth be told she was terrified of both.

'So, tell me about your mother,' Scarlet asked, curious about the work of a midwife and wanting a distraction from her thoughts. 'Did she really let you go along on visits?'

Ellie grinned. 'What, you don't believe me? Of course she did.'

Scarlet opened her bag up and took out a small parcel of food. They were fortunate to have more than most, and as she unwrapped the cold chicken she felt Ellie's eyes on her.

'Would you like to share this?' Scarlet asked.

'Can you hear my stomach growling?' Ellie quipped. 'I'd love some.'

Scarlet held it between them, content to share the cut-up pieces of cold meat. 'We have a country house, a small farm actually, so we've been lucky with food,' Scarlet confessed, knowing that Ellie was probably only just getting by on food rations from the way she'd so eagerly taken the chicken. 'We have trees laden with fruit during summer, and we've kept chickens for eggs and so forth.'

Ellie nodded, taking another bite of chicken. 'This tastes heavenly.'

Scarlet realised how grateful she should have been, how little she truly knew about suffering and making do compared to so many others.

'If I have to eat another Woolton pie I'll scream,' Ellie said. 'But this, this is amazing.'

Scarlet ate some, feeling guilty and almost ready to offer Ellie the lot. But then again she didn't know when they'd next eat, or if they'd be given only bread and dripping like they had been at the mobilising unit. She decided to have a little and let Ellie have the rest.

'So you really want to know about my ma?' Ellie asked.

Scarlet nodded. 'Please.'

She watched as Ellie pulled out a handkerchief, a plain white one with no embroidery, and dabbed the corners of her mouth. Scarlet did the same, conscious of the delicate pattern on hers and how luxurious it seemed in comparison.

'My mother liked me to learn beside her because she learnt herself going to births with her own mother. She always told me it was women's business and one day I'd understand it all, but that was mostly when she was helping country folk to birth at home.'

'So you just . . .' Scarlet cleared her throat. 'Watched?'

'Well, she usually kept me busy with fetching hot water and towels and running back and forth. I wasn't sitting there staring at the baby coming out if that's what you're asking.'

Scarlet laughed again, felt her cheeks burn as she flushed. 'Enough talk about birthing babies for me.' She knew the theory about things like having babies, but she hadn't ever talked about it openly before.

Ellie giggled and nudged her in the side. 'I had three brothers back at home and when I went with her I felt special. All grown-up instead of a tomboy wearing my brothers' hand-me-down clothes. It made me feel like a girl and then a woman.'

Scarlet nodded. 'That makes perfect sense then.' She wasn't about to mention that she'd grown up being dressed in velvet party dresses and bronze-coloured shoes for dancing lessons and only seeing her mother when taken by Nanny. All she'd ever wanted was the freedom the village children had, even though she had been left to her own devices frequently when her parents were in town. She'd have done anything to have more attention from her own mother as a child; it hadn't been until she was eleven that she'd even been allowed to dine with her parents at the table. She felt a twinge of jealousy thinking of Ellie spending so much time with her mother.

'I, er, grew up with Nanny looking after me. She did everything for us and even though I adored her, I would have loved to spend more time with my mother.'

'Even delivering babies?' Ellie teased.

'Yes,' Scarlet admitted, knowing she was telling the truth. 'Even that.'

'So what if you were sick? Or upset? Who did you go to?'

'Nanny,' Scarlet said, nodding even as Ellie's eyes widened in surprise. 'Mother would have been more likely to tell me I was being tiresome if I complained about feeling ill.'

'So no cuddles in bed with your mother?' Ellie asked, looking more shocked about this revelation than seeing the cold chicken on offer earlier. 'Bedtime stories?'

'Plenty of cuddles and stories, just not with her.' All of a sudden, Scarlet felt uncomfortable talking about her childhood. She adored her mother and had always thought they were very close. But she only had the experience of girls from families like hers to compare with. All of their parents were the same. Although she guessed the children of the servants were treated very differently by their parents, cared for by their mothers rather than anyone else. As much as she was enjoying Ellie's company, she realised they were from very different backgrounds.

'Heavens, that's dreadful,' Ellie muttered. 'At least I know how the other side lives now. We all sat around our dinner table, my brothers and me, with Ma and Pa, and at night Pa'd read to us in front of the fire. We didn't have a lot, but we had full bellies most of the time and there was plenty of laughter and hugs.'

Scarlet met her new friend's gaze. 'I never really thought about it before, the differences between some families.' Although she wished her mother had visited their quarters more, she'd always felt so loved by Nanny, and she'd had her older sister for company, so it wasn't like she'd been miserable. Far from it.

The loud noise of a train chugging into the station made Scarlet turn, her heart leaping. *It was almost time.* They'd been so busy talking and now they were about to go to London. For someone used to chaperones and chauffeurs, Scarlet was starting to feel well out of her depth.

'Is this us?' Scarlet asked.

Ellie looked as apprehensive as Scarlet felt. 'Hmmm, I think so.'

Scarlet sat up straighter, rolling her shoulders back. Her hand was slippery as she grabbed the handle of her bag, nerves sending ripples through her body.

'Don't you go changing your mind now,' Ellie cautioned, linking her arm with Scarlet's. 'We're in this together.'

Scarlet gulped. Part of her wanted to flee, to go home with her head hanging and admit her failure before her journey had even begun, but one glance up into Ellie's chocolate-brown eyes made her steel her resolve and nod instead.

'Looks like it's time to board,' Ellie said.

The noise and bustle around them amplified, made it impossible to think of anything else as they stood, bags in hand, and made their way towards the train. It had been cold outside, but now it was muggy from all the people crammed into one space and Scarlet felt flushed as she held out her ticket and finally stepped up and into the train. She'd half expected luxury, but this was anything but.

They both sat down with bags clutched to their chests, resting on their thighs. There were other women, many in pairs now, some alone, and a smattering of soldiers and civilians. Scarlet wondered what their stories were, where they were going and why, if they were searching for someone they loved. Most of all she wondered whether they'd even return.

'We're going to be fine, I promise,' Ellie said, patting her arm as a whistle blew.

Scarlet knew it was a promise Ellie couldn't possibly keep, but she took some comfort in the confident way she said the words.

'You sound so sure,' she replied.

'Or maybe I just want to make you feel better so you'll share some more food with me.'

Scarlet burst out laughing and Ellie joined in. Thank goodness for Ellie. She'd be a basket case without her seated beside her wheedling for food!

'Half an apple,' Scarlet said in a low voice. 'That's all we're having or we'll be out of food before we even get to our lodgings.'

CHAPTER TWO

Ellie

Ellie wasn't sure if her stomach was protesting more now that it had actually had some food than it had been when empty. She'd been hungry for so long that it was almost a shock to eat anything nice at all; the empty, hollow feeling was one she was starting to get used to. Her mother did her best, but making hearty meals wasn't exactly easy any longer, and Ellie was so tired of eating vegetable pies and stale bread, which was all they seemed to feed the nurses where she'd been training.

The motion of the train had made her sleepy, but she forced her eyes to stay open and stared out the window. She might be putting on a brave face for Scarlet, pretending like she was happy to be doing her bit, but inside she was scared. The thought that something could happen to her and to her brothers was all-consuming, that her mother might be left grieving for all four of her children. It was unbearable.

'I think we're almost there.' Scarlet's low voice jolted her from her thoughts.

'It's going on a boat I'm worried about. I just know we'll be going on one to somewhere,' Ellie confessed. In truth, it worried her more than the actual nursing, although she knew she might change her mind once they arrived.

'It'll be fine. I'm sure we'll be given decent food on board if we do get shipped anywhere. And surely we'll be able to sleep a lot,' Scarlet said.

Ellie doubted it. She'd been living hand to mouth for what felt like for ever now. She could tell Scarlet had lived a very privileged life, but she didn't care about that type of thing. It was the least of her worries because if Scarlet was nice then it didn't matter. They were all going to be rolling their sleeves up and getting dirty, poor or rich.

'So tell me more about this chap of yours,' Ellie said, settling back into her seat.

'Now?' Scarlet asked.

'Yes, now!'

Ellie glanced up when a soldier walked past them – the motion of the train making him unsteady on his feet. Either that or he'd had something to drink that he shouldn't have. He smiled, and she flashed him a beamer back. Poor boy was about to go to war, the least she could do was give him a grin to make his day.

'Well, he's very handsome,' Scarlet said, a pink blush taking over her cheeks as Ellie watched. 'He's tall and he looked very charming in his uniform.'

'Kind of like that handsome soldier?' Ellie raised her eyebrows when Scarlet looked away, before laughing and shaking her head. 'Well, where did you meet? How long have you been engaged?'

Scarlet sighed and Ellie sat back. 'It was at a garden party when I was presented. I didn't go to Queen Charlotte's Ball like my sister.' Scarlet had a faraway look in her eyes. 'I was wearing my white dress. I felt like a princess; and he was there and then . . .'

'He took your hand and you ran away?' Ellie knew she was being silly, but she liked making Scarlet laugh. Besides, it was all just so foreign to her. 'This is like a fairy tale for me. I want *all* the details.'

'No! I mean, no to running away, not to telling you all about it. My parents liked his family. They approved of him immediately and he was allowed to visit me, but before that we saw each other at different events while he was on leave. He was my only boyfriend. We sneaked out once to go dancing. We were back before two in the morning and no one even noticed we were gone,' Scarlet shared. 'We went on some dates, with a chaperone of course, but the best night was when Thomas was visiting when we were staying in our town house. We had to rush to the shelter during an air raid. He helped my mother and sister, but I got to sit next to him. He held my hand under the blanket and Mother didn't even know.'

Ellie listened, hanging off every word. 'And what happened? After that night I mean? When did he propose?'

She reached for Scarlet's hand when she saw her blink away tears. 'Please don't cry! I didn't mean to upset you.'

'No, it's fine. I just . . .' Scarlet's voice trailed off. 'I think of that night so often – the way he kissed me when it was dark, when no one could see. Our teeth kind of bumped and his moustache was bristly against my lips, but it was amazing. I mean . . .'

'Keep going!' Ellie begged, whispering. 'Please!'

'It was the only time he ever kissed me like that,' Scarlet whispered back. 'Every other time was just a peck on the cheek, very formal. But that night was magical, even though we were all terrified down there and cooped up like chickens. I'll never forget it because he was usually so proper.'

'And when did he propose? Was it before he was sent away?'

Scarlet nodded. 'Yes. Just before he left, he asked my father for my hand. He proposed at our house, in the garden, the day before he left. He promised me he'd write, and that we'd be married the day he came home.' She made a low noise in her throat. 'We had exactly thirty-two days in London together before he left, and he's been gone for months now.'

Ellie's oldest brother had left behind a wife and two little ones, but her middle brother had done the same as Scarlet's man – proposing right before he left – and she knew how hard it had been for his fiancée. All the waiting, wondering and, she bet, worrying about him not coming home at all and being left a spinster. Her own mother kept saying there was going to be a whole lot of young women and not enough men to go around once the blasted war was finally over.

'When was your last letter from him?' she asked gently.

'Thirteen weeks ago,' Scarlet replied quietly.

'Don't let anyone tell you you're crazy for searching for him or that you'll never find him.' Ellie meant it, with all her heart. 'If I loved a man like that, I'd be searching for him, too.'

'You might not be saying that in a few weeks' time when I've driven everyone crazy with my notices pinned everywhere and endless questions,' Scarlet said, looking glum. 'Part of me knows it might be futile, but then even if I don't find him, it won't be for nothing, will it? At least I'll be doing good along the way, tending to our soldiers.'

'Hey, you might be married to the man in a few weeks! Who knows what will happen?' Ellie said. 'Does he have a brother for me?'

Scarlet smiled. 'He does have a brother, a younger one. If my sister hadn't already been in love she'd have been begging to know more about him.'

'Good-looking?'

'I don't know. I've never met him.' Scarlet paused, her mind turning over her quest to find Thomas. 'Do you honestly believe I can find him? You're not just trying to make me feel better?'

'Honestly. He's your man, and that means if anyone is going to find him, then it'll be you.'

The train slowed, the engine noise loud and the sudden movement making Ellie stick her hand out to brace herself against the seat.

'I think we're about to arrive,' Ellie said.

Scarlet looked back at her, eyes wide. They both laughed nervously. Ellie was certain that Scarlet was as unsure as she was because they had no clue what would happen once they arrived, where they would be posted or when they'd ever see home again.

Ellie liked to be positive and make everyone around her smile and laugh, but she'd be lying if she said she didn't wish she could run for home. She hated blood – hated the smell of it – and wasn't at all good at thinking about gaping wounds and infected skin. Babies were different. It wasn't pleasant seeing what a birthing woman had to go through, but it was a process she'd known about since she was a little girl. Yes, there was blood because it was part of life, not – she sighed – not death and injuries. That was why she ended up making jokes and playing along as if she was fine about where she was going and what she was going to have to do. In truth, she was shaking in her boots about what she'd kept joking about as her big adventure away from home.

Ellie pushed her thoughts away, not wanting to worry herself even more. As the train continued to slow she clutched her bag tighter, looking down at the worn leather. It had belonged to her grandma, and then her mother, and now it was hers for her travels. Ellie brushed her fingertips across the top, looking at what was possibly the most extravagant thing she owned. They'd been told to take a carryall and she was fortunate to have it at all. Same with her uniform; if her grandmother hadn't given her most of the money to buy the two skirts, straight tunic, cap, gloves, capes and cotton dresses, not to mention all the other bits and pieces, she'd never have been able to afford it, not with what little they had to go around.

Finally, the brakes made a noise that sent goose pimples across Ellie's skin – the tiny hairs on her arm all standing alert. The train made a final lurch and she realised she'd been holding her breath.

'I think we're here.'

Ellie looked out the window. People were everywhere, in numbers she'd hardly ever seen before. She gulped then straightened her shoulders, forced a smile. *Smile and the world will see the woman you want them to see, no matter how you feel inside.* Her mother's words echoed in her mind, calming her, doing what they always did, and had done since she was a small child.

'Is your stomach twisting into knots?' Scarlet asked.

'More like an entire army kicking their boots in there,' Ellie said, linking her arm through Scarlet's.

It meant the world to her that she'd met someone to share the journey with, to talk to and make her feel less alone. All her life she'd been surrounded by her family. Until recently they'd all lived together – all of them squished into their little home. It hadn't taken long for her oldest brother to use his Irish charm and find a nice girl, but it wasn't until the other two had left to join up that the house had felt empty. She didn't like to think of how her parents would feel in bed tonight, worrying about all of their children. As much as they'd supported her decision to go, she knew it had likely broken their hearts.

Ellie and Scarlet watched and waited as people got up to leave the train, not bothering to push their way through.

'Ladies.'

Ellie smiled up at a soldier who was standing back, gesturing with his hand for them to stand and pass.

'Thank you,' she said, giggling when he winked.

Scarlet stayed close to her, head bent, as they made their way out and down on to the platform. It was a burst of noise, far louder than at the station where they'd boarded, and there was a cool wind, which made it even nicer to have Scarlet huddled close. Although, her greatcoat was very warm and her legs were equally cosy in their thick woollen stockings, so it was only her face being whipped by the late wind. She wished the spring weather weren't so cold; it had been cool and windy all month.

'I thought it would be easy to find where we were supposed to go and who to report to,' Scarlet muttered.

'Me too,' Ellie said. 'I thought Matron would be looking for us.' She stared around, not sure where to look or where to go. There were soldiers everywhere. Some of the young men were standing in groups, laughing and talking loudly, acting like they were invincible. Others were quiet, maybe more reluctant about where they were headed to, and Ellie couldn't blame them. The same feelings were running through her: on the one hand wanting to be full of life and bursting with excitement, and on the other quietly terrified about what she was about to do.

Then she spotted other Queen Alexandra's Imperial Nursing Service women. The other QA nurses were dressed just as they were, in their new scarlet-trimmed greatcoats.

'Look, over there.'

Scarlet stepped on tiptoe beside her and nodded. 'Let's go.'

They walked briskly in the direction of the other nurses, and Ellie saw there was a stern-looking matron with a clipboard, taking names.

Scarlet's name was called almost immediately. She responded, 'Present!' her voice slightly cracked with nervousness. They waited until Ellie had her name called and then finally, after much muttering, Matron announced, 'We will be travelling to Broomfield House, where you will spend the night before you are sent to your final units. There you will be working under canvas and sleeping in two-man tents, so I highly recommend that you enjoy your last night of comfort!'

There were groans, but Ellie stayed silent. She hadn't expected even one night of luxury, so she wasn't about to complain. She and Scarlet followed the others out of the station to a truck, engine running, that was waiting for them on the road. Ellie took a deep breath and climbed aboard. This was it. No turning back.

She sat beside Scarlet and another girl, who gave them a tight smile.

Ellie had spent all of her young life at home, never having been away from her family for more than a night, other than for her army training. Tears welled in her eyes, but she swallowed them down and smiled back. Everything was going to be just fine.

Ellie had to consciously keep her mouth closed, otherwise she feared her jaw might actually drop to the ground.

'Heavens,' she muttered as she stood outside the truck, staring at the grand house in front of them. The drive hadn't taken too long, but it had been bumpy, cramped and stuffy inside the truck, making her want to stretch her legs. She could see now that it had been worth the discomfort.

'Please proceed into the house. The nurses before you were stationed here for some time. However, you will only have the luxury of one night before moving on,' announced Matron.

Ellie wondered why, what news there had been. But she didn't dare ask. She walked with Scarlet, although they both stayed silent. Her bag was heavy and Ellie grasped it tighter, taking in the large pond at the front of the house and the grand entrance. She'd certainly never set foot in a place like this before. She stepped inside, eyes darting to the old portraits hanging on the walls and the huge staircase that ascended out of view. The carpet was threadbare and the house more unkempt inside than it had probably ever been prior to the war, but it was still beautiful in her eyes. *Like a grand old lady wearing finery that is a little worn around the edges,* she thought.

'I wish we could stay here a bit longer,' Ellie whispered.

Scarlet grinned. 'It's quite grand, isn't it?'

A month earlier, when she'd been issued with her uniform, Ellie had been stationed in a house with other nurses, where they'd worked at a hospital that had needed them, tending to minor cuts and burns in addition to their training. This was certainly a step up.

'Good afternoon!' a short man in uniform yelled out from the bottom of the staircase. Ellie hadn't even seen him appear, but she had to stifle a laugh; he looked too short to be a soldier, even though his shiny black boots and uniform were impeccable. He saluted them. 'This is how you should salute your sergeant!'

Ellie stood straighter, still holding her bag in one hand.

'You are lieutenants, and as such you must learn to salute correctly when in uniform. Some of you may have received instructions already, but I want you to practise!' he told them, his booming voice belying his stature. 'Salute!'

Ellie mimicked his action, doing her best to salute properly back. They might only be lieutenants, not to mention female ones at that, but she figured this particular sergeant was going to be a stickler for army procedure, and probably the sour-faced matron, too. She tried not to laugh thinking about the first lesson she'd had, back in London and wearing a cotton frock, trying hard to do as she was told without laughing at the very unimpressed sergeant instructor.

'Your stay here at Broomfield House will be short, but it will be long enough for you each to be issued with a gas mask, bedding roll and straps, two blankets, one small pillow, and a canvas bucket, bath and basin, as well as a kitbag with a stove and lamp.'

Ellie gulped. *Gas masks?* A shudder ran through her body. She hated the things, was certain she'd panic if she had to wear one.

'Questions?'

'Will we need any more injections?' one of the other nurses called out.

'Yes! Next question?'

Ellie groaned. The worst part of her training had been the injections they'd been given in preparation for the possibility of nursing abroad.

'Are we on rations here?' another asked.

'Yes, but you will receive four meals each day that you are here, and the same at your next lodgings, which will be under canvas to prepare you for war,' the sergeant replied. 'You will be shown to your quarters now. Please make your way back down promptly to collect your service items and kitbags.'

Ellie kept close to Scarlet as they followed Matron upstairs.

'Two to a room,' she announced as they passed down the corridor lined with rooms containing hospital beds. Ellie realised the house was operating as a makeshift hospital as well as providing their temporary accommodation. She'd had no idea what to expect.

'This is the bathroom you may use. Remember, five inches of hot water *only* is permitted,' Matron continued, her face devoid of any emotion. 'Further, you must be ready to leave at a moment's notice.'

They ascended the last flight of stairs, walking across stained carpet on the landing. Ellie glanced into a room through an open door, saw two men huddled around a bed and wondered what was going on.

'Excuse me.' A deep voice jolted her from her thoughts. Ellie stumbled and felt her cheeks ignite when hands grasped her elbows. She looked up, aghast, at a young man with thick dark hair and even darker eyes, wearing a white coat – obviously a doctor.

'I'm so sorry,' she muttered. 'I should have been looking where I was going.'

It seemed she'd almost walked straight into the poor doctor, who had now let her go and stepped back a foot or more.

'No trouble. There's a lot to see here.' He smiled. 'But be more careful next time, Nurse.'

Ellie tightened her hold on her bag and stepped around him, hurrying to catch up with her group. She glanced over her shoulder as she ran, still blushing as she looked at the handsome young doctor one last time. Maybe nursing was going to be fun, after all. His brown eyes were warm as he smiled at her, holding up his hand in a wave before disappearing down the hall.

'Who was that?' Scarlet whispered.

'Doctor Handsome,' Ellie whispered back. 'I walked smack bang into him!'

'Ladies, is there something you would like to share?'

Ellie cleared her throat and looked at her feet. 'No, ma'am,' she said, loud enough to be heard clearly, but her thoughts were still with the doctor who had flashed her such a sweet smile.

Ellie and Scarlet were assigned a room together and they both flopped down on the small beds. Ellie stared up at the ceiling. She was thankful they hadn't been separated.

'One of the girls was muttering something about us being sent to Burma, and another said that she'd been told we would be going to Gibraltar,' Scarlet said in a low voice.

'Nonsense. Surely they'll send us to Europe if we're going anywhere,' Ellie scoffed.

'Wherever we're heading, it's not somewhere in England, that's for sure.'

'Scarlet, can I ask you something?' Ellie said, her thoughts turning back to her mother and father. She rolled over on her stomach to stare at her new friend.

'What is it?'

'If anything happens to me, would you promise that you'll visit my family and tell them how much I love them?'

Scarlet swallowed. 'Of course. And you'll do the same for me?'

Ellie nodded. 'I think we should write letters, and sew them into each other's uniforms. That way we'll never lose them and you will always have mine and I yours, in case something terrible happens.'

The sound of other nurses walking back down the hallway towards the grand main staircase alerted them that it was time to move again.

'How about we do that tonight, then we never have to speak of not returning home again?' Scarlet suggested.

Ellie nodded in agreement. She stood and held out a hand to Scarlet, pulling her up to her feet, too. 'Let's see if we can't have some of that hot water to have a bath before bedtime,' she said, shaking off the sombre mood.

Scarlet linked arms with her and together they walked back out into the hall to join the others.

CHAPTER THREE

Scarlet

Scarlet took a deep breath and finished getting dressed in the tiny cubicle that made standing almost impossible, let alone attempting to put on clothes. She'd never realised how little five inches of water was until now, and it certainly hadn't made bathing easy. Nor had the lukewarm water. Her mind kept drifting to home, what it could have been like if she'd stayed, but she pushed away the thoughts that could so easily take over. She was here now. She was no different from any of the other nurses because it was wartime, and that meant nobody cared who you were or where you came from, only what job you did. That thought terrified her as much as it thrilled her, and she wondered how on earth she'd cope.

She needed to hurry because they were leaving soon and there was to be a briefing before they set off in the convoy of trucks that were already waiting outside. They'd been told there would only be one night at the old house, but with so many injured men to deal with, and not enough help, they'd stayed on for three more nights and it was only now they were finally moving on. Scarlet had enjoyed staying in the house, despite the restrictions on hot water, because she knew it would be a lot harder in the tents wherever it was they were going, even if she did at least have a friend to share with.

'Get a move on,' Ellie called out, her cheery voice impossible not to recognise.

Scarlet shook her head, smiling to herself before pulling the curtain back. Their room was awful, so dark and depressing, but at least she'd managed to bathe before they left. It was times like this that she thought of home, of the life she'd have with Thomas after the war – being married, having a house of her own, children to care for. It was all she'd ever wanted, a nice home and a nice husband to share it with.

'Have you spoken to Doctor Handsome yet?' Scarlet teased.

'As a matter of fact, yes,' Ellie replied, walking out of the room ahead of Scarlet. She quickly followed and they took the long walk back to their room to gather their belongings. 'I was rebandaging a patient when he came in to check the charts.'

'And?' Scarlet asked, liking to tease Ellie about this particular doctor who always seemed to make her swoon.

'He nodded and said hello, went about his rounds, then stopped to smile at me and say goodbye,' Ellie said. 'I think he's the one.'

She burst out laughing and Scarlet rolled her eyes. 'Because he's so handsome? Or because you want to marry a doctor?'

Ellie sighed. 'Sneer all you like, but the way he looked at me made my knees knock.'

'Well, let's cross our fingers that this doctor of yours will be joining us, wherever that may be.' Scarlet felt the familiar tremor of nerves beat through her stomach, but she tried her best to ignore them. Wherever they were going, they were going together, and that in itself was something to be grateful for.

'Did you hear that Charlotte isn't joining us?' Ellie said conspiratorially as they entered their room and collected their carryalls and kitbags. 'I heard that she's pregnant by a sergeant and they're having

29

a fast wedding before he leaves! I wonder how long she's even known him or been here. A month?'

'No! Surely not!' Scarlet held her breath, so pleased that she hadn't ended up pregnant before Thomas had left. She knew of some girls who were scared of even kissing their sweethearts for fear of getting pregnant, but for it to happen here and be sent home? 'Imagine if it was the little one we met that first day! What was his name – Sergeant Winters?'

Ellie giggled. 'I never thought it could be him!'

Scarlet was still smiling when they went down the stairs, gathering with the other nurses, some of whom she'd got to know well. She bet their matron would be furious that she was already losing a trained nurse.

'Have you heard where we're going?'

Scarlet turned to the girl on her right, Rose. She'd spent some time with her the night before, caring for a patient with a head injury, which meant they'd sat whispering into the early hours.

'No. What have you heard?' Scarlet asked.

Rose bent her head closer. 'That they're sending us to France.'

Scarlet gulped. She'd guessed as much, but there had been so many rumours she hadn't known what to believe.

'Ladies, listen please!'

When Matron spoke, they all knew to be quiet, and Scarlet gave the older woman her full attention, not daring to speak again.

'We are travelling today to Sussex. We will be leaving immediately and you will be staying in your two-man tents with the same person you've been sharing a bedroom with.'

'Is it true we're going to Burma?' a worried voice called out.

'You will be advised of any planned destination prior to departure, but for now you should expect to live and work under canvas to prepare for the conditions you will face.'

Once Matron had finished, Scarlet felt a hand close over her arm. It was Ellie.

'This is it, isn't it?' Ellie asked.

Scarlet nodded. 'I think she knows more than she's letting on. Surely they know where they're sending us! Why can't they say?'

Ellie shrugged. 'Wherever we're going—'

'Excuse me.'

Scarlet looked up, then glanced at Ellie and saw a wide smile break out on her friend's face, quickly replaced by a more demure expression.

'Yes,' Ellie replied.

'I'm Doctor Spencer Black. I don't think we've officially met.'

Scarlet watched as Ellie stuck out her hand and the doctor gently shook it.

'Ellie. And this is my friend, Scarlet.'

The doctor turned and Scarlet let him take her hand, too, smiling back at him. His eyes were as dark as Ellie's, and the way he ran a hand through his hair made him look ever so slightly nervous. Or maybe she was imagining it. She had to agree with Ellie that he was awfully handsome. 'Pleased to meet you.'

'Ellie, I'm going to be travelling to Sussex with your unit. My speciality is head trauma and burns, and I'm looking for a nurse to work alongside me.'

Scarlet hid her mouth with her hand, not wanting the handsome doctor to see her smirking. Ellie would be beside herself!

'I couldn't help but notice your bedside manner with the patients yesterday, and I need a kind, cheerful nurse to assist me. Someone I can trust and train accordingly.'

'I'm, well, flattered,' Ellie said in a quieter voice than Scarlet had ever heard her use before. 'And I'm truly sorry about walking into you the other day, when we first arrived. That was—'

'Nothing to worry about, it's long forgotten. Can I count on you?' Doctor Black asked.

'Of course. Thank you,' Ellie said, blushing. 'And if you need another nurse, Scarlet here is very skilled.'

He smiled kindly and Scarlet nodded back.

'If you'd prefer me to ask—' Doctor Black started.

'No!' Ellie looked horrified at how loudly she'd interrupted him. 'What I meant to say is, I would love to be your nurse. Thank you for asking.'

The doctor looked uncertain, but stepped back and held up his hand. 'I shall see you in Sussex, then.'

'So you shall,' Ellie replied.

Scarlet waited until he was a few paces away before eagerly turning back to Ellie and grabbing her hand. Ellie was so excited she had her other palm clamped over her mouth.

'I think Doctor Handsome likes you, too,' Scarlet said, raising her eyebrows at Ellie's pink cheeks.

'He doesn't. It's probably just because he saw me being nice to a patient.'

'Ellie, we're all nice to the patients. Have you seen any of the girls being unkind? We all have a lovely bedside manner.' Scarlet laughed. 'He hasn't exactly seen you do any strenuous nursing work here!' The patients at Broomfield House had already been patched up before they'd been sent on for further care.

Ellie was biting down on her lower lip and Scarlet wished she was the one falling in love, that her heart was full to brimming with anticipation rather than feeling like it was starting to break in half. But she was happy for her friend – why wouldn't she be?

'Do you really think so? That he likes me?'

'Sweetheart, a doctor just made his way over here and chose you over all these other nurses,' Scarlet told her, looking around at the dozens of women surrounding them, all dressed in uniform and chatting away as they waited. 'Who knows if he even *needs* his own nurse!'

Ellie was still chewing on her bottom lip when Matron called out and they all gathered up their bags to follow her. Scarlet looked over her shoulder, saying a silent goodbye to the old house that had been their home for the first few nights away.

Outside, trucks were lined up and waiting. Scarlet followed the nurse in front of her and climbed into one of the trucks, hauling her things and thinking for the hundredth time how she'd taken for granted having someone to carry heavy things for her in the past. But she was also becoming more aware of just how fortunate she'd been, and what a sheltered life she'd led. If she'd followed her parents' instructions she would have been hidden from the worst of the war, denied the opportunity to help like this. Thomas had been the original reason she'd signed up, but her resolve to help had strengthened with every day of training. Whether or not Thomas would have approved of her leaving home to nurse, and being sent away close to danger, was another matter entirely. She had a feeling that the answer might be no, only he didn't have a choice in the matter. She wasn't his wife yet, and if she didn't set out to try to find him, she might never be.

Tears prickled her eyes, but she refused to let them fall.

'Are you feeling all right?' Ellie asked, interrupting her thoughts as she wriggled closer beside her.

'Oh, I'm fine. Just thinking about home.'

'I miss home badly, too,' Ellie confessed. 'It's worse at night when it's dark and all I have to do is think about my family.'

Scarlet had been so tired each night that she'd fallen asleep the moment her head hit the pillow. It was during the day that her thoughts would wander. 'We never did write our letters to home, did we?'

'No. We haven't exactly had any idle time.'

Ellie was right. They'd been either nursing, learning army etiquette, eating or sleeping since they'd arrived.

The truck began to move forwards and any hope Scarlet might have had of writing in transit was dashed. 'What will you say?' she asked, curious. 'I want to tell my family, aside from that I love them, that I'm so pleased I have the chance to help our men, to do something useful, and to meet so many different people. I feel like before I hardly knew a thing, and now, after all my training, I'm like a different person.'

The truck rattled along and Scarlet looked out, admiring the countryside, wishing she was travelling for a different reason. That she and Ellie were friends exploring this beautiful country, and that they weren't about to face unimaginable horrors.

'Why do you think they are so secretive about where we're going to be sent?' Scarlet asked, waving to a woman standing by the roadside. The woman had one hand to her chest, the other raised high as she called out and waved to the trucks.

'I don't know. Why shouldn't we know instead of worrying?'

'Look,' Scarlet said, distracted at the sight of more women running down the road towards them. The trucks slowed and Scarlet realised it wasn't just women, but children, too. 'Are they running for us?'

'Look over there!' the nurse on her other side said. 'They're all waving, even from the fields!'

Scarlet admired all the women working on the farms, keeping the crops growing while the men were away. 'Are they Women's Land Army, do you think?'

'I'm certain they are. Hello!' the other nurse called out, waving back excitedly.

As some of the open-sided trucks slowly moved closer to one group of women, Scarlet could hear what they were shouting.

'It's our girls in there! Our girls are in the convoy!'

'It *is* our girls!'

Her heart leapt. She didn't know these people, but they were so excited to see them. Now she knew why they'd come running, because surely they were used to the sight of army convoys by now. She could see now that many of the older women had tears streaming down their cheeks; strong women who'd probably never shed tears so openly before were now weeping along the roadside.

'God bless!' someone called.

God bless us all, Scarlet thought. A thrill passed through her, but there was definitely terror building up inside of her as well. Terror at the unknown, excitement at what was to come, hope that she might find Thomas, or at least some clue to his location, and fear of what she might be faced with. Of the truth.

'I miss my mother so badly, seeing all these women,' Ellie murmured from beside her.

Scarlet sat back and shut her eyes for a moment, overwhelmed.

'I miss everything about home,' she whispered.

She reached for Ellie's hand and the nurse beside her suddenly clutched her other hand. They all sat in silence as they eventually passed all the well-wishers, the truck speeding up and taking them closer and closer to Sussex.

Scarlet looked up as the sun filtered through the clouds above, before turning her attention to the neatly packed tent on the ground in front of her. Watching someone else put it up had looked simple, but doing it herself was another matter entirely.

'We're going to freeze,' she announced.

Ellie pulled a face. 'I know. And to think I'll have to cuddle up to you in the night when I get cold!'

Scarlet laughed. Trust Ellie to lighten the mood when she was feeling dismal.

'I'm not Doctor Black, but I promise I don't snore,' Scarlet teased her back.

Ellie pretended to swoon. 'Oh, well if you were Doctor Handsome . . .' She burst out laughing, but the laughter only lasted until Scarlet held up part of the tent, trying to figure it out.

'Come on, let's get this over with.'

They fumbled their way through putting up the tent, helped by an orderly who was going around assisting all the nurses. Then they climbed inside and hauled in their things behind them. Scarlet sat in one corner and undid the straps on her camp bed.

'Do you think we can do anything to make these comfortable?' she muttered.

'We can only try,' Ellie replied with a sigh.

'I'd love to go exploring, walk around the farms nearby and just . . .'

'Forget the war?' Ellie asked softly.

Scarlet blinked away the tears that took her by surprise. 'Yes. That's exactly what I want to do.' She'd been having fun with Ellie, despite the hard work and conditions, had enjoyed having a friend so happy and positive about life, but then her thoughts would turn to Thomas and she'd wonder where he was all over again. Was he dead? His body lying grey and lifeless in a ditch? Or was he alive? Captured by the enemy and facing unimaginable horrors? Or injured? Was a nurse like her, somewhere out there, holding his hand and tending his wounds? Keeping him alive so that one day he'd make it home?

'Do you think about him an awful lot?' Ellie asked.

'Is it that obvious I'm thinking about Thomas?' Scarlet asked.

Ellie nodded.

'All the time,' Scarlet confessed. 'I think about him, worry about him – and then I'll become preoccupied with what we're doing, or talk to you and feel happy, and then when I stop, it all comes back again. It makes me feel so guilty, being happy and forgetting about him even for a moment.'

'Wouldn't he want you to be happy, though? No man wants to think of his sweetheart back home being miserable. He'll be remembering your beautiful smile, the smell of your hair, all the lovely, happy things about you, if he's still . . .'

Scarlet gulped when Ellie's voice halted, her sentence left unfinished, her dark eyes round as saucers.

'I'm so sorry,' Ellie whispered.

'If he's still alive,' Scarlet finished for her. 'That's what you were going to say, wasn't it?'

Ellie hung her head but Scarlet shuffled closer to her in the small tent, not wanting her to feel bad for simply stating the truth.

'I didn't mean it like that.'

'But you're right, Ellie. He might be dead.' It was a truth she had to admit, even if she didn't want to believe it.

'I don't want you to think that, though. I was—'

'Please, don't say anything more. If I don't find him, then at least I've done my best. I need to believe he could be alive, that's all.'

Ellie looked up, eyes brimming and making a fresh wave of tears fill Scarlet's.

'I believe in you. If anyone is going to find out where that man is, it's you,' Ellie said.

The sound of the bustling camp outside was getting louder, the activity of so many women setting up camp and moving around the area impossible to ignore.

'How about we sneak away as soon as we can?' Ellie said, rubbing Scarlet's arm before crawling back out of the tent. 'It might be the last time we get to have fun in a long while.'

Scarlet followed her, crawling out and emerging into the sunlight. She tilted her face up to the sky, eyes shut, breathed deep and simply enjoyed the feel of the sun's rays on her skin. *He was alive.* She had to believe it, otherwise she'd fall to the ground and never be able to stand.

The constant noise of women talking all around them was overpowering:

'Fetch water from the big kitchen Soyer stoves!'

'How long are we here for?'

'Someone said there's a farm nearby offering hot baths!'

'Did you see those new doctors?'

'I want to go home! I can't live here! It's disgusting!'

'*Have you heard about the Forgotten Army? They're stuck in Burma and they're getting eaten alive by insects in that heat!*'

It filled Scarlet's head even though she tried hard to block it out. But then she opened her eyes, straightened her shoulders and took a big breath that filled her lungs almost to bursting before slowly letting it go. She couldn't let it get to her. She had to push through and be strong.

'Come on,' she said to Ellie, who'd been standing behind her. 'Let's go.'

'Matron said we should make ourselves familiar with the place,' Ellie said. 'They're starting our training tomorrow.'

Scarlet nodded. 'I don't even want to think what they'll have us doing.' Doubts filled Scarlet again. Maybe she would have been better off making herself useful at home, working with the Red Cross and doing what she could on the home front rather than becoming a military nurse. Part of it was fear of the unknown, she knew that, and the fact she felt so overwhelmed to be living such a different life from that she was used to. When she'd said yes to marrying Thomas, she'd known she would lead the same life she'd grown up enjoying, that she'd be safe and content, looked after by a man who'd always shown her kindness. That life she'd kept imagining was so different from what was happening now. When she'd accepted his marriage proposal, she'd naively imagined that the war would be over within a few more months and everything would simply go back to normal. Her naivety embarrassed her now, made her wonder how she could ever have known so little. But she'd constantly been told by her father that war was a man's business, and that it would be over before they knew it, even after all the months then years of fighting.

They wandered slowly across the grass, away from the tents, towards a large stone house where she guessed the higher-ranking military were staying, along with the doctors. She'd heard a rumour there were even dentists posted with them, and that they could be travelling with them wherever it was they were going to end up.

'Oh my goodness, look over there.'

Scarlet followed Ellie's gaze, seeing dozens of men hauling large tin trunks up to be painted with the particular flash that identified each unit.

'It's quite a sight, isn't it?'

It was Matron speaking, and although Scarlet had found her rather stiff and intimidating back at their first lodging, the woman sounded almost motherly now.

'Ma'am, where do you think we'll be sent?' Ellie asked. 'I mean, we're going abroad, aren't we?'

Scarlet waited expectantly, hoping in this quiet moment between them that something might be said.

'We'll all find out soon enough where you're being sent,' Matron replied, back to being brisk with her words. 'It's time to get your bedding rolls and kitbags stencilled, just like those trunks. You'll be issued your battledress by the morning.'

Scarlet looked at Ellie, fear humming through every part of her body.

'So it's only a question of *where* we'll be posted offshore, not *if*?' Scarlet murmured.

'Yes. Now off you go to collect your berets; the case is outside the front door over there.'

The last time Scarlet had heard from Thomas he'd been heading to France. She knew in her heart that he was still there somewhere.

Please send us to France. Please.

They made their way quietly over to the case, being amongst the first of the nurses there as they reached in. Scarlet pulled out two berets. The first was too small so she passed it to Ellie and then tried the next one on. It seemed fine, so she tucked it under her arm and stepped back.

'We've been summoned to Matron's office!' a nurse named Holly called out, breathless as she ran up behind them.

Scarlet turned to the friendly nurse. 'What for? We were just talking to her and she didn't mention anything.'

'One of the officers ran down to see her just now, right in front of me, and she's summoning all of us!' exclaimed Holly, breathless. 'It sounded serious, they were whispering and Matron looked alarmed. We're to find our way to her office. It's in the house, through the large drawing room.'

'And you know nothing of what it was about?' Ellie asked.

Holly shook her head and ran off to tell the others. Scarlet took the lead and she and Ellie walked into the house. They hadn't had a tour yet, so she wasn't sure what to expect, but straight away she saw that it was much older and more in need of repair than where they'd previously been stationed.

Ellie tripped and Scarlet just missed catching her by the elbow.

'You all right?' Scarlet asked, holding out her hand and helping her friend up.

'Tripped over my own feet,' Ellie muttered, holding up her hand and inspecting her grazed palm.

They were about to hurry off again when suddenly Spencer appeared, a frown on his face as he approached. Ellie hovered close to Scarlet, and she wondered if Ellie was embarrassed about the conversation she'd had earlier with him before leaving.

'Do you know what's going on?' Ellie called over to him.

He gave them a tight smile and came closer. 'Matron is about to share the news with you all.'

Scarlet watched as he ran a hand through his thick brown hair. He was ruffled, she could tell. He folded his arms tightly to himself and stepped closer to Ellie.

'What have you done to your hand?' he asked, noticing the graze. He made to reach for her, then quickly pulled back. Scarlet stifled a smile, seeing how badly he had wanted to connect with her friend.

'Oh, it's nothing, just a scratch,' Ellie said.

'I'll check it for you, make sure it doesn't get infected.' He took her arm now that he had an obvious reason to and examined her hand carefully, fingertips touching the broken skin.

Ellie laughed and Scarlet tried not to do the same. 'I'll be fine. You have much more important things to worry about than me scraping my hand.'

Scarlet cleared her throat, not wanting to interrupt the tender moment between her friend and the doctor but needing to know why they'd been summoned.

'Spencer, do you know what's going on? What Matron is going to tell us?'

He turned to her, still holding Ellie's hand, the slight smile that had momentarily brightened his face turning down again into a straight, more sombre line.

'I'm sorry, ladies,' he said.

'What is it?' Ellie asked, eyes wide.

'The Allies have landed in Normandy and parachuted into Le Havre.'

CHAPTER FOUR

Lucy

Normandy, 12 June 1944

Lucy couldn't move. Her feet felt like they'd become part of the sand, etched into the soft ground. The beach was swathed in smoke, and clouds of dust billowed around her. She squinted, certain that her eyes were playing tricks on her and the dust couldn't actually be red. But this was war. She was in the middle of a war zone. Any horror was possible.

She choked, the thick air clogging her lungs, making it impossible to breathe.

'Move!'

The loud yell of a male voice close by jolted her back into action, made her spring forwards, limbs suddenly mobilised, stumbling as she carried her bag and ran after her unit. Lucy heaved, the acid burn of bile in her throat making her want to double over and be sick. But she didn't. She kept her feet moving, kept her head down, and rushed across the sand.

If they didn't get the hospital set up, more soldiers would die. There was no time for her to have a weak stomach. If she failed now, gave in to her fears, then she was only proving her father right, and there was no way she was doing that. Not for a second.

'We are the 50 Mobile field hospital with the RAF,' the same deep male voice called out. Or maybe it was someone different; Lucy's ears were ringing and her head was spinning. 'We need to be operational within hours, not days. There will be ambulances arriving from the front before nightfall, if not sooner. Our boys are relying on you, and we're their only hope for getting out of this godforsaken place alive.'

Lucy dug her nails into her palms, her fists tight. She looked back at where they'd come from, saw ships pounding the shore, heard the noise level rising. Men were shouting, running, screaming. Women in battledress were moving in all directions, not even looking like nurses other than the fact they wore the Red Cross armband. But they'd been trained for this; they were working under the RAF. If they couldn't do it, no one could, and she was more determined than any of the other nurses to prove herself.

She followed orders and moved immediately to where the orderlies had already started to set up. Working under canvas meant they could be operational fast, only they'd never actually witnessed combat, never seen soldiers with the kinds of horrific wounds she was certain they were about to be presented with. But she'd always had a strong stomach, and knew she could push past the terror of what she would see in order to do her job. It was what she'd wanted to do all her life – be a doctor and deal with wounds and surgeries, but right now she was prepared to start with being the best combat nurse she could be.

A huge booming noise rang out, making every hair on Lucy's body stand on end as she froze. It was followed by shots – noises that she didn't recognise. Was it a bomb? Was it—

'Take cover!'

Lucy ran fast, blindly escaping from a danger that could just as easily have been in front of her without her realising. When she looked back, the clouds of smoke were even thicker and she could see that the red was becoming more intense, that her eyes hadn't been deceiving her.

And then she moved straight into work mode, pushed the fear and terror aside and made herself do what she'd been trained to do. This was what she'd wanted, and she wasn't going to let anyone down. Orderlies were frantically erecting the canvas tents, setting up their hospital and making it useable. It was an army of movement, things happening everywhere, and they simply had to do whatever they could. They'd only just arrived, just come in to shore on a boat that had brought them from England, and already they were in the middle of war.

Dear God, if you can hear me, please spare the nurses. Keep us safe from harm. Without us, our boys will never make it home. Amen. Her lips moved but the prayer was silent. Unlike her heart, which was beating so loud she was certain it could be heard even over the shelling happening so close to where she was standing.

'Incoming!'

Lucy's instant reaction was to drop, until she heard the next words that were yelled from somewhere nearby.

'First ambulance is here!'

This was it.

---------- ⌇⌇⌇ ----------

Lucy was so tired she could hardly drag her feet to keep walking, but she gritted her teeth and made herself keep going. She glanced at her watch, saw that it had been almost twelve hours since they'd arrived in Normandy, and she hadn't stopped, not for a moment. There was no time; her sitting down to catch her breath or look for something to eat could mean a soldier died. Someone's son, brother, husband . . . Tears filled her eyes, but she quickly blinked them away. She was overtired, that was all. The day had been overwhelming and terrifying and she hadn't had a quiet minute to digest where she was and what they were facing. She pushed it all down, refusing to give in to her feelings. The only way to go was forward, that was what she needed to tell herself.

'Are you feeling all right?'

She looked up, bewildered for a moment, the weight of the other nurse's hand on her arm calming her.

'Of course. Just tired,' she admitted, pushing her slumped shoulders back. 'And you? How are you?' she asked, wanting to repay the kindness of someone taking a moment to ask after her. 'Can I assist you?'

The older nurse smiled kindly and they started to walk together. 'We've taken six hundred patients already. Keep up the good work.'

She nodded and took the bandages she was carrying to a doctor. The soldier he was treating started to scream, and when Lucy looked down at him more closely her body froze. His face was badly burnt, the skin red raw, like a piece of bloodied meat across one side, and yet his other cheek was clean-shaven. Perfect still, aside from a blur of dirt.

'Cut his trouser off and dress his leg wound,' the doctor ordered.

Lucy did as she was told, refusing to panic when this young man needed her so badly. She reached behind for scissors and swiftly cut off what was left of his trouser leg, taking away the bandage that had hastily been put there. His bone was exposed, the leg as gruesome as his face.

'Doctor, should we . . . ?' Her voice trailed off.

'Patch him up as best you can. Air evacuation.'

The doctor disappeared, leaving her to do what she could. Lucy reached for more bandages, but as she turned back a hand closed around her wrist. It was only for a moment. She glanced down. The touch had been so soft she wondered for a second if she'd imagined it. And then she saw something on the ground, a photo of a young woman.

'Is this yours?' she asked, bending to retrieve it, looking down at the soldier and refusing to turn away from his monster-like face, to give him the respect he deserved. 'She's beautiful. I'll get you out of here and back to her just as soon as I can.'

The noise under the canvas tent was indescribable: shelling outside, trucks pulling up, ambulances, the volume of people in one tiny space. Soldiers were moaning and screaming in pain, doctors were yelling and nurses were running madly in all directions. But Lucy pushed the noise away, focused on doing the best she could for the man on the bed in front of her.

'Sir,' she said, not sure if he was quiet because of the morphine or trying hard to be brave.

She'd finished the bandaging and touched her hand to his chest where she'd placed his photo.

'Sir?'

'Nurse! Here!'

She hesitated, didn't respond immediately to the call. Instead she bent, listened for his breath, hand still flat to his chest.

He was gone.

Lucy straightened, tears sliding silently down her cheeks. She wondered if her heart was slowly breaking, whether such a thing was even possible. In less than a day, she'd seen more men die than she could ever have imagined. She wondered if this was why her mother had silently agreed with her father, never interrupted when he had made it so clear that women shouldn't be doctors, and that she'd never have the stomach or strength to be a nurse on the front line. But she refused to think of caring as being weak. It *should* hurt to lose a patient, and she refused to think any other way, no matter how painful it was.

'Ambulance hit!'

Lucy heard the boom of gunfire before the call, dropping the bandages she was holding, ready to run. She was close to the entrance, to where the ambulances were arriving. She held her breath, terrified of what she was about to see. As she emerged, there was smoke everywhere, thick and acrid. She held her hand to her mouth, started to cough, choke, until the smoke began to slowly clear like fog – and then she simply froze.

The ambulance had been hit; she could see the vehicle on its side through the haze, not so far from where she was standing. But it was the woman's body on the ground near her that made her stop moving, made her scream silently, filling her own head with a piercing noise even though she knew no sound came from her mouth.

'We've lost nurses!' came a shout.

Lucy only took a moment to gather herself, thinking nothing of her own life, of the danger facing her, as she sprinted forward. She bent, turned the young, motionless nurse over, her tin hat discarded, blonde hair etched with blood.

'Help!' Lucy screamed.

It felt like a lifetime even though she knew it was only minutes, as she held the hand of the other nurse, staring into eyes that were slowly starting to focus. And then there were men around her: doctors, orderlies, she didn't know. She did her best to help lift the other woman, ran alongside them and into the hospital as the noise of gunfire echoed around them. She cringed at the sound of an explosion. *Would she ever make it home alive?*

CHAPTER FIVE

Scarlet

Sussex

'If I have to march again or crawl through barbed wire, I'm going to scream.'

Scarlet laughed at Ellie's moan, but the truth was she felt the same. They'd scaled ropes, marched for what felt like hours, been trained in self-defence and slept on the ground. She knew that once they were stationed somewhere, they were going to have to deal with tiring conditions, but for now it seemed unnecessary. Besides, they'd all already endured so much training before arriving here. Never in a million years had she imagined doing anything like this; it was so far removed from the life she knew it was laughable. Anyone who'd known her at home never would have believed what she was truly capable of. Even though she knew some of her friends would be stepping outside their comfort zones to help in factories or the local Red Cross, none of them would be doing anything like what she'd volunteered for.

'We'll be well prepared for anything,' Scarlet replied, instead of sharing her own concerns.

'I say we run away and find that place with the hot baths.'

Scarlet knew exactly what Ellie was talking about. They'd been in Sussex four days now, and some of the other nurses had already visited the surrounding farms. Rumour had it that an old retired colonel was taking pity on some of the nurses and offering hot water, and she was tempted to go and find out herself whether it was true or not.

'Before dinner?' Scarlet asked.

Ellie nodded. 'Maybe he'll feed us, too. Would have to be better than the slop we get here.'

Scarlet shuddered just thinking about the food they'd been eating. The poor cooks had to make four meals a day for them – but on normal civilian rations, it was almost impossible.

'I'm dreaming of eggs. And chicken. And fruit,' Scarlet muttered.

'Oooh and tea with fresh milk and sugar.'

Scarlet shut her eyes, almost able to taste it. 'Stop teasing me. I can't stand even thinking about food.'

'Dinner will be served promptly at six o'clock,' Matron barked at them.

'I think we all know that already,' Ellie muttered loudly.

Scarlet waited for them to be reprimanded, but it seemed they hadn't been heard, and soon they were trooping off after the other nurses. When they reached their tent they both retrieved their towels and toiletries, tucking them into tight balls under their arms.

'Are we going to ask anyone to join us?' Scarlet asked.

'No way. Come on.'

Scarlet followed Ellie's lead, keeping her head down, not wanting to catch any of the other nurses' eyes. They'd made some lovely friends, often chatting to many of the other women, but if they were going to have any chance of a bath, it was better if there were only two of them.

'Cathy said he is a kindly older man, and he fetched water for them straight away.'

'Sometimes I wonder if they're just teasing us. The thought of hot water . . .' Scarlet sighed, not bothering to finish her sentence. 'I think it's what I miss the most. I can't decide whether it's decent food or being scrubbed clean.'

The countryside was beautiful. With the oak trees swaying gently high above them, and the green grass stretching as far as they could see, it was almost impossible to believe they were at war. That their men were away fighting, dying; that they were going to be stationed somewhere so different, so soon.

Ellie walked along beside her, and when Scarlet glanced over she saw that her friend was looking around, too, probably thinking the same thing. It was somehow so idyllic in the midst of such chaos. They kept moving through a more forested area and over a fence that divided the properties.

'Are you ladies lost?' a deep, well-spoken man's voice said from nowhere.

Scarlet jumped and grabbed hold of Ellie's wrist. A soldier was leaning against a tree, boots crossed as he lit up a cigarette. His uniform made it clear that he was a commanding officer. He was watching them, squinting into the sun, one side of his mouth turned up in a smile.

'No, not lost,' Scarlet replied, chin up, refusing to let him see what a fright he'd given her.

Ellie gently tugged on her wrist and Scarlet folded her arms for something to do.

'I'm guessing that you're looking for a house that gives pretty nurses hot baths?'

Ellie laughed and that made the soldier laugh, too. Scarlet tried hard to keep a straight face.

'Are we that easy to read?' she asked.

He grinned again, and he seemed so at ease that Scarlet softened, letting herself smile back. She didn't know why she'd been so taken aback in the first place. He was handsome and friendly, and she needed to relax more. Things were different here from what she was used to back home.

'I hate to tell you, but you're second in line already,' he said, pushing off from the tree and stepping forward. 'Another two nurses scurried past earlier, but I'm sure they'll be almost done.'

'Are you just standing here on nurse watch then?' Ellie asked, swapping glances with Scarlet, her eyebrows raised.

'No, I'm keeping an eye out for deserters. You aren't one of those, are you?'

'There are people running away?' Scarlet asked. 'Surely not here!'

'Just joking. I'm on a twenty-four-hour pass, and I've been scrounging for some decent food. The folk around here are pretty kind to soldiers. I offer to chop wood or do some odd jobs, and just like that I'm eating again.'

'What kind of food?' Ellie asked, moving towards him. Scarlet did the same, staying close to her friend but feeling more relaxed even though she'd never spent a lot of time with strange men before.

'Just some fruit. A little bread,' he said with a shrug. 'One lady cooked me an egg.'

Scarlet couldn't help but smile at the sweet expression on his face. She would love to eat anything half-decent right now, and fruit would be heavenly. 'How did it taste?' she asked, quickly looking away when he caught her gaze.

'After months without it?' There was a twinkle in his eye that made her want to look away for good, made her uncomfortable and drew her to him all at the same time. Why was he spending so much time looking at her instead of Ellie? 'Like heaven on earth.'

'I think you need to escort us to this place,' Ellie announced, linking her arm through his like she'd known him for ever and it was the most natural thing in the world for her to do, even though he was still smiling at Scarlet, his gaze trained on her eyes. 'How about you take a couple of tired nurses to the house with all the food?'

The soldier laughed, gallantly holding out his other arm to Scarlet. His eyes dipped to her mouth for a moment, before returning to her eyes, and she felt a hot flush grace her cheeks.

'Come on. It's only proper for a gentleman to escort you both safely. I promise I'll look after you.'

She took his arm gingerly, not as sure as Ellie, but hearing in his well-heeled accent that he clearly thought it his duty to look after them. She only hoped he wasn't fooling them.

'I'm dying for a bath,' Ellie moaned.

He turned to Scarlet again, almost ignoring Ellie. 'And you? You must be missing the comforts of home, too.'

'I think I'd rather a bath than food,' Scarlet admitted, certain that he'd already figured out that she was missing luxuries more than her friend, her accent surely giving her away.

'Perhaps you lovely ladies could bathe, and I'll try to rustle you up something to eat. Although I might need you to join me if I'm going to make anyone believe that the extra food is for nurses and not me.'

'I'm Ellie,' Ellie said, ignoring his suggestion and leaning forward, giving Scarlet a stern look that she couldn't decipher. She sighed as if she was waiting for Scarlet to do something.

Scarlet realised Ellie had been prompting her to introduce herself, but the soldier had her rattled. She had to admit that he was handsome. His hair was dark and thick, his cheeks clean-shaven. He had a golden hue to his skin, no doubt from hours being under the sun since he'd joined up, and when he smiled at them his eyes crinkled just a little at the sides.

'You know, soldier, you haven't even told us your name,' Ellie said.

Scarlet smiled to herself, wishing she was as confident as Ellie.

'How rude. I'm James,' he said. 'It's my pleasure to meet you both.'

Scarlet stared at the man whose arm she was holding, wishing she could stop studying his features. Now that he'd stopped staring at her, she was doing the same back to him.

'Well, James, this here is Scarlet. She seems to have lost her voice.'

Scarlet reluctantly kept hold of his arm even though she was feeling uncomfortable about being so close to him. She shouldn't be liking his smile or his eyes, or losing her words. She was engaged to Thomas, and that meant she should be immune to the charms of other men, surely!

'Well, m'ladies, we'll be at the house shortly. Perhaps you'll permit me to escort you to the doorstep.'

James turned, a wide smile on his face, Ellie still attached to his other arm.

Scarlet giggled. She couldn't help it. It was like speaking to one of the boys from home. 'Thank you. It's very kind of you to spend your precious free time escorting us to this house,' she said.

His smile made heat flush her skin again.

'So, who's going first for the bath, and who's going to sit out here and keep me company?' James asked, grinning.

'Me!' Ellie announced, swinging away from him. 'I'm first, which means you can enjoy chatting to my beautiful friend.'

Scarlet was ready to kill her now. 'Ellie!' she hissed. She had better not tease her about the soldier once he was gone.

'You young ladies looking for a hot bath?' an old man called from his front doorstep nearby. Scarlet thought the big brick house looked like it had seen better days.

'Yes, please!' Ellie called back. Then in a quieter voice, 'I'll leave you two to have fun. See you soon!'

Scarlet watched as Ellie ran towards the house, scared of turning and looking into the eyes of the man who was making her body betray her. Why did she keep flushing hot and cold, and why did he keep giving her such a look, as if he knew exactly what effect he was having on her?

'You know, it's nice to hear a familiar voice,' he said, smiling, and somehow managing to make her relax a little. 'Meeting you has made me feel like I'm back at home, which was unexpected. Almost like I'm at one of those interminable dances my mother made me go to, only a whole lot nicer.'

She smiled. 'I know exactly what you mean.' The familiarity between them was reassuring.

'So, how are you enjoying Sussex?' he asked, dropping down to the dry grass and beckoning for her to do the same.

She did, but she purposely sat further away from him, keeping her distance. She forced a smile even though she was nervous.

'I suppose it could be worse,' she said honestly, folding her hands in her lap.

'Worse than what you're used to at home?' he asked, plucking at the grass as he watched her, his eyes never leaving hers.

'You could say that.' She laughed, and liked that he smiled straight back at her. Scarlet forced her shoulders to relax, took a deep breath, and tried to let go of whatever it was that was making her feel guilty. He was a soldier and she was a nurse, and if she couldn't talk to one friendly soldier, then how would she ever be able to treat hundreds of them? 'You could say that my parents never expected either of their daughters to ever lift a finger, let alone do work like this. My sister followed my father's wishes, she's volunteering close to home. But the longer the war has gone on, the more compelled I have felt to do something more.'

'Ahh, I see. It sounds like our families are similar.'

She met his gaze this time. 'You have sisters?'

'No, but the world we come from would definitely mean that if I did, their making the decision to nurse away from home would have been frowned upon.' He let go of the small handful of grass he'd gathered. 'Good on you for putting your name forward. It must have taken some courage to go against your family's wishes.'

'How do you know I volunteered? That I wasn't assigned to be a nurse?' she asked, becoming more curious about the handsome soldier. She wished she hadn't sat so far away from him now, now that she was feeling a pull towards him that wasn't easy to ignore.

'If your family'd had a say, and they'd made you volunteer before you were forced to do a job you didn't want to, you would have ended up doing something cute and easy close to home. Not this.'

'Sounds like you have me all figured out then,' she said, shaking her head.

'Don't I?' His eyes locked on hers again, not letting them go, and she felt the heat rise again, her skin simmering. This soldier was something else – and she knew he was dangerous company, that she didn't need to be around him when all her energy should be focused on Thomas.

'Want to take a stroll?' he asked.

Scarlet leapt up. 'Yes.' Walking meant not looking at him. It meant keeping her distance, thinking about putting one foot in front of the other.

He placed a long piece of dry grass between his lips, drawing her gaze there. Why had he done that? When he held out his arm, she shook her head; she wasn't about to be lured into getting too close to him again. He shrugged and she walked alongside him.

'Tell me, what do you miss most about home?' he asked.

Scarlet sighed. 'So many things,' she said honestly. 'My bed, food, not having to get up so early! Honestly, there are so many things, everything even, that I've always taken for granted. I won't ever again, but I'm ashamed to say I did.'

'We're all the same. We don't think about what we've got until it's taken away.'

'Do you have a wife or girlfriend you've left behind?'

James slowly shook his head, a grin kicking up one side of his mouth. 'I didn't strike you for the forward type. How wrong I was.'

'No!' She clamped her hand over her mouth, mortified. 'I'm not, I mean . . .'

'I'm teasing,' he said, raising an eyebrow and taking the grass from his lips, which only made her look at his mouth again.

'Well, it's not funny,' she huffed. 'I was simply trying to make conversation, enquiring about how you are faring without your—'

'There's no one special waiting for me. You?'

'Yes,' she said quickly as they turned back in the direction of the house, the little loop they'd walked taking them around in a misshapen sort of circle. 'My fiancé. He's serving.'

'Ah, I see.' He slowed his walk, gave her a look that she wasn't sure about. 'Well, he's a very lucky man.'

'Scarlet!' Ellie's call broke their connection, made Scarlet turn away from the deep brown gaze that had so easily captivated her.

'Coming,' she called back.

'Go have your bath, and then I'll take you both to find some real food,' James said.

'The water is heavenly!' Ellie was waving at her, gesturing for her to come over. 'If you don't get in quickly, I'm going to get back in.'

Scarlet walked towards her friend, pausing only briefly to look back over her shoulder at James. He hadn't moved: his head raised, eyes still trained on her, his smile kind. There was something about the man that unnerved her, that rattled her in a way she'd thought she'd be immune to.

'So? Tell me what you think? He's gorgeous,' Ellie whispered as she linked arms with her.

Scarlet leaned into Ellie, needing her touch. 'He's lovely. I mean, if I were single . . .' Scarlet didn't even know what she was trying to say. 'I have Thomas, though, Ellie. Please don't forget that.'

'Oh, for God's sake, just enjoy a harmless flirt!' Ellie said with a laugh.

Scarlet glared at her, not liking being teased.

'Come and meet Colonel Wright,' Ellie said, giving her a weird look and rolling her eyes. 'He's divine, and he's said we can come for a hot bath whenever we like.'

But even the thought of her impending bath couldn't take Scarlet's mind off James.

The water was luxurious, and she didn't want to think about how long it might be before she had another interlude with hot water. But it was cooling down now and she'd already taken too long.

Scarlet quickly dried herself and got dressed, and then fixed her hair as prettily as she could, thinking about their last lodgings and how she'd hardly been able to stand at all in the tiny cubicle. *Thomas.* Why wasn't she thinking about Thomas? Why was she trying to make herself look pretty for someone else? Because it was the man outside that her thoughts kept turning to, and it was making her feel every bit the unfaithful fiancée, even though she'd done absolutely nothing inappropriate. But the way he'd looked at her and the way she'd felt trapped in his gaze . . . it had stirred her and shaken her and knocked her way off balance. He was too charming, too charismatic not to be drawn to, and she hated how fast her heart had raced when she'd been with him.

She looked around, wondering what the old man's story was. It must have been a lovely home once upon a time, but given how everything could use a good dusting she had a feeling that he was a widower. Scarlet stopped in the hall, dressed and ready to head back out, and bent to look at an old photograph in a frame, sitting amongst a collection of knick-knacks.

'What a beautiful woman,' Scarlet murmured.

'She was.'

'Oh!' Scarlet leapt back, embarrassed at being discovered looking at someone else's pictures. 'I'm sorry, she just caught my eye, and I couldn't help but take a closer look.'

'She was a beauty, my Ivy,' the colonel said, rubbing his moustache as he spoke. 'Gone almost two years now.'

Scarlet reached out to touch his arm, seeing the tears shine in his eyes. 'She certainly was beautiful. I'm so sorry.' No wonder he was offering nurses hot baths; the poor old man was probably lonely as anything and liked the company.

'I've told that fella of yours to go pick some fruit. There's a bit left in the old orchard out there, though it's most likely bruised or bird pecked.'

'Oh, he's not my . . . I have a fiancé,' Scarlet stuttered. 'But you're ever so kind, thank you. And you're so generous firing up that hot water for us. You'll never know how desperately we've been dreaming of a bath.'

'You ladies will be back home soon, but for now, you come and see me whenever you get a break. I'm an old man with nothing better to do.'

'You're in uniform here,' Scarlet said, pointing to another photo, set further back. She wished she had more time to spend chatting with him.

'It was a long time ago,' he said, his smile disappearing. 'A long, long time ago.'

Scarlet hesitated, not sure what else to say. But he took the lead, gesturing for her to walk ahead of him towards the front door.

'Thank you again,' she said, hand on the doorframe, turning one last time to smile at him.

'Let's hope it's not goodbye yet. They might keep you girls here a bit longer. Keep you safe and out of harm's way.'

Scarlet could only wish. It wasn't exactly a hardship being based in Sussex, even with all the training. Not compared to where they could be.

'Bye for now,' Scarlet said, seeing Ellie sitting not far away in the grass, head tipped back in laughter, amused at something James had said to her.

She took a deep breath and propelled her feet forwards. She wasn't going to stare at James's thick dark hair, or the fit of his uniform, or the way his eyes crinkled when he smiled. Because she loved Thomas. Anything she was feeling for this handsome soldier was probably just to do with missing her fiancé, nothing more. Thomas was dependable, safe and secure, and this man . . . he might *sound* like other men she knew, but that wasn't enough to make her trust him.

Scarlet cleared her throat with a little cough and Ellie waved.

'Hi there!'

Scarlet smiled and crossed the grass, turning to give a final quick wave to their bath saviour.

'I can see why so many of the girls have been coming over here,' Scarlet said, eyes trained on Ellie so she didn't have to look at James. 'He's so kind to invite us in like that.'

'He was a real sweetheart,' Ellie agreed. 'Scarlet, have some of this fruit. James, let her have some of that apple.'

'Oh no, I'm fine.'

'Hey, I don't bite,' he said with a grin when she was forced to turn to him. 'Try it.' He was holding out the apple, and she didn't want to seem rude.

'Thank you.' Scarlet moved closer, taking it from his outstretched hand. She tried to bite delicately; it was so good, and the last fruit she'd had was what she'd brought from home and eaten on the train. She didn't even care about the brown spots all over it.

'I'd better escort you both back. Your matron looks particularly terrifying.'

Scarlet took another bite then passed the apple back to him, careful not to let their skin touch. She was feeling all kinds of jumpy, a bundle of nerves. 'We'll be fine. Thanks anyway.'

'Don't be silly, we'd love you to walk us,' Ellie interrupted. 'It's not every day a handsome soldier has time to escort nurses back to their quarters.'

James's grin was all kinds of mischievous, and Scarlet pushed away jealous thoughts about the way Ellie giggled at him. Ellie had Spencer, didn't she? Surely she didn't need to have James, too. She dug her nails into her palm, scolding herself. Only an hour earlier she'd been angry with Ellie for pushing her towards the man, and now she was acting like he was hers!

'Penny for them?'

Scarlet forced a smile and took the arm James offered. 'Oh – my fiancé. I was thinking about my fiancé,' she said, hating that she'd told a lie.

He laughed. 'Look what he has to come home to! If I was engaged to you, I'd be fighting off every damn German that came my way to get back home.'

Scarlet went to pull her hand from his arm, beyond embarrassed at his candid words. 'I, I, well.'

'Scarlet,' James said gently, hand over hers, locking it in place. 'If we can't joke about anything, we may as well all give in to the Nazis now. Come on, I'm nothing if not a gentleman. I'm just saying your fiancé is a lucky man.'

Scarlet held his arm, avoided Ellie's stare, and wished the ground would simply open up and swallow her.

'Scarlet, James told me they're going to announce a film screening tomorrow night. For everyone to attend. And the nurses will all be on army rations now, so we'll be getting bigger meals.'

'A film night?'

'It'll be amazing. I'm going to ask Spencer to come, too.'

Scarlet nodded. 'Of course. It'll be lovely.'

'So we can double date then?' Ellie asked.

Scarlet suppressed a groan at the same time as James tapped her arm with his hand. What part of 'engaged' did Ellie not understand? Or did she want two men to choose from and the whole thing was about her?

'I'd be honoured,' James said. 'Although I'm certain we'll be segregated.'

'Of course,' Scarlet mumbled.

Inside, her stomach was doing somersaults and her mind was buzzing. She should have said no. She should have made up an excuse. But it was war. There was so little to look forward to, and so much sadness surrounding them. Was it so wrong to anticipate a night of fun? She didn't have to do anything improper, after all.

'Why are they giving us a film night?' Scarlet asked, suddenly curious about why the army would decide to put on something like that now, when there had been no displays of any generosity before.

'Because soon we'll all be gone,' James said, his voice sombre now. 'One morning you'll wake up and we'll have been deployed – disappeared in the middle of the night.'

'One of the nurses said that when she was based in Scotland, they were looking forward to a dance and the boys left in the middle of the night before. Just poof, gone!' Ellie shared. 'Like they'd never even been there in the first place.'

Scarlet gulped. *Surely things wouldn't happen like that here.*

'I'd love to go to the film tomorrow night,' she announced, leaning in to James and smiling across at Ellie. No more moping or feeling guilty for being happy. She needed to enjoy the fact that she was alive and surrounded by other young people. 'It had better be something decent, because it's about time they did something fun for us.'

By the end of the week they could be gone, all of them, and they deserved something to smile about, even if it was just for one night.

CHAPTER SIX

Ellie

'You like him.'

Ellie leaned in and put her arm around Scarlet as they sat in their tiny tent. She shouldn't have kept teasing her, but it was so obvious, and she had to say something.

'Of course I like him. He was a perfectly pleasant young man,' Scarlet replied, sounding exasperated.

'No, you *like* him,' Ellie said, laughing as she fell back on to her bed.

They'd made their beds as comfortable as they could, although it wasn't exactly easy given what was available to them. But Ellie wasn't about to complain, not when she knew her brothers would have it so much worse; she was terrified every day that she'd receive word one of them hadn't made it.

'Ellie, stop it!' Scarlet scolded. 'Honestly, I don't know why you're making such a fuss about him.'

'Because he's gorgeous, for starters,' Ellie said. 'He's also charming and friendly, and I could tell he likes you.'

'He'd probably like any nurse under the age of thirty!'

'Calm down, lovely, I was only teasing.' Scarlet sighed beside her and Ellie held out a hand. 'You know, if you did like him you'd have nothing to feel guilty about.'

'But I do,' Scarlet whispered, bursting into tears. 'I have a fiancé. I made a promise to marry Thomas. I'm not one of those shallow girls who flit from one boyfriend to the next, and now I feel so guilty because I *do* like him.'

Ellie felt tears prickle in her eyes, seeing her friend so upset. She hadn't meant to push her so hard! 'I'm sorry, I was only teasing,' she said, giving her a big, tight hug. 'Don't go crying on me.'

Ellie wasn't going to say what she truly thought: that it was unlikely that Scarlet would find Thomas, or that he would still be alive after so long of no one hearing from him. She wanted to believe for Scarlet's sake, and she surely wasn't going to be the one to make her friend give up hope. But there had been something between Scarlet and James, and she'd have been a fool not to have noticed it. And if the worst was true when it came to Thomas, perhaps the memory of attraction to another man would help Scarlet believe she could find love again.

'Those dreamy eyes of his!' Ellie teased, wanting to make fun instead of upsetting Scarlet this time. 'I mean, what girl could be immune to his charm? You're only feeling what any of us would have felt, so don't go feeling guilty.'

Scarlet rolled over, their faces close as they stared at each other, both bursting into giggles.

'*Gorgeous,*' Scarlet admitted in a breathy voice. 'Soooo gorgeous.'

'If I hadn't already fallen for Spencer . . .'

'No! You can't go using any of that charm on James,' Scarlet hissed. 'Not him.'

'Hold your horses, I'm not doing anything to your James. Spencer is the one for me.' She laughed.

'He's not *my* James,' Scarlet muttered.

Ellie raised her eyebrows. 'Sweetheart, you can't tell your heart what to do. It's the one part of your body that doesn't listen to advice.' Her ma had always said it was the heart that got a woman into trouble, and to watch hers didn't go getting her into any sorts of high jinks while she was away.

'So, how about you? You've been awfully quiet about Spencer.'

Ellie rolled on to her back. 'I've hardly seen him,' she admitted. 'We spoke in the hall this morning as he dashed past, but he's been gone all day to see some soldiers with terrible burns. He said we might see a lot of that wherever we're stationed.' She laughed. 'If he keeps running his hand through his hair like he always does I think he might start to lose it!'

'I think he does that whenever he sees you,' Scarlet said with a grin.

'Oh, very funny!' Ellie rolled her eyes.

'Seriously, though, Ellie, I don't know how I'll stomach all those wounds,' Scarlet said.

It made Ellie sick just thinking about it. 'Sometimes I think how easy it would have been to stay at home and volunteer for something less gory. It sounds selfish, I know, but a factory job would have come with a lot less worries.' Although then she'd never have met Spencer.

'It's not selfish. Before the war, we'd never have thought about leaving home and doing anything like this. Never.'

'Did you hear that some of the girls are being posted elsewhere?' Ellie asked. 'They've already prepared to leave.'

'I know. Why do they do it to us? There is so much uncertainty, and if they just kept us together and told us what was going on, it would make it more bearable.'

'Did you write your letter yet?'

She looked over at Scarlet when she heard her move, watched as she took a small square of paper from her pocket.

'Yes. Do you want it?' Scarlet asked.

Ellie took her own out. She'd written it that morning, when she'd had a few moments alone. She'd have liked to have taken longer over it, but she'd been thinking about it an awfully long time, and if something did happen to her, at least her family would know how much she loved them.

'Do you want to read it to me first?' Ellie asked, keeping her voice low. They were told off for having their lamps on or talking too late, and the last thing she wanted was their surly matron to stick her head in and give them a blasting.

'If we don't read it to each other now, I guess we'll always be wondering what the note we're carrying says.'

Ellie stared at Scarlet. She felt so fortunate to have found a friend to share their journey with. There was one thing she was certain about, above all else: that if anything did happen to her friend, she would move heaven and earth to make sure Scarlet's family received her letter.

'Dear Mother and Father,
If you're reading this letter, it means something dreadful has happened to me. I know you never wanted me to leave home, but I hope you're proud of all I've achieved and done. I want you to know that I thought about you every day – it was what kept me going, knowing I would one day be home. If Thomas comes home alive, tell him how much I loved him and that I never gave up trying to find him, that I truly believed I could somehow save him and bring him home. I hope the war is over when you read this, and that you can look forward to a future of peace. All my love to Rosalie, I wish her happiness, love and children. Don't forget to tell them about their aunt and how much she would have adored them.
   All my love, your daughter,
   Scarlet.'

Ellie managed a weak smile, even though tears covered her lashes and threatened to spill. It was awful to think that they might not make it home, but she knew it was a possibility, that some nurses were so close to the front line, and the truth was that they still didn't even know where they were going to end up.

'That was beautiful,' Ellie told her, knowing how hard it must have been for Scarlet to read it aloud.

'I hope the war ends and we can burn each other's notes once we're home, knowing that they'll never be read,' Scarlet said.

'Me too. My mother – it would break her heart a hundred times over if I didn't come home to her.'

Scarlet looked haunted, the flickering light of their lamp playing shadows across her face.

'I promised her I'd make it home,' Ellie whispered. 'I looked her in the eye and told her that I would be back. She was so brave saying goodbye to me, and I don't want that to be her last memory of me.'

'Why did we volunteer for this?' Scarlet whispered. 'It seems so real now, and suddenly all I want is to go back.'

'Because it was the right thing to do,' Ellie said, summoning strength. She was not about to crumble when she'd stayed so strong until now.

'So read me yours,' Scarlet said. 'Before we get told off by Matron when she does her rounds and finds us up with the lamp on talking, when we're supposed to be sound asleep.'

Ellie knew that if she poked her head out of their tiny tent and looked around they'd be surrounded by flickering lights inside tents, with nurses chatting into the night, but Scarlet was right. Their matron was becoming more unfriendly by the minute, and she couldn't bear to be told off. Again.

Ellie opened her own letter, which she had folded into a tiny square. She carefully opened it, holding it up so she could read the words in the less than adequate light. She should have known it by heart; she'd gone through the words in her mind so many times, tried to think what to say and recited it like a speech. But it had been so hard, trying to think of how to comfort her mother, what to say to bring her family some peace if she wasn't coming home to them. It was an impossible task, although she was grateful that it was done.

> *'Dear Ma and Pa,*
> *I don't know what to say. I love you. That seems like a good place to start. I love you, I love Danny and Connor and Sam, and I love the memories I have of being with you all at home. Every night I fall asleep thinking of you all, wishing we could be together and back home, eating a big feast of roast lamb like we haven't had in years. I wish this blasted war was over and all our boys were home. I wish that I was home, too, but if it's Scarlet giving you this letter, then make her stay for tea and let her tell you all about the adventures we had together. Don't cry sad tears for me, cry happy tears knowing that I had a smile on my face every time I thought of home.*
> *Love you more than anything,*
> *Ellie.'*

She paused, still staring at the letter, wanting to keep smiling instead of breaking down in a flood of tears. Her family meant everything to her, and no matter how much she tried to smile her way through each day and have fun, she was always thinking of home.

'If I have to give them that letter, I promise I'll stay for tea. You know, any chance to talk about my best friend Ellie.'

Scarlet's soft voice soothed her, making her smile real instead of forced.

'Do you really think I'm your best friend?' Ellie asked.

'Of course. We're going to be living in a tent together for so long, I reckon we'll be as good as sisters by the end of it.'

'You think so?' Ellie asked.

'I know so. Now, give me that letter and let me tuck it away so you don't have to think about it again.'

Ellie folded it back into a small square and handed it over, taking Scarlet's from her at the same time. She tucked it into her brassiere, not wanting to risk losing it and content that it would be safe there no matter where they travelled or what she was doing. She could sew it into her uniform properly when she had a spare moment.

'I might as well put mine there, too, then,' Scarlet said, tucking Ellie's away for safekeeping.

'So, back to Thomas,' Ellie said. 'You've not told me enough. What's he like? How did it feel when you first met him? How did you know he was the one?'

Scarlet lay back again, pulling her blanket with her. 'Can we not talk about Thomas? Not tonight.'

'James then?'

Scarlet's groan, followed by the sock she threw in her friend's direction, made Ellie hide under her pillow for cover.

'Fine then, let's talk about Spencer,' Ellie said. 'Because I can't figure the man out, and it's killing me.'

'What can't you work out? Because if you're worried about whether he likes you or not, then surely I can tell you how crazy you are. That man is definitely interested.'

'Why are you so sure?'

'He singled you out and asked you to be his nurse. I think that tells you everything you need to know!' Scarlet made a clucking noise. 'Besides, I think you'll find he's a lot less friendly, and rather more brusque, with the other nurses.'

Ellie sighed. 'But, I just, well . . .' She shut her eyes, finding the words hard to put together. 'I don't know why he'd like me. I mean, why me over all those other women?'

'Oh, sweetheart,' Scarlet said, taking her hand and squeezing it. 'Because you're *you*. You're beautiful and sweet and kind, and you always have this gorgeous smile on your face. Why *wouldn't* any man pick you above anyone else?'

Ellie kept her eyes shut but squeezed Scarlet's hand back. 'Thank you.'

'For what?'

'For being the best big sister I never had.'

Ellie lay there as Scarlet put out the lamp. She meant it, too. Scarlet was everything she'd ever imagined a sister would be. She might be the funny one, the smiley one, the one who made fun of everything, but Scarlet was *hers*, her one person in the world she could count on right now, and she knew that no matter what happened or where they went, Scarlet would have her back.

'I can't believe we actually have a film to go to!' Ellie was so excited about doing something fun and taking her mind off everything they'd been learning. If she had to talk about burns with Spencer again she'd probably be sick, not to mention having to run around in her blinkin' battledress training for wherever it was they were sending them. 'I wish I had a pretty dress to wear.'

'Me too,' Scarlet groaned. 'Just one night of being normal in pretty clothes. A pretty dress freshly pressed for the evening.'

The commotion outside made Ellie hurry along, worried that they'd miss out on a good seat if they didn't get moving; and she wanted to find Spencer. He was so quiet sometimes, made her so uncertain, but he did seem to like having her near, so she wasn't giving up on him yet.

'Do you think I should kiss him?' Ellie asked.

'What?'

'Me. Kiss him. He's so bloody proper, and I want to know if he really likes me or not!'

Scarlet laughed so hard that Ellie didn't know whether to kick her or join in. 'What's so funny?'

'You! You're so impatient, and the poor man probably doesn't know what to do with you.'

'Fine. So I won't kiss him.' Ellie crawled out of the tent, stretching as she always did when she emerged.

'Kiss him,' Scarlet said, her arm looping around Ellie's shoulders. 'Make his day and kiss him. Go on.'

Ellie grinned at her as they walked away, following the other nurses towards the screening. She bet Scarlet was on the lookout for James. She would be if she was her, but she didn't mention him. Ellie already knew how upset Scarlet was with herself about the whole thing, but she could tell that there was something between them, a flicker of something that she knew Scarlet didn't want to admit to. All she wanted was to encourage her to harmlessly flirt with the man, to have a little fun, to make the days pass with a smile on her face. She'd rather see her friend happy than miserable over a missing man she doubted would ever be found, but she could understand why she was so torn. It must be so hard on her, all the not knowing.

'Ellie!'

She looked around, certain she'd heard her name called.

'Ellie! Over here!'

Ellie finally saw Spencer, waving up ahead, closer to the big house. She waved back and he immediately gestured to her, pointing inside.

'I think he needs me. Are you all right if I leave you for a bit?'

'Of course.' Scarlet gave her a little wave and she waved back. 'Just don't go making any excuses later about why you couldn't kiss him.'

Ellie couldn't help her smile broadening as she walked over to the doctor, although the sombre look on his face wasn't what she'd been expecting.

'Are you looking forward to the film?' she asked. 'I can't wait.' She looked up at him. Normally that was enough to make him break out into one of his shy smiles, but not today.

'No, Ellie, I'm not. I'm afraid they might cancel the film, unless they make the announcement after.'

She wasn't sure what he was talking about. 'Is there something we should know? What announcement?'

He took her arm, propelling her forwards and into the house beside him. 'Come with me.'

Ellie didn't argue when he guided her inside an empty room just off the hallway. She didn't know him all that well, other than that he was a kind, caring, soft-spoken young doctor, but she trusted him. If she hadn't, she never would have left the crowd alone with him.

'What is it?' she hissed.

'Ellie, we're leaving. I'm afraid we're being sent into the thick of it. I just don't know the final details yet.'

She gulped. How did he know this already? Although she was well aware the nurses would be the last to know where they were being sent.

'Tell me what you know,' she said quietly.

He reached into his pocket and pulled out a handful of red, white and blue paper money. She looked from the money in his palm back to his eyes, held his gaze.

'Is that French?' she asked, knowing in her heart that it was. Of course. Where else would they be sent? That was where they were needed. 'When are we leaving?'

He nodded, expression solemn. She yearned for his sweet smile, for the shine in his eyes when he looked at her as they worked side by side.

'Yes, it's French,' he replied. 'I think we'll be gone in forty-eight hours – maybe less. Then we'll be sailing straight into the thick of it.'

Ellie ran her hands down her trousers, the fabric feeling stiff, so different from the soft, worn dresses and skirts she was used to wearing at home. She was glad he'd been the one to tell her, his gaze taking the sting out of how fearful she might have been otherwise.

'Ellie, I don't want you going there. It's too dangerous.'

'What?' Why was he suddenly saying this now? 'Why? I'm no different from any of the other nurses going. You don't think I can cope with it?' she asked angrily.

'It's not that, Ellie. That's so far from the truth.'

He looked uncomfortable, breaking their gaze. She moved closer to him, touched her fingers to one of his hands.

'What is it?' she asked, needing him to tell her how he felt. 'What are you trying to say?'

'Because I care for you, Ellie. And if we weren't here now, with all this going on . . .'

'You never would have met me in the first place,' she said sadly.

'If I can find a way for you to stay, something for you to do here, would you—'

'No.' She shook her head. 'I'm going, Spencer, whether you want me to or not. I can't let you find me a different nursing job that lets me get out of my duty. And besides, I'm not staying behind and letting my friends go without me. I've trained hard for this.'

He took her hands, held both of them, their palms pressed together, his thumbs softly stroking her skin. 'Please, Ellie. I can't stand the thought of you getting hurt. We've only known each other a short time, but I'd very much like to ask you out, properly, one day.'

'Because you feel something for me?' She gulped, having forced the words out. 'You would actually want to . . .' For once she was completely lost.

Spencer smiled down at her, closing the distance between them, his hands still covering hers as he gently pressed a kiss to her lips. His mouth was soft, breath warm, as he kissed her again, and Ellie felt her knees buckle. His arm found her waist, holding her to him as she kissed him back.

'Yes,' he whispered when he finally pulled away. 'Isn't it obvious? You're nothing like any other girl I've met before.'

Ellie was speechless. She stared back at him, completely lost for words. He was like no other man she'd met either, but she'd never be able to tell him that.

'You are, Ellie,' he said shaking his head. When he ran his fingers through his hair it made her laugh, thinking about what she'd said to Scarlet about him losing his hair.

She smiled, her nerves disappearing. 'I don't believe you, not for a second.'

Echoing footsteps made Ellie jump back, but Spencer didn't let go of her hand straight away.

'I'm getting on that ship,' she said, not going to let him give her orders just because he'd kissed her. 'You can't sweet-talk me out of going, Spencer.'

'That's what I was afraid of,' he said. 'Then again, it's probably the reason I like you so much.'

'Ha! My father wouldn't believe any man saying those words.'

'Nurse! Are you attending the film screening or not?'

Ellie sighed and finally dragged her eyes from Spencer. How had Matron managed to find her? 'Yes, ma'am. Spencer, I mean, Doctor Black here was just instructing me about a patient's post-surgery care. I'll be getting along now.'

A hum of excitement ran through her as she walked quickly away from him, glancing over her shoulder one last time. *He'd kissed her.* Spencer had actually kissed her! And he'd talked about a proper date someday. He was so sweet, so kind, and he made her want to be a better nurse, to prove to him that he'd been right in wanting her to work alongside him.

As she skipped down the steps towards where the open-air screening was taking place, not even the thought of sailing towards a battlefield in France could ruin her good mood. She looked for Scarlet when she reached the film screening, searching the sea of uniforms to find her friend. And then she saw a soldier kneeling beside a row of nurses; the soldiers were segregated, seated to the right of the nurses, which was why he stood out.

She grinned, recognising his thick crop of dark hair as she got closer. Trust him to have found Scarlet already. She might be a hopeless romantic, but she hoped that Scarlet could simply enjoy some harmless flirting with a charming man, that it didn't upset her again. Ellie didn't like seeing her friend rattled, and she knew her feelings ran deep, but with any luck she would return to their tent happy after enjoying a fun night.

'Soldier, back to your seat!' an older officer barked.

Ellie held back her laugh and waited in the aisle for him to move. And she'd thought their matron was surly!

'Yes, sir!' he replied, but not before she caught the wink he gave Scarlet as he straightened and walked away.

Ellie waited and then slipped into the vacant seat beside Scarlet.

'The handsome soldier strikes again, huh?' she teased.

Scarlet slapped at her hand, but when Ellie grabbed hold of it she didn't pull it away.

'How was Spencer?' Scarlet whispered as the movie began, the image on the white screen flickering then coming to life.

'I'll tell you all about it later.' Ellie was bursting to tell her, but she wanted Scarlet to enjoy the film first. They had plenty of time to worry about where they were being sent and what it would be like, and she wasn't about to ruin film night for anyone. From the sound of it, they were lucky it was still being screened, given the soon-to-be-delivered announcement.

CHAPTER SEVEN

Scarlet

Scarlet felt a hand on her shoulder as the film ended, saw James's smile before anything else as he passed by her row, and for a fleeting moment they locked eyes. Swiftly, he bent his head down to her. 'Meet me by the trees outside your camp.' Startled, she nodded, but he was gone before she had the chance to say a word, moving away from the rows of seats set up in front of the large screen. A shiver ran through her body – excitement at the thought of a stolen moment alone. She'd tried so hard not to look at him tonight, not to think about him, but something about him kept drawing her in. And what if tonight was the last night she ever saw him? She was tempted, sorely tempted.

'Tell me about Spencer,' she said to Ellie, hoping she hadn't heard their exchange and wanting to make sure her attention was on her friend, not herself.

'Not until we're in our tent,' she said.

'Ladies, please report to your matrons before lights out. There will be a briefing about your posting,' an officer announced before they could all disperse.

Scarlet stared at Ellie. 'Our posting?'

Ellie pulled her closer, mouth close to her ear. 'It's happening. Spencer told me we're going to France.'

Scarlet was numb as she stared back at her friend, trying to digest her words. They were leaving? For France? She'd still been buzzing from their evening, doing something fun for once, but that happy feeling was fading fast.

'Did he know anything else?'

Ellie shook her head as they leaned into each other and began to walk back to the tent.

'No. Only that he'd been given some French money and we'd be going very soon. Then he kissed me.'

Ellie's wide eyes and huge smile made Scarlet laugh.

'Trust you to put a smile on my face at a time like this!'

'I know, but he was divine. I could kiss him all night.' Ellie let out a little squeal. 'He's so wonderful, Scarlet. Honestly, he's just . . .' Ellie sighed. 'He's lovely. I don't know what else to say.'

Scarlet envied her friend's great mood. She was already anxious about meeting James, or whether she *should* meet him, but then finding out they were going . . . Would she ever see him again? Would his unit be travelling with them? Would he end up dead or missing in action? The thought sent a chill through her.

They followed the rest of the nurses, all busy chatting, to their matron's administration tent. Matron was waiting outside, pen and paper in hand. She ran through their names to check who was present, and after what felt like an age standing in silence, shifting from one foot to the other, she finally told them. Scarlet dug her fingernails into her palms, swallowing hard as she waited to hear their fate.

'Ladies, we will be leaving the day after tomorrow at 0800 hours and setting sail that day,' she announced. 'Please collect your money, seasickness tablets and paper bag for your travels.'

Scarlet looked at the heavy paper bag being held up and hoped that either her stomach was strong enough not to need it or that the seasickness tablets worked.

'You will need to check your carry bags and ensure you have all the necessary equipment that was originally issued. The trucks will transport us directly to the port and we will be boarding almost immediately.'

Scarlet swapped glances with Ellie and wondered if her friend had the same empty, churning sensation in her stomach.

'Additional emergency rations to be collected are vitaminised chocolate, tea cubes, oat snacks, four cigarettes, a small French phrase book and four pieces of toilet paper each.'

'Bloody hell,' Ellie muttered. 'That ain't gonna last long. Four pieces for the whole journey?'

Scarlet didn't even want to think about it. She didn't know what was worse, the small amount of food or the fact that they probably wouldn't be able to shower or wash and only had such a small quantity of sanitary items. She felt nauseous all over again. Home seemed such a long way away, a distant memory, the life she'd known before like a blur that had never really existed.

'Equipment will be packed tomorrow to enable our field hospital to be operational within forty-eight hours of arrival. Your training is now over; however, you are expected to conduct yourself in an exemplary manner at all times. There will be strict segregation on the ship for this very reason, and nurses will not be permitted to undress or wash whilst aboard.'

Scarlet stifled her groan. Honestly, they couldn't wash? It seemed ridiculous to her, given the circumstances, that they were so worried about men and women being on the same ship. Although she was certain it would be cool at night on the ship below decks, so they'd likely be happy to remain clothed.

'You are dismissed. Godspeed, and be prepared for a trying journey ahead.'

Scarlet stayed rooted to the spot, watching as the women around her started to chatter and gossip, some of them crying. Shivers ran the length of her body, made her freeze, her breath coming in short pants, and it wasn't until Ellie's hand closed over her shoulder that she started to calm.

'Scarlet, are you all right?'

She nodded. She had to be all right; there was no other choice. 'I'll be fine.' She was in shock, that was all.

'It means you'll be one step closer to finding Thomas, right? This is a good thing.'

Scarlet bit down hard on her lower lip. Of course Ellie had presumed it was thoughts of Thomas upsetting her. She might finally find some answers about what had happened to him, where he could be, but that wasn't it. Apart from the fear about what they were going into, it was the reality of leaving James, a man she hardly knew but who had made her feel so alive in the couple of times she'd seen him. Her chest ached, her feelings and her guilt weighing hard on her. But deep down she knew what upset her most was her fear of the unknown, and her sadness at not getting to know James better. She should never have thought such things about him anyhow; maybe this was punishment for forgetting she was engaged to be married.

'Come on,' Ellie said, nudging her shoulder and starting to walk.

Scarlet caught up with her and kept her head down, not wanting to join in the excited chatter with the other nurses.

'I promised James that I'd meet him,' she confessed to Ellie.

'Where?'

'The trees just outside of our tents.' She hoped he'd still be there. Because he'd walked past her so quickly and she hadn't had time to answer, he might think she'd decided not to come after taking so long.

'Want me to walk you?'

Scarlet shook her head. 'I'll be fine.'

Ellie smiled at her and Scarlet forced one back. 'Have fun, and don't do anything I wouldn't do.'

Scarlet wanted to say something smart in reply, but she couldn't think of anything fast enough, and Ellie disappeared in the sea of nurses fanning out around them. Instead, she propelled herself forwards, head down as she made her way to the camp. There were people milling here and there, but she was nervous on her own, especially when she crossed the grass that stretched between where their tents were pitched and the trees that separated the property they were stationed on from the neighbouring ones.

'Over here.'

She couldn't tell for certain if it was James's voice, but she could see a silhouette ahead and she doubted anyone else would be calling for her. She fisted her hands just in case, ready to scream and hit someone if they tried anything on.

'I wasn't sure if you would come or not,' James said, reaching out to her, his voice suddenly much more familiar. She was just able to make out his face now. The moon was illuminating their surroundings enough to see by, and the fear she'd felt earlier at being alone disappeared. She felt comfortable with him already, even though she hardly knew him. There was something somehow familiar about him, something that made her comfortable with this man who made her heart race.

'You've heard the news already?' she asked.

He gestured for them to walk and she fell into step beside him. Moving was easier because she didn't have to stare at him and feel she should be averting her eyes, didn't have to think about the way something inside of her stirred every time he smiled at her or gave her a cheeky wink. But tonight, he seemed more serious than he'd been before.

'We don't have long and we'll be landing in the worst of it,' he muttered.

'So you're coming with us? I mean, we'll be travelling with your unit?'

''Fraid so,' he said, glancing at her. She could feel his eyes on her, but she didn't dare look back, focusing instead on where her feet were falling with each step.

'James, I want to find my fiancé so badly. I mean, there's nothing I want more than to discover he's alive, that he's been helped or . . .' She didn't even know what to say. 'The more I learn, the more injuries I see, I'm wondering if I've just been terribly naive this entire time. And then meeting you . . .'

James held out his arm and she couldn't ignore the action. Scarlet tucked her hand into the crook of his elbow, couldn't resist being close to him instead of feeling so alone. It was only one night. It was only one connection, one touch. By morning they'd be gone, and she could pretend it never happened.

'Hope can be a dangerous thing,' James said. 'But without hope, maybe our entire army would have broken down by now.'

She inhaled, breathed in the scent of him, wished she wasn't so drawn to him.

Scarlet slowed when James did and she saw where he'd brought her. It was a pond, once beautiful she was sure, but now overgrown and derelict. But there was still water filling its depths, glistening in the moonlight. He gestured for her to sit down, and she did, settling against a tree beside him. She tucked her legs beneath herself as he stretched his out in front.

'I know it's forward of me, but this is war. After tonight, we might never see one another again,' he said. 'I just have to tell you: you're so beautiful.'

'James, I . . .' She needed to say something, to end whatever was going on between them. This wasn't right. She couldn't do this as though she wasn't already promised to another man.

'What? I can't tell a woman she's beautiful?' His laugh was deep, his hand warm as he reached for hers. 'Sweetheart, there's every chance this is it, and there's every chance I won't make it home. What's the harm in speaking the truth, given the circumstances?' He paused, looking into her eyes. 'And it's more than that. I like you, Scarlet. You must know that?'

The harm was that she could so easily give in. If she'd met James and she wasn't already promised, if . . . She pushed the thoughts away, didn't want to imagine it. How could she even be thinking like this when she'd been so devoted to Thomas for so long? He'd been gone for over a year, and she'd never questioned her feelings for him before, not once in all those long months.

'I need to go,' she said, pushing up to stand, furious with herself. He'd told her he liked her, and her first thought should have been to tell him no instead of thinking about giving in to her feelings.

But James's warm hand closed around her wrist, anchored her to the ground. 'Please don't go. Not yet.' He kept staring into her eyes, his expression softening. 'Can we not just sit here? Away from all the horrors, all the awful things we're about to face, and just . . .' He smiled. 'Sit.'

His low voice washed over her, his fingers curled against her skin, sending impossible emotions, feelings through her body. She wanted to say yes, so badly.

'I'm engaged to be married to another man,' she croaked, forcing the words out, needing to say it.

'I know that, Scarlet. I know that and I'm not asking for anything other than a peaceful moment. I like your company and this might be the last peaceful night we see in months, maybe even years.'

'I'm sorry, I can't be here. This isn't right,' she said, biting down on her lip as she went to move again. It would have been so easy to say yes, but she wouldn't let herself.

James moved fast, so quickly that she didn't realise what was happening, not immediately. One hand was still on her wrist, but the other touched her cheek, palm flat to her skin as his body moved half over hers, lips soft when he kissed her. It was the barest of touches, the connection only lasting seconds, but it was all Scarlet needed to tell her that she was in trouble.

'Maybe it's the war, not knowing whether I'll live to come home,' James murmured against her lips. 'Or maybe it's the fact that from the moment I laid eyes on you, the only thing I've been able to think about is you.'

Scarlet waited, her breath shallow, lips parted. She wanted him to kiss her again so badly, wanted him to touch her, yet at the same time she felt like a traitor, knew she was doing the wrong thing. She should have pushed him away, told him not to touch her ever again.

'James . . .' She put her hand to his chest, wanted to push him back.

'Tell me it's not what you want and I won't do it again,' he whispered. 'I won't do something you don't want.'

She hesitated, couldn't tell a lie when she so blatantly felt the opposite. Instead she dropped her gaze to his lips – gave him permission.

His kiss was rougher this time, more urgent, not the sweet press of lips like the first one. It made Scarlet feel alive, made a tremor run down her spine, made her want more. When Thomas had kissed her that night, the one time with passion, it had felt exciting, stirring, but nothing like this. This made her want more, made her think it was worth rebelling, worth doing something she'd never thought she'd do.

Guilt washed over her as she thought of Thomas, making her pull back. James must have felt the change and sat back, too, his fingers leaving her wrist and settling more softly on her hand.

'We can't do that again,' she whispered, more to herself than him. 'We can't.'

'And if your fiancé doesn't make it home? Would you let me kiss you then?'

She pulled away from him, wrapping her arms around herself. 'Don't say that. James, don't ever say that.' Scarlet's breath shuddered through her, the guilt unbearable. 'Don't make me wish that I could be with you when doing so would mean Thomas has to be dead. I love him.'

They sat in silence and Scarlet felt pain. A stabbing in her chest that could have been her heart breaking into pieces, shattering from the decision she suddenly saw in front of her.

'Thomas?' he said, pushing back, his eyebrows drawn together. 'You said *Thomas*.'

'My fiancé,' she replied, confused about the expression on his face. 'His name is Thomas.'

'Thomas who?' he asked, voice low.

She sighed, not wanting to discuss her fiancé in detail with the man she'd just kissed. 'Thomas Sanders.'

The look on James's face scared her, worried her, made her blood run cold.

'What is it?'

'And you're *Scarlet*.'

Had he lost his mind? 'What . . . ?'

'My brother is . . . and you . . .' He shook his head and pushed himself to his feet. 'You're his Scarlet. I can't believe it. It's you, isn't it?'

'Brother? You're Thomas's brother?' Scarlet gasped, jumping up, feeling hysterical. Her fingers found her mouth, brushed her lips. She'd kissed her fiancé's brother? 'But he called you J, he never . . .'

'Because our father is James,' he said quietly, 'so to avoid confusion I've always been J at home.'

Scarlet shook her head, forcing her feet to move, even though her boots felt like they were filled with lead. She wrapped her arms around herself, hardly able to process what had just happened. How could this man, the *one* man she'd felt something for, be Thomas's brother? Or was that why she'd felt drawn to him? Similarities that she hadn't even noticed, perhaps?

'So, you're Scarlet,' he said, his voice softer than it had been before. '*The* Scarlet. I can't believe I never put two and two together.' He shook his head, shut his eyes slowly, as if he was in pain. 'I can't believe I said what I said, about him not coming home. I never would have, I mean . . .' He opened his eyes and clenched both his hands at his side. 'I'm sorry.'

She nodded, slowly turning to face him properly. She took a deep breath, her cheeks heating as she looked into his eyes. They were dark, but they were different from Thomas's, a humour there that was impossible not to notice. He made her feel all kinds of guilty – the feeling worse now that she knew the connection.

'I can't,' she finally said. 'I . . .' She was lost for words. She hastily folded her hands together. 'I can't believe it. This seems impossible.'

'The fact that we've met, or that we . . .'

'Everything!' she replied, flustered, as she positioned herself a modest distance from him. 'Meeting you in the middle of nowhere when I'm supposed to be searching for Thomas.' It seemed an almost cruel twist of fate that she'd met him instead. 'Falling—' she cut herself off. 'Doing what we did.'

'Well, Sussex is hardly the middle of nowhere,' he said, smiling as he made his stupid joke before clearing his throat. 'But yes, I don't think this is something we'll, well—'

'Ever speak of again?' Scarlet interrupted. 'Please tell me that's what you were going to say.'

'Something like that,' he said, nodding. 'I might not be close to Thomas these days, but he's my brother, and I never would have done this had I known. My lips are sealed.'

Scarlet felt the familiar heat of a blush touching her cheeks, which only annoyed her. Given the job she was doing, what she was being trained for, blushing seemed silly, and she hated not being able to control how she reacted.

'You believe he's alive then?' she asked, ignoring his other comment, needing to act as though nothing had happened between them at all. 'You speak about him in the present.'

'I speak about everyone from home, from my past, in the present,' James said, his voice quieter, more serious now. 'After what I've seen, what we've been through, the only thing left is hope. And holding on to memories of before.' He paused. 'But I won't ever tell him, and we can pretend this never happened. If that's what you want?'

'It's what I want.'

The whistle of wind passing through the trees was the only noise Scarlet heard, the only thing that connected her to the moment, when what she wanted to do, all of a sudden, was flee for home. She hadn't wanted to return home so strongly since they'd settled into a routine here, too busy learning and caring to spend time worrying about what she'd had before. Until James had spoken and reminded her of what she'd left behind, and what she was preparing to face. Why had she found him and not Thomas? How could fate be so cruel?

'Did you know all along we were going to France?'

'It wasn't my place to share the information. Not even with the woman who's going to be my sister-in-law.'

Scarlet wrapped her arms around herself again, suddenly shivering from the cold as clouds drew closer overheard, blocking out the moonlight. 'So you *do* believe he's alive?'

'I want to believe he's alive. Is that the same thing?' James asked.

Scarlet stared into his eyes, saw something of Thomas there, although maybe she was imagining it now because she wanted to. 'I feel in my bones that he's alive, but I'm prepared to admit that it could be because I so want him to be. I don't know. Maybe it's just my way of refusing to let go until I'm certain.' It was the most honest she'd been with anyone about how she truly felt.

They stood in silence, the woodland noises around them stopping it from being deafening.

'What made—'

'Were you—'

Scarlet laughed as they spoke at the same time, interrupting one another. 'You first,' she said.

He hesitated, like he was about to tell her to speak first instead. But he didn't.

'What made a young woman like you volunteer to join?' James asked. 'When you could have stayed home and been safe, done something less dangerous by choice? What I heard about the woman Thomas was to marry was more along the lines of a wealthy society girl than a roll-her-sleeves-up-and-nurse type.'

Scarlet didn't know what to say. She stared back at him, truly lost for words.

'I'm sorry, I shouldn't have said that. I didn't mean to offend you.' James ran one hand down his cheek to his mouth as he shook his head. 'What I should have said was how much it means to a soldier to have a woman care for him. What you're doing is admirable, even more so because it's not what anyone would have expected of you.'

'My family was furious with me, but I wasn't prepared to sit back and do nothing when our country and our men need us so badly. It didn't really dawn on me what I'd done until I was on the train with Ellie. Maybe it still hasn't really sunk in – reality, I mean.'

'Well, your family should be very proud of you. I hope they are. Thomas, too.' His smile was kind, warm, but she knew he must be feeling like she was, the same as before only a hundred times more guilty. 'I know I would be if . . .'

She gulped at his unfinished sentence, but tried to continue as if nothing was wrong. 'My parents would be more proud of me if I were obedient and did what they said, but I don't feel like that girl any longer. It was my determination to find Thomas myself that made me send my letter off to join in the first place.' She was only telling the truth, but it was hard to get the words out.

'He would hate you doing this, truth be told,' James said. He laughed, and for a moment she felt like they were friends instead of two people trying to pretend that they hadn't just kissed and enjoyed every guilty moment of it. 'If I know my brother, he'd much prefer you at home, baking all day and keeping a lookout of the kitchen window for him to return. Doing a little to help the Red Cross perhaps.'

Scarlet rolled her eyes, even though it was a childish thing to do. 'I don't believe you. You honestly believe that he wouldn't approve?' Scarlet asked. She was helping others and searching for him, what wrong was there in that?

'Ah, don't listen to me,' James said, starting to move away. 'What do I know? I haven't seen him in a while, so maybe my brother has become more open-minded. But me? Now, I like the fact that you're fighting Hitler alongside us boys. It's endearing.'

'Where are we going?' Scarlet asked, unsure why they were moving. 'Do you honestly think he's alive? That I have a chance of finding him?' Maybe she needed someone who knew Thomas to tell her that she was right, that she was doing the right thing; or maybe it was the complete opposite.

'I think if anyone can find him, you can,' he said softly, reaching for her hand, his touch sending unexpected chills across her skin as she started at their connection. 'I won't give up on him, not until the day this damn war is over, and you shouldn't either.'

Scarlet met his gaze, bravely staring back at him. So he didn't think she was mad, after all.

'I needed to hear you say that.' She didn't let go of his hand, not yet, even though she knew she should. 'Did he ever talk to you about me?' Scarlet asked, wanting to hear something about Thomas, to stop thinking about being with James as butterflies beat their wings in her stomach and her heart began to ache.

'He did. But you have to remember that I only saw him once since he met you, and we weren't exactly close. You must know that.' He shrugged. 'We were once, but fighting for our father's affection and respect, and butting heads constantly, kind of pulled us apart.'

'When did you last see him?' she asked. Thomas had told her something of his history and falling-out with his brother, but not a lot.

'I saw him in passing not long after he'd proposed to you. We had less than a day; a few hours on leave before we were both sent our separate ways.'

'He spoke of you fondly – talked about your childhood,' she said. 'Although he also said you hadn't been so close in recent years.'

'War changes you, makes you realise the errors of the past sometimes,' James replied. 'We were close growing up, always going on adventures, getting into trouble, fighting until we had bloody noses. But Thomas got more serious as we got older, became more interested in taking his place as the eldest son and following my father's footsteps into banking. I guess I rebelled more, didn't take life as seriously as he did. Until it was time to enlist, and then life changed.'

Scarlet slowly digested the words, put the puzzle pieces of their life together, imagined them as young boys with their dark hair and brown eyes, handsome as ever and no doubt driving their nanny mad.

'Do you want to know what he told me?' James asked, shifting beside her.

Scarlet nodded before realising he probably couldn't see the movement. 'Yes. Please.'

'He told me that there would be a wedding as soon as this war was over, and said I was to be his best man,' James shared with her. 'I laughed and asked him who'd been crazy enough to say yes to him, and he swung at me just like when we were kids! But it was nice that he wanted me to do that for him, after so long not seeing one another.'

Scarlet could almost see the exchange between the brothers.

'Thomas said you were perfect wife material – that you were from a good family, that you'd had a fast, fun courtship, and that he'd asked you before he left. I think he was worried that if he didn't ask you first, you'd be engaged to someone else before he returned. The only thing he forgot to tell me was how beautiful you are. My question is, would you have waited for him if he hadn't proposed, or would I be talking to a single woman now?'

Scarlet had been about to interrupt James and tell him that of course she would have waited for Thomas, engagement promise or not, but his last words had rattled her. Heat flooded her body, the hairs on her arms standing on end. Maybe if she'd met James before, and hadn't been formally engaged to Thomas, she might not feel as conflicted right now.

'Don't ever speak of this to Thomas. He mustn't ever know.' She stared at him. 'You meant it, didn't you? That you'd never tell?'

James's laugh was cold this time. 'That his little brother tried to steal his girl before he was even in the ground? I have a feeling he'd be more worried about me stepping into our father's role ahead of him than stealing you.'

Scarlet slapped him, hard. Her palm connected with his face in a burning slam that made her instantly recoil.

'Charming,' he muttered, stalking away.

Scarlet had never felt so alone as she stood in the dark without him, watching his silhouette walking off. What had just happened? What had she done? Why did he make her feel so . . . She didn't even know what she was feeling, what he had done to her, other than make her mad.

'You know what?' James called out, storming back towards her. 'To hell with Thomas. I'm here with you now. How long did you know him before you agreed to marry him? Was it even a month?' He glared at her, waiting. 'From what I know it wasn't even that.'

She shook her head. 'Don't talk like that. I gave your brother my word, my promise.' She wasn't about to tell him that he was right. That it had been exactly a month.

'This war is going to be full of women who fell in love with men they'll never see again. All we do is say goodbye over and over.'

She didn't know why he was telling her that, what he was trying to say, but his words washed through her anyway, making her think. He was right, and because of it women were marrying men they hardly knew, or were being left broken-hearted knowing that their chance to fall properly in love had been snatched away from them.

They stared at one another, neither of them moving. Scarlet's feelings for Thomas had been real, she knew they had, but after so long without seeing him, her mind was playing tricks on her – making her think that what she was feeling for James was more intense, making her think that maybe he was right.

'Walk me back, James. Please.'

He grunted and lit up a cigarette. She wondered if he'd also only be given four as the nurses had, or whether he had his own stash. They walked in silence, the only noise their boots colliding with branches and swishing through fallen leaves. Her mind was racing, but she wasn't about to give in to her feelings – she couldn't. She was searching for Thomas; she was engaged to the man. She owed it to him to be waiting when, or if, he returned from the depths of hell.

'I'll see you on board,' she said, rushing ahead and not looking back.

James quickly intercepted her, his cigarette gone. 'Scarlet, wait.'

She paused, refusing to look at him until he reached out and touched her shoulder. When she did, his fingers found their way to her chin, softly pushing it up so her eyes were forced to meet his.

'I'm not uncaring, if that's what you think. For all our differences, Thomas is my brother and I want him to come home. I do.'

She nodded. 'Sometimes we can't help the way we feel.'

'I'm sorry about what happened. If I'd known when I met you, if we'd realised, I never would have behaved like that.' He held out his hand.

She placed her palm to his, hating the way she was drawn to him, how badly she wanted to pull him towards her and hold him tight.

'I know.'

James shook her hand. 'Goodbye then.'

Scarlet left it at that, walking away from a man that made every bone in her body want to turn back and throw herself into his arms. Tomorrow they'd be packing, the orderlies checking that the surgical instruments were greased against rust, wrapped in oil paper, sewn in and then stencilled, along with bed pans, urinals, syringes, flags and more.

After that, she didn't know whether she'd ever even see James again. Tears burnt her eyes, the dampness hot as it hit her cheeks, curving down and into her mouth. But she never looked back. Not once.

She was too afraid of what she'd do if she did, because the way she was feeling? It wasn't right.

'Will you wait for me?'

Scarlet held his hand tight, gazing up at Thomas. He looked so dashing in his uniform – his cheeks clean-shaven, dark hair carefully parted, his eyes on hers as he reached out his fingertips to stroke the side of her face.

'Of course.' They were in the middle of a war, and all she wanted was for it to be over so he could come back home.

'Scarlet, will you marry me? I don't know when I'll return, but I need to know that we will be married when this is all over.'

His smile was so kind, his eyes full of what she was certain was love. There was nothing in the world she wanted more than to be his wife.

'Yes. A hundred times, yes,' she whispered, leaning into him as he kissed her briefly on the mouth, pulling her against him and holding her.

Scarlet breathed in the scent of him, aftershave mixed with the pressed, new smell of his jacket. He made a handsome soldier, but she still wished he didn't have to go, that there had been some reason for him to stay.

He held out a ring, a dark sapphire with a diamond at each side sparkling up at her. She let him slide it on to her finger, gazed at it, felt the weight of it against her skin. It was beautiful.

'This was my grandmother's, and I want you to have it.'

'I love it,' she said, excited about showing it to her friends. She was engaged!

'It's perfect on you. Just make sure you keep it safe, put it on a necklace around your neck if you need to keep it hidden, if anything happens.'

She nodded, hating how solemn things felt when she should have been squealing with joy, not a care in the world, excited to become the new Mrs Sanders. 'I will. I'll look after it for ever.'

'You need to sign up with the Red Cross, do work close to home. Stay safe,' he said, searching her eyes as he pulled back. 'I don't want to worry about you while I'm gone.'

She swallowed, staring back at him, not about to tell him that she wasn't sure yet about what she wanted to do. Whether she should do more, make a bigger contribution; and besides, if she didn't sign up for something soon then she'd have no choice and be drafted into any kind of work.

'I'll be here. Don't you worry about me. Just promise to write.'

The way he held her, tight to his chest, made her feel safe and loved. 'I promise,' he murmured back, mouth to her hair. 'I'm hardly going to ignore the woman who's to be my wife.'

Scarlet wanted to believe him, hoped that what he was saying was true.

'Whenever things get bad, think about us,' she whispered in his ear, arms still around him. 'Imagine our wedding day, and the beautiful little children we'll have someday.'

He kissed her cheek and stepped back, hands on hers until they slowly slipped away.

'I love you, Scarlet.'

'I love you, too,' she said, holding back a sob, watching as he walked backwards.

She didn't take her eyes off him, thought her heart was going to break seeing him walk away like that. Why now? Why did the war have to ruin her season, her engagement, all her dreams? Why did Thomas have to go?

'Goodbye!' he called out.

Scarlet raised one hand and waved, torn between wanting to chase after him and showing how strong she could be – blinking away tears and not moving from her position.

He was her Thomas, and he'd be home.

Suddenly gunshots echoed around her, the garden becoming a blur of smoke, the peace of the birds in the trees shattered by the sound of gunfire. Or was it bombs?

'Thomas!' she screamed.

Then she saw him, falling, bright red staining his back, his face bloody as he turned to her.

'Thomas!'

Scarlet screamed as hands closed over her, struggled free, searching in the dark, frantic, looking for Thomas. But he was gone.

'Scarlet, it's all right. You're fine, it was only a dream.'

Her hair was wet at the nape of her neck, her hands shaking as she stared around her, eyes adjusting to the almost-blackness. She recognised the warmth of Ellie's arm cradling her – slowly figured out where she was.

'You were calling for Thomas,' Ellie said softly. 'I had to shake you to stop you from screaming out to him again.'

Scarlet shut her eyes then quickly opened them again, the memories of what she'd seen, where her dream had taken her, coming back to her like a film playing through her mind.

'I saw him. It was the day we were engaged, the day he left. Everything was the same, perfect,' she said, then swallowed hard, finding her strength. 'But this time he died in front of me, he'd been shot, there was blood, so much blood.'

'Shhh,' Ellie murmured, rocking her, then slowly lowering her back down to the bed as if she were comforting a child. 'Everything's fine, it was only a dream.'

'It's not just a dream, Ellie. James is his brother,' she gasped. 'James is supposed to be my *brother-in-law*.'

'He's what?'

'You heard me,' Scarlet choked. 'I don't want to speak about it. Not now, not ever.'

Ellie hesitated, then quickly began rubbing her back, soothing her. 'Everything's going to be fine, Scarlet. I promise. You can tell me all about it in the morning.'

Scarlet squeezed her eyes shut again, forcing the thoughts to stay away, making herself think of happy things and stop her inner torment. Ellie's breath was steady and slow, helping to calm her as they lay pressed together on one small bed for warmth. Was it because of her feelings for James that she was dreaming like this? Was she being punished for falling for the brother of her fiancé? For being unfaithful to Thomas when she knew in her heart that she loved him so much, wanted desperately for him to come home so she could be his wife?

Tomorrow was going to be a long day, and she doubted she'd be able to find comfort in sleep again. Ellie had stopped rubbing her back, her breathing heavier now. Scarlet didn't want to disturb her friend again by trying to get up. Instead she lay there, focused on filling her lungs deep with each inhale.

She'd kissed her fiancé's brother. She was being punished. Not to mention the fact that she would have to live with that infidelity for the rest of her life.

Thomas. She was here because of him. She was looking for him. She wanted him by her side. James was handsome and charming and distracting, that was all. She'd been waiting for Thomas so long that James had managed to distract her from what she really wanted.

Her hand reached for her necklace, to find the comfort of the engagement ring there, but her skin was bare. She'd left it at home for safekeeping on her last visit back.

She swallowed, hard.

She should never have taken it off.

CHAPTER EIGHT

Lucy

Lucy shut her eyes, knowing what was about to happen, but powerless to do anything to stop it. She opened her mouth to scream, but no sound came out. *Bang.*

Everything else went silent for a moment, just one blank second, until she opened her eyes and heard the yells, the screams, the mayhem. She'd seen it happen, had watched as the doctor's hand had started to shake as he cut through the skin with the scalpel, watched in horror as he hit an artery. The blood had started to spurt, the soldier on the bed in front of them sure to bleed out if they didn't do something fast, his other leg already looking like it would need to be amputated.

The doctor had reached for his gun, held it up, the whites of his eyes flashing, before pulling the trigger and blowing half his head off.

Lucy raised her hand, wiped her cheek and found that it was sticky, saw the red stain of blood on her palm as she stared at it. Her body shook, even though she was trying her hardest to stop it. She breathed deep, eyes shut again, remembering home. The garden, walking in the breeze, sitting drinking tea with her mother on the metal chairs overlooking the roses. That was her safe place, the image she needed to draw on when the going got tough. She could do this, she *would* do this, because giving up wasn't an option here, and she certainly wasn't going to end up like that doctor.

'Nurse!'

She heard the call, a doctor elsewhere no doubt. They all seemed to call for nurses constantly, but she didn't move. She clamped her hand down, trying to stop the soldier's blood flow, but it was useless. Then the pumping blood stopped.

'He's gone,' a deep voice said. She turned and saw a doctor shaking his head as he leaned past her to check the patient. 'He's gone. Go and help the incoming.'

Lucy wiped her hands on her apron and propelled herself forwards, pushing the horror scene she'd just left from her mind as orderlies rushed past her, presumably to clean up the bodies and the blood. There was no time to care, to feel sick, to do anything other than keep going. They were a doctor down now, and as she stepped over his body, past the pool of red blood on the floor that two orderlies were scrambling to deal with, she forced down the bile burning its way up her throat and ran. She was made of tougher stuff. She'd heard her father tell her brother to keep his chin up when they'd been kids, as if he was the tougher one, the one who needed to be strong, but it was advice she was going to take now.

Outside, the air was thick and smoky, like she was in a thick, dense pea-soup fog tinged with the smell of gunpowder. Or maybe it was her imagination. After almost forty-eight hours on her feet with no sleep, she was feeling delirious, as if she were watching herself from above rather than being in control of anything.

The ambulances hadn't stopped. They kept arriving, over and over again. It was a constant circus of tending to the injured, doing what they could for some, preparing others for evacuation.

She swallowed hard, the bile rising again. And then there were the ones they patched up as best they could for evacuation, only to have them back within the hour, injured again or sometimes dead because they'd been shot again before they made it to the boats.

Lucy had no idea how they were going to survive, how she was going to pull through. But the determination she felt inside, the hatred for this war and the sadness she felt for all the men suffering, made her refuse to give in. She would hold her head high and do everything she could, for every soldier she could. This was what she was made to do, this was what she'd wanted for so long, to save lives and make a difference.

'Incoming!'

She took shelter, watched as another ambulance was shot at as it tried to make its way to the safety of their hospital. They needed protection, some sort of cover to keep their nurses safe and the ambulance drivers out of harm's way as they drove in. But she knew any sense of safety she felt under cover was silly anyway; being under canvas was no different from being out in the open.

But most of all they needed rest. They couldn't keep going like this – without sleep, without food. If more doctors started to make mistakes, had hands so shaky they couldn't hold a scalpel, then they wouldn't be any use to anyone.

She heard a louder bang, an explosion this time, and ran out from where she'd been standing, looking to the sky, searching frantically for what the noise was. Her eyes locked on the object immediately, saw a plane explode like a fiery ball of sun in the sky and come crashing down in the distance, by the shore.

Lucy said a silent prayer. Although from what she'd seen today, she was starting to doubt that there was anyone listening. For what God would let men kill men like this? Would let men butcher one another and have such little regard for human life?

Lucy ran to the next ambulance, helping as best she could. She was here to save the lives of their soldiers, and that's exactly what she was going to do until her very last breath. She wasn't going to rest until she'd done everything within her power to send these men home.

PART TWO

Normandy

CHAPTER NINE

Scarlet

The boat swayed beneath her feet, putting her off balance as it moved slowly, steadily out into the harbour. She found she was holding her breath and had to force the air in and out, clutching the handrail as she watched the men calling out to them from the docks. They were wolf-whistling, waving and singing as the ship departed, and most of the nurses around her were laughing and waving back. But Scarlet felt cold – a chill in her bones that was making her uncomfortable, not making her want to wave back and join in the fun. It wasn't just the guilt she was feeling over James, over finding out who he was, but a deep-seated worry about what they were going to encounter once they arrived in Normandy.

'Can you believe we're actually going to France?' Ellie asked breathlessly as she finally stopped waving to the men they'd left behind. 'Spencer was so certain I should find a way to stay behind, but there's no way I'd miss this adventure. Honestly, I don't know whether to be flattered or offended.'

Scarlet usually loved how positive and fun Ellie was, but today she was grating on her nerves. Was she that naive? Did she really think of this as an adventure? Maybe Ellie was simply trying to keep things feeling happy, to look forward to where they were going and their time on the ship, but Scarlet couldn't shake the feeling of unease. It was a potent mixture of fear, worries about James, and guilt over Thomas.

'Whilst aboard the HMS *Invicta*, you shall not undress at any time or wash yourselves. Any nurses disobeying this direct order will be punished accordingly.' Ellie giggled at her own imitation of Matron. 'Segregation will be strictly enforced.'

Scarlet had to smile this time, the look on Ellie's face as she mimicked the older woman making her impossible to ignore.

'I still can't believe we're travelling to France,' Ellie said in her normal voice now as she leaned into Scarlet and dropped her head to her shoulder, hands on the railing beside hers.

'Are you scared?' Scarlet asked her.

'Of course!'

'But you seem so . . .' Scarlet struggled to find the right word to say. 'Happy?'

Scarlet sighed. 'Yes. Like you don't have a care in the world.'

'Come on,' Ellie said, tugging on her arm. 'Let's take a look around. We might as well enjoy the next few days if we can, because life ain't ever going to be the same for us.'

'So you're faking it?'

'Let's just have fun, and worry about whatever we're heading into once we get there. It's better than being all doom and gloom before we even arrive.' She laughed. 'If not, we can always talk about you kissing your brother-in-law!'

Scarlet glared at her. 'Don't. Don't even . . .'

Ellie laughed, making a zipping gesture across her lips. 'I know, I know, you don't want to talk about it. My lips are sealed.'

Scarlet guessed that was Ellie's strange way of admitting that she was every bit as scared herself. She thought back to that first day waiting for the train, meeting Ellie and being thankful for finding a friend to pass the time with. It seemed like a lifetime ago, and yet it had only been weeks.

'Have you seen Spencer again?' she asked as they crossed the deck, shoes heavy on the timber beneath them.

'Not since this morning,' Ellie replied with a sigh. 'I wish I could have met him somewhere different. I mean, well, it's hard to know what to think. Or what to expect. But he's so, I don't know, different from any other man I've spent time with before.'

Scarlet was about to reply when they headed below deck, her voice lost in the sea of noise. She braced herself, gritting her teeth as she surveyed their mess quarters. It was awful. The most awful place she'd ever been. It looked dismal, it smelt damp, and it was filthy.

'Did you hear that they weren't expecting women on board?' someone said loudly as they walked past. 'The way they look at us is *hilarious*. Like they've never even *seen* women before.'

Scarlet turned and smiled at the nurse who'd spoken. 'Yeah, so much for three days of luxury at sea.'

Her dry humour made a few of the women laugh and for some reason it helped to ease the tension in Scarlet's shoulders.

'Dinner will be served at 1700 hours,' a man called out from above.

'Oooh, is it a roast?'

'Lashings of gravy for me!'

Scarlet grinned as others called out around her.

'Porridge,' came a cold grunt of a reply. 'And it won't be hot *or* warm.'

Scarlet's smile died, her lips stretching into a straight line as the room fell silent around her.

'Cold porridge. For dinner?' Holly burst into tears beside her, and the chatter that had been so lively before resumed only as a low hum.

'So much for staying positive, huh?' Ellie muttered, taking Scarlet's hand again and marching her forwards.

Scarlet had no idea where in France they were being taken, and frankly, she no longer cared. She just wanted to keep busy and not overthink anything and everything. Her emotions were swinging faster than a pendulum, and for some reason it was thoughts of James that gave her comfort, not Thomas, and she hated herself for it.

There was a loud noise above and Scarlet froze, scared, wondering if it was gunfire. And then the boat started to sway and she heard the louder lap of the waves and rain pounding on the deck. It must have been thunder.

'Great,' she murmured. Rain had been threatening as they'd boarded.

'I don't feel so good,' Ellie whispered.

Scarlet held her hand tighter. 'You'll be fine. You can take a seasickness tablet if you need to, and we'll keep talking. Maybe we could flout the rules and even try to find Spencer for you. Pretend we have an urgent medical question to ask him.'

Ellie squeezed her hand back, but Scarlet knew from the worried look on her face that she was already feeling beyond rotten.

'I'm sure Spencer would love me to vomit all over him,' Ellie said sarcastically.

'Hey, the man clearly adores you. What's a little sick between sweethearts?'

Ellie groaned and they walked on unsteady feet to their quarters. There were fifty nurses on board, and Scarlet doubted any of them would have cast-iron stomachs as the boat began to lurch more, and she knew that the further out to sea they went, the worse it would get.

It hadn't crossed her mind before, but as the storm became more intense, the wind howling already, so different from the overcast, merely cloudy weather they'd encountered as they'd stood above deck, she started to wonder about whether they'd even survive the voyage. It was a morbid thought, but the strong winds, the lashing of the rain and the big waves, coupled with a possible enemy attack, suddenly had her stomach churning and her hand reaching for the dreaded thick paper bag.

'Come on, why don't we make ourselves useful? Try to do something entertaining to keep everyone's minds off what's going on?' Scarlet suggested as she gripped the bag.

'You actually think they'll let us do something?' Ellie asked. She did look a little happier, cracking a smile as she looked back.

'So long as it's women only? I'll bet they couldn't give a hoot what we do.'

It wasn't often Ellie who needed cheering up, but Scarlet didn't like to see her so down. Besides, she liked the idea of doing anything that distracted her from the rolling motion of the boat.

'What were you thinking?' Ellie asked.

'That's the problem, I wasn't!' she said with a laugh. 'Any ideas?'

'None. But between the two of us I'm sure we'll come up with something.'

'Don't forget, Matron said we could visit her cabin if we need to for rum. A good dose of that is her cure for seasickness,' Scarlet said. 'I think at best it'd be so horrendous it would knock you out cold, but what was it she said?'

'That she didn't have the time or patience for illness amongst her nurses,' Ellie muttered.

Scarlet sighed. She'd like to see how Matron managed to keep her food down because she doubted even the strongest of stomachs wouldn't be queasy right now.

Scarlet clung to the rails and stared into the ocean. She didn't know if this was a sensible thing to do or a stupid one, but she couldn't seem to focus on anything else. The boat had been heaving for what felt like days, although she knew the wild weather had only been bad for a matter of hours – the wind howling and the rain sporadic. If there had been a worse time they could have sailed, she struggled to imagine when it would have been.

'Scarlet!'

Her name whipped on the wind, and she wondered if she was imagining it. She shut her eyes, tried to move with the boat. But even with her eyes closed she could still see the dark water, the white foam stark against the almost black waves. She didn't know why it was so dark, the violence of the storm perhaps, but she'd never seen water like it and hoped she never would again.

'Scarlet!'

This time she did turn. The voice was closer, definitely not in her imagination.

'James?' She hadn't expected to see him, not on board when there were such strict rules. Although she gathered that he was probably allowed to do things the lowlier soldiers weren't, given that he was a commanding officer.

'Ellie said I might find you out here.'

She noticed how healthy he looked, how strong. So many of the nurses had fallen dreadfully ill, not used to the conditions or the terrible food, but James certainly didn't seem to be suffering, at least not visibly.

'How are you coping?'

She shook her head, knowing they should be keeping their distance. 'Not well. Better when I'm out here, for some reason.'

Scarlet expected him to tell her off for being out, for leaning over the railing when she might fall. But he didn't.

'I wanted to make sure you were doing all right. I've been worried about you.'

Scarlet's heart was beating fast, her sick stomach forgotten as she stared into James's eyes. How did he make her feel like this every time he looked at her, spoke to her? Did he think of her as much as she did him?

Her mind was screaming out for Thomas, trying desperately to think only of him, but suddenly everything about him was a blur, a whir of snapshots that were no longer filled with the emotion or longing she'd grown used to. It was James she couldn't stop thinking about.

'I'm fine,' she stammered, eventually.

'You're too optimistic not to be faring well,' he said with a chuckle.

Scarlet looked across and fought the urge to reach out to him. It didn't matter what they were talking about, he always made her feel the same, and now, staring at his mouth, she couldn't help but think about the kiss they'd shared.

'I'm starting to feel a whole lot less optimistic now,' Scarlet admitted, raising her voice to be heard above the wind, moving closer to him as the ship heaved again.

'And if you don't find him?' James asked, taking a hand off the rail as he turned to face her.

Scarlet returned his gaze, staying strong even though he was making her feel things she didn't want to feel. Of course they were talking about Thomas again.

'I haven't thought that far ahead,' she said honestly.

James reached out to her, extended his hand and patiently waited for her to place her palm against his. Her hand was shaking, fingers locking around his, not needing any encouragement. James had been all she'd thought about as she lay in her makeshift bed the night before, as she listened to her fellow nurses and friends vomit into their bags and dry-retch, as she whispered with Ellie while they huddled close for warmth and tried to take their minds off what was happening.

And now here he was, standing before her, his expression so hard to read, his hand so warm when she was shivering cold. A wave rocked the boat and sent her spiralling towards him, tumbling into his arms as he managed to catch her.

'No,' she muttered, pushing back, not wanting to be this close to him.

He held her tight, not letting go.

'If Thomas is alive, I will come to your wedding. If I survive the war,' James said, stepping back but still holding her, staring deep into her eyes, hands to her elbows. 'I will kiss your cheek and tell you how happy I am for you, and I'll never mention what passed between us. I will be the perfect brother, the model brother-in-law.' He paused. 'We shall never speak of what happened between us.'

Scarlet should have been thrilled. Thomas would never know what had happened, that she'd wavered instead of remaining entirely devoted to him. But there was only one question circling her mind. 'What if he isn't alive?' She gulped, her feet unsteady as the boat moved up then down again. 'What if he's gone?'

'Then *I* will be the one searching for *you*,' James said simply.

Her heart had been racing before, but now it was thumping, the warmth of his body making it impossible not to think about how badly she wanted him. 'James, you don't mean that. I can't . . .'

He pulled her closer, his eyes never leaving hers, not for a beat. 'Scarlet, listen to me.' He ducked down, head lowered, mouth too close to hers. 'The day I met you, before I ever knew who you were, there was something about you. Now I'm not going to do anything I shouldn't, I wouldn't do that to Thomas, but . . .'

Now it was him not finishing his sentence.

'If I hadn't met Thomas first, if things had been different . . .' she said, then stopped herself. It was stupid to talk like this. If she hadn't been engaged to Thomas then she'd never have ended up here. She probably would have been working with the Red Cross closer to home. 'Thomas is the only reason we met. If it wasn't for him our paths might never have crossed.'

'But if we had met?' James insisted. 'Would you have said yes if I'd asked you to wait for *me* until the war was over? If I'd been the one to meet you? If you weren't engaged to any man before we'd met?'

Scarlet knew she should lie, keep her true feelings hidden, but she couldn't. 'If I'd met you first, my answer would have been yes.'

James stared at her, and she did her best to stay still as the ship moved roughly beneath their feet. The lurch came from nowhere, flinging her sideways towards the railings. She reached frantically for him as he caught her and held her close again, much closer this time. He steadied her, his heart beating so loud that with her head to his chest she could hear it pounding.

She lifted her chin to look up at him as his hands went to her arms, to push her back. Scarlet slipped her free hand around his neck, anchored herself to him as his lips met hers. She should have pulled away, but like the first time, she didn't. Who knew whether they would survive their trip to France? Who knew if she'd ever see James again, or Thomas for that matter? It was a goodbye kiss – the end – and it would never, ever happen again.

Scarlet forgot everything else and enjoyed the taste and feel of James, the warmth of his mouth and the closeness of his body as they embraced. Then the ship heaved again, lurched violently, and Scarlet completely lost her balance as a wave came crashing over the edge and on to the deck.

'You'd think we'd be spared, wouldn't you?' James muttered loudly. 'We're going into battle and I can't even get a few minutes' peace with a beautiful girl.'

Another wave crashed against the boat, and this time Scarlet screamed, the moment they'd just shared quickly forgotten.

'Below decks!' someone bellowed as James grabbed her hand tight and raced with her away from the edge and back towards the gangway.

The ship turned hard, jerked to the left, and Scarlet lost her grip on James's hand as he was thrown further away. She fell, her hip slamming into the deck.

'James!' she screamed, suddenly terrified of the water that was sporadically splashing on board, the cold wetness soaking into her clothes as she lay sprawled on the deck, instantly freezing her skin.

She scrambled up, stumbling again, until suddenly his strong arms were around her. This time they ran faster, dashing down into relative safety. But her heart was still racing and she was soaked through, which wouldn't have been so bad if it wasn't against the rules to undress.

'You all right?' he asked, still holding her tight.

She nodded. 'I'll be fine. I think.'

'I have to go,' James whispered, pressing a quick kiss to her cheek, eyes lingering on hers. 'I'm sorry.'

Scarlet nodded bravely, remembering his brother with eyes almost as dark saying the same words to her before he left for war. Only she wasn't sure whether James was saying sorry for kissing her, or for leaving. She had a feeling she wouldn't see him again, a knot of dread deep in her belly telling her that she was going to lose both of them. It might spare her the hardship of living with what she'd done, but the heartache, she knew, would be unbearable.

'They've seen enemy submarines!' someone yelled.

Scarlet turned away for the barest second, and when she looked back James was gone. She plucked at her trousers, wishing she hadn't been stupid enough to go out on deck when they'd been instructed not to. She searched for Ellie, touching her lips with her fingertips, remembering the fleeting kiss that had stolen her breath away.

'That's why we lurched suddenly. The blasted enemy is right here under the water with us. Same last night when we were sleeping,' Ellie suddenly whispered in her ear, turning up out of nowhere. 'Spencer told me. He said that's why we're zigzagging along the coast.'

Scarlet slipped her arm around her friend. 'Have you been with Spencer?'

'You'd know if you hadn't been sneaking around with lover boy.'

Ellie's arched eyebrow made Scarlet laugh. At least her friend didn't seem to think less of her for falling for her fiancé's brother; Scarlet appreciated how non-judgemental she was.

'I'm sorry. I shouldn't be making jokes like that now we know he's, well . . .'

'My fiancé's brother,' Scarlet finished for her. 'I deserved that, but I won't be seeing him again, not like that.' She shut her eyes then quickly opened them when an image of James blurred into her vision. 'What did Spencer say?'

'He told me that another ship has been lost,' Ellie murmured into her ear quietly, so no one else could hear. 'Something about a mine being dislodged from its moorings and hitting them, and everyone on board being presumed dead.'

Scarlet shuddered. 'Does he think we'll make it?' She was frightened, more than she'd ever been in her life.

'He told me to stay below decks and pray.'

Scarlet didn't want to say it, especially when she'd always believed faithfully without question, but she was starting to doubt whether there was a God up there in the sky who could help them. If He could, surely He wouldn't be letting this happen?

'Are you going to have dinner?' Scarlet asked.

Ellie groaned. 'I can't eat more porridge. I just can't.'

'The bread then. At least we know that stays down,' Scarlet said matter-of-factly, even though the stale bread was so disgusting she could barely swallow it without choking.

'Have you had your chocolate yet?' Ellie asked, eyebrows raised, eyes hopeful.

Scarlet blew out the breath she'd been holding. 'No. But now seems like as good a time as any.'

If she died tonight at the mercy of an enemy submarine, she would at least have James in her heart and chocolate on her lips. *And Thomas,* she thought to herself. She needed to hold Thomas close to her heart, too. Because without her believing that he was alive, what hope could he possibly have?

They walked together, feet unsteady but with their arms linked, back to their billet, and fell into their bunks. Around them, other nurses were already in bed, snoring softly.

Scarlet reached inside her kitbag and pulled out two little squares of chocolate, wishing she had an entire parcel of sweet treats. She gave one to Ellie, who wriggled close to her, and then they both held up their pieces.

'To making it safely to France,' Scarlet said, touching hers to Ellie's.

'To making it *home* safely from France,' Ellie said instead.

They both nibbled carefully, trying to make it last as long as possible. It wasn't the best chocolate Scarlet had ever eaten, but compared to stone-cold porridge that looked like slop for pigs, and bread so dry and stale it was almost impossible to digest, she wasn't about to complain. She only hoped that one day she'd be back home eating roast lamb with lashings of gravy and potatoes piled high, finished with any kind of pudding served with cream.

Some more nurses filed in and settled into their bunks.

'Tell me something funny,' Scarlet whispered as they lay back, huddled together. Her trousers were still damp, but even if they'd been dry she still would have been cold. Their quarters were dismal, not fit for an animal let alone fifty nurses, and the cold was a wet kind of chill, the type that was impossible to ignore. They'd all been outraged over not being able to bathe or undress, but in truth, Scarlet knew she would have been too cold to take her clothes off anyway. A quick splash of water to her face and neck had been more than enough.

Ellie made a noise deep in her throat, sighing before pushing up on one elbow beside her. Scarlet pulled the blanket up higher over both of them.

'Like what?'

'I don't know. Anything funny since the war began.' She felt her stomach heave as the boat shuddered and turned hard. 'I'm not letting this chocolate come back up! Tell me anything to keep my mind off it.'

She'd never felt so delicate, and right now she could so easily reach for her paper bag and be sick, violently sick. Over and over until there was nothing left in her stomach.

'Oh, I know something that'll make you laugh.' Ellie giggled to herself. 'It's a bomb story.'

'Sounds hil-*arious*.' Scarlet grinned back at her friend, feeling better already.

Ellie poked out her tongue. 'It was in London. I'd been doing my training and a nice man had asked me out for lunch. We were walking to the restaurant, but it wasn't going so well; he was awfully shy. Then there was this huge bang, an explosion, that sent us ducking for cover.' Ellie wriggled even closer as rain lashed above, the noise impossible to drown out even if they'd had music to play or songs to sing loudly with the others.

Scarlet hated the groans and creaks the most, as if the boat couldn't possibly withstand the unpredictable weather and sudden changes in direction. She put the last tiny bit of chocolate into her mouth and let it slowly dissolve.

'I'm supposed to laugh about you hitting the pavement during a bombing?' Scarlet asked.

'No, don't be silly. The funny part was lying there, terrified, waiting for the drone of another plane, so tired from the longest nursing shift of my life and thinking I was about to die and wondering why the sirens hadn't gone off until then, then glancing over at Matthew, my date, and seeing fluffy little white things landing on his head. I laughed, then he laughed, and we lay there looking at one another, cheeks pressed to the cold concrete, watching feathers fall all around us like soft flakes of snow.'

'I don't get it,' Scarlet said, smiling at the picture it painted, but not understanding the story fully. 'Where had the feathers come from?'

'The bomb had landed on a pillow factory nearby, and all the feathers just exploded around us. It was awful and just so, so funny at the same time. We lay there laughing until we cried.'

Scarlet laughed along with Ellie, imagining what it must have been like, reliving it with her. She'd never become used to the drone of planes or the sound of ack-ack guns, and she doubted she'd be able to hear a plane fly over without cringing ever again in her lifetime. But she could imagine how hilarious it must have been, surrounded by feathers when braced for the worst.

'Your turn,' Ellie said softly as more nurses came in, no doubt wanting to curl up into balls and try to sleep the nausea and terror away. If she wasn't talking to Ellie, she'd be trying to do the same.

'I know I asked you first, so I should have had something to share, but I can't think of anything funny,' Scarlet confessed.

The boat lurched again and Ellie rolled closer, almost landing on top of Scarlet. She wanted to make a joke that Spencer would have loved her in his quarters right now all jumpy and wanting to be comforted, but she was just too scared and couldn't get the words out.

'Anything,' Ellie whispered. 'Just talk, tell me a story, any story.'

'Well . . .' Scarlet dragged the word out, gasping when the ship pitched again. She tried not to think about enemy submarines and bombs and ships being capsized, desperately thinking back, trying to pull something from her memory that would keep them entertained.

'Talk to me about James then,' Ellie suddenly whispered, not in danger of anyone hearing them given how much chatter was going on around them now – a constant low hum of noise. 'I know he's Thomas's brother, but you can't help how you feel.'

'It's like my heart is being tugged in two completely different directions,' Scarlet said honestly. 'When I'm with him, if I forget about the fact that he is the one man who should be forbidden, I start to doubt my true feelings for Thomas. Before I knew who he was, I couldn't stop thinking about him, and now it's even worse. I am questioning why I thought Thomas was the one, whether it was only because he was leaving that I said yes so quickly to marrying him.'

'So is it true? Do you think you were really in love with him?' Ellie asked. 'Or not?'

She wished it was a simpler question, that she could make sense of what was going on in her heart and her head. 'When I close my eyes and go back in time, I know that what I felt for Thomas was true. He would have made me happy, he *did* make me happy, but it's been such a long time since I've seen him, that's all. The doubts I have only started when I met James. Maybe I love Thomas, but I'm also falling for James, if it's even possible to have feelings like that for two men at the same time.'

It was true. In her heart she'd remained faithful and determined, that Thomas would come home, that they would be married. Then James had come along and confused her. But could she feel love so quickly for a man she'd only just met? She gulped, embarrassed at her feelings and at admitting them so openly to Ellie.

'He's so different from Thomas. I suppose he's younger and more free with his words. He seems so much fun, and when he looks at me . . .' Scarlet's voice trailed off. 'Thomas used to make me feel warm inside, happy and content. But James . . .' She sighed. 'James makes me feel like I'm on fire, as if I'm burning from the inside out whenever he looks at me or touches me. It's all so silly, when I've known them both for such a short time.'

'So one is warmth and stability,' Ellie mused aloud. 'The other is fire and excitement and making your heart race.'

Scarlet nodded. 'Yes. I'm afraid that Thomas will always be the right choice, but now that I've become close to James, maybe warmth won't be enough.' It sounded pathetic, she knew that, when so many people were losing their lives to this war, losing their loved ones. But she couldn't help the internal battle she was facing. 'I want to feel that spark of crazy happiness every time my future husband kisses me, and it was so long ago that I was with Thomas, so many months, that I suppose I don't truly remember what it was like with him. To kiss him like that.'

'If you find Thomas? If he is alive?' Ellie asked. 'What then?'

'I lock away my feelings for James and live the life I was supposed to live with Thomas. I have to; I promised him. I gave him my word that we would marry upon his return.' Scarlet hoped he wasn't terribly injured or maimed, but she had told him she would marry him, and marry him she would. Her parents would never forgive her for changing her mind when she'd promised, and she would never forgive herself, either. 'James might be forward and dashing, but he's a gentleman and he's given me his word that we'll never speak of what happened between us again. I mean, if we'd known, it would never have happened in the first place!'

'So you would marry Thomas, even if it was the wrong choice?' Ellie asked, looking like she disapproved from the frown on her face.

'Thomas *is* the right choice,' Scarlet affirmed. 'As soon as I see him again, as soon as we're together, things will go back to normal. Or as normal as they can, given what we're going through.'

'What if Thomas is gone?' Ellie murmured.

Scarlet slid further down into her bed, closing her eyes as she tried to push the thoughts away.

'He's not gone,' she said, for some reason more certain than ever that he was still alive, her voice firm. 'I know that he'll come back, I just know it.' Ellie's fingers began a slow, steady stroke on her back as Scarlet turned away from her, comforting her as she quietly began to cry. She was never the girl obsessing over boys or being silly, and now she was stuck in the middle of a love triangle that felt impossible. It wasn't a matter of choosing – it wasn't that simple. She couldn't switch from one brother to another. It wasn't done. Her parents would never forgive her, and her future in-laws would think she was a terrible kind of woman, surely, and she would never be able to forgive herself. Not to mention the fact that James had promised to stand back and not pursue his feelings for her.

He threaded his fingers through hers as they walked, slowly, across the grass, the sun beating down on her face as she tilted her cheeks upwards. Quiet days were a rarity, and she was enjoying every bit of this one.

'Have you ever thought about how many children you want?'

She pressed against Thomas, a smile playing quickly across her lips. 'Two,' she replied without having to think. 'A boy and a girl.'

'How about four?'

Scarlet swatted playfully at Thomas, seeing the smirk on his face. 'I think we shall start with two in mind and see how we go.'

The thought of marrying Thomas made her giddy with happiness, knowing that one day, once this dreadful war was over, they'd be able to make a home and plan a family. There was nothing in the world she wanted more. It was all she'd ever wanted, to meet a nice man from a good family and have her own home.

'And a dog,' Thomas said. 'When I'm home for good, I want a dog.'

She didn't mind animals at all, and she liked the fact that he was thinking about their future together.

'Then a dog we shall have.'

When Thomas raised her hand, still linked with his, and pressed a gentle kiss to it, Scarlet tingled from her toes all the way up her body. Everything about this gorgeous man felt right; she only had to hope and pray now that he made it home to her, when friends were losing their husbands and fiancés faster than she could keep up with.

CHAPTER TEN

Ellie

Normandy, 22 June 1944

Ellie's stomach was doing cartwheels, and even though the ship had slowed and they were in a calmer stretch of water, she still felt like she could be sick. The cold porridge and stale bread were like permanent stodge in her stomach, making her feel thick around the middle and terribly unhealthy after so long without good food. They hadn't been at sea long, but it felt like a lifetime. The rations had been awful for so long, and she was longing for fruit, anything that wasn't stale or sloppy. Back at the hospital when she was training, they'd been permitted one orange a month, and she'd do anything to taste the sweetness of citrus now.

She squinted, looking ahead, shoulder to shoulder with so many other women all no doubt as eager as she to be on land again. There wasn't a lot to see yet, but she didn't want to miss her first true glance of France. Ellie pushed her hand into her pocket and pulled out half of an oat snack she'd been saving. Her stomach was growling violently, and she decided to enjoy it now rather than end up dropping it in the water by mistake. She had no idea how long it would be until they were allowed to rest anyway, and with the boat moving more slowly and surely through the water now, she hoped she could stomach it.

There were seemingly hundreds of other ships in the water, most heading in the same direction as they were, and Ellie wondered who was on board and what they were thinking. Whether they were a bundle of emotions like she was, or whether they were soldiers terrified of what they were about to face. She knew she was scared of what lay in wait for them, what it would be like – anxious about their fate.

A distant booming made her pulse quicken. She turned, swapping glances with one of the other nurses. The sound was followed by more distant gunfire, then another, louder bang. As they sailed closer, Ellie looked into the water, wondered what was poking out ahead. She squinted again, saw some kind of metal object half floating, and then further ahead what seemed to be the remains of a tanker.

She choked then, the oat snack stuck in her throat as something far more horrifying floated past. It was a body. A bloated human body in the water, dressed in uniform, the head covered in blood. *One of theirs.*

Ellie tried to focus on her breathing so she wasn't sick, ready to throw up what she'd just eaten straight into the sea. But when she leaned over the railing again, looked back into the water, she saw another body. Then another.

Stepping back, reeling, body shaking, she slowly tried to gather herself. Other nurses had backed away, too, were leaving the posts at the railings they'd held for so long in eager anticipation of seeing land.

'Ellie?'

Scarlet's voice soothed her, the hand she placed on her shoulder calming her.

'Did you see . . . ?' she managed, looking into Scarlet's wide eyes.

Her friend nodded. Ellie knew she didn't have to say anything else.

It was almost dusk. The light was starting to fade, and Ellie was grateful that when they disembarked the water wouldn't be so visible.

The sight of their men floating like that, men so young they could have been her brothers, was not something she would ever, *could* ever, shake.

They'd been told the drill, that they'd be pulling into the artificial Mulberry B harbour built by the Allies, that they would need to set up camp, fend for themselves and help to establish their tent hospital. But no one had said anything about bodies, about how dangerous it would be, about what to truly expect upon arrival.

'We're together,' Scarlet said beside her, voice loud and clear. 'We said that we'd be fine as long as we weren't separated, and we haven't been. Think about that and only that.'

Ellie looked at the way Scarlet was standing, her chin high, gaze fixed ahead. If she hadn't noticed the way she was clenching her other hand so tight that her knuckles were bright white, she would have thought that nothing troubled her. But she was right. They had one another – they weren't alone – and that's what mattered right now.

The ship slowed to a stop as they neared the harbour, and Ellie decided to keep her eyes trained high, not looking into the water at all as long as she stepped forward with Scarlet safely by her side. She was a nurse in the army. She had trained for this. She was a lieutenant. Without women like her, even more boys would be floating dead in the water, and she didn't want that happening on her watch.

The sound of gunfire was continuous now and although it wasn't close, it was still unnerving. But it wasn't the noise of war that made Ellie cry, tears silently slipping down her cheeks. It was the cheer that went up from soldiers standing near the harbour, waving and calling out the moment they saw all the women on board, that made the lump form in her throat. The booms echoing around died away, and the noise in her ears was more of a roaring sound that had nothing to do with the surrounding war and everything to do with emotion.

She braced herself, didn't want to break down when she was usually stronger than that. But she missed her brothers, and these men reminded her of them. She missed the way they'd always teased her, the laughter around their dinner table, their fondness when they saw her worried about something, all jokes aside. She was strong; with three brothers she'd had to be exceptionally strong, and all she wished for now was to be home safely with them. To be done with this dreadful war that she was only just entering. And to stop worrying about where on the boat Spencer was or what might happen to him before they were together at their field hospital. Her stomach heaved.

'Ladies, we will be disembarking shortly. You need to put on your life jackets and be ready to get into the landing crafts,' Matron said curtly, without any hint of emotion. 'Follow the sergeant's directions, do whatever you're told, and then on arrival please await my instructions. I expect you to wait in an orderly manner on the beach.'

Ellie stood straighter, preparing to leave the boat that had been their relatively safe haven for the past few days. It had seemed terrifying being at sea in the storms, moving haphazardly down the coast, but compared to getting off the boat right now and heading into a war zone, the old ship was starting to feel a whole lot safer than she'd given it credit for.

She put on her Mae West, their nickname for the bulky life vests they had to wear. She knew what she had to do next, they'd been briefed already, but it was still daunting. When it was her turn, she passed her bags to one sergeant to be taken over the side, then took a deep breath before approaching the edge of the boat. Only her breath didn't come back out, stuck in her lungs as a wave of terror to rival any ocean wave washed over her, clogging her throat.

'Don't look down and keep going!' she was told, the sergeant's words managing to unfreeze her. She stepped closer, letting him lower her over the edge. 'Don't look down,' he repeated as she started to climb towards the landing craft.

Cold sea spray stung her cheeks, wetting her hair and her clothes. But she kept going, didn't stop, didn't look down.

'When I say jump, you need to jump back!' another man yelled. 'Fall back into my arms!'

Ellie sucked in another breath, listened for his command, eyes shut and suppressing a scream.

'Jump!'

She let go, launching back, her vest so bulky and ungainly she imagined it was similar to feeling eight months pregnant.

'Got you,' the soldier said in her ear as strong arms caught her, holding on tight.

Ellie gasped and then struggled to stand, hating the stupid vest as the soldier helped to steady her. Her heart was beating, blood pumping through her veins, but she was alive.

'Wow,' she managed to say to him as he released her.

'It feels good letting go like that, doesn't it?' he asked with a smile that she could just make out in the semi-darkness.

Ellie smiled to herself and stood back for the next nurse to come overboard. Maybe the things she expected to be terrifying weren't going to be so bad after all.

The water was dark, black almost, and the sky above was equally inky, the bright white moon bathing their faces in a beautiful half-light. Then bright lights cascaded through the sky and the uneasy feeling in Ellie's stomach came back full force.

Ellie stared at the Tommy cooker, ignoring the flashes in the sky that had sent chills down her spine only a few hours earlier. She was already getting used to the constant, dull noise of gunfire and the distant sky being illuminated in tiny bursts as they sat there in the open. The night wind blowing across the water felt cool, and the fact that she could still vividly recall the bodies bobbing out there was making her want to heave all over again. But at the same time she was so hungry that the feeling was gnawing at her stomach as if there were an actual hole to fill. For the first time in her life, she was struggling to find any humour, any happiness, in her situation. She was lost, and even with Scarlet and the other nurses around her, she was feeling very much alone.

'Do you think we'll end up staying on the beach tonight?' Scarlet asked in a low whisper.

They were huddled together, cooking side by side, four other nurses with them in a tiny circle that was as much for comfort as warmth.

'I hope not,' Ellie replied, keeping her head down. 'I feel like we're too exposed here, not safe enough.'

Holly, who was on her other side, made a noise in her throat. 'Probably safer here than anywhere else we're headed to.'

Ellie had only caught a glimpse of Spencer since they'd arrived, and she wished he would seek her out. When she was with him she felt safe, so safe, and she needed that right now. There was something about having a man close. For so long now she felt like she'd been surrounded by women; as nurses, and at home when the men had all been sent away, when it had only been women on their own in the fields and tending the houses and everything else. And she liked how easy she found it to talk to him, how they fell into such an easy rhythm.

'What do you think this village will be like?' Ellie asked, pushing her thoughts away and not wanting to think of how close they'd be to actual fighting, how less safe it might feel compared to sitting on the beach like little ducks in a row. 'What was it? *Rice* something,' she attempted.

'Rys,' Holly corrected. 'They called it *Rys*.'

'It'll be good and safe, I'm certain,' Scarlet said. 'They wouldn't be stationing us there if it wasn't.'

The girls all finished cooking and started to eat, something hot for once instead of stone-cold slop. Then there was a commotion further down the beach, and Ellie strained to look, her eyes adjusting to the dark.

'They're Red Cross,' Scarlet said, more loudly than she'd been speaking earlier. 'They must be sending the wounded back.'

She knew Scarlet was keeping an eye out for James, but the soldiers had departed quickly and no one knew if they were already heading for the front or resting elsewhere.

'I want to get going, find out where we're staying,' she muttered to Ellie.

'Tell me about it,' Ellie said back, voice low as they kept staring at the goings-on.

The activity continued, more men moving towards the harbour and plenty of shouting, but it was too far away for them to figure out what was being said. At least it gave them all something to focus on, other than thinking about where they were going, although she guessed bundling men up to be sent home was exactly what they'd be doing, anyway.

She saw Scarlet look at her wristwatch, holding it close to her eyes as she inspected the time.

'I think we've been waiting almost three hours now,' Scarlet said.

The women seated with them groaned collectively, and Ellie felt much the same way. During their few days at sea, she hadn't expected to be parked on a beach with no information about when they were going or what they could expect. The unknown, with gunfire so close, was scaring her. Ellie was the first to admit that her nerves weren't built for suspense; she wanted to know where they were going, when they'd be working, and how close they would be to danger. She needed to know these basic things to figure out how to cope with them.

It was going to be a long night; of that she was sure. Ellie slowly started to gather up her things, systematically folding them away. She wished she'd saved an oat snack, something else to eat, but she'd been so hungry on board and nibbling it as they approached had at least made her feel better at the time.

'Get your things together, it's time to depart,' Matron announced from behind them.

Ellie looked at Scarlet, but neither of them said anything. It was time to see where they were going to be living for the next part of for ever.

'The 75th will be temporarily joining the 81st tent hospital until our site has been taken. Prepare yourselves to work alongside them, as well as to be sent to other duties.'

Ellie had no idea why they were joining another unit, and if the others had questions, they kept them quiet, too. No one said a word as they packed up. It was the most sombre mood Ellie had ever experienced.

'Do you think they mean that our soldiers haven't won the place where our hospital is to go?' Scarlet whispered in her ear as they stood, bags in hand. 'That they're fighting to secure it now?'

Ellie hadn't even put two and two together, but now that Scarlet said it, she realised that her friend was probably right. Around them, smashed amphibious vehicles littered the beach, with concrete remains that were impossible to decipher and broken tin hats and rifles. She had the daunting feeling that they'd just arrived in the depths of hell and they weren't escaping from it any time soon.

Days had started to blur into nights. Ellie couldn't remember when she'd last slept, what time she'd last eaten, or when she was supposed to finish her shift. If there wasn't so much to do, so many doctors waving at her or patients crying out to her, she would have collapsed to the ground, but something about the desperation around her kept her going. Made her keep putting one foot in front of the other.

'Please, make it stop,' she whispered to herself. '*Why can't it stop?*'

Tears burnt her eyes, but she fiercely blinked them away as she rushed to the side of a soldier calling for her. Just looking at him made Ellie want to retch, but there was nothing in her stomach, and she was determined not to. There was enough blood and bile on the floor without her adding to it.

The man was missing so much of his face; one side was near perfect, the other . . . She gulped, trying to look only at his hands. The other side was horrifying, and he was in so much pain that he kept drifting in and out of consciousness, his hand wildly flapping for hers, wanting her to hold it in the brief lucid moments that he had. He couldn't say a word, only grunt, his tongue with a stitch through it so it could be sewn to his top button to ensure he didn't swallow it.

She gave him more morphine and held his hand, letting him clutch her tightly as he slowly drifted back out again. There were more men to tend to, more coming in, but he was the worst she'd seen so far and he was still alive, so giving him an extra few minutes was not something she was going to feel bad about.

The casualty clearance station she was working in was supposed to be a temporary stop, a place to patch up the wounded and give them basic first aid before they were sent to the field hospitals for further care, recovery or evacuation, but those they'd marked for evacuation were still waiting. She had no idea what the hold-up was, and there was nothing she could do anyway.

'Nurse!'

She was used to simply being called 'Nurse'. There hadn't exactly been time to get to know everyone's names.

'Coming!'

She dropped the soldier's hand and ran. The doctors never looked at her, just barked orders, and she did her best to assist. But the blood, the mess, the skin that looked like it had been shredded . . . Her stomach lurched, just like it had constantly for the past few days.

Ellie dry-retched, bending over before forcing herself to stand.

'Hold it together, Nurse. For Christ's sake!'

She wished for Spencer, to be working alongside him instead of here, but he was operating at a field hospital helping the more badly wounded, so she wasn't going to be seeing him any time soon. His request to have her assist him had obviously fallen on deaf ears, or maybe there was simply too much to do and too few hands for special requests. She doubted she'd have coped with it anyway, after seeing what she'd seen already. Ellie only wished they'd had the chance to say goodbye; all they'd had was a few seconds to hug before he dashed away to the army truck.

'Sorry, sir,' she murmured. 'What can I do?'

'Stop the bleeding in his leg and bandage up his head once I'm finished here.'

Ellie's heart felt like it was going to break. She'd already seen so much pain, so many beautiful, strong bodies burnt and blasted and maimed. What were these men going to do if they survived? She almost hoped that they didn't, that they passed away before they reached home, so they were no longer in pain and no longer terrified of how they were going to live without limbs, without faces, without . . . The tears threatened again, an unshed gasp of them, but she refused to let them out. These were real tears, tears for the horror of war – not for her, but for the fallen and falling soldiers. She wasn't built for this, didn't have the stomach for it, even though she was trying her best.

'I have another amputation to do. Finish here and then find me to assist.'

Ellie shuddered. She couldn't. Could she? She finished stemming the blood flow as best she could and then turned to find the bandage she'd need for his head. It had been his leg that was the mess, a disgusting merger of skin and blood and what she guessed were fragments from bullets. Those would be dealt with at the field hospital, if the convoy arrived for them and didn't get blown up on the way.

'*Nurse.*'

The word was soft, kind, and a hand closed over hers when she turned back to the bed she was standing beside. She looked into bright blue eyes, eyes that reminded her of her youngest brother; they almost twinkled at her despite the pain. She let him take her hand, squeezed her fingers over his and smiled down at him.

'How bad is it?' he asked, voice hoarse.

She set the bandage down and reached instead for water, helping him to sit up a little so she could let him sip.

'It's better than a lot I've seen,' she said, referring to his leg. 'Your head wound is bloody but superficial, and I'm sure once it's stitched and tended to, it'll just be a matter of waiting for your hair to grow back.'

A boom echoed out, made the ground shudder beneath them. Ellie froze, hand shaking as she set the water back down. The gunfire had been close the entire time, but nothing that loud, nothing that terrifying.

'It'll be all right,' the soldier said, taking her hand again. She wondered if this time it was for her sake instead of his.

'I need to bandage you up, get you ready for transportation.'

'Can you talk to me? Tell me a story? I . . .' His voice trailed off as she picked up the bandage, letting go of his hand. 'It's been so long since I've had a woman to talk to. Please, just tell me what you're thinking about, anything just so I can listen to you speak.'

Ellie wasn't about to tell him what she was thinking, that with the sound of war so close she was certain they were all about to die, but she liked him. He was kind and friendly in an entirely comfortable way, and he must have been in a great deal of pain.

She looked up, across the tent, and somehow, amidst the chaos, she met Spencer's gaze. She hadn't known he was back with them yet, and it took her by surprise. He was holding up his hands, working, but for one brief moment they locked eyes and he smiled at her. It was what she needed, one smile to make her realise she had to keep going.

'Would you like me to tell you a story from home?' she asked, looking back down and knowing that she would be reprimanded for taking too long with one patient. But it was her way, and she couldn't change who she was.

'Anything. Please,' he said, pushing himself up a little on to his elbows as she carefully checked his head wound to ensure she'd bandaged it correctly.

She sighed, patting the soldier's arm before turning her full attention to his head and hoping he was starting to feel somewhat better simply from talking to her. 'Home,' Ellie admitted. 'My home back in Ireland, before we moved to England. That's what I'm thinking about.' It hadn't been, but the moment she'd thought of something to share with him, home had flooded her mind and it was the one thing she didn't mind talking about to anyone, even if it did make her sad.

'You know, I hear that Ireland is like a little safe haven,' he said. 'It's as if the war hasn't touched it; they don't even have food rations there. Or that's what they've been saying.'

Ellie smiled as she thought of home. Her real home would always be where her family was, but the house she grew up in in Ireland was always going to feel like home no matter how many years passed.

'I dream of visiting my aunt sometimes. She lived near us, and hers is a cottage much the same as ours was,' Ellie told him, keeping her voice low. 'If I arrived today to see her, she'd be dashing out to dig new potatoes straight from the soil before plunging them into a pot of salted boiling water. Then she'd serve them with freshly churned butter and meat. For breakfast it would be fresh eggs and bacon. I can almost taste it.'

The soldier chuckled. 'I think we all caught the wrong boat if that's what would await us in Ireland.'

Ellie smiled, but the truth was it wasn't just the food she craved. It was the chatter of the people, the fact that most of them were dirt poor, but rich in food because of where they lived. 'The bottom half-door of our cottage was always closed to keep the chickens out. The donkey in the paddock was always braying, and we used to run around outside barefoot on the grass with my dog chasing at our heels, or pick berries on hot summer days.' What she wouldn't give to be back there right now.

'Nurse!'

She sighed again, letting the soldier take her hand and press a kiss to it, even though she knew it was strictly forbidden. But what did she care? And more importantly, who was going to reprimand her? They needed all hands on deck, all the nurses they could, and if she couldn't comfort a soldier who'd been injured in the line of duty, then . . . She gritted her teeth. There was no point getting angry, she knew that.

'I'll remember you,' he said. 'I'll be picturing Ireland all the way just to get me through.'

She smiled and patted the soldier's hand back before dashing off. Dreams of Ireland might be the only thing to get *her* through the long days and nights, too.

Ellie almost bumped straight into Scarlet as she hurried. Her friend was carrying a tiny metal tray, her mouth set in a hard line. But when she looked up, that expressionless face broke out into a smile.

'Are you doing all right?' Scarlet leaned into her, as Ellie did to her, taking a tiny bit of weight off her feet.

'No,' Ellie whispered honestly. The truth was she was so close to slipping to the floor like a puddle.

'Me neither. Keep going, though. We can get through this.'

The moment was over as quickly as it had begun, but something about Scarlet gave Ellie strength – the determination in her eyes and the tone of her voice. Or maybe it was simply the letter sewn into her undergarments that she didn't ever want to have to give to Scarlet's family, or maybe it was knowing that she had a true friend out here who genuinely had her back. She might have been falling in love with Spencer, but the love she had for Scarlet was founded in a friendship that she knew would last until their last breaths.

'Nurse!'

'*Old women,*' she murmured. She hoped those last breaths would be as old women, and they'd look back on this as something that was never, ever to be spoken of or relived again.

CHAPTER ELEVEN

Scarlet

The sun carefully peeked through the clouds above, and Scarlet turned her face up, smiling at the sliver of brightness bathing her cheeks. It felt like for ever since she'd seen the sun. If she blocked out the noise of war in the distance, imagined herself at home, walking the gardens instead of across a street that had been damaged by tanks and gunfire, she could almost be happy.

Scarlet straightened, looked around and sighed. She was thankful to spend a day away, to not have to work at the casualty clearance station, although she felt sad to have left Ellie behind. She knew Ellie wasn't coping, could tell from how much she shook at night, not from cold, but from shock, and it worried her terribly. To her surprise, she was managing to cope, although she was finding it hard to block out the memories of what she was seeing each day. Thankfully, she was so exhausted that when she finally had the chance to sleep she fell into a deep slumber, not thinking about James or Thomas, or anything other than her bone-deep tiredness. She was finding the lack of food the hardest, serving the patients water and something to eat whilst having to go without herself. It was certainly not easy, although she doubted anything about war was supposed to be easy.

She crossed the street and recited the directions she'd been given, making her way to a convent that was housing some of the injured. From what she'd heard they'd taken in a great deal of soldiers at different times, and Scarlet had been sent to assist in any way she could.

She approached the big stone building, so far untouched by the war, and took a deep breath before entering. There was something peaceful about the old building, something nice about entering a peaceful place of God after what she'd been through lately, what she'd seen. Although she was certain the nuns would be dealing with their own fair share of atrocities here, too.

'*Bonjour?*' she called out as she entered.

Scarlet kept walking, hearing sounds but not sure where they were coming from. Then a nun appeared, a big smile greeting her the moment their eyes met.

'Thank you for coming,' the other woman said, extending her hand. She was young, far younger than Scarlet had expected, but then she hadn't really known what to expect. 'Come this way, we've been waiting for you.' Her English was thickly accented, her lilting French accent meaning that Scarlet had to listen that bit harder to each word to understand what she was saying.

Scarlet nodded, falling into step beside her. 'I'm Scarlet,' she said.

'Sister Florence,' the nun replied.

'I have to say it's nice to be here, away from the hospital,' Scarlet admitted. 'The long shifts there are tough going, and the injuries are horrific.'

Sister Florence took her arm as they walked. 'The men are fortunate to have so many caring for them. We pray every day for the nurses as much as the soldiers.'

It was comforting to be spoken to so kindly, and Scarlet was finding the convent beautifully peaceful – a reminder of times before the war perhaps.

'Through here.'

When she entered the room, closed off by a large, heavy timber door, Scarlet's breathing became shallow, the smell of injuries so familiar to her yet still so repugnant. There were men in makeshift beds, a good set-up of basic medical equipment, from what she could see, and nuns tending to the motionless patients.

'I wasn't expecting this,' she declared.

'This many men or the facilities we have?' Sister Florence asked.

Scarlet took it all in, looking around the room and back again. 'All of it.'

'We've done our best, but some of the men need more help than we can give. We're told there have been some delays with getting the soldiers back home for treatment.'

'Yes, there have been, but we should be able to move those critical ones from here almost immediately.'

Scarlet surveyed the room again, trying to see if there was any order in which the men had been placed, whether the nuns had been keeping notes about any treatments or injuries received.

'Should we look at those most critical first?' Scarlet asked.

'This way.'

The other women in the room all smiled and spoke briefly to her, some merely saying '*bonjour*', and Scarlet replied in her usual friendly manner. But she only had limited time and wanted to make sure she made the correct assessments and assisted in the most effective way she could while she was there.

'I will identify those that need immediate transportation, and report back to my superiors about the others.' As she systematically looked at each man, she decided that tomorrow she would insist on Ellie taking her place. Ellie would be more at home here, might be able to recover a little if she was removed from the front, whereas Scarlet knew she herself could continue there without being as affected. She was finding that blood and gruesome injuries didn't trouble her nearly as much as she'd feared they would, that she'd found strength in the work she was doing. It was the ones she lost that haunted her.

'Do you need help here?'

Scarlet nodded. 'If you could assist me that would be greatly appreciated. You could take notes as I make verbal assessments, and after that I'll be able to go through bandaging and stitching with the sisters, as well as any other training that you need further instruction with.'

She always feared having to show anyone how to bandage, not thinking she was very good at it, but anything she could do here, she would.

'May I ask if you've had any hot water? Been able to bathe at all?' Florence asked as they walked away from the first patient.

'Oh dear, can you tell?' Scarlet's eyebrows shot up, her cheeks warming from embarrassment.

'No! I was being polite. We can make provision for you to wash here, to say thank you for your help.'

Scarlet smiled, thankful for the offer. 'Yes, please. It would be heavenly.'

She hoped she hadn't offended Sister Florence with talk of heaven, but the idea of a bath of any kind, even merely a splash of gorgeous hot water for her face and neck, was the most glorious thing she'd been offered in weeks.

'Are there many other convents assisting the wounded?' Scarlet asked.

'Yes. Every convent still standing will open its doors to injured soldiers. We all do what we can.'

Scarlet tried not to let hope creep into her voice, to fill her mind when she should be focused only on the men in the room. 'So they could have soldiers still in their care from some time ago? Since well before this battle?'

Sister Florence had wide blue eyes, and as Scarlet looked up into them she nodded. 'Yes, of course. We would keep any person safe within our walls for as long as need be in times such as these.'

Thomas. Her thoughts were always turning back to Thomas, even if James was in her head, too. 'I lost contact with my fiancé,' she shared, wanting to be direct rather than keeping it to herself, at the very least so Sister Florence understood why she was asking. 'He was last heard from in France, and I keep hoping, praying, that he's still alive somewhere.'

Sister Florence placed a hand on her shoulder. 'We see horrible things every day, but there is always hope. There are miracles that God gives us every day, even in wartime.'

Scarlet hoped she was right, that Thomas could be one of those miracles. 'I hope he has found his way to a sister like you,' she said honestly.

'So do I.'

She felt lighter simply from admitting her hopes and fears, and continued quickly around the room. The men were in various states of injury, and when she lifted one blanket back to find a bandaged leg on a soldier that needed to be amputated, she quietly put the covers back and moved him to the top of her list for immediate evacuation.

'Do you know how long you'll be in Rys?' Sister Florence asked.

'Not much longer, I believe. We're soon to set up our field hospital, once the site has been taken.'

'God bless you, Scarlet,' the sister said, touching her shoulder.

It was one thing for an ordinary person to say those words, but another entirely to hear them from a nun. For some reason, it made them feel more meaningful to her.

'Thank you,' she said quietly.

'Don't let the horrors we are facing right now affect your belief in God. He is with us every day, and I believe women like you are evidence of that.'

It was as if Sister Florence could read her mind: the way she was feeling, the doubts she'd had. All she could do was make it through one day at a time. The hope she held for finding Thomas was helping her to put one foot in front of the other, day after day. Not to mention the prayers she was saying for James every morning and night. She had no idea where he was, but she was certain it would be far too close to the front line for her liking.

It had been a long day, and returning to their temporary lodgings was her least favourite part of it. She'd bathed at the convent, feeling terribly guilty over having access to hot water when her friends didn't, and the lovely clean feeling was with her still. Now she was back, bone-tired and dragging her feet, she doubted she'd be allowed to sneak off to bed without having to do more time in the clearance station, but at least she could enjoy the memory of her bath.

'Scarlet, do you have a minute?'

She hadn't been expecting a man to call her name, but when she looked up she saw an anxious Spencer standing near the entrance to their tent hospital. She walked over to him. He was back with them now, and it was nice for Ellie to have him near.

'Is there something I can do for you?'

He shook his head. 'Not in there.' Spencer cleared his throat, indicating that they should walk. 'It's hell in there; there's no other word for it.'

She sighed. 'It is.'

'I'm worried about Ellie. She comes across as if she's coping, that she can do it, but I worry for her. She looks like she's going to faint at any moment. That . . .' His voice trailed off. 'I feel like something isn't right with her. I might not have known her for all that long, but the spark she always had – I feel that it's fading.'

Scarlet agreed, but she didn't want to side with Spencer and get Ellie into trouble. 'We're all struggling, it's true. I don't think any of us were built for this type of work, to have to see so many injured men.' A number of women were finding it hard to keep going, and some had fallen so ill recently they were unable to work. This had left them even worse off than before, with fewer nurses to cover shifts.

'Scarlet, I'm not trying to get Ellie into trouble, far from it. I would just like your help to try to find more, well, suitable jobs for her. If I can.'

She thought about her response, chose her words carefully. 'Doctor Black, I was under the impression that she was still to assist you with your surgeries and cases, as your personal nurse.'

He smiled. 'That was my intention, but now I think you might be more suited for that role. At least for now. I'll have more authority when we take over our field hospital, but I don't want to push her.'

'This won't affect her position here? I mean, she won't be in trouble at all?'

He spoke quietly now, his eyes downcast. 'I care a great deal for Ellie, and I only want what's best for her.'

Scarlet was certain he was being truthful, and wasn't so worried about speaking freely now that he'd admitted his feelings for her friend. 'I was working at the convent today, and it crossed my mind to see if Ellie could take my place tomorrow, if there was some way of getting her on to that service. It was the nicest day I've had in a long while.'

'If I have your consent, then I'll make the change to the roster myself if I can. It won't take much for me to take charge of it.'

'I'm pleased she has you looking out for her,' Scarlet told him.

'As I am pleased she has a friend like you.'

She watched as Spencer started to walk away and hoped for Ellie's sake that something happened between them. Ellie deserved someone like him, someone whose eyes lit up every time he saw her and went out of his way to make her smile. Spencer was a great doctor, but there was something nicer about him than the other doctors, something about his manner that was almost boyish sometimes instead of the usual flippant and rude behaviour so many of the nurses were accustomed to. He'd made it very clear that he'd patch up anyone no matter who they were, that he'd become a doctor to do whatever he could to end the suffering of others, and it had made Scarlet warm to him even more.

'Excuse me.'

Scarlet turned slowly and came face to face with a nurse in uniform, her blue eyes bright, blonde hair neatly pulled back from her face. She was pretty and looked calm and collected despite the conditions.

'Yes?' Scarlet replied.

'I'm to find out who's in charge here. Of your unit,' the woman said. 'I understand there is a unit here that's temporarily joined the 81st?'

Scarlet nodded, wondering why this unfamiliar nurse was looking for her superior. 'Yes, that's right. We're waiting for our field site to be taken before setting up our mobile hospital.'

The other nurse grimaced. 'I'm afraid to say the battle has been hard-fought, but you'll be moving soon. I'm Lucy,' she said, extending her hand. 'I'm with the 50 Mobile field hospital, but I've been sent to assist with your new set-up. There will be a group of us coming to assist your unit.'

Scarlet's heart began to pound as she held her own hand out to grasp Lucy's. 'I'm Scarlet. Pleased to meet you.' It was a relief to know there would be more nurses joining them.

They stood for a moment, awkward, until Lucy spoke again. 'How are you faring here? The conditions are satisfactory?' She sighed. 'I've been nursing for some time, but nothing prepares anyone for all this.'

'We're desperate for hot water and sleep,' Scarlet replied, 'but otherwise we're all right.'

'This will seem easy compared to where you're heading, believe me.' Lucy shook her head. 'We're all in this for the long haul I suspect. I can't see things getting better any time soon.'

Lucy gave a half-smile and Scarlet attempted to do the same, not sure about this confident nurse who appeared to know everything. 'I'll take you inside, then.'

After a day that had put a genuine smile on her face for once, Scarlet had the sinking feeling that she wasn't going to have another day like it for a good long while.

'You'll be looking for our matron, over there in that office,' Scarlet told her, stopping and pointing the way. 'If you can't find her, then I'll locate a senior doctor for you.'

'Thank you.'

'Lucy?' Scarlet called, above the arrivals of ambulances and nurses shouting for assistance, the constant merry-go-round of busyness starting all over again after the short lull.

'Yes?'

'If you're joining us on your own without your unit, ask for me by name. I know how much easier it can be to have a friend when you don't know anyone.'

Months ago, she might not have said anything, wouldn't have thought about someone else's plight, her thoughts far more selfish than they could ever be now after what she'd seen. But that was then and this was now, and she would do anything she could for another if it meant making their life a little easier. Besides, Lucy was obviously experienced, which meant there was a lot she could learn from her.

Lucy nodded. 'Thank you, but I'll be fine. I have a job to do, that's why I'm here.'

Scarlet was taken aback. They all had a job to do, and she was only trying to be friendly.

'Of course,' she replied stiffly, not sure what else to say. 'Thank you for your assistance.'

It had been an awful day at their new field hospital. Scarlet rolled her sleeves up and took a deep, shuddering breath, staring at the blood that stained her hands. She'd had some horrendous moments over the past couple of weeks, but nothing, *nothing*, compared to the day she'd just had.

'I can't do it,' Ellie whispered.

When Scarlet turned, body slowly swivelling, she saw Ellie standing, tears streaming down her cheeks, hands shaking violently at her sides, teeth biting hard into her bottom lip. She hadn't seen her for hours, they'd both been attending to different doctors and patients, and she wished she'd searched for her before now. She was pressed up against a bed, clutching it as if she were about to fall.

'Come here,' Scarlet whispered, holding her arms out. 'Everything's going to be fine, I promise.'

The truth was, it was a promise she couldn't keep, but they were the words Ellie needed to hear, and if she had to soothe her then she had no problem being the one to say it.

'I want to go home,' Ellie mumbled. 'I want to go home! I want to go home! I want to go home!'

Scarlet froze. Ellie began to scream the words, louder and louder. There were so many people around them, an entire hospital full of patients and other nurses and doctors.

'Ellie, shush,' she whispered, holding her tighter as her friend stood like a statue, yelling.

'I want to go home!'

Where was Spencer? She needed help.

Ellie crumpled then, slipped straight to the ground, and Scarlet dropped beside her, holding up her limp body. Her friend's eyes were lifeless, like there was nobody home.

'Ellie, we can get through this. You need some sleep.'

They'd gone twenty-four hours with no rest, hardly a bite of food, either, and she was feeling shaky herself.

'What's going on here?' Lucy appeared, helping to scoop Ellie up and hauling her to her feet. It took both of them to hold her up.

'We need to get her into bed,' Lucy said brusquely. 'She needs a decent sleep and food, and she'll be fine. I'll take her.'

'Nurse!' the exasperated call of one of the doctors rang out, clearly needing assistance with a patient.

Scarlet sucked in a breath and stared at Lucy. She didn't know whether it was the right thing to let Ellie go with Lucy while she went to assist the doctor. Lucy hadn't exactly been friendly since she'd arrived, more interested in the work they were doing than making friends with the other nurses. The new nurse seemed insanely competent: never tired, always working, smiling to her patients but then straight-faced and serious as she attended her surgeries.

'I've seen a lot of this,' Lucy said, giving Ellie a shake that made Scarlet gasp. 'You go and answer that call. I'm more than capable of assisting her.'

She was going to protest, but if it gave Lucy time to get Ellie away without any more fuss, then she'd keep on going no matter what, although if she was honest, she was feeling shaky herself. 'Please look after her. She's struggling, and if you'd known her before – well, it's not like her.'

Scarlet would have gone looking for Spencer, asked if he could help, but it was useless. Ambulances were coming in faster than patients could be seen – they had been for hours, and the doctors hadn't had a break, either. As well as the ambulances rushing in, trucks were racing out with injured soldiers headed for the harbour, the worst of them being airlifted out. But so many had died, so many weren't going to make it, and Scarlet was finally, heartbreakingly losing her belief that Thomas could make it home alive. Part of her was starting to think that no man was going to make it out of this war alive or without body parts missing. It was the most dismal, heartbreaking thing she'd ever witnessed or imagined possible.

Scarlet turned from Lucy and Ellie and rushed to assist. The doctor who'd been yelling was still working with no nurse at his side. She had to forget about Ellie for now and believe that Lucy would look after her. The other nurse seemed capable and caring, and Scarlet had no choice but to trust the decision she'd made. From what she'd seen of her, she was as trustworthy as anyone she'd met.

'Spencer?' She hadn't recognised him when he'd called, his face smudged with blood and what appeared to be dirt, his hair full of dust. She reached for a cloth and wetted it, hastily wiping his face clean for him. Of course it was him, she chided herself. He was the only doctor who seemed capable no matter the circumstances.

'What can I do?' she asked.

'We need to amputate. I have this one and more waiting. It's the only way I can give them a chance of making it home, otherwise they'll never survive the airlift out.'

Her stomach turned but she stayed strong. There was nothing she wouldn't do if it meant helping to save a soldier's life, and there were so many to get on the boats headed for home.

'Tell me what you need,' she said.

Scarlet didn't mention that Ellie had just had to be virtually carried out. Spencer was already looking like he was on the brink of collapse, and she was certain he'd heard and seen the commotion anyway. His usually handsome face was etched with concern, lines deep around eyes that were usually bright, now dulled with tiredness. They were all struggling, even good doctors like him.

She administered morphine, prepared for surgery, did everything Spencer asked of her without faltering, but after they'd amputated both legs on one soldier and later the arm of another, Scarlet ran as soon as she was dismissed. She barely made it outside, tucked away from view, before she started to vomit – over and over again until the pain in her empty stomach was unbearable. She wondered if the smell of blood and burnt flesh would ever leave her nostrils.

Scarlet breathed hard, finally straightened and went in search of Ellie. She was worried about her friend; the fun-loving, always-smiling nurse that had kept them both full of laughter seemed to have slipped way, replaced by a shadow of the woman she'd been only a week earlier. Even on the dreadful voyage over, she'd kept her spirits up, and Scarlet was more than worried. She was terrified that Ellie might do something silly. She didn't know what, but—

'She's fine.'

Lucy appeared just as Scarlet was about to go into the tent.

'Sleeping?' Scarlet asked.

'Yes.'

Scarlet threw her arms around Lucy and pulled her in for a hug. She was not usually one for displays of affection like that, but beyond being tired, and feeling emotional, it seemed like the only thing left to do.

'Thank you.'

Lucy was stiff as she held her tight, but Scarlet didn't care. She hadn't realised how much she'd needed the contact, to touch another human being, to be held. She understood why, after so long away from home, the soldiers they cared for were desperate for the words, care and affection from their nurses. They just needed someone to hold them and tell them everything was going to be fine.

'I finally have a break. Do you have a moment?' Scarlet asked.

Lucy nodded. 'Of course. I'm going to get dinner.'

They walked side by side, Scarlet's legs so tired she feared they'd give way.

'Tell me about yourself, Lucy. You're a great nurse,' Scarlet said.

'Oh, well, you know. It's been full on here,' Lucy said. 'I arrived with my unit as part of the Royal Air Force, so I've been here since immediately after the Normandy landings.'

Scarlet nodded, impressed. 'Well, I know I've already said thank you, but I really appreciate your help with Ellie.' Scarlet paused, considering her words. 'She's not usually like this. I mean, it's not her personality to be so down; she's usually so positive. Being here has changed her.'

'It changes a lot of people,' Lucy said in a low voice. 'I've seen doctors take their own lives after making mistakes, and a nurse hang herself. I know how easily people can snap out here when they're pushed to their limits, and I don't want to see that happen to your friend. That's why I offered to assist.'

Scarlet didn't know what to say. She was numb. She'd experienced sleep deprivation and hunger pangs that hit deep inside of her, and witnessed hideous wounds, but from the glint in Lucy's eyes, she could see the other nurse had witnessed far worse.

'I don't know what to say,' Scarlet admitted.

'You don't need to say anything, and I don't want to relive it,' Lucy said simply. 'But I've seen the signs, I know when enough is enough. Not everyone is built to deal with the intensity of what we're doing here.'

'And you? How are you faring?' Scarlet probably didn't need to ask, because Lucy struck her as very capable.

'It takes some adjusting to, but I'm fine,' she said simply. 'We have a job to do, and when we get back I want to train to be a doctor.'

Scarlet stopped walking. 'A doctor?'

'Yes,' she said matter-of-factly. 'I doubt it'll be that unusual in years to come, and I like the work. It's one of the reasons why I was sent to help your unit. I have a real interest in difficult surgeries and I made a bit of a name for myself volunteering for anything and everything. I want to learn everything I can.'

Scarlet was surprised. A woman wanting to be a doctor just wasn't something she'd heard before. 'I grew up with women who dreamt of being wives and mothers,' she said. 'But the more time I spend here, the more I truly see the world, the more I realise how narrow-minded that seems.'

'There's nothing wrong with wanting to have a family,' Lucy said, her smile softening. 'I'm not saying I don't want that one day, but I don't want that to be all I'm good for. It sounds high and mighty, but I can't help how I feel.'

Scarlet smiled. 'You might be the most interesting woman I've ever met. I mean that, Lucy. You know, my family weren't exactly happy for me volunteering here, but if I'd told them I wanted to be a doctor once all this is over, I think my mother would have had kittens!'

'I know the feeling,' Lucy said with a laugh.

'So you don't have a sweetheart back home?' Scarlet asked.

'No, I don't. You?'

'It's a long story. I'll tell you all about it one day. Let's just say I'm engaged, and I'm hoping to find my fiancé while we're here.' She felt a pang from talking about Thomas when her mind had instantly jumped to James.

'I'll hold you to it,' Lucy said. 'One night when we can't sleep you can tell me every single detail.'

'I'll see you shortly,' Scarlet said, reaching out to touch Lucy's shoulder. 'Thank you again for everything you did for Ellie.'

'You're welcome. See you at dinner, unless we both fall asleep before then.'

Scarlet nodded as Lucy turned, and she decided to check on Ellie quickly before getting something to eat and then trying to get a few hours' sleep. The casualties they'd received over the past days had been horrific. What they'd been told was a battle supposed to last a day had stretched out for more than a week with little end in sight. She was so tired she felt like her very bones were weary, feet dragging with each step, and tucking up beside Ellie for even an hour sounded like heaven to her right now. But she was pleased she'd taken the time to speak with Lucy. First impressions weren't always right, she knew that, and there was a lot more to Lucy than she'd imagined.

She had been trying not to think of James, or Thomas, but as always happened when she prepared to sleep, her thoughts turned to them both. Whether she'd see them again, whether they were dead, bodies lying forlorn on the ground, or submerged in mud. Or whether someone was caring for them, a nurse with a light touch, a nun with a soft smile.

It was probably best she didn't cross paths with James, not again, not after what had been said and done. She was here for Thomas, and to serve her country – just like he was. There wasn't time to think of 'what ifs' or 'maybes' because nursing was all she needed to focus on, and she knew now it was going to be a lot tougher than she'd ever imagined to get through her time here. They'd been in France less than two weeks, and it had already been the worst two weeks of her life – without a shadow of doubt.

The night they'd arrived, sitting on the beach and watching men being rushed on to ships headed for home, part of her had wanted to leap forward and check them all, make sure one of them wasn't Thomas, but she knew there was no chance of it being that easy. If he were here, if he were still alive, wouldn't they have heard from him? Wouldn't she know? The army wouldn't have thought he'd fallen off the face of the earth if he was still fighting with his unit. The chills started to spread down her body, like they were in her bones. Thinking like that made her realise how crazy this whole thing was, how unlikely it was that she'd ever, ever find him. She bent and entered the tent.

'Needle in a haystack,' she whispered to herself.

'What?'

She leaned over and hugged Ellie. 'Nothing. Just talking to myself. I thought you were asleep.'

'My mother says that's the first sign of going crazy,' Ellie whispered, pushing back into her, starting to cry again. 'But I think I'm the one who's gone crazy. I can't stay here, Scarlet, I can't.'

'Hey, I'm the one talking to myself, so that makes me the crazy one.' Scarlet relished the extra warmth from Ellie as they huddled together. 'I don't know what to say, how to help you,' Scarlet confessed, not wanting to pretend everything was fine when it so obviously wasn't. 'But I'm worried.'

Ellie leaned back harder into her and Scarlet hugged her tighter.

'I'm so tired, and I can't get some of the things I've seen out of my head. I . . .'

'You can tell me,' Scarlet said. 'I get it, believe me, I get it.'

'I thought I'd be good at this, that I would be able to keep smiling and laughing and make these soldiers feel better. I never thought hard enough about what I was going to be dealing with, how gruesome it would be and how many men would die.'

Scarlet was certain Ellie was worried about her brothers, too, now that she'd seen the reality of war first-hand.

'No one is built for this kind of work, Ellie, no one,' she told her, her voice soft as they murmured to one another. 'You're like a ray of sunshine, and it's no wonder you're struggling. Heck, I don't know how I'm holding it together most days, especially with so little sleep.'

'So you don't think less of me?' Ellie asked. 'You don't think I'm hopeless?'

'I think it shows what a kind-hearted, lovely person you are to be so badly affected by the injuries these men have sustained, by what you're seeing them go through.'

She listened to Ellie sigh. 'I'm so tired.'

'Me too. Let's try to get some sleep.' Suddenly falling into bed seemed more important than getting anything to eat.

Scarlet knew there was only so much she could shield Ellie from, but she'd do whatever she could. If that meant covering for her and letting her get some extra sleep, then she'd do it in a heartbeat.

She shut her eyes, still tucked close to Ellie, pushing thoughts of war and injuries from her mind, the distant noises of battle so familiar to her now that she was able to block them out. She had been so determined to find Thomas while she was here, and although she'd made some enquiries, her days had been exhausting, with little time to do anything more than work, eat, sleep and then do the same all over again. But she'd not lost hope, not yet anyway.

Blackness surrounded her, soothed her, and she started to slip into slumber, thoughts of Thomas fading as she gave in to sleep.

'Scarlet!'

She jumped, eyes popping open as she quickly sat up.

'Scarlet, it's Lucy. There's a soldier asking for you.'

She rubbed at her eyes, crawling quickly over her bed and out of the tent.

Thomas.

His was the first name she thought of as she gripped Lucy's arm and, still hazy from sleep, hurried in the dark with her towards their mobile hospital. Nerves made her stomach curdle, her mind a muddle at the thought of seeing him.

Her heart skipped a beat, mouth dry, tripping as she propelled herself forwards even faster. Her boots skidded as they reached the entrance and she slowly released her vice-like grip on Lucy, following her in silently. The bustle of the station disappeared, became a blur as she walked in a straight line and watched Lucy stop beside a patient's bed. She saw Lucy hold up her hand, pointing, and Scarlet froze when a dark head lifted from the pillow, a smile crossing the lips that were smeared with dried blood.

Scarlet's body started shaking, her feet stuck.

It was James. *James.*

A tear escaped her left eye and she quickly brushed it away, the yell of a doctor bringing her back to the present, making her move to get out of the way.

'Look who it is,' James said, his smile not concealing the grunt of pain he gave when he turned in the bed. 'Trust you to come after they'd treated me.'

Scarlet gave an involuntary sigh of relief. He was already making jokes; she was taking that as a good sign.

Scarlet met Lucy's gaze and reached for her hand, squeezing it, wanting to thank her, but the words stuck in her throat.

She should have been in tears that it wasn't Thomas, but the fact that James was lying on a bed, not dead already from this awful war, made it impossible not to smile.

So she was officially the world's worst fiancée, but as she lowered herself on to a stool beside James's bed she almost didn't care.

'Tell me, what happened?' She glanced around, thankful that they weren't admitting hundreds of patients like usual, making it seem quiet, although she knew it wouldn't last. 'Where have you been? How bad is it?'

James made a loud breathing sound as he tried to sit up properly, and she quickly jumped to her feet and adjusted the pillow behind him.

'I'm sorry, I shouldn't have started interrogating you like that.'

'It's fine,' he said, but she could tell from the tone of his voice that he absolutely was not fine. 'I'm . . .' He made a hissing sound, no doubt the pain a whole lot worse than he was letting on.

'James, no,' she said. 'Let me get you something to eat and something more for the pain.'

His fingers closed over her arm, stopping her even though his touch was light. 'Stay.'

She lowered herself back to her seat, hand moving to cover his when his touch fell away.

'Are you sure there's nothing I can get you?'

He shook his head, and she could see how much of an effort it was for him, sitting up and talking to her.

'You should be resting, but then I'm guessing you already know that.'

'Mm-hmm,' he murmured.

She bent low and pressed a kiss to his forehead, not caring who saw or what anyone might say. 'For what it's worth, I'm pleased to see you. I've been so worried, looking at every soldier on the beds here and praying it wasn't you. Then I'd wish it was you because if you were here it meant you weren't dead on a field somewhere in the middle of nowhere.'

'Have you heard anything?' he asked in a low murmur.

Scarlet shook her head, knowing immediately what he was talking about without asking. 'No. Only that there are some convents in some of the more remote areas apparently harbouring injured soldiers.'

He made another grunting sound and she patted his hand.

'There's been a letter,' he managed, before coughing. 'His plane went down, but there's no report of his body having been found.'

Goose pimples rippled across Scarlet's arms. Maybe it wasn't so far-fetched to wonder if he'd been taken in by one of the convents, assuming he hadn't been captured of course. 'I'll find him,' she said. 'If he's here, we'll find him and any other soldiers being looked after by the nuns.'

She looked down at James, stroked hair from his forehead and surveyed his face. The other times they'd been together she'd felt so guilty, so scared of what she was feeling for him, but after what she'd seen since being here, something had changed inside her. Who knew whether they'd see each other again or what would happen? If she wanted to stroke his face and smile at him, kiss his skin or sit with him, then she was going to. No one else here right now, other than Ellie, knew that she was engaged to his brother.

'Get him home,' James said, staring up at her. 'I couldn't live with myself if I . . .'

His voice trailed off and she leaned over him, hand still on his. 'I'll bring him home if I can. I promise. But now we need to worry about getting *you* home.'

James made a noise, moved slightly, but it wasn't until his arm came around her that more tears pricked her eyes. She'd been so strong, hadn't wavered despite all she'd seen and done, but the moment she'd seen him and now with his arm placed around her, she melted and held him to her, just for a moment.

'You'll be the one to stitch me up properly instead of this patch-up job?' he asked, chuckling. But laughter made him cough and she pulled up to look down at him once more.

'You need to take it easy,' she reprimanded.

He coughed again. 'Says the woman who just hugged me.'

In another lifetime Scarlet would have blushed, but today she simply shook her head, blinking away unshed tears. She'd survived so much, been pushed so far out of where she was comfortable, and numerous times felt so close to giving up. She deserved to take a moment to indulge, to be with James.

'You'll be sent away soon. They'll have you headed back to England for proper treatment. But we'll do our best here before the transfer.'

He was staring at her, his dark eyes drawing her in. His face was tanned, skin dirty, but that didn't make him look any less handsome. She knew that if things were different, she could promise to look into his eyes for the rest of her life and never tire of his friendly gaze and ready smile. Instead, she'd be marrying his brother and looking at him from afar. Maybe she'd never be this close to him again.

Scarlet sighed and turned as the hospital came to life with people shouting out, men being brought in as ambulances started to arrive more frequently. She knew there was only a short time left before she was summoned, that it was unfair to spend so long talking to one soldier when so many more would need her help.

'I'll have to go soon,' she said in a low voice, fingers finding his once more.

'Stay with me until you're called?' he asked.

She nodded. Despite the fact that she hadn't eaten and would be on her feet for the rest of the day, she willingly agreed. Her meagre ration of porridge or a tinned sausage with some butter would have to wait until nightfall. It was a long time to wait, but it would be even longer before she ever saw James again.

She swallowed what felt like a rock in her throat, smiling down at him.

The next time she saw him, she might be married to his brother.

Please, God, she whispered inside her own head. *Please spare James. Look after him. Please.*

CHAPTER TWELVE

Lucy

She was finally starting to get used to the bone-deep thud of tiredness that made her wish for bed almost every hour of the day. But not the camp bed that she'd been falling into whenever she had the chance – her soft bed in her childhood bedroom, the one with the snuggly covers and feather-light pillow. Lucy sighed as she surveyed the new hospital she'd just walked back into. There wasn't any chance of her thoughts coming true any time soon. She'd been surviving on snatched moments of sleep for months now, since her last posting at a makeshift hospital back home, and the only thing to do was to keep her head down and get on with her work. Besides, if her father had his way he'd be kicking her out of his house if she defied him and insisted on training at the London Royal Free Hospital School of Medicine for Women. Not that her mother would ever let that happen, or her brother. He might agree with her father on some things, but he knew how much she wanted it. He was proud of the fact she was a surgical nurse and good at what she did.

'It's going to be a madhouse in here soon.'

Lucy turned when she heard Scarlet's soft voice. She smiled back at the other nurse.

'Don't I know it,' she replied. She hadn't told the others a lot about her first experience in Normandy, what she'd already lived through, but she had the feeling that what they were about to see would be every bit as bad. The fighting had only got worse, with more troops arriving and more men being slaughtered and injured. She shuddered just thinking about how many bodies she'd helped to stitch up and bandage before sending them off, sometimes straight back into combat.

'I don't know what's worse, to be honest. Here or where we were before.'

Scarlet had a hard-to-read look on her face, her eyes downcast. Lucy walked closer to her.

'Honestly? I think each hospital, each place we work, is just another version of awful. We get through by helping as best we can.' She shrugged. 'Nothing more, nothing less. Some of us are better at it than others.' To her, this mobile hospital they were in now was closer to the front but not much different from the last one.

'You mean Ellie?'

Lucy reached out and touched Scarlet's arm. 'Ellie has you. She'll be fine as long as we keep a close eye on her.'

Scarlet nodded and Lucy cleared her throat as a team of doctors came in the door.

'The camp is definitely worse here,' Scarlet said as they walked out, side by side. 'If this rain doesn't stop it'll be like living in a pigsty.'

They stood outside, the rain lightly falling as Lucy turned her face skywards. She didn't even care about getting wet. Before the war, she'd never have gone out in the rain and happily stood in it. Now, it was a reminder that she was alive, something to make her smile, just because she could stand and poke out her tongue and taste the wet nothingness of rain.

She straightened and looked around, wishing she'd kept her eyes shut instead of taking in the reality of their surroundings. There were twenty-five of them to a tent, which made privacy impossible, and the planks set out for them to walk around were the only things to separate their boots from the muddied, sloppy ground. She was used to such a very different environment, being more similar to Scarlet than she cared to admit.

'I know our soldiers don't have much, that they must be living in even worse conditions, but it doesn't stop me feeling sorry for myself every once in a while,' Scarlet confessed to her. 'Seeing James, seeing the pain in his face and wondering what he's been through . . . it's awful.'

Lucy nodded. She was so right. 'There is nothing selfish about the way you're feeling,' she said, thinking of how badly she wanted to go to the toilet and how desperately she was holding on to avoid the inevitable trip. 'Just remember that one day we'll think back on this and . . .' She had been about to say 'laugh', but she doubted they'd ever actually do that. 'Well, we'll be proud of the fact we made it through. How is James, by the way? Still here?'

Scarlet shook her head and Lucy saw the sadness in her gaze. 'Gone. By the time my shift was over they were already evacuating him. I kissed him goodbye moments before he left and . . .' Lucy watched as Scarlet wiped quickly at her cheeks. 'I think I'm praying more than I ever have in my life!'

A loud boom made the ground beneath them tremble and Lucy glanced at Scarlet again. There was another, more distant rumble, then the repeated noise of gunfire.

'All hell is about to break loose,' Lucy muttered.

Scarlet gave her a friendly smile and they both turned to walk across the wide plank of wood leading back to their tent. 'At least it'll keep my mind off things I can't control.'

'I'm going to the toilet first. I'll see you back there,' Lucy said, taking a different plank in the opposite direction. 'You'll see him again, Scarlet. He's going home and he's not missing any body parts. That makes him one of the lucky ones.' She envied the fact that her friend was in love, that she felt so strongly about another person. She'd never fallen for a man, had never met a man who'd made her want to question her desire to become a doctor. It wasn't that she didn't want a family or a husband, but she wanted a man who made her feel . . . She sighed. She had no idea. She was only certain that if she ever met a man who made her want to let her guard down and let him in close, she'd know it.

Scarlet smiled and waved goodbye. Lucy gritted her teeth when she finally reached the screen that was the only thing separating their toilets from the elements. She opened and closed it, keeping her eyes downcast when she realised there were two other women in there already, sitting on the board that was their makeshift toilet seat. The smell made Lucy want to gag, so she tried to breathe through her mouth only, taking little, silent gasps as she dropped on to the board of wood. There were a number of holes cut into it, just wide enough for them to sit over and do their business, suspended above the large trench. Of all the things she'd seen and done since her arrival in Normandy, this was what Lucy found the worst. And the smell of human waste and the indignity of going to the toilet seated on the same plank as two other women who were no doubt as embarrassed as herself was something she'd never forget.

'Incoming!'

Lucy grimaced, eyes shut against the yell from outside. Surely she wasn't about to be bombed off the toilet. Could life actually get any worse?

A huge boom made her forget her decision not to make eye contact with anyone else using the toilet. She looked across into a pair of eyes that appeared even more desperate than she felt.

'We'll be fine,' she said, always finding it easier to calm others than deal with her own fears.

The other nurse, one she didn't recognise immediately, nodded, but Lucy doubted she'd made her feel any better.

When she pushed the screen door aside and emerged back into rain that had become heavier in the few minutes she'd been under cover, Lucy decided to wash her hands in the hospital rather than head back to her tent. Granted, she might have been able to find food if she hadn't gone straight back, but something was telling her that they were about to be inundated with patients. *Like that first night after landing.*

After the longest weeks of her life, she was now almost immune to gunfire, but it was the booms that terrified her, reminded her of the ambulances being blown up, holding the young nurse in her arms as the life drained from her. They were the things she struggled with, the fact that even those helping the wounded weren't protected from the cold hand of death.

'Here we go!' a man yelled.

Lucy didn't know where it came from, which man had said it, but she braced herself. Waiting. Ready.

'Hi, Lucy.'

Ellie suddenly stood beside her, their shoulders almost touching.

'Oh, hi,' she replied, surprised to see the other nurse. 'Are you ready for this?'

Ellie nodded and Lucy pushed a little closer to her. It had been one of the most unexpected parts of the transfer, meeting Scarlet and Ellie and finding herself in the midst of women who had accepted her immediately. She'd thought she didn't need friends, that she needed to spend every thought and moment focused on her work, but she was starting to see that there was only so long she could rely on herself and herself alone. There was nothing wrong with accepting friends, nothing weak about enjoying the company of others.

A rumble signalled the first of the ambulances arriving, maybe more than one, and Lucy felt a familiar flutter in her stomach. Doctors were talking, someone was issuing instructions, but she was in her own world. One where she couldn't hear anything other than her own voice.

You can save them. You will do everything you can to save every soldier you treat.

'Something's happened. What's happened?'

Ellie was tugging on her arm like an insistent child, the panic in her voice pulling Lucy from her thoughts. And then she realised what was going on, that it was about to happen all over again.

Boom!

She let out a scream that she couldn't even believe came from her body and propelled herself forwards. Why was everyone standing around? Why was no one helping?

She would be damned if she'd let the enemy get away with blowing up their ambulances and the good men and women inside.

'Over my dead body,' she muttered as she ran faster than she'd ever run in her life.

Lucy ran towards the ambulance, the rain on the canvas above where she'd been sheltering the only thing she heard as she pumped her arms at her sides, desperate to help. Flames simmered orange in front of her, rising higher and turning redder, or maybe it was her eyes playing tricks on her. She didn't know and she didn't care; all she cared about was making sure another nurse or doctor didn't die because no one was brave enough to help them.

She glanced to her right, sensing someone, ready to push anyone away who tried to stop her and tell her it was too dangerous, and then she saw Doctor Black and that he was rushing to the ambulance's aid, too. The smoke was strong, sickly, and the crashing sound nearby told her she could be flattened at any moment, but she couldn't worry about that.

Spencer yanked the mangled door to the ambulance, the truck on its side in front of them as Lucy's boots skidded on the mud, stopping her abruptly.

'Help me pull this!' Spencer yelled.

She grimaced, pain tearing through her arm as she pulled as hard as she could, pressed against the doctor as they both put everything they had into opening the door. Eventually it came away, sending Lucy reeling backwards when it finally yielded.

'Help!' Lucy screamed out, looking back and seeing that more men were coming, orderlies who'd probably only just arrived for duty.

A handful of nurses stood watching, but Lucy didn't have time to think about that. The fire was in the front of the heavy truck; she knew it was only so long before it exploded.

'Help him out!' Spencer yelled at her. 'I need to check up front.'

She didn't bother to tell him to be careful, just like he hadn't told her to turn back. Instead she carefully climbed in, coughing as the smoke swirled around and filled her nostrils.

'*Help.*'

Lucy paused, certain she'd heard a whisper. Her eyes adjusted, the inside of the ambulance dark with only the one door thrown open. She saw a body, moved carefully and felt straight away for a pulse. Nothing.

'*Help.*'

The whisper was weaker now, but she'd heard it. She moved over the body, then saw another, slammed into the corner.

'I need help in here!' she called out. 'We have a live soldier to get out!'

She reached for him, touched her fingers to his. They were cold, but the slight movement of his fingertips against her hand told her he was alive, that she needed to do everything she could to get him out.

'Get that nurse out of there!'

'This thing's going to blow!'

Lucy sucked back a breath, fear starting to creep in when earlier there'd been nothing other than adrenaline.

'*Go.*' The soldier's barely audible whisper made her look up.

She shook her head. 'I'm not leaving you. We'll get you out of here, soldier.'

Hands grabbed at her, yanked her back, pulling her away from the soldier who was surely so close to death.

'No!' she screamed.

'Get that damn nurse out of there!' a man yelled, his voice cutting through her as she was dragged back.

'He's alive! He needs us!'

Spencer pushed past then and she gave up fighting, certain he wouldn't leave a man in there.

'Get everyone back. Now!' he shouted. 'If I can get him out I'll do it.' He pointed at her. 'Go back, all of you.'

She obeyed him, not about to defy his orders and distract him from hauling the soldier out. They all moved, far back, and he disappeared.

'Spencer!'

Lucy turned and saw Ellie drop to her knees, hand to her mouth as she sobbed. She quickly ran to her, all the way back to the hospital entrance, dropping beside her and putting her arms around her.

'He'll be fine,' she soothed, hoping she wasn't telling a lie as she coughed from the smoke. 'He's so brave and there's a soldier in there. *Alive.* I was holding his hand myself.'

Lucy looked back to the ambulance. Even though it must have been only a minute or less, it felt like an age since Spencer had gone back into the truck.

Then she saw him. Staggering under the weight of a man easily as big as he was, emerging from the back of the fallen ambulance.

'Help him!' she insisted, moving forward, not able to watch and do nothing.

Orderlies and doctors rushed past her, finally spurred into action and going to Spencer and taking the weight of the soldier from him. He looked like he was going to collapse and she took his arm, helped him in. It wasn't until they were all under canvas again, Spencer sitting on the ground and the injured soldier being lowered on to a bed, that the truck outside exploded, the noise deafening. Some of the nurses around her fell to the ground, covering their heads, their screams echoing past her. But Lucy simply cringed and refused to surrender to her fear, taking the hand of the soldier who'd whispered to her in the dark only moments earlier.

'Shhh,' she whispered, the noise outside and around them subsiding. 'Everything's going to be fine. We've got you.'

One of his eyes was so badly swollen he couldn't see from it, but there was a glint in his other eye that told her he might just pull through. A doctor cut through his trouser leg and she glanced down, saw it was bloody and hoped he wouldn't lose it. Then as he lifted his hand to her, the one she hadn't held earlier, she saw it was covered in blood, too.

'Your hand,' she said, 'let me—'

Lucy didn't have the chance to inspect it, the doctor across from her yelling before she finished her sentence, 'Gunshot wound! Let's get this bullet out.'

She stared at the soldier, the man she'd fought to save, saw his eye flutter, saw his dark red blood covering her hands.

Please don't die. She held her breath, feeling a connection with the man lying in front of her, wanting to do anything, *something*, to save him. She wasn't going to lose this one, not after what they'd done to save him.

'Nurse! He's losing blood.'

She moved quickly, leaning across his body, applying pressure to the wound now spurting out blood. He was losing too much; something was wrong.

'Into surgery. Let's go.'

'Lucy, you need to get some sleep.'

She blinked and focused on the person standing over her. She lifted her head, hadn't realised she'd slumped forward. How long had she been like this?

'Scarlet?' She rubbed her knuckles into her eyes.

'Come on. This might be the only chance you get to rest. You can't sit with him for ever.'

She put her hands on the side of the bed and pushed back. It was a wonder she'd been allowed to sit for so long without being reprimanded.

'I wish she could.'

The sound of a deep, husky male voice made Lucy freeze.

'He's awake!' Scarlet gasped.

Lucy stared down at the soldier, his one open eye trained on hers. 'I can't believe you've pulled through,' she said, amazed at the man staring back at her and now also feeling incredibly embarrassed about falling asleep over him.

'Water,' he managed. His accent was American.

She reached for water and Scarlet helped to hold him up slightly so she could tip a little into his mouth. He gulped it down and she let him have more.

'You're so lucky to be alive,' she muttered. 'I didn't think . . .' Her voice trailed off.

'You saved me,' he croaked. 'I'll never forget your voice. Never.'

She stared down at him, shaking her head, close to laughing. How could a man who'd been so close to death be talking to her like this?

'I hate to break this up, but your nightingale here needs some rest, and I'm going to be the one to drag her away.'

Scarlet's hand closed over her shoulder and Lucy knew there was no point fighting her. She looked around, saw how full the hospital was even though for some reason there had been a slight reprieve in wounded arriving.

'Will you make sure he has something to eat?' she asked Scarlet.

'Yes. Now go.'

Lucy took one last look at the soldier, squeezed his hand when he reached out to her, then turned and walked away. Of all the patients she'd had, all the men she'd seen die and suffer around her, there was something about him. Something that gave her hope and made her want to do anything she could to save him.

'His name,' she muttered, turning back.

She stopped, met Scarlet's gaze for a moment and saw her bend low over him.

'Soldier, what's your name?' Scarlet asked.

Lucy watched. Scarlet shook her head and lowered again.

'Soldier? Tell us your name.' Scarlet stood up. 'He keeps shaking his head. I'll ask him again later.'

Lucy slipped away then, too tired to worry. The past forty-eight hours had been a blur, with hundreds upon hundreds of injured soldiers arriving. But for some reason, the American soldier was still there, hadn't been airlifted out or sent home.

She walked across the wooden plank, numb, and so tired she could hardly lift her feet one after the other. The only thing she could think about other than sleep was that he'd better darn well still be alive when she went back.

Lucy stretched and stifled a yawn as she walked into the hospital. It had been a long week, and instead of staying in bed a little longer on the one morning she didn't have to report for work at the crack of dawn, here she was. She looked around, relieved that the number of patients being admitted had steadily slowed. If they'd kept taking in hundreds like they had been . . . She shuddered, the motion sending goose pimples down her spine. It was awful.

She walked down to where she knew she'd find him – her one and only reason for coming in so early. His outline in the bed was becoming familiar, as was the brightness in his gaze and the big smile he seemed to reserve for her. She had no idea why she was so drawn to him, but she was telling herself that it was the fact she'd helped to save him. That if it hadn't been for her actions, he might be dead instead of being nursed back to health.

'Hey, gorgeous.'

Lucy tried not to smile at his upbeat words, but it was impossible. Maybe it was his American accent, but every single time he spoke to her like that he melted her heart. She chewed her lip. All this time being immune to the charm of soldiers, and here she was, grinning like a schoolgirl. It was ridiculous, but after months of being focused on nothing other than work, she kind of liked it.

'You're sounding chipper today,' she commented, checking his chart out of habit before looking down at him.

He winked and she noticed that the swelling round his right eye was finally starting to disappear. Now she could look into a pair of gorgeous, twinkling brown eyes instead of just the one.

'It's this beautiful nurse I have. If you had her you'd be smiling all day, too.'

She turned and looked over her shoulder, playing along, pretending to look for someone. 'I can't see her. Who's this nurse you keep talking about, soldier?'

Lucy's laughter died in her throat when his fingers closed over hers, lightly but very much connecting with her. She had no idea where her witty response had come from, but it certainly didn't sound like her!

'She's right here, believe it or not,' he said in a low voice, almost a whisper.

Lucy sighed and looked into his eyes, meeting his gaze. She hated the way he made her feel and loved it at the same time. She'd never been shy around men, and had managed to hold her own through her training and the time she'd already spent abroad, but something about this man made her feel differently. She should have known better than to have feelings for a Yank; she knew all about their sweet talking, and besides, there were so many things he didn't remember, things she . . .

Lucy took a deep breath and squeezed his fingers back lightly before pulling away. She reached into his top pocket and pulled out a small photo, the image of which continued to haunt her every time she had a spare moment to herself or before she fell asleep.

'Have you thought any more about this lovely young woman?'

The woman in the picture had blonde hair, plaited into a long braid that framed a beautiful face. Her dark eyes were friendly, mouth pulled into a gentle smile.

And the handsome man in front of her had no idea who she was.

'Thought? Yes. But I still don't remember anything. I mean, I have flashes, but . . .'

The way his eyebrows knitted together, the clear confusion on his face, made Lucy pull back. She wasn't going to push him. He'd suffered a head trauma, been through hell and back, and she just had to hope for his sake that his memory started to return sooner than later.

'Whoever she is, I'm sure she's anxiously waiting for news of you.'

He smiled. 'Maybe. I just . . .' His voice trailed off. 'It's a strange thing to have a photograph of a woman on me and not recall a thing about her. Maybe it belonged to another man and I was carrying it for him.'

Lucy doubted it, but she bit her tongue to stop from speaking her thoughts.

'How is your arm?'

She glanced down at the small bandage covering the skin across her forearm before answering him. 'It was only a bad graze. It will be fine.' At the time she hadn't even realised what had happened, but with it bandaged the small wound didn't bother her.

'Doc told me I don't have to have my food all mashed up today,' he said, voice cheery again.

Lucy laughed. 'Well, good. I was getting tired of having to do that for you every time.'

They sat quietly, listening to the sounds of war that weren't so very far away.

'I have some time off this morning,' she told him. 'I'll be going to town and my friend Scarlet wants to enquire about her fiancé again – see if there's been any news.'

Her soldier nodded. She hated that she didn't know his name, that she constantly ran through different men's names in her mind trying to find one that suited him. Although compared to the mystery of the woman in the photo, this wasn't anywhere near as worrying.

'Go and get away from here,' he said, his smile kind as he looked up at her. 'It'll be hell again in here soon and if you don't go, they'll end up calling you in.'

She nodded, her cheeks flushing with heat when he caught her eye again. He was right. But for some strange reason, she didn't like the thought of leaving him, and for a girl who'd never bothered with men or spent every waking hour imagining the man of her dreams, it rattled her.

'I'll see you soon, then,' Lucy said, patting his hand as she went to move away.

His fingers caught hers again.

'What? No goodbye kiss? What if I die while you're gone and you regret not kissing me for the rest of your life?'

Lucy swatted him away, pleased that he was in such good humour today. After what he'd been through, he was so lucky simply to be alive.

'No kisses. Not with a photo of your sweetheart in your pocket.'

She patted his hand, letting her fingers linger for a moment too long and then quickly withdrawing them. This man had a sweetheart. He was flirting with her and she needed to remember that he was taken. She'd never had her heart broken before, and she wasn't about to let it happen now. Lucy sighed. Maybe she needed to talk to the girls about him. They probably knew a lot more than her about this type of thing.

She knew Scarlet would be waiting for her, so she kept walking, not looking back, trying not to think about why the man she was leaving for the day already meant so much to her. She'd assisted in his surgery, bathed him, fed him, watched over him. But then she'd done that with countless soldiers since she'd arrived – cared for them and whispered kind words as she tried to ease their suffering, doing whatever she could. Handsome men, crippled men, crying men, smiling men. But *this* man . . . maybe it was something to do with rescuing him. It had to be. Because she wasn't the kind of girl to get all hot under the collar about a man she'd just met.

'Ready to go?' Scarlet called out from up ahead, emerging from the toilets.

Lucy groaned, realising that she too needed to relieve herself before they headed off.

'Give me a couple minutes. Is Ellie coming?'

Scarlet smiled. 'I'm about to haul her out of bed. I'm so pleased we covered shifts for her because she's slowly coming out of it. I think.'

Lucy smiled back and kept walking along the plank. Getting ready was a matter of rolling out of bed and not much more here. There was precious little time to spend on ablutions before work began for the day or night, other than to brush one's hair and ensure it was neat. They had a bucket of water a day for all purposes, which usually meant there was only a small tin to spare for the quick washes they had in their overcrowded tent. But then, she'd gone weeks without hot water now, so she was starting to get used to it.

She held her breath as she gritted her teeth and pulled the screen door, entering the toilet area.

Going without water was one thing, but this . . . A bite-sized lump of vomit rose in her throat and she stoically swallowed it down.

This was the depths of hell, the bowels of disgustingness.

This was what she'd never, ever get used to.

CHAPTER THIRTEEN

Ellie

The wind was cool against her cheeks as she walked, and Ellie was the closest to happy that she'd been in a long while. She was away from the hospital, from the smell of blood and dead soldiers that usually haunted every moment of her every day. She'd woken to Scarlet shaking her gently and passing her a cup of their awful Compo tea, and it had been the first time she'd swallowed it down without wanting to moan. Maybe she was getting used to it. Rumour had it that they'd be able to pay for a hot bath and a real coffee in town, and she'd been looking forward to it for days. Anything would be better than tea made from dehydrated tea, milk and sugar that all came in one big cube and was brewed in a bucket. It made her stomach churn even thinking about the bucket being passed around the entire tent.

Some of the other nurses had already been into town for a bath and extra food, and now that they were actually getting some time off, she couldn't wait to do the same. She thought of Spencer then, how desperate he must be for a hot bath, too. The poor man had been working as hard as they, doing surgery after surgery, a constant rotation of amputations and patching men up as best he could. But even though his face was so pale and drawn, his body exhausted, he'd always managed to give her a smile, a brush of his lips to her cheek, a quick squeeze of her shoulder if she passed him. They'd hardly seen one another, but when they had, he'd made it clear that he was there for her. He was special, her Spencer, and the more she observed his manner, how he treated every single patient with such respect and dignity, the more she loved him.

'So do you know his name yet?' Scarlet asked Lucy.

'Nope. I know nothing more about him now than I did the day I met him.'

Ellie tuned into the conversation, abandoning her thoughts of Spencer to give them her attention. They'd both looked after her, been so kind and caring, and she wanted to enjoy her few hours off with them.

'Why hasn't he been sent away already?' Ellie asked.

She watched as Lucy shrugged. 'Something to do with the Yanks coming to check over any of their men we might have. There's another American soldier in the ward, too.'

'Do you still believe it's his wife in that photo?' Scarlet asked. 'Or his sweetheart?'

Ellie hoped for Lucy's sake that it wasn't, because it was clear that her friend was fond of the man. Lucy was always so focused on the job, acted like nothing could distract her, and then along had come this man with his memory loss and his cute smile.

'It has to be, doesn't it? I mean . . .' Lucy sighed. 'I don't know. I like him a lot, but then I think that has something to do with helping to save him. I want to know more and I want to make sure he pulls through. Gets home to his family.'

'Did you see the other day we had two soldiers we'd patched up and sent off only a week earlier with minor injuries, and they were already back again? Far worse this time; one might not make it.'

A shudder ran through Ellie that had nothing to do with the cold and everything to do with the amount of death and injury she'd been witness to in France.

'How about you, Scarlet?' Ellie asked, wanting to change the subject. 'Nothing more on Thomas? Any word about James?'

She saw a strange look pass over Scarlet's face, wondered what it was that was troubling her. But it was gone as quickly as it had arrived.

'More talk about some soldiers in a remote area taken in by nuns. I'm trying to figure out exactly how we can get to them.' Scarlet let out a big sigh. 'I don't think I'll hear anything about James until the day we finally get home. It's . . .' Ellie waited for her to finish her sentence, not wanting to interrupt her, wanting to hear what she was going to say. 'Complicated I guess. I feel as if I have no control over anything and I have absolutely no idea what will happen, but I can't stop thinking about him.'

'Surely the army will want to do anything they can to help them?' Lucy asked. 'The soldiers that haven't been found, I mean.'

Scarlet blew out a loud breath. 'You'd think so. But if the nuns have them and they're being kept safe from further injury, maybe they won't be a priority until the war is over.'

Ellie hung on to that thought every day: that the war would one day be over. She didn't know how much more of it she could take. The infections, the blood, the amputations and the deaths. It was so hard to face, day after day, knowing there was only so much they could do. She sucked in a breath, wrestled with her thoughts until she could push them away and focus on being out in the fresh air, away from the hospital with her friends.

'What are you thinking about?' Scarlet asked, interrupting the conversation Ellie was having in her own head about what she was and wasn't allowed to think about.

'I'm trying not to think too much about anything,' Ellie confessed. 'Everything makes me feel so down, so I try to think about home. What it will be like to be back, what I'll eat, hugging my mother. All of those nice things instead of the ugly thoughts. That's what Lucy told me to do, and it helps.'

Lucy smiled, pleased her advice had done something to help Ellie.

'How about thinking about Spencer, and how nice a little alone time with him would be,' Scarlet teased.

'Oh, I wish!' That would definitely take her mind off war. She couldn't help but wish she'd met Spencer at home, without war, so they could simply do normal things. 'He keeps telling me that one day we'll have time together, but with all the patients, with everything that keeps happening, I don't think it will ever happen.' She knew how stupid her own wishes were, given what they were living through, but she couldn't help how she felt. 'He's so nice, so . . . I don't know. In a way he reminds me of my father, even though they're from such different backgrounds. But the way he looks at me, it's the way my dad has always looked at my mother. Kind, steady, protective, I guess.'

She frowned at the grin spreading across Scarlet's face, annoyed at the way she and Lucy were glancing at each other, as if they were in on a secret.

'Why are you two looking like that?' Ellie demanded, narrowing her eyes as she stared back at them.

Scarlet moved closer, nudged her in the side. 'He's having the afternoon off. We promised to meet him somewhere with you, and he wanted it to be a surprise.'

'If *we* can't have a little wartime romance, then we're making darn sure you can,' Lucy added.

'What?' Ellie's heart was racing, fluttering away in her chest, and for once it wasn't induced by gunshots or the fear of war echoing too close for comfort.

Lucy was grinning back at her. 'He's so sweet. The poor man wanted to do something nice for you, as a surprise, and even though we were sworn to secrecy Scarlet said you'd hate not knowing.'

Scarlet had definitely got that part right. She *hated* surprises. Although now that she knew what was about to happen . . . She gulped, finding it hard to breathe all of a sudden.

'You're not kidding, are you? Please tell me you're not having me on,' she said.

'Ellie, it's not the type of thing I'd joke about, I promise,' Scarlet said. 'Although it is kind of amusing being the one to tease you. When we first met, that was your role.' She laughed. 'Seems I learnt from the best.'

Ellie smiled back at Scarlet. It felt like a long, long time ago, that first time they'd met at the railway station. Another lifetime even. So much had changed, she didn't even feel like the same person any longer; that fun, always-happy, energetic girl had slowly disappeared. When she was with Spencer, a spark of her real self seemed to emerge, but it was a struggle putting on a brave face. For the first time in her life, smiles didn't come as easily.

'I've never actually been alone with him,' she confessed. 'I mean, we've been alone, but there's always been someone close by or someone listening or . . .' Her voice trailed off.

'You're nervous,' Lucy said matter-of-factly. 'It's perfectly normal.'

'I'm not nervous,' Ellie insisted. Was she nervous? She'd never been nervous around him before, but the way her stomach was flipping and her pulse was racing, she was worried she was about to collapse.

'Look, the man wants to spend time with you. Simple as that,' Scarlet said, her smile so kind that Ellie's nerves started to settle.

'I want to spend time with him,' she said, wrapping her arms tightly around herself. 'But the way I've been feeling lately, the trauma of it all, I don't know.' She didn't even know how to express what she had been going through in her mind. 'I've started to wonder if he feels sorry for me, after everything that's happened. If he doesn't actually like me that way any longer.'

Scarlet and Lucy both made a type of sighing noise, instantly shuffling closer to her as if by doing so they could protect her.

'Sweetheart, anyone can see what he feels for you, and it's not pity.'

'Scarlet's right. I've only been here a short while, but the way he looks at you? It doesn't take a genius to figure that out.'

Ellie blinked away tears. It was so unusual for her to feel like this, but something about their time in Normandy had affected her deeply, from the moment she'd seen those bodies bobbing in the water – water red with the blood of their fallen soldiers.

'He's been worried about you, too,' Scarlet said, her voice tinged with sadness. 'We all have. But that's not why he wants to see you. He told me that if he'd met you back in London, he'd have taken you for lovely dinners and long walks. I think this is his way of trying to be romantic.'

'So it's not a pity date?' Ellie asked, making herself laugh. It had been so long since she'd simply giggled and been silly, joked around and made fun. 'Please tell me I'm not a pity date,' she moaned.

The other girls laughed and Ellie linked her arms through theirs, taking a big lungful of air. It was cold and it was dreary outside, but something inside of her was finally starting to thaw.

'I don't know where I'd be without you two,' she confessed.

'Bored, that's where you'd be,' Lucy quipped.

Scarlet dropped her head to Ellie's shoulder for a moment, and Ellie knew that despite all the jokes, her friends felt the same. They'd looked after her in her darkest moments – times that she'd been so sleep-deprived and tormented by her thoughts, she didn't know how she'd have survived without them.

'I think today you'll finally see how much you mean to him,' Scarlet said in a low voice.

'If I manage to get a bath first, you mean?'

Ellie and Scarlet burst out laughing at the same time.

'Hey, I wasn't going to say anything, but let's be honest. I wouldn't let a man near me right now!' Lucy giggled.

'Even your gorgeous soldier?' Scarlet asked, still laughing.

'One whiff of me and he'd probably lose his memory all over again.'

Ellie burst out laughing. 'You girls,' she muttered, shaking her head. 'Heavens, I'd forgotten how good it was to laugh.'

They all looked up as a truck came rumbling down the road, the noise making them pause. Ellie was so used to being cautious now that it came as second nature, on alert at the first sign of danger.

'It's one of ours, we're fine,' Scarlet said quickly.

The truck passed slowly, the weary-looking soldiers raising their hands as it went by them. Ellie wasn't attention hungry, but she thought it was sad when a group of young men didn't say anything or even whistle at three nurses on the side of the road. They might all be in need of a bath, but her friends were pretty, and the soldiers they'd waved goodbye to back in London wouldn't have missed the chance to wolf-whistle or wink at a pretty nurse. Now, those same soldiers had a defeated look in their eyes that she saw countless times in the hospital, and it made her so sad.

'So where do you think we should go? I mean, to find what we need?' Scarlet asked.

Lucy was the first to start walking again and Ellie quickly fell in beside her.

'Some of the girls said to head to a large white farmhouse, one with the flag flying on the front porch. Someone said something about the people there having a soft spot for nurses, so they're often willing to sell food cheap, like eggs.'

Ellie listened to Lucy then turned to Scarlet when she started to speak.

'I think we should hitch a ride to the convent. The one in Bayeux. If I had to choose, I'd rather have a shower than something to eat.'

Ellie didn't mention that she'd heard how long the queues could be there because she knew how desperately Scarlet wanted to find word about Thomas. Her friend might have had feelings for the man who was supposed to become her brother-in-law, but it hadn't curbed her determination to find her fiancé. Maybe her guilt was making her more determined.

'So the option is to get one of those jeeps to take us,' Lucy said, frowning, 'and spend the better part of the day travelling, or head straight to a local farmhouse and beg them to feed us?'

Scarlet made a kind of clucking noise in her throat that reminded Ellie of a chicken. Ellie stifled a laugh. 'I know it would be cold, but couldn't we just bathe in a river or something? I'm ready to beg for food!'

Scarlet scowled and stuck her thumb out as soon as the distant rumble of a vehicle sounded out on the road, most likely heading straight for them. 'You two can do as you like, but Ellie? If I were you and I had a fine man like Spencer all excited about an afternoon alone with me, I'd be choosing the hot bath first.'

Ellie clamped her hand over her mouth. The Scarlet she'd met all those months ago would *never* have said anything like that. 'You're trouble,' she teased.

'Me?' Scarlet laughed. 'If you think I'm trouble you obviously haven't met my friend Ellie.'

Ellie poked out her tongue before looking back and seeing the jeep heading straight for them, going slow enough to make her think it was stopping for them. 'Fine. But don't moan if we end up standing in queue for hours.'

Not to mention if they ended up taking so long that she missed the time she was supposed to have with Spencer.

Ellie was a ball of nerves. They'd finally made their way back after their baths, which had only cost a few francs but had made Ellie feel like a million dollars. She'd forgotten how incredible it felt to have every part of her body clean and scrubbed. Her hair was long dry, and she'd pinned it up with some help from Scarlet and Lucy, since she didn't have a mirror. Now all she could do was wait, and perhaps pay for another cup of real coffee. It had been her other highlight of the day, drinking real coffee with real milk. She smiled just thinking about the difference between what she'd finished drinking to what she'd survived on at camp.

But now Lucy and Scarlet had gone off in search of food to take back to camp, with eggs top of the list, and she was waiting for Spencer to arrive. Part of her wondered if it was a cruel joke, that he wasn't truly coming and her friends had only been teasing, but she knew them better than that. They would never have waved her goodbye and left her to wait for no one.

'Ellie.'

She jumped at the sound of his voice, turning slowly. She was standing outside the little place where she'd had coffee, not minding the cool breeze.

'I'm so sorry to keep you waiting like this.'

Spencer's smile was kind, his face open as he looked down at her.

'I've hardly been waiting. We only arrived back from Bayeux less than an hour ago.'

He moved closer, his arm extended like he wasn't quite sure what to do, and it made her laugh. She grabbed his hand and smiled up at him. Today was the first day in a long while that she'd felt a little like her old self, and she was going to make the most of it.

He laughed back and drew her closer, palm to palm. 'I hope you don't mind sitting and drinking coffee awhile,' he said. 'I've been craving anything other than that hideous Compo blend.'

'I thought the fancy doctors would get the real stuff,' she said, walking through the door ahead of him when he held it open with one hand.

'I'm afraid not. Don't you think I'd have smuggled you some in if I did?'

'A girl can only hope.'

They ordered their coffee and sat down, and Ellie was struck by how ordinary everything seemed. There was terrible damage all around, roads ruined and buildings blasted beyond recovery, but in this little café, the world seemed almost perfect. As if she was a regular girl on a regular date, about to sip coffee and talk. She leaned closer to Spencer, head bent and wishing she was sitting beside him instead of across the table.

'I was worried Scarlet was tricking me,' she confessed.

Spencer looked up and stared straight into her eyes. 'I've been wanting a moment alone with you since the very first time we spoke.'

'When I bumped into you in the hall that day?' she asked, feeling some of her old confidence returning.

'Well, maybe the second time. That first time I was just struck by your beautiful big eyes.' He gave her a half-smile. 'I even told my mother about the beautiful nurse who'd taken me by surprise.'

She giggled, like a silly little girl. *And if felt wonderful.* 'You did?'

'Of course. I couldn't write a letter home and not mention that I might have someone to introduce her to when we get back.'

'Tell me what you have planned for us today,' she said, eyes averted, not wanting to know what he'd told his mother. She couldn't believe he'd done it in the first place!

He raised an eyebrow and made her laugh again. This was a different Spencer, one she hadn't had the opportunity to enjoy with everything that had been happening.

'What would you say if you found out that I'd made up a story about needing you for an evening shift at the local convent?'

His wry smile made her blush. 'You have?'

'Are you angry?'

'I can't be angry yet because I don't know what you have in store for me!'

Spencer leaned back when their coffee was placed on the table, the steaming hot cups looking as good this time as her first one had.

'There's a stream that runs through a farm near here. I thought we could sit down there and talk,' he said simply. 'I like you, Ellie. Despite everything we're dealing with, I met you, and that makes everything I've had to deal with worth it.'

'How did you find this stream?' she asked, wishing she had the nerve to tell him that she liked him straight back.

'Do you remember when I had to leave last week?' he asked. 'I went to the other hospital.'

'Of course.'

'Well, I had a few hours off, after a shift that ended up being almost two days with not a moment of sleep,' Spencer said, taking a sip of his coffee. The taste made him smile and she sipped her own. 'I came here, to this very café, and met a woman. She was crying and I asked what was wrong. It turns out her son had broken his arm and her daughter was sick, and she had no one to help her.'

'So you, dashing doctor that you are, helped her, didn't you?'

He nodded. 'I bought her a coffee, since I had a pocket full of francs, then went back to her house. She has a lovely little home, full of warmth, but her son's arm hadn't been set and I was able to check both her children over. Today, I called in to check on them all and I happened to mention you.'

Ellie's heart leapt. 'What about me?' What could he possibly have told this woman about her?

'That I finally had a date of sorts with you. She offered to make us a simple meal to say thank you, and told me that there is a lovely stream at the bottom of her property, with a hut of sorts that her husband made for the children long before the war. She said she will leave the food for us there, should we wish for some time away from everything.'

Ellie was speechless. She didn't know what to say, how to react; but she did want to say yes.

'Are we, er, are we going there soon?' she asked when Spencer didn't say anything else.

'Yes,' he said. 'Unless you want to go back instead?'

'Spencer,' she whispered, 'there is nothing I want to do more than forget this war and spend every stolen moment with you.'

He leaned forward, hesitated, then pressed his lips softly to her, his kiss barely touching her mouth it was so gentle.

'Well, good then,' he muttered.

She was kissing her man in front of anyone who cared to watch, and she didn't give a damn.

CHAPTER FOURTEEN

Ellie

'Is this too much?' Spencer asked, his voice soft.

Ellie stared in amazement around her. It was definitely too much, but it was also perfect. The stream was pretty as a picture, the water trickling gently and long grass tickling its way right down to the bank. She looked up at Spencer, their hands linked, the smile on her face impossible to stifle.

'It's perfect,' she said.

'I wasn't sure if you'd want to be here alone with me,' he said, dropping her hand and stroking her back instead. 'But compared to being stuck in the hospital, it seemed the better option.'

She exhaled and leaned into him, more comfortable with Spencer than she could explain. There was something so lovely about him. He was charming, but strong; capable, but also so easy-going and not at all pushy. Not to mention he was an amazing doctor, which made her admire him all the more. He genuinely cared, she could see that, and it showed her the type of person he was.

'Hungry?' he asked.

She sighed. 'Starving. But I'd give you the same answer any hour of any day. I don't think I'll ever get used to the lack of food.'

He grunted. 'I see you feeding the patients sometimes and think how hard it must be. Giving them food when you know how many hours it'll be until you have a meal.'

They stood a moment longer before turning together. There were oak trees dotted around them, long grass scattered amongst areas of dirt and stone. But it was the little house that caught her eye; it was almost like a miniature log cabin it was so perfect.

'Can you believe this?'

Spencer chuckled, looking straight ahead. 'It's like a beautiful house that's been shrunk.'

'Did you say her husband built it for their children?' she asked.

He nodded. 'Yes. Lucky kids.'

'I hope for their sakes that he makes it home,' Ellie whispered, wishing she wasn't thinking about war again. But it was impossible not to. 'To think of all those families . . .'

Her voice trailed off and Spencer squeezed her hand. 'Come on. Let's see what she left for us to eat.'

She followed his lead and she waited as he pushed open the door to the wooden playhouse. They both had to duck their heads to get inside, but it was cute, with a little table and two children's chairs to one side, and a picnic basket in the middle waiting for them.

'It might be a low ceiling, but if it rains we could at least huddle together and have a tea party.' Ellie giggled. 'Makes me feel like a little girl again being in here.'

When he turned to her, eyes meeting hers and staying locked, she suddenly felt anything *but* a little girl. She gulped, holding his gaze, her body flooded with warmth as he stared at her. It was only a moment, but it felt like hours that she stood basking in his gaze.

Spencer took a step towards her, head ducked low, his frame far too tall for the small space. His eyes dropped to her mouth and her lips parted, her breathing shallow as he placed one hand to her cheek. He dipped down, pressed a soft kiss to her lips that made her forget everything except his mouth on hers.

Ellie kissed him back, not wanting it to end, wanting the kiss to last for ever. Slowly he backed her up, lips still locked as they moved outside. The cool breeze brushed against her skin, in contrast to the warmth of the sun as it kissed them from above. Spencer's arms went around her, his mouth firmer against hers now, their bodies close.

'Ellie, are you sure . . . ?' he muttered against her mouth.

She clutched his shirt, pulled him closer as her back hit the little house. Spencer's body blocked her from the world, protected her as he kissed her deeply. His hands skimmed her hips, touched down her body, and she'd never felt more alive.

Everything about Spencer felt so right. There was no part of her that wanted him to stop.

Her fingers found the buttons on the front of his shirt and she worked them impatiently. She wanted to touch his skin, *needed* to touch his skin. Spencer's hands were still on her, and when he groaned it only urged her on more. She hadn't been with a man like this before, never felt so strongly about a man, but Spencer was driving her out of her mind.

'Ellie, please . . .'

She shook her head. 'Don't stop.'

'Ellie, no,' he said, pushing back, hair dishevelled as he looked into her eyes, his body braced against hers, one hand pressed to the house behind her.

She was breathing heavily, staring up at him.

'I love you, Ellie,' he murmured, his voice raspy and barely louder than a whisper. He stroked a strand of hair from her face. 'I love you.'

She looked up at him, still breathing hard, studying every inch of his face. He'd had no need to say those words to her, it wasn't as if she'd needed encouragement, and yet he'd stopped her to say it.

'I love you, too,' she whispered back, tears in her eyes that took her by surprise.

Spencer gently stroked her face, his eyes never leaving hers, body pressing tighter, warming her. This time when he kissed her, it was gentle. The urgency had gone, his touch lighter. Ellie slipped her arms around his neck, stroked his hair with one set of fingers before running her hands down his back.

'Why rush?' he asked, murmuring against her skin as he took his lips from her mouth and dipped them into the hollow of her neck instead.

Ellie smiled to herself, pressing into him, loving the way his hands felt on her. Spencer was right, why rush? But what if this was the only time together, alone, that they ever had?

'Are you still hungry?' he asked, his voice a husky whisper.

She kissed his lips when he pulled back, watching her face. 'The food can wait,' she said against his mouth, kissing him again and starting to undo the remaining buttons on his shirt, having only succeeded in loosening two of them earlier.

Spencer scooped her up in his arms, making her giggle as her feet left the ground, and he carried her over to the grass. His breath was hot against her cheek as he lowered her down, taking off his shirt and placing it behind her before dropping to his knees and gently pushing her back.

Ellie laughed when he lowered down on top of her. And when he paused and gave her a quizzical look, she grabbed his shoulders and pulled him closer. Laughter was not something that came so easily to her now, but today she'd smiled and laughed so much that her cheeks ached.

'This is your first time?' Spencer asked gently as his hand ran up her leg, sending shivers through her body as it arched up in response to his touch.

'Yes,' she whispered.

'Tell me if you want me to stop,' he said, kissing her, making her forget everything.

She wouldn't. Ellie loved Spencer, with all her heart. He made her smile when everything else around her made her shudder. She only hoped that when the war was over he still wanted her.

Spencer smiled at her in such a knowing way that she blushed. Ellie was fully dressed again, the air curling its chilled embrace all the way into the little cabin they were sitting in now that the sun had gone down. A shiver ran through her, but she ignored it, content to snuggle closer to Spencer and enjoy the last of the food.

'I wish we didn't have to go back,' she admitted.

Spencer placed his arm around her and dropped a kiss into her hair. 'Me too.'

They'd eaten hard-boiled eggs and bread covered in butter, and a small bowl of preserved fruit as well. It was the biggest meal she'd had in what was starting to feel like for ever, and the taste of real eggs had been heavenly.

'Spencer, I should have asked before now, but . . .'

He looked down at her, waiting expectantly.

'What is it?' he asked.

'You don't have someone at home waiting for you, do you?' Ellie felt silly asking him, knowing that what they had might well just be a wartime fling for him. But it meant more to her, so much more.

'Ellie, my love, I wouldn't be here with you now if I did,' he told her, stroking her hair. It was loose over her shoulders – she hadn't bothered to pin it back up yet – and his fingers caressing each strand was nice. She leaned into him, hoping he'd keep doing it. 'I certainly wouldn't have written home to my mother about you if I was supposed to be with another woman.'

'It's not so unusual for men to—'

He stopped stroking, interrupting her sentence and using his other hand to touch her chin and tip her head up.

'I wouldn't have gone to so much trouble if that's all I wanted from you. Surely you know that?'

She nodded. He was right, she did know, but asking made her feel more certain about his intentions.

'What about when we go home?'

He kissed her head again and went back to stroking her hair when she dropped her cheek to his shoulder.

'When we're back in London I'll be taking you for dinner with my mother. She'll love you just like I do.'

'You sound so sure.'

'If I love you, she'll love you. Simple as that.'

Ellie doubted she'd ever tire of him saying those words. She loved him right back, only she wasn't quite so certain that his mother would automatically adore the nurse he'd fallen for while away on active service. Only time would tell, but right now she'd have to take his word for it, and hope that he didn't fall out of love with her once the war was over and everything went back to normal back home.

'Spencer, why did you become a doctor?'

'Because it was a good career choice, and because I like helping people. Simple as that.'

'You're a good man, you know that?' She held him close. He was like her father, warm and caring, open and strong, and she liked that. She didn't know what she'd done to make him like her so much, but she wasn't going to waste time worrying about it any longer.

CHAPTER FIFTEEN

Scarlet

'James!'

Scarlet ran so fast she skidded and almost landed on top of the stretcher being carried in.

'James, what . . . ?' she gasped when she saw his gaping wound, the blood oozing from not only his side but his leg as well.

She ran alongside him, assisted as he was transferred into a bed. Her head was thumping from working all night after the long day out with her friends, not to mention the nightmare she'd woken from the previous night, dripping in sweat and screaming his name.

'What happened to you?' she asked as she applied pressure to his side, a doctor coming over to check his leg.

Scarlet prayed that it wasn't too bad, didn't want to look for fear that it would be an amputation. She'd started to wonder if too many limbs were being cut off, if the doctors thought they had no other option, when if they'd been back home, if they'd been able to evacuate them fast enough, they might have been able to save arms and legs aplenty.

'I got shot again,' he gasped as she pushed harder at his side, concerned at how quickly the fabric was soaked a dark, violent red.

'You went back to the front?' she fumed.

The grimace he made told her she was right, and she was tempted to slap him hard across the face. Except she knew how much pain he was already in, and how stupid men could be when it meant getting back to their units and helping their men.

'I believed you were going home, that you were going to be safe.'

'Should have . . .' he gasped, 'followed orders. This bloody wound reopened as soon as I started running and shooting.'

She tried impossibly hard to suppress her anger with him. 'You'll be evacuated within the day now,' she told him. 'Don't go having any more hare-brained ideas about getting back out there. Your fighting days are over, for now at least.'

'Wanted to . . .' he started, taking a deep breath, 'find out more. Thomas.'

Scarlet nodded. 'I see.'

He might have feelings for her, but Thomas was his brother. Of course he was desperate to find him, see if there were any way he could get him home. What they'd had between them was banished to memories, and she needed to remember that. Part of her was devastated that he hadn't said anything about returning for her, but she knew that was silly. They'd sworn never to speak of what had happened again. It was as simple as that.

'I have a plan, James. Trust me.'

She wasn't lying. She'd had a plan for days now, had even gone as far as discussing it with Spencer, and she was certain it would work. If Thomas were where she thought he could be, then she'd find him. And if not him? Then at least she'd find someone else's Thomas and help to bring him home. She trembled with fear at the very thought of finding Thomas now, scared of how her feelings had changed, but she couldn't back down now, not now that she'd come so far.

'Doctor!' she cried, her breath catching in her throat as she watched James's eyes flutter, as if he were slowly slipping away from her. 'Help, please!'

Not James. Not her James.

'Prepare this man for surgery. Nurse! Attend to him!' the doctor barked at her as she stood, dead still, staring at James on the bed before her. His uniform was filthy, her hand was covered in his blood, the colour seeping across her skin and making it look like her own hands were bleeding.

'Nurse!'

The second bark made Scarlet snap out of it. Thomas might be a long shot. But James? James was here. James she could do everything within her power to save.

———— ∂~∿∾ ————

Scarlet had been working all day. Her hands were sore and red, and she wasn't sure if that was from overwork or because they were stained with the blood of the men she'd been tending to. She stared down; her hands started to shake, body slowly beginning to tremble as she looked around.

They'd had hundreds of men. Hundreds. The ambulances hadn't stopped arriving, the blood hadn't stopped spurting, and she still hadn't eaten anything. And even though she knew that every soldier was someone's loved one, that her focus should have been purely on the injured man lying in front of her, all she'd thought about was James. Not Thomas. Not the man she was promised to. *James.*

'Where is he?' she murmured to herself, not sure whether anyone else could hear them. The room spun around her, everything a blur, her stomach churning as she inhaled, trying to breathe when all she could manage were rapid gasps.

Where was he?

'Nurse, out of the way!'

The shout from behind made her lurch forward, tripping. She was so hungry, so tired, so . . . She needed to find James.

'Lucy!' she called, seeing her friend standing over a patient. She recognised her blonde hair pulled back into a tight bun.

Scarlet rushed over to her, the blood starting to pump through her body again as she moved. He couldn't be gone. She needed one more moment with him, one last stolen moment before he left and she had to pretend all over again not to have feelings for him.

'You're looking for him?' Lucy called. 'For James?'

Scarlet nodded, catching her breath. If she'd had the chance she would have stayed with him, cared for him and been there when he came out of surgery. Instead she'd been rushing around trying to do everything she could, and she didn't even know if he was still here.

'I saw him being taken out of surgery. I made sure to ask after him the moment I had the chance and I went to see him with my own eyes. They haven't evacuated anyone since then.'

Scarlet nodded, relief washing through her, and touched Lucy's arm, looking down at the man she was standing with. 'You doing all right?' she asked, talking to Lucy as her friend hovered over the American soldier.

Lucy let out a long, shuddering, deep sigh. 'Given the circumstances? I guess you could say that. Although I'm sick of doctors acting like we're no more important than orderlies when we have to work like dogs and assist them at every turn.'

Scarlet kept her hand on Lucy's arm for a heartbeat longer, but she saw the way the soldier was looking at her friend, and she wanted to leave them alone. 'It can't keep going on like this. We have to keep telling ourselves that.' She didn't go on, didn't tell her that sometimes she worried that it wouldn't stop, that they were stuck in France for the rest of their lives until they, too, were blown up by a bomb or shot down by the enemy.

'Go find your man,' Lucy ordered, turning back to the soldier on the bed, leaning low and whispering words that Scarlet couldn't hear.

Scarlet left her to finish her work and started to scan the beds. It was her worst nightmare to think that she'd missed him, that he could have been taken away after surgery before she'd had the chance to say goodbye. Seeing the soldiers go, once upon a time, had made her think they would be safe, that they were going to make it home safe and be looked after, that they were the lucky ones to get away. Now she knew better.

Those lucky ones often ended up dead or more badly injured before they got to their transportation. She swallowed a lump in her throat. So why, when she knew the reality of what happened every single day, had she been so certain that James had been safe?

She surveyed more beds, started to look more frantically, wondering where he'd gone, and then her eyes landed on a mop of dark, almost black hair. Her heartbeat slowed from its rapid pounding as she moved towards him, relief hitting her hard.

Within moments she was by his side, taking in the steady rise and fall of his chest, the bandaging that she could see under his cut uniform. It hit her how close he'd been to dying, and the thought that she might never have seen him again hurt her more than she wanted to admit.

'Hi,' she whispered when his eyes opened, carefully, like he was cautious of what he was going to see.

When he groaned, loudly, she realised it was probably more to do with the pain he was feeling than not wanting to see what was above him.

'Don't speak,' she whispered, taking his hand and stroking his skin lightly with her fingertips. 'I wanted to check on you, in case they took you without my knowing.' She smiled when his lips parted, the upward tilt of his mouth telling her he was happy to see her. 'My shift is only finishing now, it's been a long day, and I thought I'd come looking for you and then I thought you'd gone.'

'I'm . . .' He hissed out a breath; she hated seeing him in pain.

'Let me get you water,' she said, reaching for the cup so she could soothe his cracked, dry lips. She turned back and dripped a little into his mouth, more when he swallowed it down.

'Thank you,' he muttered, looking better for having had something to drink.

'Your surgery must have gone well. You look good,' she said.

'Liar.' He chuckled, cringing when his body moved with the laughter. 'I look like . . .' He pushed up a little and she helped him, the blood soaking through his bandage too much for her liking. She bit her tongue instead of saying anything.

'Hell,' he finally said. 'Turns out bullets hurt a whole lot more than I thought they would.'

Scarlet didn't know if it was from exhaustion, hunger or both, but she burst into tears. Not the silent, quiet type of tears that slowly ran down her cheeks like they usually would if she cried, but a gasp of tears that made a choking noise sound out in her throat and a torrent of unshed emotion shudder from her. She tried to stop, tried to swallow it all away, but the more she cried, the harder it was to stem.

'Scarlet.'

She heard James say her name as she fought and lost the battle she was waging with herself.

'Sweetheart, is it me you're worried about? Because I'm tough. A bullet or two won't keep me down.'

She tried to laugh at him, but it came out as more of a snort and only made her want to cry more.

'Unless you were hoping I'd be dead?'

His voice was still weak and when he started to cough she wiped frantically at her face with the heels of her hands, then used her sleeve. She was being silly, and it certainly wasn't like her to be so overly emotional.

'Don't you ever say that,' she said, looking around, surprised she hadn't been reprimanded or called to attend anything. She was crying because she was supposed to be looking for one brother, and instead her thoughts were consumed with the one in front of her. It wasn't right, but no matter what she tried to tell herself, nothing could change the way she felt.

'I'm worried about you,' he said quietly, his fingers moving against hers when she touched him, threading her fingers so they were lying in between each of his on his right hand.

'Don't be,' she insisted, trying to focus on each inhale of air, slowly letting each breath go. 'We don't get a lot to eat and the days are long, that's all. I'm so tired and beyond hungry.'

He grunted. 'Fair enough.'

'But don't for a moment think I'm not happy that you pulled through. My greatest fear is losing you, too.'

She cringed. They'd circled straight back around to Thomas again even though she'd been doing everything she could to avoid thinking about the news James had shared. Why had she had to say that, that she was scared of losing him, *too*? Maybe it was the world's way of reminding her that she was already supposed to be worried about another man, a man that wasn't James.

'Any chance you'll be heading home soon?' he asked, his voice low but not quite as strained as it had been before.

'No.' She sighed, giving herself permission to look into his eyes. 'I doubt that very, very much.' Some days she wondered if the war would ever end or they'd ever get the chance to go home. Maybe home wasn't even going to be there; it could be bombed and flattened for all she knew.

'It'd be nice to have you coming home with me,' James said, mouth curling up into a mischievous smile. 'I could do with a private nurse.'

'Joking like that makes me doubt you're even that badly injured!' Scarlet said with a laugh, hands on her hips. But the movement sent her off balance, made her dizzy. She reached for the bed and steadied herself.

'Scarlet?' All teasing was gone from James's voice, but she flapped her hands at him when he tried to haul himself up, not wanting him to do further damage.

'No,' she managed, slowing her breathing, doing what she could to stop the room from spinning.

'Damn,' James swore, lowering back down.

'We're both in a bad way.' Scarlet held on to his hand again and he stared back at her. 'I'm not sure which one of us is in the worse state.'

'You need to get something to eat,' James told her. 'Then you need to sleep.'

'It's not as easy as just finding something to eat,' she said, grimacing. If only it were that simple. 'But yes, you're right.'

'Is there food for the patients?' he asked.

Scarlet nodded. 'Of course. I can get something for you. We need to keep up your strength and I can even mash it with a fork for you if you need.'

He chuckled. 'Scarlet, you're not mashing my food for me.'

She shrugged. 'I do it for half the other soldiers. It doesn't matter.'

'Go get food, tell them it's for me, and you can have it. I won't get an ounce of rest tonight if I'm worrying about you.'

'I can't do that. It's forbidden.'

'What are they going to do? Fire you? Send you home?' He shook his head. 'I doubt that very much.'

'Rules are rules.' She thought he'd have been a stickler for them, given his position in the army. But then plenty of men and women were doing things they'd never have considered before.

'Go get the food. You can bend low over me, share some with me, and no one will know if you're taking mouthfuls or bending to spoon something into me.'

Scarlet sighed. He was right. She did need sustenance. It wasn't her fault that she'd had to work all day and night without a break, without so much as a spoonful of food to see her through. She had eggs still to cook from the day before, but she hadn't even had a chance to take them from her jacket pocket.

'Why do you have to be so . . .' She blew out a deep, long breath. 'Lovely.'

'Lovely?' He laughed. 'Is that supposed to be a bad thing? Because if you were trying to offend me, you're failing.'

'Caring,' she said. 'I don't know. I just wish you weren't so nice. It'd make this whole thing easier.'

'Why?'

She stared at him, ran her fingers over his hand, feeling less guilty now. Maybe she was so overtired that she didn't care, or maybe after everything she'd been through she'd simply stopped judging herself so harshly or by such high standards.

'Because then it would be so much easier not to like you,' she told him honestly. 'I've tried so hard. I don't want to like you, but I do.'

'Go get the food,' he said. But Scarlet didn't miss his smile, the way he relaxed back into the bed, eyes still holding her gaze.

He liked her, too. He didn't need to say it. Every look, every touch, every minute they spent together told her everything she needed to know. One day she could go back to worrying, but as long as she kept looking for Thomas and didn't give up her search, she could live with herself.

'I'll go get that food then,' Scarlet said. She looked around, noticed that the noise level had dropped to a low hum. She prayed that it would be a slow night, that soldiers wouldn't be falling as fast as they had been during the day.

She saw Lucy, smiled at her, raising her hand as she went in search of something she could share with James. For a girl who'd always played by the rules and stayed true to her promises, she was fast turning into someone she no longer recognised. Scarlet bit her lip, amused by her own thoughts. Maybe she even liked this new version of herself.

'Nurse!'

She cringed, her smile falling away as quickly as it had appeared. *Please, Lord, not now.* She should have staved off her hunger and stayed at James's bedside. It would have been better than a doctor calling out to her and begging her to work.

Scarlet kept her head down, kept walking, ignoring the call.

'Scarlet!'

This time, a heavy hand fell on her shoulder, gripping her, forcing her to stop. She spun around, angry, ready to tell the damn doctor to get his hands off her.

'Don't . . .' The words died the moment she looked into Spencer's face, his expression a mix of exhaustion and uncertainty. Heck, she'd have been scared of the look she'd given him. 'I'm so sorry, I thought . . .'

He ignored her words. 'Scarlet, there's been word. Confirmation of some British soldiers' existence among the ones being cared for at one of the convents you asked me to enquire about.'

Her heartbeat picked up speed, mouth dry as she stared at him. 'Thomas?'

'Look, all I know is that there are soldiers of ours there. They needed a doctor to attend and I've volunteered to go.' He paused. 'And I've asked to take my own nurse.'

Scarlet gulped, swallowing what felt like a rock in her throat. She almost didn't want it to be true, had started hoping that she was wrong, that she'd never find him. 'Me?'

'I've requested you. I made it clear that you can work fast and that I can trust you with any task.' He placed a hand on her arm, and this time the touch comforted her instead of alarming her. 'That is, if you want to go?'

'Yes,' she murmured, knowing she couldn't falter now, even if she wanted to. 'Yes,' she said again, this time in a stronger voice. 'I'll go.'

James was here. She was tending to one brother and now planning a possible rescue mission for another.

'I don't want to get your hopes up, this is a long shot, but there is a chance he's there.'

Scarlet nodded. 'I'll be ready.' She needed the food more than ever now, light-headed from the news she'd just received as well as her growling stomach.

'I haven't told Ellie yet. I don't want her to worry,' Spencer said as she took a step back before turning. 'I'll tell her when we have confirmed plans.'

'I understand.' Scarlet had no intention of worrying Ellie unless it was absolutely necessary. 'And thank you, Spencer. Thank you for caring.'

'Ellie would never forgive me if I didn't do everything I could to help you,' he said. 'Turns out I'll do anything to make her happy.'

'Even embark on a crazy trip to locate a handful of soldiers?'

It sounded crazy, even to her.

'Yes.'

He smiled one last time before going back to his patients, and she walked quietly off. She needed to get back to James, and she needed to forget all about what Spencer had told her and enjoy her last hours or days with James before he was sent back home. If they found Thomas, it might be the last time she could hold his hand and look into his eyes without being unfaithful, before her heart was broken into a million pieces that she doubted could ever be placed back together. She'd almost convinced herself that Thomas was gone, that finding him was a fantasy that would never come true. Truth be told, she could barely remember how she felt about him, her memories of him hazy, starting to blur the more she tried to draw on them. Or maybe it was simply that all the old feelings had disappeared the moment she'd laid eyes upon James and felt alive like she'd never felt before.

CHAPTER SIXTEEN

Lucy

'Check out the Yanks!'

Lucy looked up when one of the nurses nearby whispered excitedly. She'd been dressing a wound and studying how well it had healed. When she looked up, she could see that she'd missed quite a commotion.

Three American soldiers were standing inside the entrance to their tent hospital, talking to a doctor. He looked uptight and they appeared relaxed, one of them casually standing there with his hands in his pockets looking around. Lucy smiled, nervous but excited, too. She had been waiting for them to arrive, had known for days to expect them, which meant that today was the day she might find out exactly who her Patient X was.

She wiped her hands on her apron and glanced at the man in question. He was sitting up, laughing about something to another nurse, but when he noticed her standing there he gave her a slow wink that made her heart fall to her toes and leap back up again. She had no idea how he managed to do it, but every glance or touch or smile from him sent her spiralling. She laughed to herself and turned her attention back to the soldiers. Gosh, her mother would be in fits if she could see the effect he had on her, after years of trying to convince her that one day, mark her words, a man would come along and knock her socks off. Well, one finally had, and her mother would love it. Only this one belonged to another, and the ache in her heart was only going to get worse.

The doctor beckoned her and Lucy crossed over to them. The relaxed soldier who'd caught her eye originally was staring at her, smiling. He raised an eyebrow and let out a low whistle.

'Why *hello*, lovely nurse,' he said, making the other two turn to face her.

Lucy's cheeks flushed hot but she tried to appear unrattled. She wasn't used to that type of attention. 'Gentlemen,' she said, addressing them in what she hoped was a strong voice when they all turned to look at her. 'Sorry to interrupt. Are you here to see our American patients?'

They nodded, and it was the same soldier who was still staring at her, his smile fixed in place, who responded. 'We sure are.'

'This is the nurse who has been caring for one of your men who's been suffering memory lapses,' the doctor said.

'That's right,' confirmed Lucy. 'Or more accurately, he can't recall all that much from his past, his long-term memory I should say.'

The soldier laughed. 'I'll bet he's liking you taking care of him.'

She gave a tight smile and motioned for him to follow her. 'Would you like to come and see him?' She made an attempt to bat her eyelashes, trying not to laugh at herself. 'Please?'

He shrugged and followed her, and she walked quickly. What she wanted was to have a moment alone with this soldier, to see if he knew anything, to find out everything she could about the man she had become so fond of, before the doctors came over and she was ushered out of the way. Or more likely ignored altogether. Real life was about to step in, and the flutter in her chest was telling her exactly how badly the truth was going to hurt.

'How long's he been here?'

'A couple of weeks,' she said. 'The ambulance coming in was hit and I was part of the, er, well, rescue team I suppose you'd call us.'

'You helped rescue one of our boys?' he asked, incredulous.

She thought about that day constantly, second-guessed what she'd done and wondered how differently things could have turned out. 'It was one of those moments,' she said, not wanting to explain it all to him. 'I only wish he could have told me more about who he was.'

'Jack!'

Lucy was interrupted by the soldier pushing past her, running to the patient she was taking him to.

'Jack! We thought you were dead!'

The soldier was shaking hands with her patient, then grabbed him by the shoulders and hugged him. She quickly intervened, touching his arm.

'He's still in recovery,' she said, watching her patient's face, wanting to see any recognition.

'This, this . . . Oh wow,' the soldier gasped. 'This is *Jack*! Captain John Colton.'

'Jack,' she repeated, smiling down at him. His face was crumpled, half frown, half smile, and she watched as he silently mouthed the name. 'At least we have a name.'

'He's been missing so long, we thought he was dead or taken.' The soldier slapped him on the shoulder again and Lucy cringed. 'Instead he's been here in the lap of luxury with a beautiful nurse tending to him.'

She didn't mind the beautiful part, but she did want Jack to stop being manhandled. Men were like that, she knew, but still. It seemed that American men were a lot more physical than she was used to.

'Jack,' she started, feeling peculiar addressing him by an actual name after days of trying out every male name she could think of to see if it seemed to fit him or not, 'had a photo in his pocket, something that was obviously important to him. We were certain it was a wife or sweetheart from back home, and we kept it safe for him.'

She reached for it and tentatively passed it over. A smile broke out instantly on the soldier's face, and she held her breath, waiting, hoping it wasn't a wife.

'This is Susie,' he said with a chuckle. 'We always hassle him about having a photo of his damn sister on him, but he didn't have a sweetheart back home and he liked having her near. They're twins.' He paused. 'Well, we don't all make fun. Anyone lower than an officer would have been whipped for teasing him about her.'

Lucy let out a swoosh of air so loud she had to plant her hand over her mouth. *His sister?* She couldn't believe it hadn't crossed her mind that it could be his sister! His wife, his fiancée, his sweetheart, someone he loved . . . but *never* his sister.

'You're certain?' she asked.

The soldier laughed. 'Believe me, it's his sister. I know that as surely as I know his name.'

She stared down at Jack, smiling so hard she was almost ready to burst out laughing; a hysterical, ridiculous kind of laughter.

'Well, now you have a name *and* a sister,' she said, patting his hand.

'We'd better figure out how to get you out of here,' the soldier said, shaking his head and turning back in the direction they'd come from.

Lucy hoped the soldier would disappear, that he'd go back to the others and have to talk it all out, because she needed more time with Jack. She couldn't stand the thought of finally finding out who he was only to have him disappear straight away.

'Does it make you remember anything?' she asked in a hushed tone once they were alone, reaching for his hand, needing to make a connection with him.

His eyes were fixed on hers. 'The name made me smile, I guess. Things are hazy, but I think I'm starting to make some sense of my jumble of thoughts. Memories hit me like flashes, jigsaw puzzle pieces I have to piece back together.'

Lucy was happy for him, she truly was. She only hoped that he wouldn't forget her, which was silly since they were never likely to see one another again.

'What about your sister? You're a twin!' she said, still excited about the fact that the man she'd been holding hands with and whispering to late each night as she told him stories from home and fed him his meals didn't already belong to another woman. Her greatest fear had been that he was married with a family.

'Can you pass me the photo please?' Jack asked.

Lucy reached for where she'd tucked it into his jacket, folded beneath the bed. 'Here you go.'

She stared at the woman as she passed it over, looking at her differently now, wanting to know more about her instead of pretending she didn't exist. His face didn't change, his expression the same as before.

'Jack, my boy!'

The soldiers appeared without warning from behind her, making her jump with their loud words. They crowded around his bed, only to be hushed by a much older nurse and a doctor working nearby. They didn't seem to mind, but Lucy took a hesitant step back even as Jack's eyes met hers again, one look telling her everything she needed to know.

She was about to lose him, and she hated it. Of all the things she'd lost in this war, of all the things she'd wished for and wanted, Jack was the one thing she didn't want taken from her. After each long shift, she'd been excited to go and talk to him, even when her eyes had been so blurry and weary that it had been almost impossible to keep them open. To sit and talk with him, to care for him, had given her something to smile about. Knowing that she'd done the right thing, helped to save a man who was so kind and funny, even though he couldn't even remember his own name. And the way he looked at her, it softened her. Made her realise that personal connections *were* as important as her work.

'We'll get you out of here in no time,' she heard one of the soldiers say, tuning back in. 'We just need to check on the other Americans here and you'll be our top priority, sir.'

Lucy stared at him through a gap between two of the soldiers in their handsome uniforms. He was staring back at her still, seemingly ignoring everything they were saying, his eyes trained firmly on hers.

'Give me a minute,' he said, clearing his throat and interrupting whoever was talking.

His voice, although hoarse, was full of more authority than she'd ever heard from him. This was the officer talking, no longer an unnamed patient.

'Yes, sir.'

Even the soldier who'd been joking earlier left him, and Lucy stood still, feet locked to the floor.

'Lucy,' he said, voice softer this time.

She nodded, not trusting her voice, not ready to say goodbye to him, even though she'd said goodbye to hundreds of soldiers since they'd been in France, even though she knew that she had no claim over this man and that he needed to go soon.

'Come here.'

Lucy wrapped her arms around herself, cold, shivers taking over her body as she moved slowly to his side once more.

'I don't know how to say goodbye to the woman who helped to rescue me from a burning ambulance and has nursed me every day since,' he said, taking her hand. He was sitting upright, staring at her, his fingers interlinked with hers. 'Leaving you ain't going to be easy, that's for sure.'

'You'll forget all about me the moment they take you away from here,' she said, trying to be brave even as a single tear slipped down her cheek.

Jack reached up, gently wiping it away and taking her other hand in his, pressing a kiss to her skin. He never blinked once their eyes met again.

'Lucy, there is no part of me that could ever forget you.'

His words washed over her, made it almost impossible to breathe. Why did he have to be so nice? Why did he have to say things like this when they were never going to see one another again?

'Don't say that. You don't even know . . .'

'I don't need to know anything more than I already know,' he said. 'I want you to write down your address, I want to know every detail about you and your family so that one day, when all this is over, I can find you.' His smile was warm. 'I will find you, Lucy, mark my words.'

Lucy didn't believe him, didn't want to believe him, because it only made the hurt worse, the pain shooting through her chest already unbearable.

'Don't go making promises you can't keep,' she said.

He squeezed her hand tighter. 'Unless I die in a field out there or end up in another burning ambulance with no Lucy to rescue me, I promise that I will find you. One day, somehow, I will find you.'

She folded forward, arms around him. She'd be scolded for this, for what she was doing in plain sight of every other person in the hospital, but she didn't care. No one was going to take these last moments from her.

'Goodbye, Lucy,' he whispered into her hair.

Lucy raised her head, found her face too close to his, her mouth too near his. When Jack leaned forward, only a touch, it was all it took for their lips to meet; the most gentle press of his lips on hers – a soft, sweet kiss that she'd never forget for as long as she lived.

'Goodbye,' she whispered against his mouth.

The soldiers returned and she stood, holding Jack's hand still until the very last moment, until their fingers slid from one another's and her hand was left cold. She clutched it to her chest, a chill wrapping its icy touch around her.

'Men, I need pen and paper.'

She knew that even when she took the pen from one of them, hand shaking as she scrawled her address, she still wouldn't believe that he'd ever come for her. She'd be a nurse he'd smile about, think of fondly, but there was no possible way that this handsome American officer was ever going to come to London in search of her. Every breath in her body hoped it was so, but she wasn't stupid and she certainly wasn't naive.

She loved a man she'd never, ever lay eyes upon again, and it hurt.

———— ໒ ໒ ————

Lucy lay in her bed, the cold seeping into her bones as it always did now that the weather had become cooler. Living like this was something she'd never get used to, not to mention the rain, or the constant mud beneath the planks they had to walk upon. She'd always kept her complaints to herself, never wanting to make a fuss, but everything was starting to annoy her tonight. Previously, she'd cared about her work and doing her best and learning all she could. She'd seen things, but then so had everyone, and she got on with whatever task was at hand to keep things moving forward. But tonight, she didn't want to do anything, and she certainly didn't want to be part of any banter with the other nurses.

The girls were all talking about moving camp at the end of the week. The last shift had been so much quieter than usual, meaning that they weren't as bone-tired as on other nights. She had been starting to wonder how long they'd be here, when they'd be packing up to move to another location. They all knew the drill, how the patients were moved and the hospital slowly closed down until they were able to pack it up and move closer to the fighting that no longer terrified her as it once had. But this time they were moving further away, and no one knew what to expect. Tonight she felt numb, like she was watching the world go by from outside of her own body, listening to her friends talk without truly hearing what they were even saying.

'Lucy?'

She lifted her head, hearing her name. It pulled her back to the present. When she looked around, she saw that Scarlet and Ellie were both looking at her, waiting for her to say something.

'Sorry, I wasn't even listening,' she admitted, seeing no point in pretending that she even knew what they'd been talking about.

'One of the doctors said that you were responsible for setting up a convent hospital before you came to work with us.'

She nodded. 'Yes, I was.' It was one of the reasons she'd been sent to help with the 75th, that and the fact she'd proven herself as a surgical nurse in the field. She liked to get on with her work and do her best, and the last thing she'd wanted was to be paraded around as if she were someone important when she felt anything but, most of the time.

'So you save soldiers from fires *and* set up special hospitals?' Scarlet's eyebrows were drawn together, her mouth hovering between a frown and a smile. 'Why have you never told us about it? Is there more about you that we don't know?'

Lucy wasn't in a mood to talk about herself, and she certainly didn't want her friends thinking she was anything other than ordinary. She tried to be brave and do her job well, nothing more, nothing less.

'There's not a lot to tell. I did my job,' she said with a shrug, picking at the edge of the blanket resting over her knees. 'I don't need help from anyone, I don't need special pats on the back, I simply do what I have to do.'

Scarlet stared at her, frowning, and Lucy instantly regretted her words. There had been no need to be so blunt to the women who'd been so kind to her. She was taking it out on Scarlet when she was upset with herself. Letting her guard down with Jack had happened too easily, and the pain at trying to rebuild that wall around her heart was crippling.

'I'm sorry,' she muttered.

'It's fine,' Ellie said, her smile kind, and Lucy was certain they both understood how hard she'd found it, saying goodbye to Jack.

'From what Spencer told me, it's not me who should be going on this rescue mission to the hill convent,' Scarlet said. 'It's you.'

'What mission?' asked Ellie.

Scarlet looked at her, eyes wide, and Lucy forgot all about feeling sorry for herself.

'You mean the, er, drive to the convent to do a routine patient check?' Lucy asked, her voice at a higher pitch than usual, trying desperately to save Scarlet. She might have been snappy before, but she wasn't going to let Scarlet be thrown under the bus.

Ellie had been so fragile for so long, but the last month, after her day away with Spencer, she'd been smiling and so much happier. Lucy didn't want to do anything to make her lose her smile again. She'd never cared about making friends with the other nurses before, but now she wanted to keep the ones she had.

'Yes, that's, ah, right,' Scarlet said, her shoulders visibly rising then falling.

'Is Spencer going on this trip? Are you?' Ellie asked Scarlet. 'Why is this the first I've heard of it, if you both know and Spencer knows?'

Lucy stayed quiet, leaving it to Scarlet to decide what to tell her. She contemplated getting up to scoop a cup of Compo tea from the bucket being passed around, but thought better of it. Her stomach was starting to churn thinking about the wretched taste of it; she preferred the sick feeling of dread over her goodbye to Jack.

'Ellie, we didn't want to worry you, but I suppose we were going to have to tell you sooner or later,' Scarlet admitted. 'Spencer has had confirmation that we will be travelling to a convent that is at least a day's drive away. In fact, it could take longer depending on the conditions.'

'You're going with him? *Both* you and Spencer are going?' Ellie's voice had raised to a higher pitch now.

'Yes. I'm going because word has been received that they've been hiding and caring for a small number of soldiers. Convents everywhere have. There is a chance Thomas could be among them, although I'm not counting my chickens yet.'

Lucy thought Scarlet sounded more and more as if she were trying to convince herself that she wanted to see Thomas, or maybe that was just her reading too much into it. The poor girl was probably terrified of what state he might be in after all this time.

'Thomas? Thomas could be there and you kept this from me?' Ellie shrilled.

Lucy wished she could help Scarlet out, but she didn't know what to say. She decided to try. 'Spencer didn't want to worry you, and neither did Scarlet. I only found out because Spencer had enquired about me joining them. He didn't get permission to take another nurse, though, so I'm staying put.'

'Which is why I now know more about Lucy's time nursing before we met her,' Scarlet finished.

'You're both leaving me?' Ellie asked in a low voice.

'I need to do everything I can to find Thomas,' Scarlet said. 'You know I do.'

'I feel sick,' Ellie complained, pulling her blanket up higher and lying down.

'Ellie, please,' Lucy said, reaching for her.

'No, I mean I actually feel sick. I've been nauseous all day and it's starting to get worse.'

'I hope you aren't getting the stomach flu or some awful virus,' Lucy said, leaning over her to place a hand to her forehead. 'You're not burning up, though, which is good.'

'I haven't heard of anything going around,' Scarlet said, before suddenly looking wide-eyed at Lucy.

Lucy mouthed, *What?* She wasn't sure what Scarlet was silently trying to tell her. Scarlet dropped a hand to her belly and patted it, but Lucy still had no clue.

'Um, sweetheart, the afternoon you spent with Spencer . . .'

Lucy sat bolt upright then, knowing exactly what Scarlet had been hinting at. If she hadn't been so preoccupied with her own thoughts she'd have put two and two together herself.

'Oh, that'll make me forget the nasties,' Ellie said with a giggle.

'Ellie, I think what Scarlet is trying to say is that, well, you might be . . .' She looked at Scarlet again. '*Pregnant.*'

Ellie fell silent. She didn't move. Then she sat up, staring down at her stomach.

'No!'

Lucy didn't know whether to laugh or cry for her, so she kept a straight face. This had definitely taken her mind off Jack.

'Don't go worrying yet,' she told her. 'If you are, well then there's nothing you can do about it anyway. And if you are?' She grinned. 'I'm godmother!'

'No!' Scarlet thumped her on the arm. 'I'm the one who needs a little baby to cuddle and squish. I'm godmother for sure.'

Ellie shook her head, but Lucy could see the little smile hiding on her lips. 'You really think . . . ?'

Lucy raised her brows and she grinned at Scarlet as they both looked back at Ellie.

Ellie groaned. 'I've been around pregnant women and babies my whole life. How did I not think about this when I started feeling sick this morning? I don't want to be one of the women sent home for getting pregnant!'

Lucy didn't know what to say to make her feel better, so she decided to change the subject. 'Did I tell you that Jack promised to find me after the war?' It hurt her to even say it, but she knew Scarlet or Ellie would have done the same for her.

A smile immediately broke out on Ellie's face and Scarlet grinned. Saying those words out loud was like twisting a knife into her heart, but if it stopped Ellie worrying about being pregnant or being left alone for even an hour, she'd do anything. These girls had been her friends when she knew no one else, had shown her the importance of having her own family away from home, something she'd thought she didn't need, which meant there was little she wouldn't do for them.

'Tell me everything he said,' Ellie insisted. 'I want word for word.'

Lucy didn't think for a moment that Ellie wasn't still worrying about being left and bringing a baby into the world, but at least this would keep her smiling for a little longer. And if it meant she could think about Jack, even cry about him openly, instead of all on her own after dark, when no one could see her pain, then maybe it was for the best anyway.

CHAPTER SEVENTEEN

Ellie

Ellie groaned as she vomited, again. It felt like she'd been sick for hours, even though she knew that wasn't true. Her body was heaving, stomach so empty, but the vomiting was better than the plain nausea. That had gone on for two days already, but at least vomiting meant she was doing something.

'I'm so sorry,' she said as she slowly stood back up. 'I can't believe you've had to hear all that.'

Scarlet stroked her hair, fingers still holding it back from her face. She'd been there for her the entire time, rubbing her back, keeping her hair from her face, whispering soothing words. It had been embarrassing to start with, but now she was just grateful to have her friend by her side. Other nurses had got pregnant, it wasn't like she was the only one, but she still felt ashamed that she was going to have to walk away from her duties.

'I'm going to have to tell him,' Ellie said, dabbing at her mouth, wishing she wasn't in the disgusting toilet block. Being sick was bad enough, but being sick here was revolting. 'I can't keep hiding it.'

'You're certain?' Scarlet asked, her eyes full of concern.

'There ain't no chance this is a stomach flu,' Ellie said, rubbing in gentle circles across her belly. She couldn't believe how unlucky she'd been, for this to happen after their one and only time together.

Scarlet smiled. 'Everything is going to be fine. I promise you. Spencer will be thrilled.'

Scarlet looked so certain, as if she genuinely believed Spencer would be happy when she told him. Ellie herself wasn't so certain, had no idea how she would tell him. Had he meant what he'd said? Would his mother really think she was good enough for him? The last thing she wanted was . . . She didn't know what she wanted. But she was pregnant now; there was a tiny, beautiful baby growing inside of her, and there was nothing she could do about it other than be happy. Even if she was terrified.

'Why don't we go find him,' Scarlet suggested, pushing open the door for Ellie to follow. 'I can't stay in here a moment longer; the smell is horrible.'

They stepped out on to the timber planks, the weather still dreary, the mud still deep. There were plenty of horrible things here, and the fact she was pregnant wasn't going to be one of them.

'What will they do with me? I mean, will I have to return home immediately? Will I stay here until I'm showing?' Ellie whispered, wishing she was pressed against Scarlet for warmth and comfort instead of following behind her.

'I don't know, but Spencer will.' Scarlet's smile was kind. 'Look, it's not like you're the first, and you won't be the last. It's one of those things and there hasn't been all that much fuss made about it when others have had to leave for the very same reason.'

Ellie stopped, turned her face up, the gloomy grey sky drawing her in. It wasn't sunny, it wasn't warm, but the sky was still somewhere to escape to. It looked so peaceful today. If she stared at it for long enough, she could almost pretend she was back in England.

'Ellie?'

She straightened, sighed and started to put one foot in front of the other again. Soon she'd be gone. Soon she'd be heading back home, away from here, the place she'd grown to hate, the place she had dreamt of leaving. Only she'd never wanted to leave without her friends, or without Spencer. But the pain she'd felt, the struggle that had wound like a cord around her neck, threatening to strangle her . . . She pushed the thoughts away. She was better now, and she needed to stay positive for the baby, not dwell on the painful thoughts and the desperation she'd felt during much of her time here.

She sighed again, something she had being doing constantly of late. She'd also dreamt of a life with Spencer, but it hadn't involved her getting pregnant and being sent away, perhaps never to see him again, and to raise his child on her own, without a husband. Because she knew how easily something terrible could happen to him, that he might not make it back.

She walked behind Scarlet until they were back at the hospital, wishing she could head back to their tent instead of going in to find Spencer.

'He loves you, Ellie,' Scarlet said as she linked arms with her. 'He loves you, and he'll love this baby.'

Ellie looked at Scarlet, took strength from her, then headed straight towards the familiar silhouette of Spencer as Scarlet went to her patients. She'd spotted him straight away, and now that the hospital wasn't as chaotic with so many patients arriving every hour, it was easier to approach him. She forced herself to smile, didn't want to appear as nervous as she felt inside. It had been so busy since their afternoon together, with no more days of leave, and they'd only had a snatched few minutes here and there between patients.

'Spencer?' she said, pausing a few steps from him.

He turned slowly, a smile breaking out on his face when he saw her.

'Hello, Ellie,' he said, his gaze somehow warming her and taking her nerves away at the same time.

'Spencer, when you have a moment we need to talk,' she said bravely.

'Is everything all right?' He turned back to his patient, said something that she didn't hear and then put down the board he'd been holding.

Ellie waited, not sure what to say. No, everything was not all right, but then she didn't want to make a fuss and worry him, either.

'Ellie, come this way,' he said, taking her arm and leading her away from the patients and the prying eyes and ears of the other nurses. They moved to the far corner of their large tented hospital, his eyes searching her face.

'Spencer, I'm sorry, I don't even know how to tell you this, but . . .'

'What is it, Ellie? What's wrong? Tell me.'

A fresh wave of nausea hit her but she forced it down, refused to give in to it right at this moment.

'Ellie, you're worrying me. Are you ill?' He took her hand again, held them gently. 'You know I can help you if you're sick, don't you? There's no need to be embarrassed if you need me to treat you.'

'Spencer,' she said, eyes filling with tears that she tried so hard to fight, desperate to stay strong. 'I'm pregnant.'

He didn't move, didn't speak, simply stared at her as if she'd said nothing at all. Ellie opened her mouth, about to repeat her words, when he came back to life.

'Ellie,' he said, his mouth fixed in a line that was almost a smile. 'I, well, I don't know what to say.'

He stood stock-still, his hands still holding hers.

'Just say it's not the worst news you've heard all day,' she mumbled, trying so hard not to sob.

'Oh, Ellie, don't say that. It's' – he blew out a breath, smiling – 'wonderful news. Or at least it would be wonderful if we weren't here.'

She nodded, wondering if he was only saying nice things to spare her feelings. 'I know. I'll be sent away, I don't know when, but I wanted you to know before someone realised, or before I have to tell anyone about my' – she hesitated – 'condition. I know they have rules about this.'

'We need to get married,' he said, his face more serious again, tone deeper. 'I will organise an army chaplain and we'll be married immediately. It's the only thing to do.'

'No. No!' she said. 'This is not how it was supposed to happen. It's not what I wanted.'

'You don't want to marry me?' he asked, eyebrows drawing together. 'Ellie, this is the right thing to do.'

She gripped his hand tighter, hating how matter-of-fact he was being. 'Of course I want to marry you,' she said. 'But not like this, because it's the *right* thing to do.'

'Ellie, I was never going to let you go,' he said, leaning forward, stroking her face with the back of his fingers, sounding more like himself again and less like he was reading from a script with the right words to say. 'I was going to wait, make sure we survived this wretched place, and ask you to marry me when we returned home. But what does it matter when? You're the best thing to happen to me during this war.' He cleared his throat. 'Heck, you're the best thing to happen in my life, Ellie.'

She held on tight, hearing his words, wanting to believe that he'd honestly want to marry her if they hadn't got a baby on the way. 'Truly?' she asked.

'Truly.' He kept hold of her hand as he lowered, bending to one knee. 'And that was no way for me to propose before.' Spencer cleared his throat. 'Ellie, will you do me the honour of becoming my wife?'

She burst into tears, frantically wiping them away. 'Yes. Yes, Spencer, I will. Of course I will.'

'We'll be married tomorrow, or as soon as can be arranged. Then we'll find out how to send you home,' he said, dropping a kiss into her hair as she fell against him, exhausted and still feeling sick. 'I'll write to my mother. She'll await your arrival in London, and you'll have somewhere to stay and be looked after until I return.'

Ellie froze. 'Your mother?' she mumbled against him. She'd imagined herself going back to her own home, to her own family.

'We can discuss the arrangements later,' he said, brushing hair from her eyes as she looked up at him. 'My mother will adore you, and you'll be safe and cared for with her. She can arrange anything you need, I promise.' He grinned at her, looking more boy than man in that moment. 'I've told her all about you, Ellie. Don't look so surprised.'

She touched his shoulder, wished it was the two of them somewhere private instead of here. Anywhere but here.

'We're moving at the end of the week,' she said. 'We can't possibly do it then.' In a few days' time they were supposed to start packing up. They'd been told they would be working in a proper building this time, rather than under canvas, which would make a nice change.

They'd already moved camp once, from their casualty clearance station to their field hospital, when the Allies had advanced further into France, and now they were moving again to be of more help. They were going to stop admitting new patients before the end of the day, which meant she had a long shift ahead of preparing patients to move to other hospitals. The army trucks would start arriving, patients would start being moved, and then somehow everything would be packed up and relocated within hours at the new site for them to be up and running, admitting patients immediately upon set-up. She could hardly stand the thought of what was ahead of them, just when things had become less frantic.

Once she finished her Thursday shift, it would be a short rest before they started packing up, getting everything prepared for the orderlies to travel with all the equipment. Her stomach wasn't likely to help her, and she hated the thought of vomiting around others, of not having any privacy. She could only imagine the gossip amongst the other nurses when they put two and two together, if they saw her being sick ahead of her wedding.

'Ellie, my love, everything is going to be fine,' Spencer told her, echoing what Scarlet had said only moments earlier as they'd walked in. 'This baby, it's a blessing, not a burden. One day, when we're old and sitting in our rocking chairs, we'll look back and smile about my hasty proposal. I promise. You're not to worry about what anyone else thinks, either, because this has happened countless times at hospitals everywhere.'

They were sweet words, but they weren't enough to stop her from worrying.

'I had better get to work before Matron comes looking for me and gives me a telling-off,' Ellie murmured, lifting her face to look at Spencer.

'We wouldn't want that now, would we?' Spencer chuckled and kissed the back of her hand, before leaving her.

She was to be married. She was having a baby.

The war didn't look as if it was going to be over any time soon, and yet here she was with another life growing inside of her. Ellie placed a hand flat to her stomach, took in a few deep breaths, before heading out to do her job. She only hoped she could keep what little was left in her stomach down for the entirety of her shift.

The others were going to bathe in the river later, or so they'd planned, despite the freezing cold. She'd do anything to freshen up, although the way she was feeling, she might be better off sitting it out and being the lookout for snipers.

For some reason, the nausea Ellie had been feeling didn't have its usual hold over her as she stood and waited for Spencer. She was so nervous, ridiculously nervous, about what was about to happen, but later that day they were moving to a new camp. Before then, she was to be married. Her hands were shaking, and even with Scarlet and Lucy to keep her calm, she was a nervous wreck.

'You look beautiful,' Scarlet said, looking so excited even though all that was about to happen was a hurried set of vows being recited before an army chaplain.

Ellie looked down at her dress. For the first time since she'd arrived, she was wearing something other than her battledress uniform. It was simple, but it made her feel beautiful, even if she was freezing cold.

'I can't believe you found this for me,' she said. 'Thank you. A hundred times over.'

'You were lucky there was another nurse who'd needed one before you,' Scarlet said, reaching out to stroke the fabric. 'Makes me miss all my lovely dresses back home all the more.'

It was made from parachute silk, and even though it wasn't much, Ellie felt special. She hoped Spencer would like it, and that this was how he'd remember her once she was gone. The next time he saw her, she could be as huge as a house. Ellie shuddered, another thought crossing her mind: or she might not be. She might already have a baby in her arms, a child that had grown up without a father for years. There was such uncertainty; she had no idea at all.

'I still don't know when I'm to go home,' Ellie said, looking for Spencer.

'You'll find out soon. Don't spend time worrying about it,' Scarlet said, always full of practical advice. 'Focus on you and Spencer and how lovely this will all be for you once the war is over.'

Spencer appeared from behind one of the tents, his smile wide when he saw her. It was all so wrong, not at all what she'd imagined for her wedding day, but she was going to be with Spencer, and that was all she could think about.

'Matron told me I have to go around sniffing wounds for gangrene after this,' Lucy muttered. 'Punishment, I'm sure, for taking an hour off.'

Ellie ignored the chatter between Lucy and Scarlet, watching Spencer, hands extended when he reached her.

'You look beautiful,' he said, pressing a warm kiss to her cheek. 'Absolutely beautiful.' Spencer held her out at arm's length, admiration in his gaze. 'I'm the luckiest man here.'

'You do realise you're supposed to wait until after you're married to kiss the bride?' Lucy quipped.

'Hey, it's my wedding day,' Ellie joked, laughing back at her over her shoulder. 'The man can kiss me if he wants!'

They were to meet the chaplain in the open, outside one of the tents, and Ellie was praying it didn't rain. All they needed were a few moments, the two of them standing together, supported by Scarlet and Lucy, and the officer standing before them. Then perhaps being pregnant wouldn't seem so scary.

As they neared the spot, her hand still locked in Spencer's, she saw a man in uniform rushing out of a tent. She knew instantly that it was the officer charged with marrying them, and her heart started to beat that little bit faster, her mouth dry.

'Doctor Black, over here,' the officer called. 'We need to hurry this along.'

Ellie glanced at Lucy and Scarlet one last time, before stepping up with Spencer and preparing to say the vows that would change her life for ever. They stood in front of the officer, with his straight back and immaculately trimmed moustache. It always amused her that, despite all the atrocities, the perfect keeping of one's moustache and hair was so important.

'The vows you are about to take are to be made in the presence of God, who is the judge of all and knows the secrets of your hearts; therefore, if either of you knows a reason why you may not lawfully marry, you must declare it now.' The officer cleared his throat and Ellie looked up at Spencer. Less than two days ago she'd told him she was expecting, and now here they were, about to become man and wife.

Ellie gripped Spencer's hands even tighter, nervous for no good reason. The officer recited words she'd heard so many times before at other weddings, and as she answered she gazed into Spencer's eyes. And then it was their turn to repeat their vows.

She listened while the officer said a short prayer, holding hands with Spencer still. She glanced beneath hooded lashes over to where her friends stood, side by side with their heads bent. Then suddenly it was Spencer's turn to say his vows and she had a lump in her throat simply listening to him. Then it was her turn, and the words were so hard to force out even though she'd been practising them in her mind all night.

'I, Ellie O'Sullivan, take thee, Spencer Black, to be my wedded husband, to have and to hold from this day forward.' She took a breath, slowing down, smiling. 'For better or worse, for richer or poorer, in sickness and in health; to love, cherish and obey, till death do us part, according to God's holy ordinance. And thereto I plight thee my troth.'

They made their way through the ring ceremony, and when Ellie held out her finger, Spencer whispered to her, 'When all this is over and we're back in London, I promise I'll have something nicer for you.'

She shook her head, not caring what he was giving her. She hadn't expected a ring at all, given the short time since Spencer had proposed.

'I convinced an engineer to make it for me. It's gold from my watch.'

Ellie clapped her hand over her mouth. 'You melted your watch to make me a ring?' He couldn't have, could he?

'I got him to make one for me, too, so it wasn't all for you,' he said teasingly.

If she hadn't been sure about marrying Spencer hurriedly before, she certainly was now. She doubted she'd ever meet a better man in all her life. As the final words of the ceremony were said, there was only one sentence Ellie was waiting for.

'I pronounce that they be man and wife. In Jesus's name, amen.'

Ellie let out a little squeal as Spencer leaned forward to press a kiss to her lips. She looped her arms around his neck and sighed into his mouth when he pulled back, drawing him back in for another, longer kiss. She could hear Lucy and Scarlet clapping and when they finally pulled apart, Ellie blushed as the officer stepped back and cleared his throat. She couldn't believe that they were actually married.

'I apologise to you both that you won't be having a honeymoon at this time; the moving of our camps and the limited personnel means it is not possible to grant you leave,' Captain Grant said. 'However, I understand that provision is being made for you to depart for home at the next opportunity?'

Ellie nodded, her body going numb, goose pimples covering every inch of her skin. 'Yes, that is right.' She presumed he knew that she was expecting.

'God bless you both, and I wish you a safe passage home,' he said, before turning sharply on his heel and beginning to walk away. 'There will be a great need for trained, capable nurses back in London,' he called back.

Safe passage home. Ellie had been so worried about the baby and Spencer that she hadn't even thought about the forthcoming voyage. It had been bad enough coming over, but . . .

'What if I don't make it?' she whispered, her bottom lip trembling.

'You'll make it home just fine,' Spencer said firmly. 'Now, come with me. I'll be damned if we're not at least going into town for a decent cup of coffee to celebrate.'

Scarlet and Lucy waved their goodbyes and hurried back to the hospital to check on their patients, doing their final rounds on those that were yet to be transported.

'Come along, wife,' Spencer teased, once they had gone, catching Ellie's chin in his fingers and tilting her face up, dropping a soft kiss to her lips.

Ellie kissed him back, his words soothing her, making everything else leave her mind. 'I like the sound of that, *husband.*'

They both laughed, then she picked up the hem of her dress so it didn't get muddy and they went off in search of a ride to town.

CHAPTER EIGHTEEN

Scarlet

There was a knot of fear in her stomach that Scarlet had never felt before. She wasn't sure if it was the fact that she was about to leave what she knew, or that she might actually find Thomas. All she'd ever wanted was to find her fiancé, it was the very reason she was here, and now it terrified her. She knew in her heart that it was because of James, that he'd changed something inside of her. She still loved Thomas, fiercely, and she would give anything to find him and take him home to his family, but her heart was pulling her towards James, making it impossible not to think about him. Sometimes she wondered if she thought of anything else at night, when it was quiet and dark and she was lost to her own thoughts.

'I can't believe it's really time for me to go,' Ellie said, tears in her eyes as she enveloped Scarlet in a big hug.

Scarlet snapped out of her daydream and hugged Ellie back. Her friend was leaving, and come morning she and Spencer would have left, too. Everything was changing, and she had a feeling nothing would ever be the same again. Normandy might have been dreadful in so many ways, but they'd been a team. She'd spent the past months glued to Ellie, sleeping side by side, working side by side, sharing everything together, and then Lucy had come along and become part of their little unit, a friend she'd never forget. She'd been so cool and capable, as if she didn't need them, but in the end Scarlet had become as close to her as she had to Ellie.

'Tell me exactly when you're embarking,' Scarlet asked, wanting to know all the details, not ready to let Ellie go even though she knew it was the right thing. 'Surely there must be some additional supplies you need to take with you.'

Ellie's smile was sweet, tears still filling her eyes. 'Stop worrying about me. I'll be absolutely fine. It's you lot staying behind I'm worried about.'

Scarlet touched her arm, knowing she needed to give Spencer and Ellie a moment alone but needing to say one last thing to her friend before she left. She kept wondering if this was the last time they'd see one another again – if this was it. Ellie might not make it home; she herself could be killed working, or on her own way home one day.

'I promise I'll keep your letter for you. Until this blasted war is over,' Scarlet said in a low voice. It didn't matter who heard; it wasn't so much a secret as something that for some reason felt private between them.

'Thank you.' Ellie pressed a quick kiss to her cheek and gave her a hug. 'I'm pleased you'll have something of mine tucked against your body every day. It'll be a little bit of me still here with you.'

Scarlet hugged her back, not wanting to let go. 'You'll keep mine? In case of the worst?' she asked.

Ellie squeezed her one last time then stepped back. 'Of course I will. I will keep it safe until the day you come looking for me. I'll only give it back to you in person, so you'd better find me!'

'I promise,' Scarlet said, biting her bottom lip, not wanting to cry.

'I'll have tea and scones waiting,' Ellie said, 'or dinner bubbling away in a pot. Either way we'll be drinking something and eating something even better. I can't wait.'

Scarlet hoped that was true, that she could look forward to it over the months or maybe even years ahead. She longed for the day they could give their letters back, for neither of them to have to make the pilgrimage to one another's families, to deliver the worst kind of message.

'Stay strong and look after that baby,' Scarlet said.

Ellie gave her a sweet little wave and Scarlet started to walk backwards, ready to give her some space and say her goodbyes to her new husband. Whoever would have thought that Ellie would be married to the doctor she'd bumped into in a hallway at their first lodgings, and expecting his baby? Certainly not her, but Scarlet was happy for her. If anyone deserved some happiness, it was Ellie. She had changed a lot from that girl she'd first met, had matured from a girl full of energy and optimism to a more mature woman. She was still Ellie, but they'd endured a lot, and Scarlet only hoped it had made her stronger in the end, even though she'd been so close to breaking.

Scarlet watched as Lucy spoke to Ellie and hugged her, and then they were both trudging back to the hospital. Saying goodbye was always hard, but this was tougher, especially after they'd both been through some hard times with Ellie, when they'd both wondered if she would pull through after being so traumatised by what she'd been seeing and doing.

'I still can't believe she's pregnant,' Lucy said as Scarlet turned back to give Ellie one last wave. 'Imagine what they must have been up to that afternoon we left them in town!' she quipped.

Scarlet laughed – it was impossible not to – but she didn't exactly want to think about what Ellie and Spencer had been doing. 'Well, the poor lovebirds didn't get a lot of private time for starters, and other than that I don't want to think about it.'

'You've got to admit that it's pretty funny, though, right? I mean—'

'La-la-la-la-la,' Scarlet started to sing loudly, elbowing Lucy in the side. She wasn't used to talking about intimate matters, and she wasn't about to start, no matter how much more worldly she was now than before she'd begun nursing.

Lucy poked her tongue out and they walked back into the hospital. It was going to be another long day, that was always a given, only today would end with her climbing into an army truck and heading off on an adventure that could mean finding Thomas. Her doubts were mounting. It was almost impossible to believe that after all this time it could be him.

She'd only just started to do her rounds, checking her patients, sniffing for gangrene and checking for fevers, when a hand closed on her shoulder. A strong, masculine hand that made her turn.

'Scarlet.'

Scarlet turned and stared into the sombre face of Spencer, his eyes sad, mouth bracketed by a frown. She knew it must have been hard for him saying goodbye to Ellie, knowing she was carrying their unborn child, too.

'I didn't want to worry Ellie unnecessarily by mentioning this before, but we're leaving pronto,' he said. 'Gather your things and be ready to depart in an hour.'

Scarlet stared up at him, incredulous, certain he was mistaken. 'An hour from *now*?' But she still had all her rounds to do. She had thought they weren't leaving until after her shift.

He nodded, looking weary as he stood before her, arms folded.

'But my rounds, my patients, I will need to tell Matron and . . .'

'Everything is organised, Scarlet,' he said. 'Gather your things; meet me at the commanding officer's tent in an hour, and then we'll both be briefed before departure.'

Scarlet was certain her knees were actually knocking together, legs most definitely beginning to shake. She bit down hard on her lower lip. She felt incredibly anxious. Maybe she didn't even want to find Thomas.

'Yes, Doctor,' she said, slowly stepping back from the patient's bed she'd been hovering beside. She took a slow, shaky breath and looked around, wondering when she'd be back and how different everything might be once she was.

By nightfall, she might know whether Thomas was dead or alive.

It had been only hours since she'd said goodbye to Ellie, but it already felt like days. The soldiers she was travelling with had been pleasant enough, much like the lovely men she was used to treating, but being the only woman amongst a group of men wasn't something she would have volunteered for. They'd already had a convenience stop once, and while they couldn't have cared less about relieving themselves around others, she had been red-faced and horribly embarrassed. They wouldn't let her go far from their sight, and knowing they were so close had been awful, but they were being careful with her safety. They had to be.

But Spencer was his usual friendly self despite everything, and she was comforted by the fact that he was travelling with her. She doubted she could have gone without him, even if the soldiers had been friendly enough. Spencer was in love with her best friend, and she trusted him like she would have trusted a brother; she had no doubt that he'd protect her and demand that she be treated respectfully if he needed to.

'Do you know how long the trip will take?' Scarlet asked, clearing her throat and speaking up in a moment of silence between the men. They hadn't told her why they'd left ahead of schedule, but she could only imagine it had something to do with their safety. She'd been told not to ask questions.

'It'll be a while longer yet,' one of the men said, glancing across at her. 'I suggest you get some sleep.'

She was exhausted, but the road was bumpy, the truck uncomfortable, and she doubted she'd be getting any sleep any time soon. Her imagination was running wild, too, thinking about what they might find, whether they'd see Thomas, what he would be like. She didn't know how she felt, other than that she wanted to get him home, to do her duty by him in that respect.

'Would you mind explaining to me how these soldiers ended up at the convent?' she asked, speaking loudly over the noise of the truck. 'I understand they were taken in by the nuns and kept safe there, but do we know what actually happened? I've been told more than one plane might have been lost in the area.'

The soldier driving answered her questions, calling back to her.

'There were two planes shot down, and we believe that before the soldiers could be taken by the enemy, some brave locals helped to save them. They were taken to a convent, but we don't know if any of those men are still alive or not.'

Spencer spoke up then. 'Scarlet, all we know is that there were soldiers taken to safety. We do not know how badly injured they were, whether any of them could have survived even,' he explained. 'The only thing we know for certain is that local intelligence has confirmed that some of them were alive following their planes being shot down, which is a miracle in itself.'

'So we could arrive there and find they are all dead?' she asked, hardly able to believe what she was saying.

'Yes, ma'am, that's right,' one of the soldiers answered.

Scarlet did shut her eyes then, because all the hopes she'd had, the scenes she'd imagined, might be so far from the truth that they were impossible. Thomas might be there, or he might not. He might have survived; he might be dead. He might be injured, he could be a prisoner of war, or he might have perished when his plane was shot down – a fiery ball of metal in the air that he didn't have a hope of surviving. But some soldiers had survived at least the initial crash, and there was no reason why one of them couldn't have been Thomas.

She listened to Spencer talking, wished she knew him well enough to reach for his hand and hold it, but instead she folded her hands in her lap and squeezed her eyes shut even tighter, hoping sleep would wrap its arms of slumber around her.

'Oh hell!'

Scarlet's eyes snapped open as the soldier cursed, Spencer's arm thrusting in front of her as her body rose off her seat. She was thrown violently upwards, her head hitting something hard, something . . . She groaned, as everything started to go bright colours – every colour of the rainbow splashing through her vision.

'Scarlet?'

She reached up, a swirl of blackness taking hold.

'Damn it! Scarlet!'

The voice made her smile. She recognised that voice.

'James?' she whispered, smiling, feeling the change in her lips as she slowly became more aware of her surroundings. 'James!' she gasped.

'Scarlet?' the voice said again. 'Who's James?'

She blinked, reached for the face hovering in front of her. 'James?'

'We need to keep moving!' someone yelled.

'She'll be fine, I've got her,' the man's voice said again as her eyes began to focus, the pounding in her head almost unbearable. 'Scarlet, it's Spencer.'

She groaned and let him help pull her up.

'What happened?'

'We hit something in the road,' he muttered. 'Who's James?'

Scarlet swallowed, wrapped her arms tight around herself. 'Ah, sorry?'

'You were asking for someone called James?'

She went to shake her head then groaned. 'I don't know what you're talking about,' she lied.

Scarlet hated that it was James her thoughts always turned to, and not Thomas.

'Go to sleep. Once we're there I'll look you over more thoroughly, but for now I can at least see there's no blood.'

Scarlet huddled down, hugging herself to try to stay warm. *Thomas*, she told herself. *Thomas*. She was supposed to be thinking about Thomas.

By the time she woke, roused by the bumping of the truck beneath her and Spencer calling her name, the sky was black and her neck was sore from the position it had been locked in. She had no idea how long she'd been out, from when she'd first thought she'd never fall asleep to obviously falling into a deep slumber.

'We're here?' she croaked, straightening and staring out of the window into blackness. She glanced at her wristwatch and saw that they'd been travelling for hours.

'Yes,' Spencer said, looking weary as he rubbed a hand over his stubbly chin and then pressed the back of his knuckles into his eyes. 'Once the area has been secured, we'll head straight in and make our assessments.'

Scarlet nodded, her mouth feeling like even more cotton wool had been stuffed in than it had when she'd woken up moments earlier, her head still throbbing. This was it. This was the moment when she actually might find Thomas – the man she was engaged to, the man she'd been waiting almost two years now to even lay eyes upon again. The man whom she almost hoped she wasn't about to find.

'Is our plan still to evaluate the patients based on their injuries first, identify whether any need immediate evacuation, and then to look at those that are less injured?' she asked.

Spencer managed a smile and for some reason it helped to relax her, settled the caged butterflies beating their wings in her belly.

'Yes, pretty much. If you recognise him, if one of these men is your Thomas' – he nodded at her, as if wanting her to do the same to acknowledge what he was saying – 'you don't freeze, you keep going, you do your job, then you can fall apart after our work is done.'

The soldiers had started talking, doors were opened, commands were issued and Scarlet sat and waited, completely immobile as the soldiers who'd been in the same vehicle as her for hours disappeared into the inky blackness outside. She focused on her breath, the silent inhale and exhale as her lungs worked.

'I'm thinking about Ellie,' Spencer said quietly, his voice barely more than a whisper. 'I know what it feels like to have that kind of pain in your chest.'

Scarlet didn't care how well she did or didn't know Spencer now, or the fact that he was her superior; she slid her hand across the seat and touched her fingers to his, clutching them as they sat side by side, both staring straight ahead. His fingers locked around hers, too, until there was a sudden bang on the window that made her jump.

'It's time,' he said, releasing his grasp and pushing open his door. 'Oh, and Scarlet, I took a good look at your head while you were sleeping. There's a bump, but I'm sure it'll simply be a headache and nothing more.'

Scarlet touched the side of her head and waited, watched as he moved, and then followed him out, a soldier reaching for her in the dark and taking her hand, helping her jump down and catching her before she hit the dirt.

'Is it grim in there?' she asked, terrified of what they might find.

'No,' the soldier said, letting her take his arm so she didn't stumble in the dark. She felt fortunate they were all such gentlemen. 'There's only two of the men in there.'

Scarlet's heart sank, a roaring sound in her ears that made it impossible to hear anything else. She opened her mouth to say something, anything, but any words there died in her throat.

Only two of them in there. There was no chance Thomas could be one of those two, not with odds that bad.

There were lights on in the convent, the small stone building untouched by war. Any soldiers who'd been kept there were lucky to have been so far from the fighting, so far from everything that was terrifying.

Spencer walked up the steps ahead of her with the soldier who'd been driving, the others posted outside, guns slung across their chests, held loosely in their arms. It settled Scarlet, their relaxed stance, the cigarette hanging from one of their mouths as if there were nothing in the world to worry about here.

Her feet were like lead, her movements slow as she followed behind the others, finally walking through a door held open by an elderly woman in a habit. Her smile was kind, her hand reaching for her. Scarlet took it immediately, holding on tight, needing to draw strength from someone.

'We didn't think we would have soldiers here looking for these men until the war ended,' the nun said, her expression kind as she led them through the entrance. The flickering of candles catching Scarlet's eye. It was as cold in the hall as it was outside, her breath billowing like frost before her, but the room they walked into had a fireplace going, with at least five candles burning for light. 'We'll miss the company once they've gone.'

She could imagine Ellie laughing and teasing that nuns shouldn't be enjoying the company of strange men so much, but her gaze was locked on the two chairs in the room. Needing to see. Wanting to see if one of them was Thomas.

Spencer was striding ahead, his black bag in hand, full of whatever he might need to help these soldiers.

'How long have they been here?' Scarlet asked, her footsteps slow, knowing she wasn't supposed to freeze.

'Months, my dear. Months and months,' the kindly nun said. 'There were five of them here, but the first three passed away even after everything we tried to do for them. They were so badly injured, but . . .'

'Where are they?' a deep voice asked, one of the soldiers'.

'Buried,' the nun said, her voice matter-of-fact. 'We prayed for them and buried them, as we would have anyone's loved ones. They were given all the love and care we could, and then when it was time to let them go, we were there to hold them.'

Scarlet was still listening, the soothing voice of the older woman like a lullaby that kept her moving. Spencer's eyes met hers; she knew she was supposed to be at his side, doing her job, but she was holding her breath, unable to focus.

The first soldier had light, sandy-coloured hair, and the side of his face was covered in old burns, healed, but still bad enough to make her gasp. His arm was in a sling, but he didn't look too bad, the worst of his injuries obviously healed, or at least from what she could see. But he was asleep, his mouth slightly parted, his body slumped.

'This man is doing well?' Spencer asked.

'Very,' the nurse said. 'It's the other man we've had more trouble with.'

Scarlet turned, slowly, her feet swivelling on the spot as she turned to the other chair positioned slightly further from the fire. She hadn't been able to see him in the shadows and she moved closer. The thick dark hair caught her eye instantly, the dark brown, almost black eyes that met hers – haunted, troubled, almost dead.

The room spun, her face was on fire, she opened her mouth but nothing came out . . .

Scarlet looked back at Spencer, which only made the spinning worse, the dizziness making her stumble as she tried to turn again to the soldier, trying so hard not to fall, not to faint right there on the mat in front of the burning embers of the fire.

'*Scarlet?*'

CHAPTER NINETEEN

Lucy

It had only been two days since Ellie had left and Scarlet had headed off in search of the missing soldiers with Spencer, but for Lucy it had felt like a lifetime. The days had been long, sending off all the remaining patients, and she'd had mixed feelings about saying goodbye to their field hospital. But she'd moved hospitals before and she knew that before long they'd be settled into their new location and busy again with more casualties. If her heart wouldn't stop thumping away like mad as she fretted about her friends, she'd be fine. So much for not getting attached to anyone! Jack had broken her heart and her friends were gone, and she hated it.

The orderlies had already left with the equipment, so by the time she reached their new location the hospital would be set up again within hours. It was amazing how quickly they could leave one site and be operational in another.

'Did you hear that we'll be back wearing our scarlet uniform again?' Holly asked as she passed, bag in hand.

Lucy lifted her own and followed the other nurse out. 'I know. It'll be nice to be in a more fixed hospital,' she said. 'Can't say I'll miss working under canvas.'

'Any word on Scarlet and Doctor Black?' Holly asked.

Lucy shook her head. 'Nothing as yet. I'm hoping they'll be meeting us in Brussels, though, at our new hospital, all being well.'

They had a long trip ahead of them, and as she walked to the big covered army lorry with Holly, she wished she had Scarlet with her to chat to on the journey. The other nurses were all nice enough, but it was Scarlet whom she felt closest to. They were heading further from the front, which was in itself reassuring, and there had been murmurs of better living conditions, which she'd believe when she saw them with her own eyes.

'Come on, ladies, let's get a move on,' a soldier called out.

Lucy climbed up when it was her turn, gratefully taking the arm of an officer who was standing to help the nurses up into the truck. She settled in, knowing her bottom would be numb within the hour, and they'd be travelling for the better part of the day, hopefully arriving before nightfall, but perhaps not.

'Do you think we'll be home before Christmas?' Holly asked, her question taking Lucy by surprise.

'Honestly? I don't know,' Lucy said, as another nurse sat down beside her. 'Sometimes I wonder if we'll ever be going home. When's it all going to end?'

'Oh, don't talk like that. I need to believe I'll be home in time for my mother's Christmas cooking,' Holly scolded.

As the truck rumbled to life, juddering and jolting as they started off on their journey, Lucy shut her eyes and remembered what home was like. Her father's kind embrace, awkward but welcoming; her mother standing at the door, listening to her fail terribly at playing the piano, which always exasperated her mother and made Lucy giggle; the room she'd shared with her sister growing up, even though they could have had their own spaces had they wished. Her books, crammed into every inch of her bedroom shelves, her saviours when she felt like no one understood her.

Home was a memory she had to grasp hold of tight. Because if she didn't, she was afraid it might disappear from her mind for ever, and she needed to remember what she'd left behind.

'Did you hear there's no rationing in Brussels?' another nurse said excitedly. 'I've heard there's fresh vegetables, fruit and even champagne to drink there.'

'Champagne would be heavenly,' Holly chimed in. 'Can you honestly imagine how good it will taste after all that hideous Compo tea we've been drinking?'

'We're staying in an old coat-hanger factory,' another nurse said. 'I know it's true because I heard Matron talking and confirming all the details. We're actually going to be inside, two to a room. Imagine it!'

Lucy wasn't going to get her hopes up in case Brussels was even worse than everywhere else she had been. They might be safer there, but she wasn't going to start setting her heart on anything other than being thankful they were all still alive.

A nurse with a lovely voice started to sing then, a song that Lucy didn't recognise. Her voice carried through the lorry, and a few others joined in. Lucy was content listening as more women started to sing along, too. Then they started another song, one she knew straight away, and she opened her mouth to sing, but found the words wouldn't come out. Tears prickled her eyes, but she fought them, not about to let a little song make her get all silly and emotional.

Her mother had sung it, softly under her breath as she'd worked in the kitchen, and when Lucy closed her eyes she was back there, watching her mother and listening closely to hear her sing. They'd had help at home, but her mother took pride in everything that went on their table, and she'd always been in that kitchen cooking. Perhaps it was her mother's way of expressing herself; she'd been so guarded of her emotions, so strong and proper, but cooking was what she'd loved, and it was also the only time Lucy ever heard her mother sing. She forced herself to join in the second verse of *April Showers*, not content with listening without singing, too.

There was so much she missed, memories she refused to let close to the surface. Lucy wasn't sure what she was afraid of; maybe it was simply the fact that thinking of the past might make it too hard to put one foot in front of the other each day and keep going. When she'd left home, she'd thought her parents didn't care, that they hadn't shown her the love she'd craved and the support for her dreams that she'd needed. But in hindsight, maybe it had taken leaving to make her see what she'd missed.

But it didn't mean she didn't pray every single night for this war to be over. She wanted to go home, too. She wanted to laugh with friends and eat decent food. She wanted to make more memories with her family, to kiss her father's warm cheek and throw her arms around her mother. She wanted to talk to her sister and laugh about what it would be like one day to have their own children. She wanted to see her friends.

Lucy brushed tears from her cheeks as they dripped silently, wetting her skin and falling down to her mouth. Most of all, she wanted to believe that she'd see Jack again one day, too, even though she knew it was a silly dream to have. There was no way her American soldier would ever come looking for her. He was gone, a beautiful memory from her time nursing, and nothing more. He had his own life to remember and get back to. One day she'd forget about him, but with all the other awful things happening around her, for now she was going to hold him close and let herself dream of what could have been.

'Help!'

Lucy jolted awake, her head lifting from Holly's shoulder as she tried to figure out what was going on. There was some sort of commotion going on around them, but none of the nurses around her were bothering to get out and find out what was going on, or at least that's how it seemed.

'What's happening?' Lucy asked.

She looked around, but the other women were all shrugging and shaking their heads, with many of them still sleeping.

'We've been told to stay seated,' someone said.

'Something's going on out there, but Matron told us we were to stay put and wait it out. The officers didn't want to risk our safety,' Holly said in a hushed tone.

Lucy sat still, listened and tried to make out what was going on.

'Is it safe here?' someone muttered. 'I mean, aren't we in danger being immobile on the side of the road like this?'

Lucy stood, not able to sit a moment longer and not know what was going on. Curiosity always got the better of her, and she didn't like sitting helpless if there was something she could do to help a situation.

'Excuse me,' she murmured, making her way to the side of the lorry. They were under canvas to protect them from the elements, but it didn't take much for her to open the side and look out.

Lucy surveyed the situation, watched as soldiers from their lorry and the one ahead stood and talked. They were chatting like nothing much was going on, although a few of them were standing to attention, guns at the ready.

She climbed down, which was awkward without any assistance, but she managed to do it fine. She cleared her throat, not wanting to take the men unawares and be mistakenly shot in the process.

'Excuse me,' she said politely.

At least half a dozen uniformed soldiers turned at her and glared, their faces furious. She gulped, feeling as if she were shrinking before them as an officer pointed to the truck and barked at her.

'You were told not to move!' he shouted. 'Get back into the truck.'

But even as Lucy cowered at his loud voice and intimidating body language, she heard the muffled cries of a child. Her head turned, body snapping around with it. There were three children. She could only just see them. They were in the grass, far enough away that their screams were muffled, the wind carrying them to Lucy and forcing her to listen. Two were on the ground, sobbing, and a third was standing, crying out for help. Further away there were dead cattle in the fields, with the remains of a charred-black army vehicle haphazardly abandoned on the side of the road. Lucy dragged her eyes away from the vehicle, away from wondering whether soldiers had perished or whether their bodies were burnt to a crisp inside.

'Sir, those children! We need to help them,' she cried, spinning back to look at him.

She saw a coolness in his gaze that surprised her, saddened her. Surely they weren't all standing here looking and listening without doing anything?

'Get back in the truck,' he ordered.

'Are you honestly going to leave them there? Young children with no one to help them?' she pleaded, finding a strength that was coming in such strong waves she knew she wouldn't back down. 'Are we not here to assist the French people? Our allies?'

His expression was fuelled by anger now, and she knew it was most likely for her questioning his decision in front of the other men.

'Look here, *little lady*,' another soldier said, interrupting their conversation, maybe trying to defuse it. 'This place could be crawling with SS for all we know. We're checking the situation, making sure it's safe to proceed, then we'll be on our way.'

Soraya M. Lane

She understood safety, and making practical decisions, but she still disagreed with standing by and doing nothing when there were children involved. She wasn't going to stand for it; they could drag her kicking and screaming back to the lorry but she was going to make her point heard.

'Let me go to them,' she said.

'No,' barked the angry officer. 'You are to follow your orders and get back in the bloody truck!'

'Please,' she begged, glancing at the other soldier, hoping he might be more understanding. A handful of the men were staring at her now, or more like glaring. 'Those children could be injured, they need help, and it is my duty to offer it to them. Your men can stay here, but send me. I'm wearing the Red Cross armband; no German is going to shoot me in cold blood if I pose no threat.'

'They're bloody pigs those SS,' a soldier snarled. 'They'd shoot their own mothers.'

'This is the last time I'm going to tell you to get back in the vehicle.'

She took a big breath and flashed her sweetest smile. 'Please let me tend to them. I will be quick, and then it won't play on your mind for the rest of the day that you let small children bleed out in a field whilst you stood by and did nothing.' She paused. 'I will run over to them with a medical bag, tend to their injuries, and then come straight back.'

Lucy looked around. She knew the sensible thing would have been to get straight back in the truck, but that wasn't the type of person she was. She was a nurse and she knew how to save lives. If she'd stopped to ask questions before running to the burning ambulance, Jack would be dead. She preferred to listen to her instincts, and her instincts were screaming at her right now to do something to help the children calling so desperately for them.

'Sir, please,' she tried again.

'If you die out there, it'll be your own fault,' he said, voice gravelly. She wasn't sure if he wanted her to die or actually cared, but she wasn't about to stand around asking questions. 'We call you back? You listen

244

to instructions and follow orders. I'm not risking the life of a good soldier to save you.'

She understood, loud and clear. 'Yes, sir.' From what she could tell, he thought her life wasn't anywhere near as valuable as those of his soldiers, even though she was trained to save those very men should they need her.

'What are you waiting for?' he asked.

Lucy glanced over her shoulder, saw some of the nurses were now looking out from the truck, and she was pleased that none of them were trying to talk her out of what she was doing. Or maybe they actually had no idea what was even going on, which was highly likely.

'May I take my nursing supplies?' she asked.

'No.'

His voice was harsh, flat, and Lucy decided not to press him. She would walk calmly, slowly over to the children. Once there she could assess the situation, and then come back and beg for whatever she needed to assist them.

Lucy nodded and started moving. She focused on her breathing and putting one foot in front of the other.

'I'm coming,' she called out, trying to make her voice sound as warm and friendly as possible. '*Bonjour!*' She switched to French, her knowledge of the language limited, but she doubted young children living out here in the country would understand English.

'*Bonjour. Je m'appelle Lucy,*' she called out again, not wanting them to be scared of her.

'*S'il vous plaît. Aidez-nous!*' the eldest girl cried out.

Lucy understood her words, knew she was begging for help, and she hurried the rest of the way.

'I'm coming,' she called out. '*Oui.*'

Lucy was met by wide, tear-filled eyes when she finally reached the children. She dropped to her knees and gently touched the eldest girl, the one who'd called to her, on the shoulder.

Her gaze dropped to the first child lying on the ground. His leg was bleeding badly, the pain in his face heartbreaking for anyone to see. When she looked at him, his mouth open as he let out a sob, she blocked it all out; the noise, the metallic smell of blood, the gruesomeness of his wounded flesh. All she concentrated on was fixing him, assessing the situation, making a diagnosis. The doctors might be the highly trained and skilled ones, but she'd been making practical decisions and dealing with wounds since she'd arrived in Normandy that terrifying night on the beach, and she'd spent the better part of six months listening to everything the doctors around her had said. She was as capable as anyone when it came to wounds now.

Lucy looked at the bone protruding through flesh, checked to see if it was obviously broken, then she looked across at the older girl to tell her that she was going back for supplies. It was only then that she laid eyes upon the other child, another girl who had been sitting silently, almost invisible until now. Her blue eyes were brimming with unshed tears, hand to her side, pressed there tight as she stared back at Lucy.

'What's wrong?' Lucy asked, knowing something wasn't right, knowing she needed to stop and check over this child before she ran back to the truck. '*Qu'est-ce que le problème?*' she tried.

The child slowly took her hands from her side, parting her fingers and then pulling her palms away. Lucy gasped as crimson red spread like a fast-moving cloud across the girl's top, seeping out.

'No!' Lucy shouted, leaping forwards, stumbling as she frantically tried to reach her. How could anyone have gunned these children down like this? Injured them so terribly with no adults around to pose a threat? Or maybe there had been and they were dead.

'Pressure,' she said, unable to think of the French word for it. As she showed her what to do. 'Hold.'

She looked behind her at the older girl, nodded with her head, but the poor child looked terrified.

Lucy thrust one hand against the child's side and reached back for the other girl, grabbing her and tugging her forwards. She replaced her hand with the girl's, pushing hard, showing her what to do.

'Help!' Lucy screamed. 'We need help here!' Why were the soldiers not coming over? Why was no one helping her? Why did no one else care about these poor children, alone and so terribly injured?

'Wait,' she said, nodding at the children. 'I will come back. I promise.'

Lucy stood, glanced at her bloodstained hands for a moment before turning back to the army trucks. They were watching her, the soldiers standing there, the lorries in the background. She opened her mouth to yell at them, to scream that she needed more hands, that they needed to get these children out of here to safety.

She lifted one foot, about to move, wondering who had done this, whether there were SS soldiers close by or . . . Lucy stopped. She watched as one of the soldiers lifted his gun. There was a yell and then all the soldiers suddenly had their rifles cocked. What were they doing? Were they about to shoot her?

Everything moved in slow motion then, from the rising of guns to the piercing scream behind her, a blur that made her feel as if she were watching everything unfold from above. Lucy dragged her eyes from the soldiers, head turning as she looked back. A feeling of dread washed through her – empty, silent blackness taking hold as everything paused around her.

The distinctive grey-green SS uniforms caught her eye first, the cruel expression of a soldier with his gun cocked at the children she'd just fought so desperately to save. The yells from her own soldiers behind her, her mouth open as she tried to scream and instead made no noise at all.

Burning heat burst through her body. The ground vomited dirt as it flew up to meet her, a blast echoing through her ears, throwing her off her feet, making her feel as if she was caught in the centre of a tornado.

'No!' she screamed, the word rocketing through her mind as everything blurred. Her neck was on fire, her arm burning. She looked down, expecting to see flames, expecting to be in an actual fire, the heat was so bad.

But she didn't see her arm. She saw blackness, blackness everywhere like a charred log from a fire, and bubbling flesh where her skin should have been. Lucy tried to sit up, tried to move, tried to speak, but nothing happened.

She forced her feet to move, clumsy, managing to rise on to all fours and move like a dog for a step or two until she fell to the ground, not even having the strength to raise her face from the dirt.

There was a loud ringing in her ears that was deafening. Lucy managed to roll over, just a little, her body heavy as lead, skin burning so hot she wanted to scream at the top of her lungs. But all she managed was a guttural groan as she lay, stagnant, one eye open, smoke and debris billowing around her.

She shut her eyes, trying to push away the pain, trying to remember what it was like back in London, imagined her mother's arms around her, whispering a song in her ear. She was in bed, a child, wrapped in a warm blanket, her mother's body a comforting weight beside her.

Twinkle, twinkle, little star, how I wonder what you are.

Lucy smiled up at her mother as everything else went dark. She was home. She was safe. She could close her eyes now.

CHAPTER TWENTY

Ellie

Ellie placed a hand flat on her stomach, looking down at it. There was nothing to see, but knowing that so much was changing within her was making her so curious, and touching it made her feel more content. It gave her the feeling that she might just be able to protect this baby, if she could only make it home safe, if she could arrive back in London in one piece, go to her family, and then meet Spencer's mother.

The thought of meeting her sent a shiver through Ellie that she found hard to ignore. Despite Spencer's constant reassurances, she doubted she would be good enough for his mother, given that her son was such a dashing young doctor, so well-spoken and obviously from a very good family. An Irish farm lass was most likely not what Mrs Black had expected for her boy, no matter what he'd told her to the contrary. But maybe she was used to Spencer being different. He always seemed to care so little about who he was treating or talking to. He cared about people, no matter who they were, and that was one of the reasons she'd been drawn to him. He was the kind of man she'd dreamt of, the type of man she wanted to make a life with once all this was over.

But for now, she had to simply survive the boat ride. She'd been told they should have a safe passage, that the most dangerous part was getting to the ship and boarding, but she wasn't so sure about how safe anything felt any more. If only her friends were with her to talk to, to pass the time and chat about what awaited them back home. Then again, she had to admit that she was grateful to be travelling home at all.

Ellie twirled the ring on her finger, smiled when she thought of the effort that Spencer must have gone to in order to have had it made at such short notice. It was simple, plain as plain could be, but it was hers and it reminded her every time she looked at it or felt its weight against her skin that she was married. To Spencer. She had only to hope that Spencer would make it home from France to meet his little baby.

Ellie stretched and then made her way from the quarters where she was staying with the other nurses, some on leave and others being transferred back to England, back to the hospital area. It didn't seem to matter that she was pregnant; they were desperate for nurses on board and she was more than happy to do her bit. There was something less daunting about nursing in this way; perhaps she felt safer, or less connected to the immediacy of war. The daily terror of dying had drained so much of her confidence and happiness, but now, heading for home, she could feel more of her old self slowly coming back. Their job was to assist the wounded and care for them, tend to their wounds and make sure their journey was as comfortable as possible, and she liked not having the worry of patching them up only to have them sent back to the front.

'Nurse, can you assist here please?'

She smiled to herself. Perhaps even the doctors were feeling more at ease on board, for it had been a long time since she'd heard anyone superior to her say the word 'please' in the same sentence as 'nurse'.

'What can I do for you?' she asked.

Ellie looked down at the man on the bed closest to her and fought the urge not to retch. The poor soldier was covered in the most terrible burns. She wondered why he'd been earmarked for sea travel instead of an emergency air evacuation.

Taking a deep breath and smiling, not wanting to scare the poor young soldier further, she touched his hand, the one part of him poking out that was miraculously unscathed. 'Would you like me to assist in the bandage changes?'

'Yes. I'll need his dressings changed regularly. Once you're done here, I'd like you on my service to assist with some of the other burns victims, changing dressings first and then overseeing their meals.'

Ellie nodded, feeling nauseous. The baby and the moving of the ship had been bad enough, but preparing to change the dressings of a severely burnt soldier, knowing how terribly he'd start to scream once she started, was unbearable. Perhaps her job hadn't got better after all.

'This is going to hurt, I'm so sorry,' she told him, still holding his hand.

The soldier nodded and she turned to gather what she needed from the nearby nurses' station. When she turned back, she noticed tears slipping silently down the soldier's cheeks, knowing what was coming, what pain he was about to endure. Ellie felt tears slide down her own cheeks, but she didn't stop what she was doing, kept preparing, not wanting to delay the inevitable. She told herself that it was fine to cry with him; all it did was show how much she cared, that she was sharing his pain. There was nothing wrong with compassion.

She'd have preferred to be fork-mashing his dinner and murmuring stories to him to pass the time, but that could come later.

'Here goes,' she muttered, using her forceps to slowly, painstakingly, remove the first of his old bandages as he started to scream.

CHAPTER TWENTY-ONE

Scarlet

Scarlet knew she should be crying. She should be wailing or sobbing or something other than what she was doing right now. Which was standing very, very still, body shaking, as she stared at the man she'd been waiting so long to find.

Thomas. It was actually Thomas.

'I never expected to hear your voice again.' His voice was lower, quieter than she remembered. 'Let alone see you here.'

Scarlet looked at Spencer. He was staring at her, not saying anything, and Scarlet knew she had to do something. Her body was so numb, her hands like lead at her sides as she tried but failed to lift them.

'Thomas?' she whispered. 'Thomas, it's truly you?'

He made a grunting noise and she forced her feet forward, dropping down in front of him and placing her head against his knees, arms around him. She wanted to be happy, she wanted to kiss him and squeal and be so, so happy to have found the fiancé that everybody else had presumed dead. She'd believed for so long, and now she was touching him, the man who by all accounts should be dead, and instead of being overjoyed, all she could think about was James. The brother she wished was in her arms right now. James, who was on his way back to London. James, who had whispered to her and kissed her and made her feel things she'd never in her lifetime forget.

'I can't believe I've found you,' Scarlet said – the only honest words that she could say out loud.

'Doctor, may I have a word?' The nun spoke to Spencer, but it gave Scarlet an excuse to pull away, to look back at Spencer and hope that her presence would be requested, too. But it wasn't. Spencer gave her a long look that she couldn't read, then disappeared.

Scarlet slowly turned back to Thomas, rose enough to shuffle sideways and move into the chair beside him. She held out her hand to him and when he didn't take it she reached for him, gently stroking his skin.

Thomas flinched. She saw it, but she didn't stop. She'd been nursing soldiers long enough to know that they didn't want people to act differently around them even though they felt so different within themselves.

'Thomas, I was so sure I'd find you,' Scarlet told him quietly. 'From the moment I knew we were being posted to France, I had this feeling that I would find you myself. Everything I've done, I did to find you.'

He stared at her, a half-smile on his face. He was so deeply troubled, she could see that, but he was still the same man she'd promised to marry, who she'd fallen in love with before waving him off and swearing that she'd always wait for him.

'When your letters stopped coming I feared you'd met someone else, that you'd fallen for a beautiful Frenchwoman, perhaps, but when your family told me it had been months since your last letter, and then being told you were missing . . .' Scarlet's voice cracked, all the strength that had been keeping her going, that had made her believe he was alive and to nurse through such tough conditions, seeping from her body.

'I'm so happy we've found you,' she said, blinking away her tears and clearing her husky throat. 'Your family will be so thrilled to know you're safe, that we'll be bringing you home.'

'No,' Thomas said, his voice as hostile as the glare he was giving her.

'Of course they'll be happy!' she insisted. 'I met your brother, I nursed him, and he's—'

'James?' Thomas choked on the word.

'James is alive,' she told him, squeezing his hand, hating that he tried to pull it away, flinching as if she'd hurt him. 'I met him by chance and we were both posted here. But he was injured, twice in fact, and he's been sent home now. Nothing he won't fully recover from, although he was shot pretty badly the second time.'

The snigger took Scarlet by surprise, the hate, or maybe it was pain, as it passed across Thomas's face, making her snatch her hand back and dig her nails hard into her palm.

'So he's not a cripple like me?' he sneered. 'Is that what you're trying to tell me?'

Thomas pulled back the blanket that had been covering him, showing the legs, the knees that Scarlet had embraced only moments before. They didn't move. She didn't ask him whether he could move them or not, they were covered by trousers, but given the way he'd spoken to her she doubted very much that he could. She discreetly sniffed the air, couldn't detect any obvious gangrene.

'You can't walk?' she asked gently.

'If I could bloody well walk I would have stood up when my fiancée walked into the room!' he barked.

Scarlet recoiled as if he'd slapped her across the cheek, his words as powerful as any punch. This was not the Thomas she'd fought for. This was not the man she'd promised to marry. Memories of him flooded her mind, reminded her of the man he was: good and steadfast, decent and kind.

'Thomas, we have excellent doctors on staff at our hospital and Doctor Black . . .'

The man who she'd once felt such deep love for, such desperation to find, started to sob before her. His body was shaking, heaving, crumpling over as he cried like a baby torn from its mother. Scarlet reached for him, didn't hesitate, couldn't do anything but be there for him. Before the war, she didn't recall ever seeing a man cry, never once, but since she'd been nursing she'd seen hundreds of men sob. Mourning the loss of friends or brothers, their limbs or sight, or simply crying with gratitude that they'd been saved. That they were going to be safe, perhaps even to be sent home, with food in their bellies and the warm hand of a nurse to hold when they were at their worst.

Scarlet wrapped her arms around Thomas and held him tight, letting him cry as she soothed him and made shushing sounds in his ear as she would to comfort a child. This was the last time she could think about James, romantically at least. Thomas was her fiancé. Thomas needed her. Thomas was her priority now, and she would do everything in her power to heal him and get him home, to be there for him and nurse him back to health. It was Thomas to whom she was promised, not James, and what had happened with James needed to be remembered as a wartime lapse of judgement and nothing more.

'What are you even doing here?' he muttered. 'Why are you nursing?'

She sighed. 'I'm doing my duty, just like everyone else.'

'Scarlet?'

She eased herself away from him, enough to lift her chin and look up at Spencer, who was saying her name from the other side of the room. She met his gaze and knew she had to step away from Thomas.

'We need to discuss something,' Spencer said, his smile tight.

Scarlet stood, pressed a quick, light kiss to Thomas's cheek and followed Spencer back out into the hall. 'He's not in a good way,' she blurted out before the doctor had a chance to speak. 'He doesn't seem like himself.'

'Scarlet. We've been advised to wait until morning, then we'll drive directly to Brussels to our new hospital there. They'll be well set up by then, and we can give your Thomas all the medical assistance he needs.'

She nodded, the only thing she felt truly capable of right now. 'You're not going to examine him now?'

Spencer's face was grim. 'I am, but from what I've been told he's in denial about his injuries, perhaps even about what happened in the first place. All we know is that he was dragged from the plane before it exploded, and somehow brought here safely. The fact he's still alive is a miracle.'

Scarlet didn't know what was wrong with him, what the extent of his injuries were, but the fact that his legs weren't working properly was terrifying. To her and certainly to him. But he was her responsibility, and whatever was wrong, whatever happened, she wasn't going to leave his side. She looked at him and felt only duty, a sense of helping a friend, but her feelings didn't matter. She'd made him a promise, and there was nothing more to it than that.

'So we stay here for the night?' she asked.

'Yes,' Spencer said, touching her shoulder. She was so pleased he was here with her, that she wasn't with any other doctor. 'I want to examine him alone, in privacy, man to man,' he said. 'I think that given the circumstances we can afford him that luxury.'

'Thank you,' Scarlet said.

'Now you go and take a bath. I've managed to negotiate hot water into our accommodation.'

Spencer said the words with a smile and she had to fight the urge to throw her arms around him. He had so much to worry about himself, yet here he was being so kind and not letting on to anyone his personal concerns. She caught a glimpse of the band around his finger, the ring that reminded her he was married to her friend making her feel somehow that Ellie was here with them.

'I can't say no to a bath now, can I?' she replied.

Spencer turned to go back into the room and Scarlet hated how easily she kept her back turned and went in search of the nun instead of returning to see Thomas. The possibility of submerging herself in a tub of warm water was a luxury like no other.

'Come,' the nun said, emerging from another room. 'I've drawn you a bath and I have some bread and butter for you.'

Scarlet was surprised at how good her English was as she followed behind the kindly woman. This woman had kept Thomas alive, nursed him and cared for him, fed him and most likely bathed him. And now she was taking care of her as a mother would a daughter. She tried to find the words to tell her thank you, wanted to say the right thing, searched her mind for the French words she knew that would make sense and not come out of her mouth a jumble. She failed.

'Thank you,' she mumbled instead, barely more than a whisper.

The nun turned, took her hand and looked into her eyes. 'You're welcome,' she replied, her words simple, but her gaze full of so much more.

Scarlet smiled as tears lined her lashes. If only they could stay safely tucked away in the convent for more than one short night.

The bath had been nothing short of heaven-sent. Scarlet had washed her hair, scrubbed her skin, lain still and let the water wash over her, submerged just deep enough to cover her body. It had been warm, and she'd been so desperate to get in that she'd eaten her bread in the bath instead of beforehand. If she hadn't been so desperately hungry she'd have waited until afterwards, but she was as famished for food as she was for being clean.

As she walked down the cold hall, shivering from her wet hair that she'd pinned back up tidily, she focused only on placing one foot in front of the other. Whatever she was about to face, whatever life she now had to walk into, she would keep her chin up. She had a lot to be thankful for, and she wasn't going to mourn the rest of her days for a man she had briefly fallen in love with, because what had happened with James couldn't happen again, no matter what love her heart was brimming to full with. She had to be dutiful. It was the only option.

Scarlet walked through the door at the same time as a plate was hurled from one side of the room to the other. She stopped, frozen mid-step. Spencer was standing in the middle of the room and Thomas was still seated, his arm raised from hurling the plate. She took a breath and forced herself to keep going.

'Goodness, that was a mighty good throw,' she said, walking straight over to Thomas and smiling down at him. It seemed the other soldier was still asleep, although she was certain the noise would have made him stir. 'Perhaps I should have made it clear that Doctor Black is a dear friend of mine. He's married to Ellie, a nurse I've worked alongside since London.'

Thomas stared up at her, his eyes empty, as if a light had gone out with no hope of it being switched back on.

'I want another doctor,' Thomas said flatly, looking away.

Scarlet turned her eyes to Spencer, saw nothing but kindness there and knew he must have been the bearer of bad news.

'Don't be silly,' Scarlet continued, wanting to keep talking for something to do, and hopefully to settle Thomas, to make him feel more like himself again, a connection to the past drawing him out of his shell. 'You were so very lucky to be rescued.'

'I'd be better off dead.'

Scarlet had heard those words a lot; they'd often echoed through her mind as she sterilised a bone saw in preparation for surgery, knowing she was about to assist in the amputation of a young man's leg or arm. Maybe two limbs. Then afterwards, once the doctors and the anaesthetist were gone, they were the words that filtered through her again as she cleaned up all the blood – blood that seemed to splatter everywhere, as if to remind her with every speck of what they'd taken from a man.

She'd talked soldiers through this before, and she was equipped to talk Thomas through it, too.

'If you were dead you wouldn't be able to marry me,' Scarlet said softly. 'I've come all this way, believed you were alive for so long, and now you're telling me that instead of looking forward to a life with me, you'd rather be dead?'

Thomas didn't look at her, but she continued anyway.

'Those men buried in the yard didn't get any choice, Thomas. Those soldiers who died would give anything to get another chance to be with their families, and yet here you are moaning about injuries that won't stop you from living. They certainly won't stop me from loving you.'

He still looked away, his gaze levelled on the fire, the embers still burning. She knew she was playing on his memories of the friends he'd lost, making him feel guilty for wishing for death instead of a life with her, but it was the only way she knew how to get through to him.

'Thomas, I need you to change your attitude. I need you to be strong and look forward to going home. To seeing your family again and celebrating the fact that you made it. That, against all odds, I found you.' She paused, lowering herself slowly into the seat beside him. 'I need you to see that for the miracle it is.'

Thomas finally turned to her, stared at her. 'Leave me,' he said coldly.

Scarlet opened her mouth to speak again, to reassure him. But the deathly stare he gave her made her press her lips together instead.

'Leave me!' he shouted.

She glanced at Spencer and then rose, refusing to cry or show any other emotion. His words were cold, cruel even, but he was battling demons that only he could face. If he didn't want her by his side, then there was nothing she could do about it other than do as he asked. One day she'd be pledging to obey him, so she may as well get some practice in now.

Spencer ushered her from the room and she held it together as best she could, refusing to give in to the torrent of unhappiness that was surging helpless inside of her.

'Scarlet, he's struggling, and it's easier to lash out at you than face what he's going through,' he told her. 'Most of the time the men we operate on – they don't get time to think about what's happened to them, haven't had time to dwell on their situation. We certainly don't even talk to them half the time about their amputations because we are coping as best we can with patient after patient, making fast decisions to save their lives.'

She knew that. It was what she'd been living day after day, week after week, month after month. Only she was the one talking to the patients and nursing them, wiping away their tears and mashing their food so they could swallow it. It was the nurses dealing with the soldiers when the doctors were gone, so she did understand what Thomas was going through.

'Have you examined him already?' she asked, weary as she stood in the cold, arms wrapped around herself.

'The plate-throwing was the aftermath,' Spencer said, rubbing his head as if it were sore.

'And?'

He shook his head. 'It's not good. There's no gangrene that I can detect, the nuns have been fastidious with their care, but my concern is that he may develop an infection and that his spine has suffered a terrible trauma. Most likely the impact from the crash. He has some movement, but not a lot, and it seems he's partially sighted in one eye now.' Spencer's shoulders rose then fell. 'Whether he will make a recovery from this and walks again is unknown. His legs haven't completely wasted away yet, but I will need to do a more thorough examination when we're at the hospital. The other patient is doing well, and with sufficient rest and medical attention should be able to return to active duty in the near future.'

Scarlet nodded. It was hard to believe that the other men they'd been with were dead, despite every effort being made to save their lives. It was equally a miracle that Thomas had survived the crash, let alone been taken to safety and then found by her. She'd been right to believe he'd survive.

She was ready for bed. She wanted to close her eyes, block everything out and think of nothing. But one thought kept circling her mind, one thing that she couldn't shake no matter how much she tried.

Thomas would have made it home even without her being here. Eventually. The war would one day be over and he would have been found or taken into town by the nuns. Which meant the outcome would have been the same for her whether she'd personally found him or not. She would still be engaged to him, she would still be expected to marry him, and she would still be having to forget all about James and every thought and dream she'd had since being with him that maybe, just maybe, they would end up together.

CHAPTER TWENTY-TWO

Lucy

Lucy heard yelling. Something was pulling at her leg, tugging her, trying to move her. She tried to look up, but she couldn't lift her head. The smell of smoke made her choke as it swirled around her, and as she tried to sit, tried so hard to move, blackness started to engulf her again.

The children. Where were the children? It was all she could remember; the children she'd been trying to save, the wound in the girl's side, the supplies she needed. The pain hit her, an intense burning that raged across her skin. Why was her skin on fire? Why was she so hot?

She could still feel pulling; was someone trying to lift her? Lucy raised her hand, touched something on her neck, something that was making her burn so bad. She touched something gooey, the pain intensifying, like sandpaper over her nerves.

It was her. Where was her skin? What was that?

She screamed, the noise rasping her throat.

The pain swirled, like a knife edge across every inch of her skin. She felt like she was bubbling, boiling from the outside in, and when she opened her mouth again nothing else came out.

'We're getting you out of here, love.'

The muffled voice soothed her, reassured her that she wasn't alone. Until the voice moved her, pulled at her again, and the scream that echoed from deep within her sounded more animal than human.

Lucy gasped for air, gulping frantically before everything slowly faded to black around her and breathing no longer seemed so important.

CHAPTER TWENTY-THREE

Scarlet

There had been moments at the convent and during their journey to Brussels that Scarlet had felt numb, but it was nothing to the numbness that had coursed through her body, through every vein and every inch of her, since she'd collapsed, puddling like water on the ground, when she'd been told that Lucy was gone.

She'd missed her by less than a day, and no one seemed to know if she was going to make it. She was being sent home by ambulance train, which by all accounts Thomas would be, too, depending on the outcome of his assessments. Instead of cherishing the fact that she was now working under a real roof, *sleeping* under a real roof, her heart was breaking open all over again. Lucy and Ellie meant everything to her, and now they were both gone. She needed them, and they needed her, and instead she had nobody. She'd already felt as if her heart had been ripped open, the pain so deep after finding Thomas – this new version of Thomas making it even harder – and she wanted her friends.

She touched her chest, feeling the tiny crinkle of paper there. It was the only thing that proved Ellie was real, that she hadn't imagined her. She only hoped that she'd be handing over the letter to her sooner than later, and not passing it to her parents. Scarlet gulped. Or Ellie passing her letter to her parents. But what of Lucy? Why hadn't they made her write a letter? Why had they seemed to think that because she was so strong and brave and capable, she was somehow not as mortal as they were?

Scarlet pulled herself together, changing her stance and straightening her shoulders. She had to put all her energy into Thomas. He was here and he was her responsibility, and he was the only person close to her that she had any power to help right now. She needed to be thankful for the small luxuries, the fact she wasn't starving hungry every moment of the day as she had become so used to. Or the fact that they were in a proper building and weren't trooping through mud into makeshift toilets, with a smell so foul she'd forever be able to recall it.

She turned around, and kept her chin up as she crossed the room. They weren't full of patients yet, and she made herself appreciate the small things in here, too, like the fact that the cold air wasn't lashing its cool grasp around her ankles as it had done when they were under canvas.

'Thomas,' she called out affectionately when she neared.

He gave her a half-smile that she took as a victory. 'The doctors think that time should heal me,' he said in a quiet voice. 'I don't need an . . .'

She finished his sentence for him, returning his firm grip when he grasped her hand. 'Amputation,' she said, voice shaky as she said the word for him. 'Thank goodness.'

She wondered if time would truly heal him, but she kept her thoughts to herself. She knew first-hand that doctors liked to keep morale up whenever they could.

'Your eye?' she asked, looking down at him and remembering how and why she'd fallen for him in the first place. He was handsome, undisputedly so, and even though he'd been cool and unpredictable since they'd been reunited, she knew it was the pain and fear talking. Beneath all that, he was the same man she'd desperately been searching for, the man she'd been so excited about marrying.

'I can still see you out of my good eye just fine,' he said, sounding more like the old Thomas for the first time, a hint of friendliness there instead of coldness. 'That will have to do.'

She stared down at him, feelings she'd long thought abandoned coming back in a rush. Maybe it truly was possible to love two men, even though she'd never have believed it before now. If she kept seeing glimpses of this Thomas, if she could keep drawing on her memories and reminding herself of all the reasons why she'd loved him, why he'd make a good husband . . .

'Scarlet, I've asked for an army chaplain to marry us at once,' Thomas said, coughing as he tried to pull himself more upright. 'I'm told you never gave up on finding me, and it's proper that we're married at once.'

Scarlet's heart started to pound. The whooshing of her blood flooded her ears.

'Pardon?' she asked, voice shaky as she forcibly expelled the word.

'I want us to be married at once,' he said. 'This war has taken everything from me already, but it seems the one thing it hasn't taken is you. And besides, when I left I expected you to stay at home with your family. I don't want you unmarried around so many men.'

'Would it matter so terribly? Surely after all this time you can trust in me and my decisions.' They were words that choked in her throat, but hearing him say that had made her blood boil!

'Scarlet, you're not made for this type of work. I'm surprised to see you here, and that your family allowed it. It would be improper for you to be unmarried and continue being in such close contact with all these soldiers.'

Unshed tears hugged her lashes as she tried to smile through them, pretending he wasn't hurting her, that his words made her feel so lowly when all this time she'd felt so empowered, in charge of her own destiny. So he wanted to marry her to make it clear she was his? It might have even seemed romantic to her once, but now it only made her sad. She was so much more than a girl waiting for a man now. She was a nurse, a capable, confident nurse who'd put status aside to work shoulder to shoulder with any nurse or doctor, to tend to any soldier regardless of his injuries.

'We're . . .' she stuttered, clearing her throat, pushing her thoughts aside, knowing he'd never understand. 'We're to be married immediately?' She must have heard him wrong. Surely she had heard him wrong. Convincing herself about her *fiancé* was one thing, but marrying him now? Before they even dealt with his injuries or returned home?

She didn't even let herself whisper the words inside her own mind, even though they were fighting to be let free, her thoughts drowning in her head.

Deep inside, in her heart, she was still torn. It broke her heart to think of James. But Thomas was her fiancé. Thomas was her intended. Which meant, if Thomas had indeed requested the army chaplain already, James would officially become her brother-in-law and nothing more. She'd known the time would come, but Thomas's words had still managed to hit her hard. Once she went home, who would care about what she'd done here? Her family would expect her to perform her function as a dutiful wife. No more, no less. She doubted they'd even believe how capable she'd been.

'Scarlet?'

She drew her shaking hands together, trying to stop the quiver before it took over her entire body. 'I'm sorry. It's all been such a shock, finding you and then hearing of my friend's terrible injuries and return to England.' It wasn't an excuse, her words were true, her explanation entirely accurate. But this man, this man lying on the bed, he seemed more a stranger than her fiancé right now.

'Then a wedding will cheer you up,' he said bluntly.

No kind words, no soft touch. The Thomas she remembered would have been more gracious, would have comforted her. Or maybe that was just the Thomas she'd created in her imagination, just like she'd never realised how cold her upbringing had been or how truly wonderful a man could make her feel. They had only spent a handful of days together – hazy, happy days with a smattering of stolen moments between them. In all truth, it was James she knew better, whose actions and emotions she had seen in the most trying of circumstances. He would have comforted her.

She patted Thomas's arm before turning to walk away, forcing her movements to be slow even though she wanted so desperately to run.

She was about to be married. With no family or friends present, just a man whom she'd been so desperate to find and who, right now, felt more of a stranger than half the soldiers whose wounds she'd tended to all these months.

Scarlet had already talked with her matron, and had had a strong feeling that Thomas would insist on a marriage, but not so soon as this. Now, she would be travelling home by sea with him, accompanying him back to England as his wife. He would never return to the front, which in itself was a godsend, and she'd already set the wheels in motion to transfer him to a London hospital. The news of the shortage of nurses was already making its way to them, and it seemed the country was grateful to have some highly trained nurses from the front return home. But instead of accompanying him in a military convoy to a hospital when they returned, then taking a few days' leave with her family before being given a new posting, she'd be married. Thomas's wife. Which meant she had no idea how things might change or what that would mean.

Or maybe she did and she just didn't want to accept it.

PART THREE

London

April, 1945

CHAPTER TWENTY-FOUR

Ellie

Ellie stood at the window, the curtain clutched between her fingers as she stared out into the dim light. Every time her baby moved it made her restless, not because she didn't enjoy feeling the little kicks and turns, but because it made her wish for Spencer all the more. Where was he now? In the hospital in Brussels still? Or somewhere more dangerous? The not knowing was what kept her awake long into the night, kept her tossing and turning, trying to get comfortable with her ever-growing bump. Now she realised how hard it must have been for her own parents when she left and was sent to another country.

'Come away from the window, my dear.'

She turned and let her hand drop from the fabric. Thank goodness for Lily. She'd been terrified of meeting her mother-in-law, and the prospect of staying with her had been beyond daunting. But from the moment she'd arrived Ellie had been drawn into her arms and treated like the daughter Lily had never had, and it had made her fall in love with Spencer even more. Because in that first moment, that first warm embrace, she'd seen him; in the attentive way Lily listened, the kindness, the understanding. Far from being the upper-class woman looking down her nose that Ellie had been expecting, Lily had been anything but. Spencer had a strong sense of social justice, and now she knew where it came from.

Lily gestured to the tea she'd placed on the low table. 'Did your mother ever laugh and tell you a watched pot never boils?'

Ellie rolled her eyes. 'Very funny. One of these days I'll be watching and he'll walk straight up that path.'

The both laughed. Theirs was an easy relationship, and given Spencer was her only son, Lily seemed comforted by the fact that his wife was with her, with all the happiness that a new baby brings.

'Are you missing your family terribly?' Lily asked, raising her cup and taking a small sip.

Ellie watched her, always watching, wanting to be as refined as the delicate Lily one day. She raised her teacup just as gently, taking a tiny sip. Every time she sipped real tea and not the ghastly brew they'd subsisted on in France, the flavour made her smile. In fact, it reminded her of drinking real coffee with Spencer that day in the village.

'I'm looking forward to going back to see them again soon,' she said, setting her cup down. 'But if you're asking whether I'm comfortable here, then the answer is yes.'

Her own mother was busy on the farm, working beside her father, and one of her brothers was at home convalescing and enjoying having their mother clucking over him. Had her mother been alone, then Ellie would have felt differently about leaving her so quickly to come back to London, especially after losing her brother, Connor. She blinked away tears as she thought about her lovely big brother, wondering if he'd had a nurse holding his hand before he'd passed away. It had been lovely seeing her family again; lovely but bittersweet.

'I love having you here, Ellie. I would be terribly sad if you left, but your family deserve the chance to spend time with you, too.'

Ellie nodded. 'Spencer liked the idea of me being here. He had the strange idea that you'd be better at looking after me than my own mother. Even though I repeatedly told him she was a midwife!' She suspected the truth was more to do with his worries about his mother here alone. He probably liked the thought of Ellie keeping her company while he couldn't.

Lily grinned over her teacup, and not for the first time Ellie thought how youthful she seemed. Widowed before the war and with her only son away, it must have been so lonely for her waiting for news. But she was far from being an old spinster, and Ellie was more than happy to play the role of surrogate daughter.

'Has little baby been moving today?'

'Yes.' Ellie's hand dropped to her stomach. She was six months along now and her stomach was round and protruding. 'I'm certain he's a big bouncing boy.'

'Heaven help us,' Lily teased. 'Although if his father doesn't make it home in time to hold him as a newborn, he'll get mighty sick of his grandmother clucking and never letting anyone else have a hold.'

Ellie leaned back into the sofa and let her head rest back. Her sleep was always troubled, not only because of Spencer, but also because of the memories that haunted her. This was why she was always tired, the exhaustion bone deep, even though it was a different type of exhausted to how she'd felt nursing. If it wasn't the past or the baby, it was her brother. Even happy childhood memories of him were enough to keep her up all night.

'Are you going to visit your friend again now she's home?'

Ellie sat forwards to reach for her tea. 'I'm desperate to see her, but after last time . . .' She sighed. Lucy had been the most independent and capable of them all, and to think of her so badly injured and refusing to see even her friends was almost impossible. It took hours to get to Lucy's house and as much as she wanted to see her, she hadn't been home all that long and the last thing Ellie wanted to do was push her too soon to receive a visitor.

'It takes time adjusting after an injury,' Lily said. 'Give her time. One day she'll be so happy to see you, I promise.'

'I have written to her every week,' Ellie said. 'Next time I will turn up unannounced and force her to see me.' Once the war was over, she wouldn't give her a choice, but for now while travel was difficult all that way, letters would have to do.

'If you'd like me to go with you, I'd be more than happy to.' Lily raised her teacup and took a sip. 'Anything you need, all you have to do is ask.'

Ellie considered her words. Maybe she should take up Lily's offer and go to see Lucy. It would be hard once the baby was here, or in her last few weeks of pregnancy.

'He'll be back before you know it,' Lily said. 'I know how hard it is, waiting and hoping, but he will come back.'

Ellie hoped she was right. It was moments like this that she wished she had stayed with her own family, out in the country and away from everything else. Maybe there she wouldn't feel like she was being constantly reminded of Spencer. She rubbed her hand in circles over her belly. No, that wasn't true. Her baby would be a constant reminder even without the photos of Spencer surrounding her, his clothes hanging in his room, looking back at her whenever she reached for something of her own.

'I suppose it feels extremely odd, being a married woman with a baby on the way, yet no husband in sight.'

Ellie grinned. 'Are you wondering if this ring is a fake?'

Lily tut-tutted at her. 'Perhaps I should let you read the letters my son sent. Maybe then you'd realise why I was so ready to welcome you with open arms.'

'He really said such lovely things about me?' Ellie asked, remembering the day he'd told her of the letters he'd written home.

'My dear, come with me,' Lily said, gesturing for her to follow as she stood and walked into the library. 'I have every letter tucked away in here. I reread them whenever I'm feeling lonely, which hasn't been often lately, given that I have you for company.'

Ellie appreciated the offer, but she didn't want to intrude. 'Lily, please. You don't need to share personal letters with me.'

'They're here,' Lily said, pulling a neat stack from an ornate metal box. 'Whenever you want to read them, whenever you need something to put a smile on your face, come in here and be with Spencer. His words will help keep him alive in your mind.'

Ellie stared at the letters. On the one hand she was desperate to read them, to devour every word immediately. But the other part of her was scared of reading letters he'd written to his mother, not sure if she wanted to see words Spencer had written that weren't for her eyes.

'You're his wife, my dear. He was taken with you from the moment he met you, and the Ellie he told me about was all guns blazing and wouldn't have thought twice about reading them!'

It was true – when they'd first met she'd been far more outspoken and fun. The war had changed her, as it had many soldiers and nurses, but being here was starting to make her feel more like her old self again. Or at least a version of her old self. She forgot sometimes that Lily didn't know the details of what they'd all been through, what had happened to her when she'd broken down.

'Sometimes I worry that he only married me because . . .' She swallowed, not wanting to discuss this with the woman who'd been so open with her, who had surely pondered the same question before her daughter-in-law even arrived. She was certain Lily would have guessed that she was pregnant before they were married, but it still wasn't something she wanted to speak of.

'Read the letters,' Lily said, stepping back and waving towards them. 'Once you've read them, you'll have no doubts that my son wanted to marry you of his own free will. Perhaps he would have preferred a London wedding than a rushed ceremony in France. Who knows? All I know is that you're married with a beautiful baby on the way, and any woman who managed to steal my boy's heart like you did . . .' Tears filled Lily's eyes and Ellie felt a pull at her own heartstrings, a fluttering of emotion inside her so intense as she worried all over again that Spencer might not make it home.

'Thank you,' she said simply. 'I'm going to sit here and read for a bit, if you're certain you don't mind?'

Lily nodded. 'Enjoy yourself. I'll be in the other room if you need me.' She paused then spoke more quietly. 'You'll find a ring there, in the box. Spencer asked for permission to give it to you. It belonged to his grandmother. I suspect he'd have liked to give it to you himself, but given how long you've been waiting for him, I think it's only proper that you have it now.'

Ellie waited until her mother-in-law was gone before slowly moving over to the small table, hand hovering over the letters that were waiting to be read. She tried not to think about the ring, but curiosity got the better of her and she lifted the letters out to find it. She gasped, hand flying to cover her mouth as she stared down at the gold and diamond ring. It was beautiful, absolutely beautiful. The type of jewellery that she'd certainly never imagined herself having.

Ellie slipped it on to her finger, held it out and admired the shine of the diamonds in the light of the lamps. But the moment felt surreal, especially without Spencer at her side, and she slid it off as quickly as she'd put it on, placing it carefully back in the box. She wanted it, would love to have the weight of it on her finger, but she wanted Spencer to give it to her, to wear it once he returned. For now, the melted-down links of his gold watch were more than sufficient, and they'd hold a place on her finger for ever.

Turning to the letters once more, Ellie recognised the familiar scrawl of Spencer's handwriting, and she lowered herself into the chair after plucking the first letter from the pile. The ring was beautiful, but the thought of reading his words was comforting, and it was comfort she was craving. Ellie took a deep breath and touched a hand to her stomach, intending on reading aloud so their baby could hear words penned by his father's hand.

> *Dear Mother,*
> *Would you believe that I've met a girl? A lovely nurse named Ellie. I can't tell you exactly where we are, but I can tell you that, despite the horrors of what I'm seeing on a daily basis, she is making it impossible for me not to smile. I know you'd like her. She's different, a strong Irish-born lass, but there is something so happy and bright about her, as if she were put on my service to make each day bearable. I hope you get to meet her one day, because if we both make it home in one piece, I will certainly be bringing her home for supper. I miss you terribly, and I think of you often all alone. Stay strong for me, as I will stay strong for you. Perhaps the thought of a daughter-in-law once the war is over will be enough to bring a smile to your face.*
> *With all my love,*
> *Spencer*

Ellie fell forward, the letter clutched in her hand as she started to sob. For all the nights she'd spent without him, for the future they'd both imagined that could so easily be snatched away by the war, and for the bouncing baby kicking away, oblivious to the world he or she would enter. Perhaps a world without a father.

'Ellie, it's so lovely to see you, but I'm afraid Lucy isn't, well, up to having visitors.'

Ellie straightened her shoulders, not prepared to walk away for a second time. It wasn't Lucy's mother's fault, she was only the gatekeeper, but she'd come all this way and she was going to see Lucy.

'Lucy's stubborn, I already know that,' Ellie said, smiling. 'She forgets that I spent months with her acting like she was a doctor, not a nurse. When she makes her mind up, I'm well aware it's not easy to change it.'

That made her mother laugh. 'That's my daughter for you. Nearly drove her father to drink before the war with all that talk about women being able to do anything and wanting to be a doctor herself.'

Ellie reached out, placed her hand over the older woman's arm. 'Lucy means the world to me, and I need to see her. Let her tell me herself that she doesn't want company, and I promise I'll walk straight back out of that door and not bother you again.'

She kept her hand there, their eyes locked, until Lucy's mother stepped back. 'In some ways she's lost herself, lost the spark that used to make her so strong. But she's angry, too, Ellie. I'll apologise now for anything she says to hurt you.'

'I'm stronger than I look,' Ellie said with a grin. 'Besides, Lucy was there for me when I was at my lowest; now it's my turn.'

Ellie let herself be led down the hall, stopping when Lucy's mother paused to push open a door. She stood back and Ellie stepped in, surprised at the cloak of darkness. It was past midday yet the curtains were still drawn, a small lamp the only ray of light in the corner of the room.

'Lucy?' she asked, stepping forward.

'I told you already, I don't want to see you or anyone else.'

Ellie strode across the room and pushed back the curtains. 'You can say that till the cows come home, but I'm not listening.'

'No!' Lucy screamed.

Ellie spun around, eyes finding Lucy, seeing her for the first time. A gasp caught in her throat as she stared, fighting to avert her eyes from Lucy's skin. Now she understood why the room was dark.

'I look like a monster, don't I?' Lucy whispered.

Ellie walked slowly towards her, the shock still humming through her body as she felt her friend's pain. 'No, Lucy. You don't.'

'Just go home. I don't want to talk, I don't want you to look at me, and I don't want your pity or sympathy.'

Ellie unbuttoned her jacket and pulled it back, pointing at her large, rounded stomach. 'You see this?' she asked, staring at Lucy.

Lucy looked up, arms folded as she sat on the bed.

'This means that I'm the one wanting sympathy! You think I came here to give it, then you are very, very wrong. I thought you knew me better than that.'

Lucy's mouth turned up at the corners, but the faint smile was gone as quickly as it had appeared.

'I'm carrying a baby around in here, he moves constantly, I have to go to the toilet a hundred times every night and I can't sleep,' Ellie continued, sitting down on the single chair in the room near the bed. 'So now that I've hauled this stomach of mine all the way here, you do not get to play the sympathy card. Not to me.'

'I'm sorry,' Lucy mumbled. 'I . . . I . . .' she stuttered, something the Lucy in France would never have done. 'I don't want anyone to see me because I don't know how to behave, how to be this new version of me.'

'Sweetheart, you're still the same you,' Ellie said softly. 'So your skin is all burnt. It doesn't change who you are!'

'It does,' Lucy said, sounding miserable. 'It changes everything.'

'What are you afraid of?' Ellie asked.

'People staring at me, other women making fun of me,' she whispered, tears falling like big dollops of rain down her cheeks. 'Nothing used to scare me, and now everything does.'

Ellie sighed. 'Let me see properly,' she said. Of all the girls, she'd had the weakest stomach, but Lucy's burns were healed; they were nothing like what they'd had to deal with.

'No.'

'Lucy, it's skin. Yours looks a little different, that's all, and if you're so worried about what strangers would think, then let me see and tell you the truth.'

Lucy shook her head, but Ellie looked anyway, saw what she could. It was bad, it was heartbreaking, but it wasn't the end of the world. 'It's bad,' she said honestly, knowing Lucy would see through her if she lied. 'But so much of you is still unchanged. It's how you feel on the inside that's making you scared.'

Lucy was playing with the edge of her blanket, not saying a word.

'When I was at my lowest, you were there for me. You helped me find my way, covered my shifts and guided me. I will never forget that, and I want to do the same for you.'

'Then leave me,' Lucy muttered. 'Please, leave me and get on with your life and enjoy your baby.'

'No,' Ellie replied.

'Pull the curtains on your way out. I don't want to catch sight of myself in the mirror.'

Ellie watched her, saw her turn away, her shoulders slumped. Lucy looked defeated, and it broke her heart, but if she didn't want her there, then she wasn't going to stay.

'Fine,' she said. 'But I'm not burying you in darkness just because you're afraid of your reflection.' Ellie pulled a blanket from the back of the chair and draped it over the one mirror in the room. 'The dark is far more scary than looking at your beautiful, brave self.'

She bent to drop a kiss to Lucy's head, lips touching her silky soft hair, before standing and walking from the room. She'd be back, but for now she was going to respect Lucy's wishes.

CHAPTER TWENTY-FIVE

Lucy

'Lucy, there's a gentleman here to see you.'

Lucy looked up from where she was sitting. She spent most days in her chair, reading, knitting what she could for the hospital to keep soldiers and new babies warm, and drinking tea. Cup after cup of tea – tea she enjoyed every sip of compared to the shudder-worthy Compo tea they'd all suffered. She wasn't used to having visitors, and the ones who had come, well, they hadn't kept coming back. She was wallowing in her own self-pity and she knew it, but it didn't change how she felt, even if the guilt from pushing Ellie away the week before was still weighing on her. One day she'd tell her that she'd helped, that it was she who'd made her get up each day, let the sun in, and do her best to help the war effort from home. But she wasn't ready to reach out yet.

'Lucy!'

'I heard you, Mother. Whoever he is, tell him to go away.' Her mother had barely spoken to her after her violent reaction the last time she'd suggested an outing. She didn't seem to get that she wasn't about to walk out of that door, that she wasn't ready to face the world. Everything she'd planned had been taken away, because she certainly wasn't going to go to medical school and face the stares and whispers of others.

There was a shuffle in the hallway and then her mother's head appeared around the door. 'Dear, it's an American soldier. He said his name was Captain Jack Colton.'

Lucy froze. She then carefully took the book from her lap and placed it on the table beside her. 'You're certain?' she asked, staring at her mother. But there was no reason for her mother to be playing games; Lucy had never once mentioned Jack to her. Unless she'd mumbled it when she'd been heavily sedated in hospital.

Her mother nodded, looking uncertain.

'Please tell him I'm unavailable.'

'Lucy, there is an extremely handsome soldier standing at our door. Don't make me leave him standing there! I've had it with having to pretend you're as good as dead!'

Lucy summoned all her courage, all her determination, despite the rapid beat of her heart. She'd never been so desperate to see another human being in her entire life, but there was no way she was letting him ever see her like this. Anyone but Jack! Why had he come looking for her? After all these months of telling herself that it had been an empty promise, and here he was standing on her doorstep. Asking for her. Waiting for her.

'Mother, please. I'm not seeing him, so tell him to leave.'

Lucy could only guess how hard her mother had found it having her home like this, caring for her and most likely wondering when her happy, strong girl was going to come back. She wished for her old self some days, too, and she certainly wasn't going to let Jack see her like this.

'Lucy . . .'

She turned away, looked out of the window, at the curtains blowing in the breeze, the world looking so sunny and leafy today, it was almost impossible to believe there was still a war going on.

Lucy sat still, then couldn't stand it any longer, knowing he was out there and not being able to catch even a glimpse of him. She touched her hand to her face then slowly let her fingers trail down her neck, stalling when they touched the edge of her burn scars before bravely following the path down to her collarbone. She knew there were a million reasons to be thankful – that she was alive, that most of her face had been spared. But the burns slicing across her jawline, down her neck and her arm, her hand, they were impossible to ignore and even harder to forget about. She was a different person now.

She rose, walking so quietly across the carpet and leaning into the window. She could hear them, her mother being friendly, and then the deep voice that she'd never forget, no matter how hard she tried.

'I don't know what to tell you. I'm sorry, but she's – well – Lucy has been through a lot.'

'You tell her that I'll be waiting here,' he said, so confident and strong. 'I don't mean to be a nuisance, ma'am, but I owe your daughter my life, and I'll just sit and wait her out until she's ready to see me.'

'Oh no, I couldn't have you sitting out here,' her mother gasped. 'You can come on in, maybe you could tell me all about how my little daughter managed to save a soldier like you.'

He laughed and Lucy found it impossible not to smile. He was charming her mother, a woman certainly not used to the charms of Yanks in uniforms.

'I'm fine waiting out here, and that'll be her story to tell you, ma'am,' he said with a chuckle. 'But your little daughter, well, she's got the heart and courage of a lion if you ask me.'

Lucy wanted to call out to him, to give in and follow her heart, but she couldn't bear to see the look on his face. She'd rather exist in his memory, a pretty nurse with perfect skin. She hadn't thought so back then, but now she could understand just how lovely her skin had once been, something she'd always taken for granted. She wanted him to remember the person she'd been then, the nurse with more determination and courage than she could ever summon now.

'You're certain? You'll sit out here?'

'Tell her I'll wait. I'll be waiting for her, all night if I have to.'

Lucy heard her mother shut the door. It closed with a soft thud, and then she listened to footfalls echo down the hall before her mother appeared in the room again.

'Lucy, please,' she begged, voice soft but full of desperation.

'Mother, that man out there, that handsome soldier . . .' She inhaled, releasing a shaky breath before continuing. 'Do you honestly believe he'd still feel the same about me if he saw this?' She extended her neck, letting her mother get an eyeful of her daily reminder from that awful day, the day she'd almost burnt alive, or at least that's what it had felt like. 'This?' She held out her arm.

Her mother turned then, a sad look on her face as she walked out of the room. Lucy knew she was hurting her and she hated it. But she sat back down, picked up her book, and pretended to read. Because it wasn't only her burns, it was the broken feeling inside of her that made her feel a hundred times removed from the woman she'd once been.

———— ✺✺ ————

'Lucy?' her mother muttered, marching into the room, hands in fists at her sides.

She tried to appear unrattled even though it upset her to see her mother so worried. 'Yes?'

'He's still sitting out there. In the cold.'

Lucy shrugged. 'Perhaps it will get cold enough that he'll leave.'

Her mother threw up her hands in desperation. 'It's been six hours. *Six hours*, Lucy!' She folded her arms crossly. 'I've taken him tea, and now supper. Please, just go out there and see him or he might still be there come morning. It's ridiculous.'

Lucy closed her eyes, squeezed away the tears. Crying was for dealing with skin grafts and pain, not for worries concerning a man.

'Please tell him again, Mother, I don't want to see him.'

'Lucy, enough,' her mother said, walking closer, her eyes full of her own tears. 'If you want him to go, then you march out there and tell him yourself. Whatever it is you think has changed about you. Whatever it is that's making you think you're not good enough.' She leaned forward, touched her finger to the side of Lucy's head. 'The change is in here,' she said, moving her fingers, reaching for her hand. 'Not here.'

Lucy stared up at her mother, knowing she'd been awful to live with, awful to care for. She stood, throwing her arms around her and holding her tight.

'I'm so sorry,' she whispered. 'I am so, so sorry, Mother. I regret every harsh word, every time I've lashed out at you, but I can't seem to help it. Please tell him to go, please do that for me.'

Her mother held her then kissed her head. 'No. Go and make peace with him. He told me you saved his life, and I don't think he's leaving until he says whatever it is that's brought him all this way.'

Lucy wiped her eyes with the backs of her hands, trying to steady herself. Her mother was right, she needed to be the one to tell him to go. Only she knew why he'd come, and she was going to have to show him that she wasn't the nurse he remembered, far from it. Once he saw her, spoke to her, he'd understand.

She stepped past her mother and pressed her hands against her skirt, smoothing out the fabric, then ran her fingers carefully against her hair. She wasn't going to make an effort to disguise or hide her burns; it was an impossible task and besides, it was dark outside. Perhaps he wouldn't see them and she could convince him to go regardless.

Lucy walked slowly but steadily forwards. She turned the knob and pulled the door open, her eyes taking a moment to adjust to the dim light outside. It was after dark, but the moon was high in the sky, bathing the porch in enough light to see by once her eyes focused. And there he was, leaning against the railings and looking out at the street.

She wished she could run to him, throw her arms around him and pretend nothing had changed. She wished the war was over, that things were different.

'Hi, Jack,' she said simply.

When he turned to her, his smile was so big it almost broke her heart. In a few fast steps, he'd know. He'd see how different she looked, what had happened to her.

'Lucy!' He closed the distance between them in four short strides, scooping her up into his arms. 'You kept me waiting long enough!'

Lucy refused to give in to his warm embrace, stayed stiff, pushing him away when he let go enough for her to do so.

'Jack, you need to go,' she told him.

'What? Why?' He looked confused. He was so dashing in his dress uniform, the jacket firm over his wide shoulders, his dark hair a handsome contrast against the olive of his skin. She wished she didn't have to act so cold when all she wanted was to hold him close.

'You can't be here. Please, just go,' she said, her voice breaking, the crack in her softly spoken words impossible to miss.

'No. Not unless you give me a good reason.' He took her hand and openly studied her fingers and then met her gaze. 'You're not married. Are you engaged? Because whoever it is, whoever beat me to it . . .'

'There's no one else, Jack. That's not it.'

'Then what?' he asked. 'I've been playing this moment through my head ever since I went back to active duty, imagining your face, your smile, everything about you. It's what kept me going. You're what kept me alive.' He paused. 'I slowly remembered everything, time healed that, but I never once forgot about you.'

Lucy sobbed then, she couldn't help it. One big, heart-wrenching sob escaped from her mouth, depleting all her energy and making her double over.

'Lucy, what is it? Why are you . . . ?'

'Look,' she sobbed, holding out her other hand, letting him see her skin, all tortured and pink. '*Look*,' she whispered this time, standing up and moving into the moonlight, turning her face so he could see the mangled skin that made its way up her neck, almost to her jaw. She had it over her stomach, too, on the same side. Her skin had literally burnt off her body the day she was trying to help those children, children that had been blown apart when the SS soldiers had started shooting and a grenade had exploded, parts of them sprayed on to her as she lay burning on the grass.

Jack didn't say anything. He looked at her, held her gaze, his eyes damp as he then turned his stare back to her arm and neck. He was quiet, so quiet, and she bit down hard on her bottom lip, trying to stop the sobs, trying to quiet the emotion that was so raw within her.

He reached for her hand, paused, then stepped back, his hands now both by his sides.

'I'm sorry,' he said simply.

Lucy nodded. 'Now you know.'

'This is the reason you didn't want to see me?' he asked. 'This is why you've kept me waiting half the day and night?'

She nodded again.

'I see.'

They stood there a moment longer, awkwardly. She looked down and she wondered if he did, too.

'Lucy, I don't know what happened to you over there, but I have a feeling you did that for someone else. To save someone else.' He cleared his throat. 'You risked your life to save me. I know what you're capable of. Is it true? Am I right?'

She stepped back to lean against the front door, her body braced against it for fear she might collapse otherwise.

'Yes.'

'So tell me,' he said firmly. 'I want to know what happened.'

Lucy stared at her hands and took a shaky breath, hating the idea of reliving the moment that had changed everything. 'We were transferring from our field hospital to Brussels,' she told him. 'It was supposed to be a nice change, somewhere with better facilities and plenty to look forward to, and instead I ended up being rushed there as a patient with burns that almost killed me.' She stopped, nails digging into her fisted palms as she fought to find the words to continue. 'I was injured in an enemy blast when I was trying to save the lives of some young children on the side of the road. There were SS troops hidden. They must have injured the children in the first place.'

'I can't imagine what you've been through,' Jack said.

She smiled. 'But you can, Jack. You've been there, you've been injured for your bravery, lived through hell over there. I was doing nothing more than what so many of our soldiers have done, yet I'm a woman and somehow that's seen as different.'

Jack took a step forward and she went to move back before realising that she couldn't back up any further.

'You are nothing like most of the soldiers I know, I promise you that. You're the woman who bravely told me she was going to be a doctor one day and be damned with what anyone else thought,' he murmured. 'And *I* don't give a damn about your burns. You deserve them, Lucy, because you risked your life to save another. They should remind you every day of your bravery.'

She wanted to believe his words, to believe that he didn't see her any differently. But she couldn't, because she knew the reality, knew how ugly she looked.

'Please, Jack. Can't you leave me in peace?'

He leaned in, cupped her chin and pressed a soft, warm kiss to her lips. The feel of his mouth brushing hers almost made her feel like herself again, even though she knew it was a goodbye kiss.

'It was good seeing you, Lucy.'

Jack walked backwards, holding up his hand, a smile on his face that she knew she'd never forget. This was it. This was goodbye. One last kiss, in the dark as if she were still normal, unmarred by war, and now he was gone.

She held up her hand in a wave, knowing that her mother was probably watching from inside, hoping she didn't ask her too many questions until she'd had the chance to pull herself together.

'I'll see you tomorrow!' he called out.

Lucy blinked, wondered if she'd heard him right. Her right ear was damaged, but she'd thought she'd heard him say . . .

'Pardon?' she yelled out.

'You heard me,' he replied, before whistling and disappearing down the road.

CHAPTER TWENTY-SIX

Scarlet

Scarlet rushed inside, the washing hanging on the line forgotten. Her heart was beating so fast she could hardly breathe, her arms pumping at her sides as she ran.

'Thomas!' she called, bursting into the house. 'Thomas! Germany has surrendered!'

She couldn't hear him, wasn't sure where he was in the house. She walked through, stopping outside the front room when she saw his silhouette. Of course he was in there. He could have moved his wheelchair on his own to another room or even another spot, there was nothing wrong with his arms, but she was used to him not doing anything without her assistance. Being told her husband could walk if he set his mind to it was one thing, but forcing him to do it? She had decided it was an impossible task.

'Thomas, did you hear me?' she said, breathless, as she stood pressed against the doorjamb. 'Thomas, Germany has surrendered. It's over.'

He didn't say anything, back turned to her, not even a flicker of movement that showed he'd heard her. She'd preferred it when his mother was staying with them, but she'd returned home and now here she was trying to pretend everything was fine. Every day was a struggle, every hour of every day driving her a little further into a desperate kind of sadness that she wondered if she'd ever manage to emerge from. But this was news to celebrate.

She walked around, placed a hand on his shoulder, and tried to summon the strength to be sweet, kind and patient with him. Every day it was harder to pretend that she was happy to be married to him, harder to remember why she'd ever wanted to marry this man who was equal parts cruel, miserable and depressed. But then she'd remind herself what he'd been through and try to be patient all over again. She nursed her arm, glancing down at the bruise. Being patient to a man who tried to hurt her, who grabbed her around the wrist so tight sometimes she'd been certain he'd snap it, was starting to become tiresome.

'The news just came through on the wireless,' she told him, stroking the back of his neck, trying to push her thoughts and fears away. 'Mr Grey next door told me. I was out hanging the washing and—'

'Leave me,' he muttered, smacking away her hand.

'Thomas, I know you're suffering, but it wouldn't hurt you to make an effort. *Please.*'

'Leave,' he muttered again.

Scarlet couldn't stand another moment in the stuffy room. He wouldn't let her air it, complaining of the cold, and he never wanted to come out into the sunshine with her on a nice day and sit in the garden, or simply sit and enjoy a cup of tea with her and ask her about her day – about anything.

She was nursing as many days a week as she could, doing whatever was needed, but because Thomas refused to do anything, she was his nurse, too, which was a job in itself. The only things that saved her were the letters she received from Ellie. Scarlet hadn't been able to visit her, not being able to leave Thomas for long and with every day so full to bursting with nursing and caring. But now that Germany had surrendered, it gave her hope that the war and all its atrocities would well and truly be over soon. Their elderly neighbour, Mr Grey, had had tears in his eyes when he'd told her, a smile on his face so wide that it alone had made Scarlet rush over to him. To hear the news, to know that no more innocent people would die at the hands of the Nazis – it took a weight from her shoulders.

She heard the post being pushed through the letter box. She ran into the hall, grabbed the single letter and hurried out to call to the postman.

'Did you hear the news?' she cried.

The kindly older man raised his hand in the air and waved to her. 'Best news an old man could wish for!' he called back.

'Scarlet.'

She turned, a letter in her hand, wondering who was saying her name. The envelope dropped the moment her eyes fell upon James. He was standing in the street, in uniform, his eyes locked on hers. Scarlet froze; she couldn't have moved if she'd wanted to. How was he here? Why was he here?

'You've heard the news?' he asked, as if they hadn't just seen each other for the first time in months, since the day he'd been sent home from France.

'James, I . . .' She couldn't stop staring at him. Tears prickled her eyes, made her wish she never had to see him again, the man that reminded her of what could have been. 'It's so good to see you again,' she managed.

'And you,' he said, stepping forward and brushing a kiss to her cheek. 'I've missed you.'

Scarlet wanted to cling on to him, to dig her nails into his jacket and hold him tight. She needed a touch, a kindness, some tenderness to balance out the pain that was in her home and her heart, but she fought to keep it all down, to not show how badly she was struggling.

'I would have come sooner to see Thomas, but I was reposted almost the same time as he was sent home,' James said.

Of course she knew all this, had listened to his mother talk about her other son when she'd been to visit. That he was in England still, that his duties had changed. Every time he was mentioned she'd silently tucked away every snippet of information into her memory to savour later.

'Please, come in and see him,' she said, hating how formal and stiff she sounded. 'You're always welcome to visit, and I'm sure he'll be so happy to see you.'

James laughed. 'Mother has made it more than clear to me that he's not happy about anything.'

She nodded, not about to lie to the one person who'd surely see through any falseness.

'How are you?' he asked quietly as they walked inside, him slightly behind her. 'Is Thomas at least treating you well?'

Scarlet forced a smile. 'We're doing the best we can,' she dissembled.

'Who are you talking to?' Thomas yelled out.

'Your brother is here!' she called back, trying to sound happy. 'James has called to see you.'

James moved past her, glancing back and smiling at her, so soft and kind, making every bit of strength within her threaten to shatter like glass.

'Thomas! I hear the war didn't treat you so well, my brother.'

'Get out, J,' Thomas snarled, turning his chair around to stare at his younger brother. 'I don't want to see your uniform or your legs or your smug face.'

James glanced at her again and she gave him a tight smile. It was all she could do.

'Thomas, come on now. Is it so bad to have a visitor?' James said. 'It's good to see you.'

Thomas glared at him from his seat as James walked over, closer to him. 'You've got what you always wanted now. You win.'

'I haven't won anything,' James said in a low voice. 'You think I've won something? That it doesn't kill me that my brother is in a wheelchair and my friends died? That I saw what I saw over there? Did what I did?'

Thomas had a look pass over his face, a sadness that made Scarlet wonder if James was going to be the breakthrough that he so sorely needed.

'Darling, would you like me to get us something?' Scarlet asked, refusing to look at James as she moved closer and slung an arm around Thomas, leaning low so that she was part of the conversation. 'Tea perhaps?'

He shoved her roughly, pushed at her so hard that she stumbled back, recoiling. James reached for her, catching her and quickly righting her.

'Thomas!' she scolded.

'It's one thing to feel sorry for yourself, and another thing entirely to take it out on your wife,' James said, glaring at his brother.

'She's *my* wife, and I'll treat her as I damn well please,' Thomas said. 'I think you've overstayed your welcome.'

Scarlet looked at James. She hated that he'd seen that. It had been hard enough for her adjusting to being a wife, being a personal nurse and emotional punching bag to the person who was supposed to love her and care for her, but this was too much. Going from society girl to nurse had been tough, but it was another thing entirely to return home and be in her own personal hell, to be trapped in a marriage. Her family liked to pretend everything was fine, her mother sympathetic but telling her to remain stoic no matter how hard things became.

'What happened to you, Thomas? What made you like this?' she heard James ask as she walked away.

'Look at my damn legs!' Thomas bellowed.

'I'm talking about the way you spoke to your wife. The monster that you've turned into. Where is my brother?' James demanded. Then he added, 'Have you hurt her before?'

Scarlet walked straight out of the front door and stood, trembling as she tried to calm down. She didn't want to see James again, and she desperately needed to get out of the house.

'Scarlet, wait.'

She paused, took a deep breath before turning around and looking straight into James's eyes. She'd been wrong. She couldn't be happy to see him, she couldn't have him close without wanting what she would never have.

'I'm sorry. For the way he's treating you, I'm so, so sorry.'

'I need you to not come back here, James,' she said, her voice wobbling as she tried to get the words out. 'You're only making things worse, for both of us.'

He opened his mouth to say something else but she couldn't stay to listen. Tears flooded her eyes and she turned and ran, away from the one man she wished she didn't ever have to part from.

The sun was shining and Scarlet turned her face up to it for a moment, enjoying the warmth on her skin. Her favourite thing when she wasn't working was to get out into the fresh air, for even a few minutes, any excuse to leave the confines of her house, to linger in the garden and feel the sun or wind against her skin. And every time it reminded her of the day she'd heard James's voice behind her, seen his face for the first time in months. She'd relived that moment every single day since.

With one last sigh, she reluctantly went back into the house. As she shut the door, she saw a letter poking out from the letter box that she hadn't noticed before. She smiled to herself, wondering who it was from. She'd been hoping for a letter from Lucy to stop her worrying about her all the time, or a nice happy letter from Ellie to enjoy, but this one was in a hand she didn't recognise. It was also addressed only to her. She frowned and quickly ripped it open. When she scanned to the end to see who it was from, her legs weakened beneath her. *James.* The letter was from James.

She had tried so hard not to think about him these past two weeks, not to imagine how different things could have been. Because if she did that, if she remembered how sweet and fun and exciting he was, every day with Thomas would be even more torturous that it already was. Besides, she was still ashamed of what he'd seen that day, when Thomas had been so deliberately cruel.

> *Dear Scarlet,*
>
> *I know I promised to leave you be if you ever married my brother, and although I'm pleased that he has returned, I can't say I'm pleased to have to keep that promise. The unwavering belief you held that he was alive still amazes me, and after all that time I cannot believe it turned out you were right. My parents told me bits about what he is like now that he's home, and how hard it must be on you caring for a man who no longer resembles the brother I once knew, but it wasn't until I saw him for myself that I truly believed them. I should visit again, but I doubt I could stand in your home and play the role of loving brother if he dared to speak to you or touch you like that again. It breaks my own mother's heart to see how distant and miserable Thomas is, and to see the husband he has become to such a loving, wonderful woman.*
>
> *Scarlet, I need you to know that I love you. Not a day has passed since I left you in France that I haven't thought about you, and if you ever tire of my brother's loathsome behaviour, if it becomes worse or you can no*

longer stand to put up with his treatment of you, then I want you to know that my home is your home. If ever you walk through my door, well, I want you to know that my feelings about you haven't wavered.

The war changes all of us. I will never be the same again after what I've seen; I'm sure you feel the same. But surely, after all we've suffered, we deserve happiness as a reward for living? I'm writing to you from my garden, and I can imagine you here with me, picking flowers and smiling, bringing brightness and happiness to everyone and everything around you. Don't spend your life worrying about what others think, or trying to do what is best, if it is slowly draining the life from you. You deserve more.

If this letter finds you happy and content, if you truly love my brother and want to endure it all with him, then toss it away or burn it and never think of me again. But if not, then my address is on the envelope. No one will think less of you for walking away from such an intolerable situation.

With all my love,
James

Scarlet stared at his name long after she finished reading his words. James was asking her to go to him. He wanted her with him. Two weeks to the day that Germany had surrendered, he was asking her to surrender her own marriage. To walk away from the vows she'd made to Thomas.

She quickly folded the paper and placed it in her pocket. She slowly glanced behind her, having the most awful feeling that Thomas could be watching. He was in the front room, he *could* have seen her, but he didn't seem very interested in anything she did so she knew it was unlikely.

He couldn't seriously believe that she would go? Walk out on Thomas, leave him alone and leave their marriage? It wasn't that she hadn't thought about it; it was something she dreamt about every night as she struggled to fall asleep. Worse, she sometimes imagined what it would be like if she woke up and he was gone. She squeezed her eyes shut, hating herself for her thoughts. One morning, when he'd not spoken to her for days, had refused to even acknowledge her when she'd made him dinner, she'd wished he would die. And that thought returned more and more when he slapped her, shoved her, spat at her.

But Thomas was her husband, and her life was what it was. She would ignore the letter from James, pretend she'd never read it, and soldier on. Thomas needed her, and she hadn't searched for him for so long to give up on him now. What she had to do was believe that this was a stage that would pass, that he'd slowly come to terms with what had happened and let her back in.

Scarlet gathered herself together, pushed all thoughts of James aside, and placed a smile back on her face. She walked into the kitchen, determined to make lunch and perhaps take Thomas out into the sunshine, read to him.

'Thomas, darling, I'm going to get lunch,' she called out, doing her best to sound bright.

If she didn't pretend to be happy, then she'd only end up as miserable as her husband.

———— ❦ ————

'Mary! It's so good to see you again.' Scarlet took the small case from her mother-in-law and embraced her with one arm. What she wanted to do was collapse into a heap at her feet and beg her to take care of her son for the rest of the day, but instead she kept her smile fixed and stood back, gesturing down the hall.

Her own parents had been to visit several times, as had her sister, but they'd found it hard to talk to Thomas, his discontent so obvious, and in the past month she'd only received letters. She'd naively imagined that her mother would frequently come from their house in the country to stay, but it hadn't happened. Her parents' favourite saying of 'chin up' kept ringing through her mind; she wished they knew what it meant to truly keep her chin up around her husband. She doubted they understood this any more than the horrors of what she'd seen and experienced abroad, imagining their daughter well fed and working ladies' hours.

'How has he been?'

Scarlet looked at Thomas's mother, certain she would be able to see straight through her if she lied.

'Well, you know, he's . . .' She didn't know what to say, couldn't even conjure a lie. There was nothing for her to say unless she wanted to break his mother's heart.

'Scarlet, why don't you go for a walk? It's a lovely sunny day out there and I'm sure you could do with a break and some fresh air.'

Mary was so kind, she always had been, and she truly did seem to understand how hard things had been. Often Scarlet wondered if James had ever said anything, if he'd let slip how he felt, but his mother had never mentioned it and neither had she. Scarlet gave her a grateful smile, not trusting her voice, and touched her arm before turning and reaching for her coat. She opened the door and gratefully breathed in a burst of air.

'He's in the front room as usual,' she called out. 'I won't be long.'

Scarlet shut the door behind her, hurrying out into the open and stumbling down her front steps. She was failing as a wife. There was no other word for what was happening in her home other than to call it failing. All the months she'd dreamt of finding Thomas, remembering the soft touch of his lips to hers that night so long ago as they sat in the shelter during a bombing raid, how dashing he'd been. She'd dreamt of a wedding surrounded by their family, children filling the halls of their home with laughter, happiness once the war had ended. She doubted now that they'd even be able to have children, given that Thomas wouldn't see a doctor and made no effort to do his exercises to even try to learn to walk again. They hadn't even been able to consummate their marriage.

She dug her fingernails into her palms. The entire war was so close to being over, and yet her marriage was on the brink of its own kind of collapse.

She couldn't do it. The weight of her own admission hit her, forced her to stop. Her breath was rapid, her chest rising and falling heavily. *She couldn't stand another day in that house with that man.* She'd promised to love and obey a man who was a stranger to her, so far removed from the Thomas she'd been promised to. Was James right? After all they'd done, all they'd survived, didn't they deserve to make a decision based on happiness? But what kind of woman would she be if she walked out on her crippled husband?

Scarlet forced herself to keep moving, to walk as if she wasn't dying inside. She didn't want to alert anyone to the fact that something was wrong, and standing on the roadside or collapsing to her knees wasn't exactly normal behaviour. She walked a few more steps before turning around and going back the way she'd come. She was going to try harder, she would make this work. She needed to stop thinking about James and the letter that seemed to burn a constant hole in her pocket.

She walked back into her house, closing the door and hanging up her coat again. She'd only taken a few steps down the hall when the smash of glass made her jump. Scarlet ran into the front room, worried something had happened to Thomas, only to find his mother standing there, glass smashed around her, and Thomas glaring at her. She'd obviously walked in on an argument with his mother, the only other person in the world who cared about him enough to be a constant presence in his life.

'Mary? Is everything all right here?' Scarlet asked in a low voice.

'Get her out of my house!' Thomas bellowed.

Scarlet took a step towards Mary, worried for her. But she received a tight smile in response. 'I was telling my son that he might want to be more grateful to his attentive, caring wife,' Mary said. 'I'll clean this up.'

Thomas stared at Scarlet. 'Don't just stand there,' he muttered.

'No,' Scarlet said, shaking her head. 'You don't get to sit there and bark orders at me as if I'm no more than your servant. I will do anything for you, Thomas, and yet you'll do nothing for yourself, and certainly nothing for me. A kind word wouldn't go amiss every once in a while.'

'You dare say that to me when I'm stuck in this chair?' he said coldly.

'Your legs would be getting stronger if you'd let me help you with your exercises, but instead you sit there and refuse to so much as speak to me,' Scarlet said, terrified of how quickly the words were flying from her mouth, words she'd kept locked away for so many weeks and months. 'I am still hoping that the Thomas I know is in there will come back, that this will have all been a bad dream. I don't want us to be like this,' she pleaded.

He was quiet, his gaze focused on something outside.

'Thomas!' she demanded. 'Don't ignore me. We are talking about this now whether you like it or not.'

She marched over to him, stopped in front of him.

'Thomas, please!' she insisted.

He lunged at her from his seat, swung his closed fist at her face so fast she barely managed to turn as his knuckles crashed into her cheek, the full force of his punch sending her flying backwards. She hit the window, her head smashing against the window pane so hard she wondered how it hadn't shattered.

'Thomas!' she heard his mother scream.

'Get out of my house,' he yelled, slumped forward, half out of his chair. 'Get out!'

'What?' Scarlet stared at him, reaching for his mother's hand to help her from her sprawled position on the carpet. '*What* did you say?' she managed, the thumping of her head beating like a pulse.

'You heard me. I said get out,' Thomas repeated.

Scarlet stood there, recoiling as much from his words as his punch. She should have told him that the house had belonged to *her* parents, that it was their wedding gift to her and therefore was as much her home as his. But she didn't. Her mouth opened and no words came out.

Scarlet gingerly touched her fingertips to her cheek. She was better than this. She was a nurse who'd saved numerous lives and cared for so many men. Served her country and survived. Searched tirelessly for the fiancé she'd so desperately wanted to marry. She deserved more, and she was not a woman who could suffer a marriage like this and be told to leave her own home.

'Fine,' she said, a warm sense of calm settling upon her. '*Fine.*'

Thomas was back to staring out of the window again.

'This is your last chance, Thomas. You say sorry, you apologise for the way you've treated me since we returned, for hitting me just then. I've done everything I can to show you love and affection, to care for you and prove how dedicated I am to making this marriage work. But I can only put up with so much.'

Thomas said nothing – just continued to stare blankly out of the window.

Scarlet's mother-in-law was also silent, and the only guilt Scarlet felt in that moment was for leaving her to care for her son. But he was her son, he was the boy she'd raised into a man, and if anyone should care for him, then it should be her.

'I'm sorry, Mary, but I can't stay here,' Scarlet said as she folded her hands together. 'If Thomas wants me gone that badly, then I shall go and stay with a friend.'

'Scarlet, please, I . . .' Mary's eyes pleaded with her, but she never finished her sentence. Scarlet was certain it was because she didn't know what to say. What could she possibly come up with that would make her want to stay? They both knew the reality of living with Thomas, and no matter how many times Mary apologised for him, it didn't mean anything if it wasn't coming from him.

She embraced Mary quickly, before walking out and up the stairs to her bedroom. Scarlet never looked back at her husband, thinking only of packing her case and taking her essential belongings with her. Then it struck her that if she would never return then she would have to make sure she had everything she needed. Changing her mind, she found her leather carryall that she'd taken to Normandy, deciding to fill that as well. She went to her bedside table and took out the letter she'd kept in there, the one she'd carried for Ellie all those months. She needed to take it with her.

Scarlet hurriedly packed her things, not bothering to fold them. It was still only morning, which meant she had plenty of time to make her way to the station and be on her way. She would sit in a train all day and night if she had to; anything would be better than staying here. She carefully slid her ring off, the engagement ring she'd missed so much in France, and left it on the table.

Once she was done, Scarlet took her bag and case, hurrying down the stairs and out of the house without a backward glance. She didn't call out goodbye, didn't think about what she was leaving behind, although the muffled crying of her mother-in-law was impossible not to hear, and she was certain the sound of her sobs would haunt her for ever.

She was never coming back.

CHAPTER TWENTY-SEVEN

Lucy

'Your young man is back. Please don't let me see him waiting all day again to see you.'

Lucy peered out of the window, surprised to see Jack standing there. She'd started to wonder if she really had misheard him – couldn't understand why he'd want to come back to see her again. Maybe he wanted to thank her for saving his life, to talk about that day. She knew many people preferred to keep everything they'd experienced at war bottled up inside, like she did about that awful day of the blast, but perhaps Jack needed to ask her questions. They'd talked so much at the hospital, before she'd even known who he was, but that was a year ago when he'd been struggling with his memory.

She checked her hair was in place and studied her face for a moment before heading out to greet him. She'd been up early, preparing herself in case he did, in fact, appear, but now that he was here she felt anything but prepared. It was one thing to be brave in the dark, like she had been the night before, and another thing entirely to front up to Jack in broad daylight.

She swung open the door, certain her mother would be eavesdropping from nearby. The last few months had been terribly hard for her mother, and Lucy was still working on her proper apology. She'd put her through a lot simply because she'd been easy to take her frustration out on, and she wished she could take back every curt word.

'Good morning,' she said, eyes meeting Jack's dark gaze.

'Good morning,' he replied, taking his hand from behind his back and passing her a large bunch of assorted flowers. They were tied rather crudely with a piece of thin grass.

'Oh, they're beautiful.' Lucy reached for them, using her right hand and forgetting for a split second that she'd meant to keep it hidden. She went to snatch it back before Jack could see her ugly deep pink scars, the marred skin, but he deftly caught her around the wrist.

'Almost as beautiful as you,' he said smoothly, his words low and only for her.

'Jack, please. You don't have to say things like that to me now,' she protested.

'I like telling the truth,' he said with a grin. 'You see, I stole these flowers from your neighbours. The truth.'

She laughed. 'You didn't!'

'You are beautiful. Another truth.'

Lucy laughed as he dropped the flowers on to the floor of the porch and caught her other wrist, gently sliding his fingers to her hands.

'Does that hurt? Touching the skin?'

She blinked up at him, all joking aside. 'Not like that, no.'

Jack smiled and lifted her left hand first, kissing her wrist, lips so soft as they brushed her skin. Then he lifted her right, pausing when she flinched, before pressing a soft kiss there, too.

'My memory slowly came back,' Jack said, voice more serious now. 'My sister would never have forgiven me if I'd never remembered her. And it was just as well. I needed someone to write to about you, and I told her all about the beautiful nurse who'd cared for me until my unit found me.'

'You did?' Lucy asked, wishing she was still that same girl who'd nursed him, the one who was brave and courageous, no matter what.

'Do you know what she said to me?'

Lucy shook her head, holding Jack's hands back, looking into his eyes and thinking how easily she could become lost in that welcoming gaze.

'She told me that once the war was over, I was to find you. No argument. I was to go to the address you'd given me and camp outside your house until . . .'

She smiled. 'So that's why you stayed for so long yesterday. Because your sister told you to?' Lucy sighed. 'She couldn't have known about what happened to me, Jack, so I'm sure she'd release you from that promise.'

Jack ignored her words, dropping to one knee in front of her. 'Until I could convince you to marry me,' he finished, as if she hadn't even spoken. 'So here I am, asking you, Lucy, to be my wife.'

'Jack, no!' Lucy tried to pull her hands from his but he didn't let go. 'Get up!'

'Marry me, Lucy. Do me the honour of becoming my wife.'

She cried then, tears falling heavily down her cheeks, her eyes so moist she couldn't see through the blur. 'You don't want to marry me. Not like this,' she sobbed.

'Yes, yes I do,' Jack whispered, carefully stroking her skin and wiping the tears from her face as he stood up. 'And you're wrong about my sister. She wouldn't care less about some burns – scars that are a constant reminder of how brave you were during the war. Don't you see?' he said. 'They show what kind of woman you are, and I will kiss those burns every single day if you'll say yes to me. If you'll marry me.'

Lucy finally lifted her head, looked at Jack again. 'After all this, after . . .' Her voice broke. 'You *still* want to marry me?'

He grinned. 'Yes. Is it that hard to believe?'

'Yes,' she admitted. 'I don't know if I'll ever believe it. Why didn't you walk away after you saw me last night? You never had to see me again. You could have disappeared.'

He shook his head. 'I couldn't walk away from you, Lucy. Don't you see? I fell in love with you before I could see you, when my head was bandaged and all I could hear was your voice because my head was so blurry. And we have so many dates to go on! We're starting backwards, but we need to go out for lunch and dinner, to the pictures, on walks. I promise you I'll be romantic.'

'Truly?' she asked.

'You're not taking her back to America with you. Please tell me you're not going to America with him?'

Lucy spun in Jack's arms, her mother's voice taking her by surprise. So she'd been listening all that time after all.

'Jack?' Lucy asked, turning back to him instead of scolding her mother for listening in. Why had she never thought of that? 'If I married you, would you want us to go back to America?'

He stared at her long and hard. 'London is your home. Perhaps it can be mine, too.'

She would move for him. When all was said and done he'd come back for her, and she'd never felt love before she'd met him. Lucy had always been the one laughing at other nurses falling head over heels for soldiers or doctors. She'd always been too focused on her work, more concerned about doing her job well and caring for others. But from the day she'd helped to save Jack, something inside her had changed.

'Mother?' Lucy said, looking back at her standing there in the open doorway.

'I think you'd make a lovely couple, but before we go talking about a wedding, it's high time you invited this man inside.'

Lucy didn't get time to reply before Jack took her arm. 'Another piece of that delicious pie would be nice, Mrs Anderson,' he said with a grin.

Her mother laughed at the same time as she did.

'You Yanks and your charm,' she said, cheeks flushing, which amused Lucy. 'No wonder you like my Lucy. She's probably the only girl who didn't fall for your fancy words – made you try a little harder.'

'Mother!' Lucy protested. But her mother wasn't wrong and she knew it.

Jack let go of Lucy, winking at her before taking her mother's arm instead. 'Your Lucy was as brave as a soldier in Normandy. I hope you have all day because I have a lot of stories to tell about her. Did you know how we met?'

Lucy groaned. It was one thing him proposing on her doorstep, and another entirely to have him in her own home, telling her mother all sorts of tales about their time in France.

'Do we have to go back there?' She understood why so many soldiers didn't like to talk about what they'd been through. She stopped, the hot blast rushing back to her, the feeling of her skin crawling with fire.

'Lucy?' Jack was at her side, hand on her arm.

'It's . . .' she breathed, pushed the memories away. Her burns were the physical reminder, but her memories were equally as bad – the way they surprised her when she was least expecting them, like a wave crashing through her mind out of the blue.

'We all have skeletons in our closet, Lucy,' he said gently, stroking her arm as he looked into her eyes, not afraid of whatever she was going through. Her mother was so kind, tried so hard, but she didn't know what to do when Lucy was hit with an attack like this. Jack's soft, smooth words started to soothe her, his fingers a steady rhythm against her. 'Acknowledge them, remember the pain, then don't let it back in. Don't let it take hold.'

She shook as he held her, his arms circling her now, embracing her even though her mother was standing quietly only a few steps away.

'We don't ever want to forget the things we did. They make us who we are, each and every one of us,' he told her. 'The men I killed will haunt me for ever, just like the day you got your burns will for you. But we survived, Lucy. We survived it and we're getting our second chance.'

She looked back up, came back to the present, away from the memories and the pain. 'Yes,' she said. 'Yes to marrying you, and yes to living again.'

He lifted her hand and kissed her red raw skin, something she was going to have to get used to accepting instead of flinching away from.

'Good,' he replied with another wink. 'Now, let's stop scaring your mother and go and tell her all about how we met, and how you nursed me back to health.'

Lucy clutched his arm, drawing on his strength, wondering how on earth she'd been fortunate enough to meet a man like Jack. He was right, though; she did need to get on with living. She needed to help returned soldiers and put her nursing skills to good use; she needed to talk to women about what their husbands and sons might have experienced so they could better understand them; and most of all she needed to believe in herself. Jack said he loved her, and instead of doubting him and letting herself be plagued with questions, she needed to believe in him. Instead of running for the hills when he'd seen her, burns and all, he'd returned with open arms, and that wasn't something she'd ever expected.

'Jack, you'll have to ask Lucy's father's permission. He won't have you asking her on the porch like that as a proper proposal.' Her mother tut-tutted.

'It can be our little secret,' he said with a laugh. 'Can I call you *Mother*?' he asked, putting on a hilarious English accent.

They went inside and Lucy dropped into a chair at the table as her mother almost tripped over her own feet reaching for the teacups.

Jack was definitely the breath of fresh air her family needed after putting up with her for the better part of six months, that was for sure.

'Oh, and sweetheart? I'm not like other men,' Jack said with a grin. 'If my fiancée still wants to be a doctor, then she has my blessing.' He laughed. 'I haven't forgotten all the things you told me when I was slipping in and out of consciousness and you were keeping a bedside vigil.'

CHAPTER TWENTY-EIGHT

Scarlet

She couldn't do it. Scarlet's hand hovered, but she couldn't bring herself to knock. Why was she here? What had she done?

She lowered her hand and fisted it to stop it from shaking. What if he'd met someone else by now? What if he no longer felt the same way, despite the letter he'd sent her? What if . . . ?

'Scarlet?'

She dropped the bag she'd been holding in her other hand the moment she heard his voice. Scarlet turned, and when she saw him, everything changed. All the fears disappeared when James ran the distance between them and embraced her, arms around her as he lifted her from the ground and swung her around. She was safe in his embrace; wanted, loved, needed. All the things she'd been craving and desperate for she knew were now within her grasp, yet not from the man she was married to.

'You have your bags,' James stated when he finally set her back on her feet, staring down at her, mouth so close to hers as he glanced from her eyes to her lips and back again. 'Does that mean . . . ?'

Scarlet nodded, braving his gaze, refusing to look away even though the pull to do so was strong. She'd spent so many long months trying not to think about him, refusing to acknowledge that she'd made the wrong decision. Yet here she was, with James instead of Thomas.

'Did he do this to you?' James asked, reaching up so carefully to skim his fingers across her cheek, the pain in his expression impossible not to notice.

Scarlet nodded. 'He doesn't know I've left him,' she said, voice quavering. 'I, well, your mother was there and he was yelling at both of us. When he told me to go I left, but I said I was staying with a friend.'

James shook his head. 'I'm not your friend.'

She blinked twice, staring at him. 'What? I mean . . .' She'd said 'friend' as a cover when she'd left, but still she thought he'd consider himself her friend.

He moved closer, into her space again, his hands running down her upper arms as he ducked his head, lips closing the distance left between them as he kissed her. Scarlet let him, didn't consider pulling away as her mouth hungrily met his, kissing him like she hadn't kissed a man since the night on the boat, when she'd been wide-eyed and innocent about what awaited them in France. Thomas hadn't kissed her like this even on the day they'd been married. But James . . . James made her feel alive. James made her want to live instead of hide herself away from the world, trapped inside that house. Only she wasn't trapped any longer.

'I don't want to be your friend,' James said when his lips parted from hers. 'I have no interest in being friends.'

She saw the glint in his eye, understood his words. 'I'm married,' she whispered. 'Nothing can change that.'

He pressed his forehead to hers. 'I don't care. And if you cared, you wouldn't have turned up here, unaccompanied, with your bags packed.'

He was right. Of course he was right. But she was realistic enough to know that their families mattered to them both, and a woman from a good family didn't walk away from a marriage and take up with another man. Certainly not her husband's brother!

'Your mother will never forgive me.' *Her mother would never forgive her.*

'She will,' he insisted. 'And if our parents don't, then it doesn't matter.'

They stood together, so close, outside his house. She hadn't even had time to acknowledge how pretty it was, with a big garden, away from other houses. It was pretty and perfect – a home rather than a house, despite the fact that he lived here alone.

'What now?' she asked, looking up at him expectantly, hoping he had all the answers. He'd lured her here, told her that he'd be waiting, so she could only expect he'd figured everything out.

'I have absolutely no idea,' he said.

'James!' She slapped at his chest and he caught her wrist, eyebrows raised. It made her heart pound, wondering what that look meant, and knowing they were all alone . . . She gulped. His place was so pretty and overgrown that she couldn't even see any of the neighbouring houses.

'I never actually thought you'd come,' he admitted, shrugging, as he reached for her case and then her bag.

'You had me from the first day we met, James. You honestly did.'

He grunted. 'If only we'd known, huh?'

He was right. Perhaps she should have made a different choice, but at least she could put her hand on her heart and know that she'd tried her best to be loyal and faithful to Thomas. To keep her word.

'Come on,' he said, walking ahead of her and using his boot to kick the door open. She hadn't even noticed earlier that it wasn't properly latched.

'Are you going to show me around?' she asked.

'No,' he said, dropping her bags to the floor. They landed with a thud on the polished wooden floor. 'I'm taking you to our bedroom.'

Scarlet felt her eyes go wide, worry streaming through her as he strode back the few steps between them and scooped her up in his arms. He kissed her again, his lips rougher this time as he claimed her mouth. If she'd pushed at him, resisted a little, she was certain he would have put her straight back down on her feet, but she didn't want that. She'd dreamt of being in his arms for too long to let fear get the better of her now.

'James,' she murmured, his breath hot against hers when she pulled back a touch.

He stopped walking, held her still in his arms.

'What if we can't ever get married? What if he comes looking for me?' she whispered.

'I can handle my own brother,' he muttered, 'and right now I don't give a damn about marriage. All I know is that he hurt you and he sure as hell doesn't deserve you.'

She knew she would care, though, one day. That being a mistress, an adulteress, wasn't something she could live with for ever, but for now, being in James's arms was enough.

───── ❦ ─────

'Scarlet,' James called. 'Scarlet!'

She paused, stopping cutting the roses that curled out on to the path that led to the house. She'd been on her knees, settled upon a folded towel, but she carefully put down her cutting tools and stood, concerned by the worried tone in James's call. It had been an idyllic week with him – almost like a holiday away from the life she'd been forced to live since arriving home from France.

'I'm here,' she called back, seeing him come through the gate.

'Scarlet, I just received a telegram,' he said, his face full of anguish like she'd never seen before. 'It was from my father.'

She crossed her arms and then changed her mind and wrapped them around herself instead. His words had sent a chill through her that she couldn't explain.

'What's happened? Is it your mother? Oh no,' she gasped. 'Have they found out I'm here?'

James shook his head, reaching for her and pulling her into his arms. 'No,' he murmured. 'It's Thomas.'

She leaned back, pushed him away so she could look at his face. Her body went cold.

'Tell me,' she insisted, her voice sounding stronger than she felt inside.

'He took his own life, Scarlet,' James said as he blinked away tears, his body visibly shaking. 'By his own hand, he killed himself. Shot himself dead. He's gone.'

'No,' she gasped, falling, her knees giving way beneath her. 'No!'

She'd killed him. There was no other explanation. She'd left him, and as soon as she wasn't there to care for him, to be the wife she'd promised to be, he'd blown his own brains out.

She sobbed, crying as James dropped to the ground beside her and held her tight. She wanted to fight him, push him away and grieve alone. Because she shouldn't have been here, she shouldn't have put herself first, shouldn't have given in and come to James instead of being there for Thomas.

'This is my fault,' she told him, wiping furiously at her face, refusing to cry any more tears even as emotion pulsed through her body. She'd made her choice, and she needed to live with what she'd done for the rest of her life. This was her punishment.

'It's not,' he said gently. 'Nothing about Thomas's behaviour, now or before you left, is your fault.'

'But he's dead because of me.'

'No,' James said firmly. 'He's dead because of the war. That man I saw that day, in your home? He wasn't my brother, and I'll be damned if that's the way I'll remember him.'

CHAPTER TWENTY-NINE

Ellie

'I'm worried that we haven't heard from him,' Ellie said, taking some scones from the oven and transferring them to a wire rack to cool. She sighed. Baking and cooking were the only things that calmed her these days, and with the baby so close to coming she knew she should be spending more time with her feet up instead of trying to find things to do constantly.

'Ellie, you're exhausting me with all that jittering,' her mother-in-law said. 'Now come and sit down.'

She spun around, hands searching for the counter to hold on to as she stared back at Lily. She was going crazy. She was actually going stark raving bonkers thinking about Spencer, and the more she tried to stop thinking about him, the more she did the exact opposite.

'You don't think he's . . .'

'No!' Lily set down her teacup with a clatter. 'Don't you ever say that, not once, do you hear me? Don't even think it.'

Ellie nodded. It was the only time her mother-in-law had ever spoken to her like that.

'I don't want to go back home and wonder if he might be here, if he's going to surprise us. I mean, what if he comes for me and I've left?'

'My dear, you make it sound like you're leaving the country,' Lily said, her voice full of warmth again, tone soft. Ellie had the feeling she was always trying to soothe her, knowing how rattled she was. 'Your mother needs to see you, and you're better being with her now you're due. There's no need to worry at all. And if Spencer comes home, then I shall whisk him straight over to you.'

Ellie took a deep breath, ready to collapse. Her ankles were swollen, her stomach was huge and she was starting to breathe heavier than usual. They were all signs she needed to slow down, despite the fact that she was doing her best to ignore them.

'I wish Lucy had written back. I would have liked to see her again before I go. But I can't exactly trot off to see her at nine months pregnant!'

'What of your other friend? Scarlet?'

She nodded. 'I'd hoped to see her, too. In fact, she's said she will try to call on me tomorrow if she can. I don't know where she's been, but she mentioned in her letter coming back from somewhere and needing to see me.'

'Well, you tell your friends they're welcome here whenever they want to call. I can't think of anything nicer than having my home filled with visitors and happy chatter.'

Ellie looked back at her scones and decided to wrap them in a tea towel to keep them warm for tea before finally sitting down. She was desperately doing her best to knit for the baby, even though she'd never been talented when it came to homely tasks.

Lily had gone and Ellie had only settled for a moment when there was a knock at the door. She set down her knitting needles, hoping for a moment that it could be Spencer, heart racing as she wondered if he might have come to surprise them. But she quickly pushed those thoughts away. Surely Spencer would have walked straight through the door without knocking.

'I'll get it,' Ellie called out, not sure where Lily had disappeared to.

She walked to the door, waddling now, which infuriated her. There was a knock again and she wondered who would be so impatient.

'Scarlet!' She gasped her friend's name when she opened the door, letting the handle go and opening her arms.

'Oh, Ellie, look at you!' Scarlet hugged her tight, their stomachs pressed together to allow them to do so.

'Larger than last time you saw me,' she joked, before noticing how drained Scarlet looked. Her friend's cheeks were ghostly white, like chalk, and her eyes were hollow, her face thin. She didn't resemble the Scarlet that she'd known for all those months, even when they'd both been at their thinnest on their substandard daily rations. 'Scarlet, what's happened? You don't look like yourself.'

Scarlet's face crumpled as she lost her composure, but she quickly righted herself, reaching for Ellie's hand and holding tight to it. 'Can I come in?'

'Of course.' Ellie closed the door and led Scarlet through the house to the kitchen, still holding her hand. 'How about we have a cup of tea? I've made scones so we can have jam with them. It's a little tart as we made it from our strawberries without a lot of sugar, but it's still nice.'

Scarlet had sat down at the table and Ellie kept glancing at her as she boiled water, made tea and prepared the scones. Scarlet was rubbing her thumb over a ball of wool that had been left on the table.

'This is a beautiful home,' Scarlet said.

'It is,' Ellie agreed. 'I wish we'd been able to see more of each other, but with so much going on for you with Thomas and your nursing, and me with this huge stomach . . .' Ellie laughed to herself. 'Now the war is over we'll have no excuse but to have regular get-togethers. How is Thomas getting along?'

Scarlet stared down into her tea when Ellie set it in front of her. 'Thomas is dead,' she said quietly.

'Dead?' Ellie dropped into the seat beside Scarlet. '*Dead?*'

Scarlet nodded, brushing tears from her cheek with the back of her fingers then picking up her cup and wrapping her hands around it. 'We buried him only five days ago. I'm officially a widow.'

'But, what . . . ?' Ellie didn't know what to say, whether it was even proper for her to ask what had happened. But Scarlet was her friend, and she'd obviously come here to talk. 'Tell me everything, Scarlet. What happened to him?'

Her friend met her gaze and even her eyes seemed paler than usual. 'Thomas was unbearable, there's no reason to pretend otherwise simply because he's dead. He couldn't live with himself, not being able to walk and stuck in that wheelchair with no answer about why his legs wouldn't work. He hurt me over and over again, so I left and he . . .' She swallowed. 'He took his own life.'

Ellie's hand flew to her mouth. 'He didn't!'

'Shot himself, sitting there in his chair in the front room of our house.'

'I'm so sorry,' Ellie whispered, reaching for Scarlet's hand again.

'I'd left him,' Scarlet said. 'I'd left him for James and he didn't even know.'

'It's not your fault,' Ellie told her.

'Isn't it? James keeps telling me the same thing.'

They sat there, sipping their tea, quiet for a long while.

'You fell in love with James when no one else believed Thomas had a chance of being alive, and yet you turned your back on your heart and followed through with the promise you'd made. If he couldn't see how lucky he was to have you, or he couldn't live with his demons from the war, then that was his burden, not yours.'

'You honestly believe that?' Scarlet asked, chewing on her bottom lip the moment she stopped talking.

'Yes, yes I do,' Ellie insisted. 'I've never met a person as loyal and loving as you.'

Her stomach twinged, but she ignored it. She'd been getting small contractions for days and, as unsettling as it was, she wanted to give Scarlet her full attention.

'I needed to tell someone, someone other than James. He keeps telling me not to blame myself, he wants me back with him, but I can't pretend I'm staying with a friend any longer.' She sighed. 'He is mourning his brother, the brother he remembers from their younger years, and I'm mourning the husband I wished I'd had, but it doesn't change the way we feel about each other.'

'So don't let it,' Ellie said, grimacing as a stronger pain squeezed through her stomach. 'Stay put, let yourself be the grieving widow for a time, and then let his family and everyone else see you slowly fall in love with his brother when you're ready. No one but you, Lucy, James and me has to know the truth. And if you need time away from him, he'll understand that. Heck, he's already waited all this time, what's a few more months?'

A light came back into Scarlet's eyes as she looked up, her shoulders rising, and what she could only presume was hope filling her friend's gaze.

'You honestly believe all that? Everything you just said?'

Ellie smiled, but it was cut short by another tightening. 'Yes. His family would probably be overjoyed at another marriage, so long as it all looked proper, and no one would ever guess the truth. But before that you need time to grieve. You both do.'

Scarlet went to say something else but Ellie flapped her hand at her, trying not to moan.

'I think I'm going to need some help here,' she confessed, starting to think that the contractions were no longer false ones. 'I have a feeling this baby has made up his mind that today is the day – and it's not a day too soon for my liking.'

CHAPTER THIRTY

Lucy

10 September 1945

Dear Scarlet and Ellie,
I'm sending this exact letter to both of you, which is why I've addressed it as such. I'd best keep it short, otherwise my hand will be cramping when I have to write the second copy out!

Would you believe that Jack turned up on my doorstep? I mean that literally. He sat there in the cold outside our house until I agreed to see him! So much has changed, so much has happened, but the one thing I know for sure is that I want you both here on our wedding day. Yes, you heard that right. He proposed to me, and we've already set a date, and I want you both as my bridesmaids. I have friends I've had my entire life, who I love dearly, but none of them know me as well as you do. We went through so much together, and I want us to be together when I marry Jack. I wish I hadn't pushed you away, Ellie, with your baby on the way and all, but I was so down about my injuries, about my scars, and everything that had happened. I will forever be sorry, truly sorry, that we haven't seen one another during the last months since I returned home. After your visit I think I was too ashamed to write to you, and now I'm worried I've missed news of your baby, Ellie! You must have had your little one by now, and I can't wait to hear all about him or her. And Scarlet, I hope all is well with you. You're in my thoughts constantly.

I do hope this letter finds its way to you both easily enough, because if not, well, Jack will be furious as I've told him that without you both being able to attend, there will be no wedding. We survived the war, girls. We did it and we served our country well. Now it's time for us to just be friends. Three young women with their lives ahead of them, even if we do carry memories enough for a lifetime of nightmares.

Keep the date free, ladies: New Year's Eve. I want us to celebrate the new year together. Please write back to me when you can.

Much love,

Lucy

CHAPTER THIRTY-ONE

Scarlet

Three months later

'It's so lovely to see you again, James,' Scarlet said, letting him kiss her cheek as she greeted him with a quick hug, before smiling at his parents and greeting them with hugs and kisses, too.

James winked at her, only for her eyes, and she knew a hot red flush had spread up her neck and no doubt across her cheeks. The first six weeks had been the hardest, full of tears and hatred, regrets and loneliness, but she was ready to smile again. She was ready to accept her feelings for James again now without guilt weighing so heavily on her shoulders.

'It's wonderful to see you looking so bright,' his mother said, bustling past her and through into the sitting room.

'Well, I feel like I've mourned until I can't cry any longer,' Scarlet told them, without a hint of a lie. The fact that she was in love with James had nothing to do with the terrible grief she'd suffered over Thomas. She still cried for the man she'd once loved, furious that he'd had to lose himself during the war, but she no longer felt sorry for herself or blamed herself for what he'd done. She couldn't, because then she'd become lost, too, and the men she nursed each day were suffering through so many traumas, many of them no longer physical, that she was gaining a stronger understanding of how affected these former soldiers were from what they'd seen.

She cast a quick glance at James and saw he was watching her, and she was certain his mother had seen it this time. At least some time had passed now, and besides, Ellie had probably been right. She was starting to see that a new relationship with James might even be welcomed, so long as they went about it the right way, because as much as his parents were still grieving deeply for their lost son, they adored James and only wanted him to be happy.

'James has been telling us that you nursed him at the front,' his father said, stroking his moustache as he often did when he was talking. 'It sounds as if he was rather fond of his pretty sister-in-law-to-be.'

Scarlet did blush then, but it was only right that she did. James had been making it more than obvious that he enjoyed her company, and she was starting to feel more comfortable about it herself.

'How about we let you two young people talk,' his mother said, making a gesture at her husband for him to get moving. 'We do want to walk in the garden and get some fresh air, don't we, Roger?'

Poor Roger looked as if he had no idea what was going on, and Scarlet stifled a laugh as he grunted and followed his wife, doing as he was told. It was freezing cold outside, which made it beyond obvious that they were being left alone on purpose. She stood still, not moving, hardly breathing until the room was empty, except for her and James standing on the far side. A door shut, the bang making her jump, but still she didn't move forwards.

'I think my parents are starting to understand my intentions,' James murmured as he strode towards her, footsteps light on the carpet. 'My mother gave me a very knowing smile earlier.'

'And what exactly are your intentions, James?' she asked in her most demure tone.

'To have my wicked way with you,' he muttered, one hand lost in her hair as the other wrapped around her waist, tugging her to him.

'I'm not sure this is what your mother had in mind when she decided to leave us alone together.' Scarlet laughed, lips finding his and kissing him hungrily.

'Let's not waste time then,' he said, pulling away for a moment before kissing her again, the warmth of his lips, the press of his body making her want even more of him. They'd gone weeks without seeing one another after the funeral, but he'd been calling on her in the past several weeks, and she'd loved every moment with him, loved feeling like herself again after so long.

'James, stop,' she whispered back, hearing a noise and pushing him away. She ran her hands against her hair to check it was in place around her face. 'I'm pregnant.'

James went silent, stepping back as his mother cleared her throat in the hallway, obviously wanting to alert them to the fact that they were about to be disturbed.

'Lovely garden out there, my dear,' she called out. 'It will be delightful in spring.'

James was still staring at her and Scarlet didn't know whether to laugh or feel sorry for him. She'd never seen a man look so shocked.

'Mother, Father,' he called out, standing straighter and no longer looking so daunted by the news she'd just shared with him.

His father ambled into the room, followed by his mother.

'Scarlet and I have news to share,' James said.

Scarlet shook her head. He wasn't? Oh no, surely he wouldn't . . . '*James*,' she cautioned.

'I know it's soon after Thomas, but my intention is to ask Scarlet to marry me. I cannot see the point in delaying simply for the sake of being polite, because in the weeks that have passed I've realised what

Thomas couldn't.' He smiled. 'This woman deserves a husband to adore her, and that man is me.'

She let out a breath. For a moment there she'd been certain he was going to share that she was pregnant!

'Oh, that's wonderful news,' his mother enthused, stepping forward to envelop Scarlet in a hug. 'I will never forget my Thomas, but, my dear, after what he put you through . . .' She sighed. 'I didn't raise my son to treat a woman the way he treated you, and even though I know he saw and experienced so many horrors over there, it doesn't mean I ever accepted the man he returned as.'

Scarlet held her tight. 'We don't need to speak of it,' she said, not wanting to delve back into the past. 'Let's all remember the man we knew before the war rather than the one at the end.'

'You were a good wife to him, Scarlet. Better than good,' the other woman whispered. 'You deserve to be happy.'

Scarlet looked at James over his mother's head, receiving a devilish wink in reply, and a smile that made him look like the cat with the cream before he hugged his father.

He was a devil, her James, but he was hers, and for the first time since she'd met him, she no longer had to hide it. It didn't mean they would ever forget Thomas, or the man he could have been. But Thomas was gone now, and she wasn't going to spend the rest of her life wondering what could have been.

CHAPTER THIRTY-TWO

Ellie

'Anybody home?'

Ellie heard the man's voice call out, and she carefully slid her baby into her cot, wondering who it would be, coming in unannounced like that. It sounded so like her husband, but . . . She walked on light feet out of the nursery, not quite closing the door behind her. And then she saw him.

'*Spencer?*' His name was only a whisper on her lips; she could hardly believe her own eyes. 'Spencer!'

He dropped his bag and strode down the hall as she ran down the stairs into his arms, looping her legs and arms around him as she squealed and showered him with kisses.

'Hello, wife,' he said, voice husky as he held her back.

'Oh my goodness! *Spencer!*' Ellie squealed, forgetting all about her sleeping baby. 'What are you doing here? You were supposed to be another day away.'

'Well, I'm here,' he said, and she noticed for the first time how weary he looked. 'And you . . .'

She looked down at herself, realised in horror that she was covered in baby sick, all over her shoulder and now all over Spencer. She probably smelt horrendous, too, and her hair was a mess.

'You're not pregnant,' he blurted, still staring at her. 'I mean, I know you're not still pregnant, it's just that's how I've imagined you all this time, with a rounded stomach.'

'No! But I'm a mess to look at, aren't I?' Ellie shook her head, annoyed with herself that Spencer had arrived home to find her so dishevelled.

He reached for her, smiling, but he paused when a soft cry rang out. It quickly turned into a wail and Ellie sighed, exhausted.

'You'd better come meet your baby girl, then,' she said.

'I can't believe we have a daughter!' he said, eyes wide.

'Yes, darling, we have a daughter, and she has a set of lungs on her that she exercises all day and night.'

He grinned, looping his arm around her and dropping a kiss into her hair. 'Poor little girl has just been waiting for her daddy to get home, that's all. I'll bet she'll be quiet as a mouse now.'

Ellie laughed and hugged him tight to her side. Spencer was home, they had a healthy baby girl, and the war was over. Finally, everything was back in its rightful place.

EPILOGUE

Scarlet

New Year's Eve, 1945

The day was unseasonably warm, the sun shining down on them all as they stood outside the church. A gentle breeze touched Scarlet's cheeks. It had been a beautiful service – a small gathering, which had made it feel intimate – and there was not a person in the church with dry eyes after watching the happy couple recite their vows and celebrate with an exuberant kiss.

'Ready to help me celebrate?' Lucy asked as her hand landed on Scarlet's shoulder.

Scarlet smiled at her, beyond happy for her friend. They'd been through such a lot together, and to know how much Lucy had suffered and how much she'd overcome to even be here today brought fresh tears to Scarlet's eyes.

'You look so beautiful,' Scarlet told her. 'I know I've told you already, but you do.'

Lucy sighed. 'I feel like everyone is telling me that to make me feel better about my scars,' she said.

'I know you think that, but it's not true,' Scarlet told her, eyes sweeping over Lucy's flushed cheeks, hair down and curled rather than fashioned into an updo, so as to cover her neck. It was true that her hand and wrist were an ugly deep red, as was a large part of her neck and jawline, but none of that detracted from how pretty she looked in her beautiful off-white gown. 'You look alive today, truly alive, so happy and content.'

'How do *you* feel?' Lucy asked in a low voice so no one else could hear. 'You're not woozy or anything?'

Scarlet shook her head, smiling. Lucy and Ellie were the only two people, other than her husband, who knew that she was pregnant. They were waiting to tell everyone, wanted to wait a few more weeks since they'd only just been married. It had been a small ceremony, only their parents had been there to witness it, and given what had happened to Thomas, it was what Scarlet had wanted. Lucy's wedding today had made her a little sad that she hadn't had her own lovely ceremony in a church, wearing an amazing dress, but it didn't matter. She looked past Lucy to James, saw him standing there talking to Spencer. She might not have had the fairy-tale wedding, but she had James, and that was what mattered.

'Come on, let's get you to your reception.'

The church was within walking distance of Lucy's family home, where the wedding breakfast was being held. Scarlet lifted Lucy's train and held it off the ground.

'Wait for me!' Ellie called out, hurrying down to walk with them. 'I'm ready for champagne.'

Scarlet laughed. 'We weren't going to celebrate without you.'

'It seems like such a long time since we were all together. I don't want to miss a moment,' Ellie said.

Lucy turned back, her smile wide. 'I was as excited about seeing you two today as I was about marrying Jack.'

To anyone else, her words might have seemed peculiar, but after all they'd been through together, what they'd seen and done side by side during the hardest months of their lives, it made complete sense to Scarlet.

'I have something of yours,' Scarlet said to Ellie as they walked.

'Me too.'

They walked to Lucy's house, the groom having run along to join in and link his arm through Lucy's. It was a picture-perfect moment for Scarlet, seeing her friend with her new husband, knowing how they'd met and for how many painful days they'd seen Lucy caring so much for a man without knowing his name or whether he was already promised to another.

Once they were at the house, with Lucy's family and other friends filling up the interior and heading straight through to the large table that was being set for a feast, Scarlet waved Ellie over and they made their way outside. There was a seat in the garden, and Scarlet sat down in it, wishing her dress wasn't so tight around the middle. Everything was starting to feel a little snug, although she hadn't only the baby to blame. Since they'd been home and with more food than they'd had in France, she'd been making up for lost time and enjoying every meal, and it wasn't doing her figure any favours. Ellie sat down next to her.

'This is for you,' Scarlet said, reaching inside her brassiere for the letter that had spent most of its life close to her body. 'I'm so pleased that I never had to find your family to give it to them.'

Ellie did the same, holding out the letter that she'd held for safekeeping. 'Do you ever wonder how we made it? I mean, did you ever truly imagine it could be that bad?'

Scarlet leaned against her friend, dropping her head to her shoulder. 'Never. Not for a moment.'

'Do you ever think about how many men we lost?' Ellie asked her, her voice quavering. 'On our watch?'

Scarlet put her arm around her and squeezed. 'I have certain patients who haunt me, I suppose they always will, but most days I think about the ones we saved. I have to think happy thoughts, especially after Thomas.'

'Do you still blame yourself?' Ellie asked.

Scarlet didn't sit up; she didn't want to look at Ellie and let the emotion hit her hard, as she knew it would, so instead she kept her head on her shoulder. 'I don't think that's something I'll ever move past, but I try not to think about it.' What she did often think about was that letter she'd written to Thomas, the one she'd let be taken by the wind, never to be posted to him. Then, she'd thought nursing would be fun, that it would be nothing more than character-building, that she'd find Thomas and they could get on with being married and living happily ever after. She'd been so wrong. But then again, when she looked at James, everything felt somehow right, as if she'd lived the journey that had been made for her.

'I feel like we started out as girls and somehow became women, even though that sounds so silly and we didn't exactly behave like typical teenagers back then.'

'But we *were* girls, in a way,' Scarlet said, her gaze settling on a pretty robin perched on the fence. Sitting there, looking out at the garden, it was almost possible to believe that the war had never happened. In the city and the streets where she worked, the war had touched everything; there was evidence everywhere of what they'd been through, what London and all her people had suffered. But not here, in this quiet garden. 'I was so certain that I knew what I wanted, what my future looked like back then.'

'And now?' Ellie asked.

'It's a different kind of future,' Scarlet replied, shifting to look at her friend. 'I'm content, but I'm still . . .' She wasn't sure how to finish her sentence.

'You're still haunted by what happened, aren't you?' Ellie said.

'Yes,' Scarlet agreed. 'Yes, I am.'

'I think we all are. I honestly don't think anyone could have seen what we saw and not be kept awake at night thinking about it,' Ellie said as she unfolded her letter. Scarlet watched as she stared at the words. 'When we wrote these, we had no idea what we were about to face, but we knew there was a chance we wouldn't make it home.'

'Girls!' a breathless Lucy called out to them from the door. 'I've been looking everywhere for you.'

Scarlet touched Ellie's shoulder and then tucked her little folded-up letter into her hand, holding it tight. 'We were just reminiscing.'

'Well, come and reminisce inside,' Lucy said. 'The food is almost ready, but Jack and I are going to have our first dance now.'

Scarlet smiled to herself. Trust Lucy to already be in her husband's arms. It was lovely to see her smiling again, after everything that had happened to her, after all they'd been through.

'Come on,' Scarlet said to Ellie. 'We have men to dance with.'

'I'm missing Rose,' Ellie said, frowning. 'It's the first time I've left her.'

'And her grandmother will be in heaven having her all to herself,' Scarlet scolded. 'It's high time you enjoyed a few hours out with your friends. We might not all be together again for a while.'

They followed Lucy in, watched as Jack pulled her into his arms, dipping her back and kissing her. Scarlet had studied him, seen the way he looked at Lucy. She knew there were men who'd have been repulsed by Lucy's burns; they were horrific and they would mark her for life. But Lucy had saved Jack; she'd been his lifeline when he'd woken up not knowing who he was or where he was from. She deserved him like no woman had ever deserved happiness before, because she was Lucy. She was the nurse who'd braved fire to save another's life, and they were all lucky to have her in their lives.

'Hello, beautiful.' James surprised her, catching her in his arms from behind and whispering into her ear. They stood there, Scarlet leaning back into him as Lucy enjoyed her first dance as a married woman. All the furniture had been pushed back to make way for the happy couple. Scarlet waved at them, and when they laughingly asked them to join her, James twirled her around so they could dance, too.

'Are you happy?' he asked, murmuring against her cheek, his skin pressed to hers.

'Yes,' she answered, honestly. 'I am.' She wasn't stretching the truth, either. She would forever shoulder some responsibility for Thomas's death, warranted or not, but she was happy, and she needed to stop feeling guilty and let herself enjoy her future. If James had pushed past it, then so could she.

'Good,' he said simply.

Scarlet curled her arms around his neck, held her new husband close. Past his shoulder she could see Ellie dancing with Spencer, holding him tight. Anyone looking at them all now would have no idea what they'd been through, how far they'd all been pushed. She shut her eyes and listened to the steady beat of James's heart. She'd found her happy place, and she only hoped they'd never have to face another war ever again.

———— ∽⌒⌒⌒∽ ————

Scarlet looked up when someone tapped a spoon to a glass. She'd been leaning past her husband to chat to Ellie and Lucy since they'd all swapped chairs after the meal, but it seemed the groom was ready to make a speech.

'On behalf of my lovely new wife,' Jack said, his American drawl making Scarlet smile, it sounded so smooth, 'I'd like to thank you all for joining us today.'

Scarlet raised her glass of champagne, one of a few bottles that Lucy's father had brought up from the cellar where he'd had them hidden since before the war. She took a slow sip.

'My family would have loved to be here today from New York, in fact they'd love to meet my beautiful wife, period, but I was in a bit of a hurry to marry this gorgeous girl before she realised what a mistake she was making.' He laughed. 'The truth is that they couldn't make it here due to my sister expecting her first baby any day, but they'll be visiting as soon as they can.'

Scarlet smiled along with everyone else seated around the table. Jack was always entertaining; he had been even when he'd been lying on a hospital bed without his memory and so obviously trying to court Lucy, the one nurse who'd always been immune to a soldier's charm.

'Anyway, my sister sent a letter, and she wanted me to read it today, so here goes. *To my future sister-in-law, thank you for marrying my brother. If you're anything like he's told me, we're both lucky to have you in our lives, and I can't wait to meet you one day. I wish you a lifetime of happiness, and I want to thank you with all my heart for your bravery. I know that you are the reason he's here today. Without you, he wouldn't be alive, and I will forever be thankful for your decision that day to help save him. He's told me you have scars, that you were badly burnt, but he's also told me that they're a sign of your bravery and of what you went through. I don't even know you yet, but I do know that I'm proud to call you my sister. Yours truly, Susie.*'

Scarlet wiped her eyes, smiled through her tears as she reached for her glass. She stood, urging Ellie to do the same. She wasn't one to speak in front of others, but this was different. This was Lucy's wedding, and they were surrounded only by her family and a handful of her other friends. This was something she needed to do.

'Lucy is one of the bravest and most talented nurses we met in France, and we are so happy that she found Jack. We suffered through her constant worries about this man, certain that a photo in his pocket was his sweetheart, when in fact it was this lovely new sister of hers, Susie.' Everyone laughed and Scarlet smiled over at Lucy. 'One day the memories of what we saw over there will start to fade, but I will never forget you or Ellie. I am forever grateful to have met you both, and I am so, so happy to be here today to see you marry Jack.'

Lucy held up her glass, eyes twinkling as she whispered, '*Thank you.*'

Scarlet sat back down and leaned into her husband, sighing when he dropped a kiss into her hair. A few months ago, she was certain the war would never be over, that she would never be home. But she'd found her home now, with James and her friends. Her hand fluttered to rest on her belly.

They were all wives to this war, but somehow they'd managed to survive it and find happiness on the other side. Despite it all, despite everything, they'd survived.

ACKNOWLEDGMENTS

I have taken small liberties to make this story fit within the confines of real-life events, although almost all of what you read in this book is accurate in place and chronological order. The 75th Mobile Field Hospital, and the depictions of the nurses landing in Normandy, living at the camp and working under canvas, are as accurate as possible. I read the true accounts of many nurses to ensure these scenes were as true to life as could be, and I must thank my research assistant, Jai Patel, for his great work in providing me with much of my background information. However, there were times where I had to depart from the exact path the nurses from the 75th followed, such as when the lorry stops en route to Brussels and faces enemy attack by a small band of SS soldiers – this was entirely my imagination.

This was an amazing book to write because it was set in such a fascinating time in history. It was a period when women were stepping up to fill roles they had been prevented from doing in the past, and often finding an inner strength they never knew they had. I applaud all the women who pushed themselves outside of their comfort zone, either of necessity or choice, during World War II. I cannot imagine the fear of waving a husband off to war, alone with my children and with a farm or business to tend to; or the bravery of nurses like my characters from this story, leaving the relative safety of their families to care for soldiers abroad.

As with all my acknowledgements, I have a core group of people to thank. I'd be lost without my personal and professional support crew, so I must thank them all individually. First, thank to you to my editors, Sammia Hamer and Sophie Wilson, who are always full of great ideas to help make my books stronger, and offer so much encouragement through the editing process. My agent Laura Bradford is also vital to my writing process, not only for handling contracts and negotiations, but also for general hand-holding and advice! I also have a fantastic extended team at Amazon Publishing, including Emilie Marneur and Bekah Graham, as well as my copyeditor and proofreader, and many others behind the scenes.

I would also like to say a special thank you to my mother, Maureen, for all the daily childcare help. If I can be half the mother she was to me growing up, then I'll know I'm doing a good job! Thank you to my gorgeous sons, Mackenzie and Hunter, for being so much fun to spend time with, although I'm looking forward to Hunter's fascination with pushing buttons on my laptop coming to an end. More than once I was terrified he'd deleted this entire file! Thanks also to Hamish, my husband, for all the hours playing *Star Wars* with the boys. One day I'm going to make you put down the lightsabre, though, and read one of my books . . . And while I'm on that topic, Dad, it's about time you read one of your daughter's books, too!

Natalie Anderson, Nicola Marsh and Yvonne Lindsay – I'd be lost without you all. Sometimes I wonder how I'd ever get a book written without your emails and messages, especially my daily writing sprints with Yvonne that keep me on the straight and narrow each day.

I'm also very fortunate that my children have such lovely teachers, which means I don't have to worry about them when they're at school and preschool. Given how easy it is as a writer to become distracted, it's hugely important to me to know my children are happy and cared for when I'm not with them, and I am so fortunate that my children have their own great support crew. I will continue to show my thanks by giving you all books to read.

And finally, to all my readers: without you, I wouldn't have a job. Thank you for every book of mine you purchase. I hope you continue to enjoy the stories I write as much as I enjoy creating them. Every email you send me, every time you tell me how much you've loved a story – it honestly brings a smile to my face that lasts for hours.

ABOUT THE AUTHOR

Photo © 2014 Carys Monteath

Soraya M. Lane graduated with a law degree before realising that law wasn't the career for her and that her future was in writing. She is the author of historical and contemporary women's fiction, and her most recent historical novel, *Voyage of the Heart*, was an Amazon bestseller.

Soraya lives on a small farm in her native New Zealand with her husband, their two young sons and a collection of four-legged friends. When she's not writing, she loves to be outside playing make-believe with her children or snuggled up inside reading.

For more information about Soraya and her books, visit www.sorayalane.com or www.facebook.com/SorayaLaneAuthor, or follow her on Twitter at @Soraya_Lane.